To Carey and Wendy

UNQUIET BONES

DAVID J. GATWARD

WEIRDSTONE PUBLISHING

Unquiet Bones
by
David J. Gatward

 Created with Vellum

Grimm: nickname for a dour and forbidding individual, from Old High German grim [meaning] 'stern', 'severe'. From a Germanic personal name, Grima, [meaning] 'mask'. (*www.ancestory.co.uk*)

CHAPTER ONE

The caravan sat alone in the field, a long-ago holiday destination once filled with happy memories, now rotting in the mire. A guest book rested on the side by the small, stained kitchen sink, its pages damp. Blotches of mould warped words that spoke of good times and promises to return. But for years now no one had, and time and decay had instead taken up residence, peeling wood and Formica from the cupboards and doors, rusting hinges, rotting the carpet. Which was why it was the perfect location for a murder.

The killer had chosen the caravan because it was forgotten. The farmer was an old man, weary of working the land. This small attempt to diversify the business was probably little more than an abandoned idea lost in a ledger at the back of a cupboard. Access was down a track overgrown with weeds and thorns, and no public footpath ambled past. Only shadows gathered near, trapped beneath trees leaning over the caravan in some vain attempt to hide it from view, as though embarrassed by its presence.

As for the victim, if such a word could be used to describe him, considering the pain and hurt he had caused so many others, well, he had it coming. He wasn't the first, wouldn't be the last.

The killer had done this before, played the long game with

each new project, become a part of their lives just enough to give them the chance to end it themselves. Not that they often did, but it was always fun to see if they would.

How it had all started, the killer wasn't entirely sure. Was it their past which had caused them to take this road? Perhaps. But there was also no denying the thrill of it now. Not so much at the kill, watching it unfold and knowing their work had been instrumental in bringing it about, but that knowledge of doing good by removing the rubbish. These were people the world was better off without, and no one could argue any different; the killer knew that better than most.

Not that it had ever been about just bringing the lives of the worst kind of people to an end. If it was, then there were easier ways to go about it. After all, a knife in the dark was tempting, but where was the payoff, the admission of guilt? Murder was easy, but meaningless. Messy, too, if you became so involved as to ram in the knife, or pull the trigger. This, though, had purpose, and that purpose was confession; the victim needed to take responsibility for what they had done, understand the pain they had caused, then either remove themselves from it permanently, or be removed despite them.

Persuasion was key to convincing them that nowhere was truly safe, and that a refuge of sorts was needed. A location so out of the way and invisible that no one would find them or even think to look for them. The caravan was perfect. Other locations had suited just as well; a derelict warehouse, a quiet cellar of an empty house, but this was perhaps the favourite so far.

Throw in a willing ear to listen, a shoulder to cry on, a supply of alcohol and subtle drugs, and even the toughest of criminals would crack. And the funny thing was, they never even realised, always believing in their own invincibility, the armour of the hard, mean, and violent lives they'd led until cracks started to show.

The hardened criminal wasn't always the target, however. Sometimes, it was those whose lives and actions had simply caused too much pain to others for them to be allowed to continue. Variety was the spice of life, after all, and there was no point sticking to only one type when it came to such important work.

So, once again, another line was to be drawn in the sand, between the good and the bad. And when it came to being bad, the man now sitting at the table in front of them had, over the years, redefined that word many times over. The things he had done were unspeakable. The world deserved better than to have him still in it. Which was why he wouldn't be for much longer.

'Here,' the killer said, passing the man a glass of vodka from the cool box carried in from the car.

The clear liquid was laced with a little something to help with what was to come, and that little something was a healthy dose of the cocaine the man had built his empire on. So many lives were destroyed to fund his hedonism, buy him houses and cars and boats and power. Not anymore.

As the man emptied the glass, throwing the contents down his throat hard enough to not even touch the sides, the killer hummed a little tune, the words dancing in their head: *Just a spoonful of sugar...*

'I know that one,' the man said.

'Everyone knows that one.' The killer smiled.

'Mary Poppins, right?'

The killer gave a nod.

'Used to watch it with the kids.'

'Those must have been happy days.'

'They were.'

'Hold that memory. It'll be a comfort.'

The man smiled.

'It is,' he said, then the smile broke and tears fell, sliding down his cheeks like streams on a mountainside after a storm.

It was an odd sight, the killer thought, to see this man hardened by evil, break so easily.

The killer said, 'You don't have to do this, you know.'

It was a lie, of course. They had to do it, because that was the whole point, after all. But saying it reinforced the decision already made. Clever and so very subtle.

'I do. You've helped me realise that. The pain I've caused. The hurt. It has to stop. It has to.'

The killer nodded, one so drenched in faux understanding that they almost believed it themselves.

'You won't leave me, will you?'

'Of course not,' the killer replied, reaching out with both hands to clasp the man's calloused paws. 'I'm here, as I promised I would be.'

'Thank you.'

Silence then, but not so much the absence of sound, as the soft symphony of a world going about its business, of waiting for someone to finally leave.

The man leaned back, reached into one pocket to remove an envelope, then drew from another a small pistol.

'Here,' he said, sliding the envelope across the table. 'You'll make sure my family gets this, won't you?'

The killer took the envelope, then lied, 'Of course, I'll hand it to them personally.'

'You promise?'

'I promise.'

'It's important. They have to know. How sorry I am, I mean. For all of it.'

'I know.'

Silence descended once again, though this time a new sound filled it; the deep breaths of someone preparing for a final journey.

The man lifted the gun.

The killer noticed how it seemed heavy in his grip, as though the weight of what it was about to do had somehow manifested itself in the awful device, putting extra strain on the muscles holding it.

'Somehow, I always knew it would come to this.'

'Then why, Mr Nightingale, did you not stop it all sooner?'

The killer expected an answer, a discussion. Instead, the man shrugged, then tucked the barrel of the gun under his chin and pulled the trigger. The top of his head exploded in a rush of red and covered the ceiling in brain matter and fragments of skull.

The killer leaned back and stared at the dead meat in the seat opposite. The man had slumped back, his arms at his side, lifeless eyes staring blankly into whatever Hell now welcomed him. The air between them had changed colour a little, filled as it was with a faint pink mist. And behind it lay the invisible scent of blood and the propellant from the gunshot; the metallic tang of haemoglobin mixed with the pungent stench of nitroglycerine.

One final act remained.

The killer stood and from a pocket, pulled out three slim aluminium tubes, each only a few millimetres in diameter, and connected to the others by a length of elastic threaded through the middle. With a flick of the wrist, the tubes sprung out and slotted together with a soft snick.

Pulling on a pair of surgical gloves, the killer then reached for the envelope on the table and slipped it into a small plastic Ziploc bag, before moving round to stand beside the body, clasping the ruined jaw and gently easing it open.

CHAPTER TWO

Police Constable Jadyn Okri arrived in Hawes more than a little nervous about the day ahead. Not because of work, though, so that was something, at least. In fact, work had been fairly quiet of late, which was no bad thing. Life had been busier than he'd ever expected it to be when he'd joined the team in Hawes, so he welcomed the quiet.

There had been a few things to deal with, but nothing too taxing. Mostly, the team had been able to catch up on paperwork, in between various trips out to deal with everything from the occasional domestic argument, which had got out of hand, and a traffic incident or two, to a missing person who hadn't actually been missing at all, just at the wrong pub and a bit grumpy, and a fight on a school bus involving the end results of a domestic science class, in particular, scones hard enough to draw blood when thrown at a soft, young face.

No, work was not the issue. Family was. And the thought of what was to come grabbed hold of Jadyn's guts and gave them an unexpectedly violent twist.

With a deep breath to calm himself, Jadyn slowed his vehicle, eased it off the main road, and parked up in the marketplace. Being a Saturday, the town would soon get busy, so he'd hit the gym extra early to ensure that he was able to get to Hawes before all of the parking was taken close to the community centre.

Not that having to park further away was ever really a bind. A walk to work in the Dales, even in the worst of weather, was infinitely better, he imagined, than having to take the Underground in London every day. He'd experienced that enough times, during training and on various school trips and weekends away with friends, to know that it was something he never wanted to do on a regular basis. Ever.

Engine off, Jadyn climbed out into a November day heavy with the promise of bad weather and worse to come. The sky was low and grey clouds jostled with others more menacing, their edges already feathering with rain and ill will. A gust of wind threw itself down the road, bringing with it a few damp paper wrappers from the chippy at the end of town, no doubt discarded by a careless customer from the night before. The roadworks, which had done little more than cause congestion and arguments through Hawes the past couple of months, were now gone. Somewhere in the distance, sheep called out into the morning, their voices swept away on the breeze and into the dark, ancient fells beyond.

'Officer Okri!'

Jadyn turned at the call of his name to see Detective Sergeant Matt Dinsdale approaching. The man was an inch or two smaller than Jadyn, stocky, and walked with an air of casual purpose, which Jadyn had never been able to quite pull off himself. The DS seemed to exist in such a constant state of calm that Jadyn sometimes found himself seeing the man not so much as a commanding officer, but more as a caring uncle. He was always looking out for everyone, checking up on how things were at home as well as work, and he also worked particularly well as a mediator between their moderately irascible boss, DCI Grimm, and the team.

'Morning,' Jadyn replied.

'And a gloomy one it is at that,' Matt said, glancing upwards.

'That sky doesn't look too happy now, does it? You hungry? I know I am. Just heading along to the Penny Garth Café, if you want to join me, like.'

Another thing about the DS was that when it came to food, his mind showed the focus of a special forces soldier behind enemy lines.

'Actually, I think I'm okay,' Jadyn said, and he immediately saw confusion write itself across the DS's face as clear as if it had been scrawled there in ink.

'Is something the matter, Constable?'

Jadyn shook his head, perhaps a little too enthusiastically.

'No, I'm fine, honestly. Just not that hungry this morning.'

Matt shook his head, narrowed his eyes, and leaned in a little closer, as though carrying out a medical examination.

'There's something you're not telling me, isn't there?'

'Not at all.'

Matt stood back and folded his arms across his chest.

'Out with it, lad. Come on.'

Perceptive, too, Jadyn thought.

'Honestly, there isn't. I just don't fancy bacon right now, that's all.'

'What about sausage? Or egg?'

Jadyn shook his head.

'Or—and this is only if you're feeling adventurous, mind—sausage and egg, but with a bit of black pudding thrown in, nice and crispy like? You'll be hard pushed to find a better way to start the day than that.'

Jadyn laughed at the DS's inability to understand why anyone would turn down breakfast.

'Maybe later, Sarge.'

The DS narrowed his eyes for a final stare at the police constable.

'Only if you're sure.'

'I am.'

He turned and headed off up the street, leaving Jadyn to walk the rest of the way along to the office. When he arrived, he found the doors already open and pushed on through to be attacked by a ball of fur.

'Down, Fly! Get down!'

Jadyn dropped to his heels and the young sheepdog flopped over on his back, offering up its tummy for a rub.

'Morning, Jim,' Jadyn said, catching sight of PCSO James Metcalf over in the corner by the kettle.

'Now then,' said Jim, greeting Jadyn. 'Sorry about that. He's getting better at not being such an idiot, at least that's what I tell myself.'

Jim was a year or two older than Jadyn and they got on well. Though that was the case with the whole team really, wasn't it? They were more family than work colleagues, and a little easier to deal with than his real family, that was for sure.

Not that he didn't love his family, just that they took a little getting used to. Actually no, that wasn't fair. His older brother and sister—one in finance, the other a marketing director—had set the bar rather high for him and his younger sister. Isioma was fine and surprisingly communicative for a seventeen-year-old. They'd always got on well, Jadyn enjoying the role of older brother, Izzy relishing being the pestering younger sister. Their parents, though, particularly their mum, well, she was ... enthusiastic. Yes, that was probably the best way to describe her, Jadyn thought.

'Big day today,' said Jim, as Jadyn joined him beside the large teapot.

'Is it?'

For a moment, Jadyn thought Jim was talking about what was on his mind—the imminent visit by his sister, Izzy, and his parents—but then he remembered that no one knew. He hadn't known himself either, not until a couple of days ago. As surprises went, it wasn't the best, or one to share around if it could be helped. So, he'd kept it to himself. The team would find out in good time. Maybe he should warn them, though, he thought. Then again, perhaps not.

Jim paused mid-pour.

'You've not forgotten, surely,' he said.

'No, of course I haven't,' Jadyn replied. Then added, 'Forgotten what, exactly?'

Jim finished filling the teapot.

'Harry ,' he said.

'Harry ? What about—' Then he remembered. 'The move. Of course.'

'There you go,' Jim said. 'Knew it was in there somewhere.'

'That's come around quick, hasn't it?'

'Just a bit.'

'What has?'

The interruption came from DS Dinsdale, who pushed into the office with a white paper bag in his hand. He opened it to reveal a large roll filled with sausage and egg.

'Harry , the move,' Jim said, eying the bag. 'You hungry, then?'

'Always.'

Jim poured out three mugs of tea.

'Do you think he's packed?'

'Don't think there was that much to pack, really,' Matt said. 'He's got the week off anyway to be on with it all. Picks the keys up this morning at ten, I think.'

The office door opened again and in walked PCSO Liz Coates and Detective Constable Jenny Blades. They were both carrying small parcels wrapped neatly in brown paper and string. Liz had probably chased Jenny over on her motorbike from where they both lived in Middleham, down at the other end of the dale.

'Did you travel back in time for those?' the DS asked, looking at the parcels.

'They're Harry 's housewarming presents,' Liz said. 'Remember?'

'And we thought plain wrapping was, you know, more "Harry ,"' said Jen, throwing quotation marks in the air with her fingers around the name of their boss.

'Would've been funny to see his face, though, wouldn't it?' said Matt. 'If you'd gone for something a little fancier?'

'Like this, you mean?'

Everyone turned to see Detective Inspector Gordanian Haig standing in the doorway, in her hand a shiny helium balloon in the shape of a big, pink heart.

CHAPTER THREE

'AND JUST WHAT THE HELL IS THAT?' MATT SAID, POINTING AT the balloon.

As well as the balloon, Gordy was holding a bottle of Prosecco and a box of chocolates, both covered in bright, colourful twists of ribbon.

'It's all they had, is what it is,' said Gordy with a shrug. 'No, that's a lie. It was either this, which is at least plain, or one saying something about being engaged. And that seemed a little premature, I thought.'

Jadyn, like everyone else in the room, laughed at the thought of Harry being presented with the balloon.

'Well, I'm sure he'll appreciate it,' said Liz.

'I'm not,' said Matt. 'Which is all the more reason to give it to him, if you ask me. Pity you didn't purchase a few more.'

With the whole team together, everyone gathered round, grabbing a seat for a chat about the day ahead, the DI took centre stage.

After a quick *how's everyone doing,* she then said, 'You remember what we've all agreed on for today, yes? We all know that Harry made it very clear he'd prefer to be left to move in on his own. However, I don't think that's fair to either him or Grace, who will, I'm sure, be over there helping him not be too grumpy about it all.'

'We'll just take it in turns,' Matt explained. 'Instead of all turning up *en masse,* as it were.'

'Exactly,' said Gordy. 'Offer a helping hand, move a few boxes, make some tea, turn up with food, that kind of thing.'

'He's going to hate it,' said Liz.

'That's half the fun, though, surely?' said Jen with a grin.

With the team's help decided for Harry 's move, Gordy then asked Matt about the action book.

'Not much to be going on with today,' Matt said. 'But to my mind, it's the quiet before the storm, seeing as there's only a few days to go.'

'A few days till what?' asked Jadyn.

Matt pointed at the calendar.

'Today is October thirty-first, and we all know what that means, don't we?'

Jim said, 'That it's Halloween and Jadyn will be out trick-or-treating?'

Everyone laughed.

Matt shook his head.

'November fourth is just round the corner,' he said.

'Mischief Night,' said Gordy.

Matt gave a nod as everyone in the room groaned.

'I know it's pretty much just kids having fun, but I can't help feeling it's one tradition that could do with just buggering off.'

'It's not the kids that are the problem,' said Jen. 'Or the teenagers. A few eggs and bags of flour thrown at doors, a missing gate or two, that we can handle. It's the idiots who are a bit older and should know better that are the problem.'

'Don't really remember it being a thing back home in Bradford,' Jadyn said.

'Well, it's a thing up here and has been for as long as anyone can remember,' Matt said. 'And Jen's got a point. There's no fun in having sheep let loose or tractors having their handbrakes let off.'

'We've even caught people who've driven in for the night from over in Darlington and goodness knows where else, just to run riot,' said Liz.

'And don't get me started on the havoc caused by fireworks.'

'Not as many folk go in for it now, really,' Jen said. 'But you're right, it doesn't stop a small number of idiots from causing damage. Happens elsewhere in the country, too. Not sure many folk like it, really. It's dying, I think.'

'Kids would rather be sitting at home on their computer games than out on a cold night annoying the neighbours,' said Gordy. 'Anyway, we've all done the talks in schools over the past few weeks about it, so that's something. The warning's out there, and generally, parents support it.'

Jadyn had been lumped with speaking at the secondary school in Leyburn. Standing in front of a few hundred teenagers and trying to explain to them that it wasn't a good idea to sneak around terrifying people by door-knocking and egg-throwing. It had been one of his toughest assignments to date.

'Some actively don't, though,' Jim said. 'Even see it as a rite of passage when their kids hit thirteen.'

'Well, we're all on duty that night,' Matt said, 'and we'll just need to be out and about and ready to respond if we need to.'

The chat continued for a few minutes on how to deal with any kids found causing a disturbance or what could potentially be seen as criminal damage. Once that was done, Gordy asked if there was anything else for the team to be aware of.

Matt raised a hand.

'Not sure how to say this, but I think something's up with Jadyn,' he said, screwing up the now empty paper bag.

'Really? Why?' Gordy asked, and she turned to look at Jadyn, concern in her eyes.

Jadyn went to speak, but Matt got in there first.

'Earlier this morning, I offered him three different types of breakfast rolls and he turned them all down.'

A palpable gasp rippled through the team.

'You're kidding,' said Jim.

'I never kid about food.'

'I don't believe it,' said Jen. 'Big strapping lad like you needs to eat.'

'I just wasn't hungry, that's all,' said Jadyn.

Matt shook his head.

'No one, and I mean no one, turns down black pudding.'

'I do,' Jadyn said. 'I did. It's not like I'm wasting away, is it?'

That made everyone laugh. Jadyn's large but not overly imposing physique was built on weight training, a good diet, and plenty of protein shakes.

Jadyn felt a hand rest on his shoulder and turned to see Jen staring at him.

'Is everything okay?' she asked, mischief in her eyes.

'Yes, everything's okay,' Jadyn replied. 'Of course it is.'

'Don't mind admitting I'm a little worried,' Matt said.

And Jadyn didn't mind getting his leg pulled, but he didn't need this. Not today.

'Honestly, I'm fine,' he said. 'If it'll make you happy, I'll have a roll once we're done. How's that?'

'You're just saying that to make me feel better.' Matt huffed.

'I'm really not.'

Liz joined in.

'Look, if there is something up, then ...'

'There really isn't!' Jadyn said. 'It's just that with my fam—'

Jadyn stopped speaking, acutely aware he was about to say too much. Matt was staring at him expectantly. He was about to explain when there was a knock at the door.

Being the closest, and pleased that something had distracted everyone from what he'd just said, he stood up and opened it to reveal a black woman in a police uniform. She looked about the same age as Gordy, Jadyn thought, though he wasn't entirely sure what that age actually was. Rude to ask, and all that.

'Good morning.' The woman smiled, her accent northern, but a little softer than the likes of Matt, as though it had been gradually worn away, the edges smoothed off over the years. She reached out a hand. Jadyn shook it.

'Hi,' said Jadyn, not exactly sure what to say next, and letting go of the woman's hand. Then he caught sight of the insignia on the epaulettes of her uniform: a single crown. 'Oh,' he said. Then added, 'Ma'am.'

The woman smiled.

'Can I come in?'

Jadyn stepped back.

'Make yourself at home ... I mean ... yes, of course.'

The woman slipped past Jadyn and walked over to Gordy, once again reaching out a hand.

'Detective Superintendent Eileen Walker,' she said. 'I'm here to replace Detective Superintendent Graham Swift, temporarily anyway, until something more permanent can be arranged.'

Gordy walked over.

'Good to see you,' she said. 'Though, we were expecting someone else.'

'Things sometimes get swapped around in situations like this,' Walker said. 'So, I'm just standing in for now, though that may change, as things often do. Right now, I'm not sure how long I'll be working with you exactly, so we'll just muddle along as best we can.'

'That's a slippery slope, that is,' Matt said.

Walker turned to Matt with a slight frown.

'How so?'

'Our DCI didn't think he'd be here for long either. Next thing you know, he's buying a house.'

'Well, I'll stay away from estate agents for now, how does that sound?'

Gordy said, 'Well, it's good to see you. You're a few days early, though; we weren't expecting someone till at least next week.'

'We've even got it in the diary,' added Matt. 'Properly organised, that is.'

Walker shrugged. 'Sorry to just turn up with no warning, but

I'm afraid something rather urgent has come up. I need to speak with DCI Grimm.'

'I'm afraid he has a few days off,' said Gordy. 'The whole week, actually. Though it's hardly a holiday. Not sure the man knows what that word even means.'

'I know, I've already checked,' Walker replied. 'Moving into the house you just mentioned, I believe, yes? Do you know where he is at this moment?'

'Up in Gayle, I should think,' said Jadyn. 'Well, he will be soon enough.'

Walker turned to look at Jadyn but continued to speak to Gordy.

'Can you spare your constable here to take me to speak with DCI Grimm?'

Jadyn saw worry momentarily flash in the DI's eyes.

'Is there anything we should know?' Gordy asked. 'Surprise visits from Detective Superintendents are rare, if you know what I mean.'

'I do indeed,' Walker said, 'but all I can say is that I need to speak to Grimm rather urgently.' She then walked over to Jadyn and gestured towards the door. 'After you, Constable.'

Jadyn headed out of the office.

CHAPTER FOUR

A few minutes' walk from where the team were gathered in the community office, Harry was in his flat and growing grumpier by the second. He was close to deciding that moving house would be a whole lot easier, and considerably more enjoyable, if he just threw everything away and started again. And he voiced as much to Grace.

'I do see where you're coming from,' she said, 'but there is a downside to that plan that I feel I should point out.'

'Really? And what's that, then?' Harry asked. 'Because I don't see one.'

'Shops,' Grace replied.

'Not sure I see what you're getting at.'

'You'd have to go in them again to replace what you've thrown away, wouldn't you? And we both know how much fun you were just getting the bare minimum of new stuff you needed for the house.'

Harry let out a grunt of disapproval.

'And there'd be more online shopping, too, don't forget that. All that sitting in front of a computer screen, scrolling through this and that, putting things in a basket, having to fill in your bank details.'

'Bollocks,' Harry grumbled.

'Exactly.'

Dropping down to grab the box sitting at his feet, Harry then headed out of the door. His old Rav4 was almost full, but he was going to squeeze this next box in, whether it liked it or not.

Outside, Hawes was still quiet, though Harry knew that it wouldn't stay that way for long. For a small and fairly isolated town, completely surrounded by fells and moorland, it was a constant surprise to him just how busy the place always seemed to be. The quiet times were little more than regular lulls at the start and end of the day, and those were often cut short by the moving of animals and farm machinery, sometimes right through the centre of town, or the influx of visitors heading out to fill up the pubs and restaurants for the evening.

As he pushed the box into the back of his vehicle, Harry was very aware of the change in the weather. Not just over the last few weeks either, with autumn succumbing to the creeping cold of winter's claws sinking into the earth, but the in last forty-eight hours. The bright mornings everyone had been enjoying had been replaced by something considerably gloomier, with grey clouds sitting low in the sky and that invigorating scent of rain in the air. The world was hunkering down for winter, pulling low blankets of fog over the hills and fields as protection from the cold.

Harry slammed the rear door when a voice called over and he looked up to see a young man approaching.

'Ben,' he said, sending a wave over to his brother. 'I'll warn you now, I'm not in the best of moods.'

Ben laughed.

'No change there then, right? Just thought I'd pop over to see if you need a hand. Liz is on duty today.'

Harry shook his head.

'No, I'll be fine. Nearly done. Anyway, you'd only get in the way.'

Grace trotted out of the flat, pulling the door shut behind her.

'Weather's turning,' she said. 'Which means our dogs will be in front of my dad's fire, making damned sure they don't go out in it.'

She looked at Ben, an eyebrow raised. 'I'd stay away if I were you,' she said. 'He's a bit, well, you know.'

'I do,' Ben said.

Harry laughed.

'Smudge doesn't mind the bad weather.'

'Given the choice, though.'

Ben asked, 'You sure you don't need a hand? I've not much to do this morning. I was going to pop into the garage, do a bit of overtime, but I don't have to.'

'Got something on this afternoon, then?' Harry asked.

'A bit of that online counselling,' Ben said. 'Remember?' He pulled out his wallet and removed a card, handing it to Harry .

Harry looked at the card, which had in elegant script *Words Heal*, beneath a simple image of what Harry assumed was a white quill.

'How's it going?' Harry asked.

Having completed his probation, Ben had been doing amazingly well with adjusting to a normal life. His probation officer, however, had advised him to look at having some counselling anyway, just to continue with a bit of support. Harry was impressed that his brother was sticking with it. He'd made use of similar himself over the years, both during his army days and while in the police, and had never found it easy. It had helped though, of that he had no doubt.

Ben shrugged.

'I'm not one for talking much, if you know what I mean.'

'Can't imagine where you get that from,' said Grace, raising an eyebrow at Harry .

'I think it's useful, though. Certainly seems to be. Not really sure why or how, but it is, if that makes sense.'

Harry knew how difficult it could be to open up about trauma, experiences which seemed to follow you like a shadow, always waiting around a corner to pounce.

'Well, Ben, I'm impressed,' he said. 'And what's the counsellor like?'

'She seems alright, I guess,' said Ben. 'Chatty and friendly and always interested in what I'm doing. Anyway, if you don't need me …'

'Escape while you can,' said Grace, shooing Ben away. 'It's for the best.'

'I'll give you a call later,' added Harry , handing the counsellor's card back to Ben. 'Let you know how we're doing.'

'Keep it,' Ben said with a faint smile. 'After this, you might need it yourself.' He turned and headed off back into town, calling back with, 'I'll come over for a nosy tomorrow as well.'

Harry watched Ben walk away, then climbed into his vehicle, slipping the card into his pocket. Grace climbed in beside him.

'He's doing alright, isn't he?'

'He is that,' Harry said.

'You should be proud.'

'I am.'

Grace reached out and rested a hand on Harry 's leg.

'Right then,' she said. 'You ready for this?'

'Not much I can do about it if I'm not, is there?' Harry replied.

'Not really, no.'

Harry started the engine.

'Best we go and collect that key then, hadn't we?' he said.

'I thought the estate agent was meeting you at the house?'

Harry shook his head.

'So did I, but they're short on staff, so I said I'd head over and pick it up.'

'From Leyburn.'

'Yes.'

'For a house you're buying in Gayle.'

'Again, yes.'

'Bit of a round trip, don't you think? I mean, Gayle's not even a mile from where we're now sitting, is it? And Leyburn's at the other end of the dale.'

'The best-laid plans, and all that, right?' Harry said.

Grace frowned, though Harry could see a smile threatening to break it.

'If this is you having second thoughts, I hate to point it out, but it's a little late now, don't you think? You've exchanged contracts, the house is yours.'

Harry started the engine.

'There's Jadyn,' he said, as they pulled out onto the road.

The constable was walking through the marketplace with a woman in uniform who Harry didn't recognise.

'Who's that with him?' Grace asked.

'Haven't the faintest idea,' Harry said, and drove on, ignoring the police constable's waving hand as they drove past.

'You're not going to stop?' Grace asked.

'Whatever he wants, and whoever that is with him, can wait,' Harry said.

As Hawes slipped away behind them, Harry knew that Grace had a point, that in some ways he was having second thoughts. But they weren't ones he could act on, or even ones he wanted to. So, instead, he'd leapt at the chance to take a little drive that morning before finally stepping across the threshold of a house he now owned. He wasn't thinking of bolting at this last moment, not least because of the large sums of money he'd spent on the purchase.

What he was thinking, however, was a little hard to explain. What he'd finally pinned it down to was a need to put himself in the mind of someone coming to the area afresh. If he could approach Hawes from down dale on the morning he moved in, it might just help settle those odd little nerves fluttering around his gut.

'I could've picked the keys up for you, you know,' Grace said. 'I'm sure that wouldn't have been a problem. Carperby is considerably closer to Leyburn than Hawes is.'

'No, this is fine,' Harry said, as Bainbridge rose to meet them. 'Left or right?'

'What?'

'Do you want to go the Askrigg and Carperby way, past your place, or on through Aysgarth?'

'Let's do both,' Grace said. 'Head left to Askrigg, then we'll come back the other way when you've got your keys.'

Harry drove on, and the weather, he noticed, not only followed them, but swept around to greet them.

The weather, Harry knew as well as anyone, was a big deal in England. If you couldn't think of something to talk about, then two subjects were always bound to get people going: route choice on British roads and the weather. But in Wensleydale, the weather was something altogether different. This was a place where it was almost a physical presence, perhaps even some ethereal spirit that treated the fells as a place to just run amok.

He'd once ventured this idea to Matt over a couple of pints at The Fountain. Matt had, in no uncertain terms, told him to stop talking bollocks, which had been fair enough. His point had been, though, that instead of complaining about the weather, no matter if it was hot or cold or wet or dry, Dales folk instead seemed to celebrate it more. Though perhaps celebrate was too strong a term, Harry thought. Appreciate, served better, maybe. They understood the weather, knew the importance of the rough days as well as the good.

One of the greatest sights around was the rivers in spate after a storm, the waters brown with peat from the fells. Gayle Beck storming its way through Hawes, chucking itself down the waterfalls to smash itself to pieces under the bridge before rushing on into the fields and beyond. He'd yet to see Aysgarth Falls after similar, but that was something he'd be doing for sure the next time the rains came in. And judging by the clouds jostling above, that was looking to be sooner rather than later.

'You've quite the week ahead of you, haven't you?' Grace said, interrupting Harry 's thoughts.

'I suppose so, yes,' Harry replied. 'Though, I'm still in two minds about that other thing.'

Harry had hoped the week would go by and this other thing would be forgotten. Grace clearly had other ideas.

'It's a reunion of old army buddies, that's all,' Grace said. 'It'll be fun.'

'I've not seen any of them for over twenty years, not since I left the Paras and joined the police. That's a long time, Grace. The only contact we've had since then is the rare text message, and now this.'

'Exactly.'

The invite had arrived a few weeks ago, sent by Amy, the wife of Anthony Stratton, one of the lads Harry had served with. Anthony was turning forty, so a reunion was being planned. Harry just wasn't convinced it was a good idea.

Neither Harry nor Grace spoke for a minute or two, until Grace said, 'You've not been keen on it since the invite arrived. Why? What's the problem?'

'Just not my kind of thing, that's all,' Harry said, not really wanting to go into it.

'After what you've told me, I get the idea you'd be noticeable by your absence. Seems a shame to not go. I know it'll be hard ...'

Harry stayed quiet. Hard didn't even come close to it. He'd been close to death numerous times, but one occasion had changed his life forever. And of the original six in his team, only four were still alive.

CHAPTER FIVE

Arriving in Leyburn, and thankful to not be talking about the reunion, Harry left Grace in the car as he nipped out to collect the keys to his new house. The estate agent, Mr Brian Sunter, a man somehow blessed with all the charm of a brick, and who wore his hair in much the same way as a child would wear a novelty hat, was at the door when Harry arrived.

'Yes?'

'Morning,' Harry said, aware now of rain in the wind.

'I'm on my own today,' Brian said, every word spoken with the same tone, the same volume, no inflection, no emotion. Almost, Harry thought, robotic. 'So, this is the last thing I need.'

'Is it?' Harry said, a little taken aback.

'Of course.'

'But I'm only here for my keys.'

'I'm sorry, what?'

'My keys,' Harry said. 'Someone was going to drop them off for me this morning, but I arranged to come over and get them instead.'

Brian stared at Harry for a moment, eyes post-box narrow.

'So, you're not on duty, then?'

'No, I'm not,' said Harry .

'Then you can't help, can you?'

Harry could feel the already thin threads of his patience beginning to fray.

'I'm just here for my keys,' he repeated. 'That's all. Then I can be on my way and let you get on with whatever it is that I've obviously interrupted.'

'But you're the police,' Brian said. 'So, really, you should help, don't you think? Or do I need to call someone? But that will take an age, I'm sure, and I really don't have the time to be sitting on the phone waiting and waiting and waiting. Don't people know Mischief Night isn't for another four days? It's just not funny. Never has been. Do you see me laughing? Of course you don't.'

'I think we may be talking at cross purposes, here,' Harry said, then found himself asking the question he didn't want to, because usually the answer to it, and those much like it, would ruin any chance of a day off. 'What appears to be the problem?'

'The door,' Brian said, stepping back now to point at it. 'Look.'

Harry stared. For a moment, he saw nothing. Then he spotted the door handle and lock, and could see that both were damaged.

'You've been broken into.'

'I have.'

'When did this happen?'

'Last night.'

'Has anything been taken?'

'The key safe has been drilled open. And as far as I can tell, a key has been taken from each set, which is quite the problem, isn't it?'

'Is it?' Harry asked.

'Of course it is! Take yours for example.'

'Mine? What about them?'

'Well, if someone has a spare key to your house, you're going to have to change the locks, aren't you? Obviously, insurance will cover it, but you're just one house, aren't you? We have dozens of properties on our list. So, I'll be sorting that all out for the rest of the weekend and most of next week as well, no doubt.'

For the moment, Harry wasn't too fussed about someone

having a key to his house, seeing as there was nothing there yet worth stealing. But that would change the moment he moved in. He'd just need to see what lock he needed, then replace it himself; from what he could recall, it wasn't exactly high-end.

'What about your alarm?' he asked.

'I don't have one.'

Harry groaned.

'You can't be serious.'

'Well, I do, it's just not connected, that's all. Haven't quite got around to it. One of those jobs that just keeps getting put off. You know how it is.'

Harry wanted his key. He did not want to be messing around with a break-in and a business owner who didn't see the importance of security and then wanted the police to sort everything out when something went wrong. Neither did he want to have to interview Brian about it, simply because the man's monotone voice might push him a little too far.

Asking Brian to step back, Harry moved in for a closer look. The lock had been drilled out, which rather surprised him. A spur-of-the-moment break-in, in the middle of the night, was one thing, but one planned to such a degree that the perpetrator brought their own drill? Now that was strange. And what was there to take from an estate agent, anyway? They were hardly places where vast sums of money were stored, or anything of any real value.

He stared through the window in the door, then through the windows to each side, but could see no sign of damage inside at all. It looked untouched.

'I need to call this in,' said Harry .

'Yes, that sounds like a good idea,' Brian agreed. 'Call it in. Will it take long?'

Harry shook his head.

'I'll have one of my team come out and check everything over, see if we have any fingerprints, that kind of thing, and look at the damage. You'll need to contact your insurance company as well.'

'I already have.'

Of course you have, Harry thought, though he wondered what they would have to say about the alarm.

'Oh, and here you are. These are yours, I believe.'

Harry saw a set of keys in Brian's hand.

'Thank you,' Harry said. 'You've been inside, then?'

'I'd left a sandwich in the fridge yesterday,' Brian explained. 'I didn't want it smelling the place out if it had gone off. Not a good customer experience that, is it?'

'No, it isn't,' Harry found himself agreeing.

'Exactly.'

Harry lifted the keys in front of his face. So, this was it then, he thought.

'I'll call this in now,' Harry said.

'This has made an already busy day considerably busier,' Brian said.

Harry pulled out his phone. A few seconds later, his call was answered.

'Boss?'

'Police Constable Okri,' Harry said. 'You busy at all?'

'You drove straight past us,' Jadyn said. 'I waved and everything.'

'Did we?' Harry said. 'Must've missed you completely. Sorry about that.'

'Where are you?'

'Leyburn,' Harry said.

'Why?'

'Pardon?'

'I thought you'd be up in Gayle. That's why we're there.'

'What?'

'We're at Gayle,' Jadyn said. 'Where I thought you'd be.'

'Who's this we?' Harry asked, a little confused by Jadyn's call. 'Anyway, I'm the one who called you, so I'll be asking the questions. Are you busy?'

'No, I mean yes, I mean ...'

'Which is it?'

'I've someone here who wants to speak with you,' Jadyn said. 'It's urgent, Boss.'

'Well, that doesn't sound good.'

'I don't know how it sounds,' Jadyn replied, 'just that she needs to speak with you. Are you coming back up the dale?'

'You're asking those questions again,' Harry said. 'There's been a break-in at the estate agents' over in Leyburn, the one I bought my house through. Are you able to come over and sort it out? I think the owner, Mr Brian Sunter, would greatly appreciate it if you could.'

Harry heard mumbling as Jadyn spoke to someone else, though Harry couldn't make out the other voice.

'I've been told to send someone else,' Jadyn said, coming back on the phone.

'Who by?'

More mumbling, then a rustling sound, as though Jadyn was swapping his phone to his other hand.

'DCI Grimm?'

Harry didn't recognise the voice.

'What's happened to Constable Okri? Is he okay?'

'He's fine,' the new voice said.

'Who is this?' Harry asked.

'Detective Superintendent Eileen Walker,' came the reply. 'I'm Mr Swift's temporary replacement.'

'But you're not due to visit for another week.'

'So I've been told,' Walker said, and Harry heard a faint smile in her voice. But the smile was soon gone when she spoke again. 'However, something has come up.'

'That doesn't sound good, now, does it?'

'I think it would be better if we talked in person. Are you coming back this way now?'

Harry wanted to say no.

'Yes. I'll be there in about half an hour.'

'Good,' said Walker. 'I'll see you at the office, then.'

'No, you won't,' Harry replied, very aware that he was being somewhat curt in his response. 'I'm moving house today. You can meet me there. Officer Okri has the address.'

There was a pause and then Walker said, 'I'm sorry to have called in on such an important day. I will do my best to take as little of your time as I have to.'

'I'll see you there,' Harry said and hung up.

Back in his vehicle, Harry dropped the keys in Grace's palm.

'Everything okay?' she asked.

'Unsurprisingly, no,' said Harry , and keyed the ignition. 'I've not even moved in, and I already need a new door lock.'

Grace looked baffled.

'I'll explain on the way,' Harry said, as the clouds broke, and rain threw itself at the windscreen. 'Just perfect.' He sighed, and headed off back up the dale.

CHAPTER SIX

The drive from Leyburn to Hawes wasn't exactly how Harry had hoped. He had wanted to be able to relax and enjoy the journey, take in the numerous shades of green that painted Wensleydale into a masterpiece. Perhaps even stop at a layby and just look down on it all and think to himself that yes, moving here, and now buying a house, had been the best thing to ever happen to him. Instead, he'd floored it, or at least tried to anyway, the Rav4 not exactly excelling when it came to being either nippy or fast. But it had pulled them home with a confidence unhindered by its age.

West Witton zipped up to meet him far sooner than he had expected and only a gasp from Grace at the speed with which he was approaching the village had him slow down.

'Sorry about that,' Harry said, rolling into the thirty-mph speed limit at the right speed after some rather dramatic braking.

'You going to tell me what's up, or am I supposed to guess?' Grace asked.

'It's the new DSup,' Harry said. 'Swift's replacement. That was her on the phone.'

'I thought you weren't due a visit for another week or so.'

'I wasn't,' Harry said.

'Oh.'

'Oh, indeed.'

Harry drove on in silence, eventually heading down along Temple Lane, then back up the hill towards Aysgarth. The vast range of green hues the dale wore so well were deeper now, he noticed. Trees were falling bare, gathered together as silent skeletal armies stood fast on sodden fells and fields to face the coming winter.

'Any idea why?'

'Not a clue,' Harry said. 'Can't imagine it's good, though.'

'It might be,' Grace said. 'Maybe it's a promotion, more money, that kind of thing.'

Harry laughed, and the sound was deep and cheerful enough to lighten the atmosphere a little.

'And maybe it isn't,' he said.

'You never know.'

'Oh, but I think I do. I'm in the Dales because the powers that be wanted me out of the way. They're hardly likely to come along now and push me to the front again, are they?'

'But didn't Swift say he thought you should replace him?'

Grace was right, Swift had indeed suggested that. And Harry had quickly gone about seeing him off the idea. There had been more than enough change in his life over the past year or two. The last thing he needed was more responsibility, more meetings, more reasons to end up trapped behind a desk, hating every single day.

'I've never known of a surprise meeting with a senior officer, in either the army or the police, to be a good thing,' Harry said. 'That's just not the way it works. No one ever turns up with a pay rise, a handshake, and a bottle of champagne, trust me. Well, not unless you're leaving. Which I'm not.'

'So, what's it about, then?'

Harry shook his head. He hadn't the faintest idea.

'And you're sure it'll be bad news?'

'I didn't say bad. I just said that it wouldn't be good.'

'That's double talk.'

Harry didn't reply and focused instead on driving them back

up the dale. Aysgarth was quiet, as it always was. Harry spotted smoke curling up from chimneys to bunch up into tufts like grey candy floss, fires already lit in hearths against the turn in the weather. Then they were out the other side and heading down the hill, speed picking up again. The road was making its way towards becoming a river now, water flowing in streams down the sides, gathering in puddles, brown and plentiful.

'Actually,' Harry said eventually, 'thinking about it, I'm not sure I've ever had a senior officer turn up unannounced like this.'

'What, ever?'

'Strange, right? Maybe something's come up with an old case,' he suggested. 'That could be it, I guess. Needs my help on something I was involved in, that kind of thing.'

'You don't sound entirely convinced.'

'It's the best I can come up with.'

A few miles later, Harry swept them down into Bainbridge, dropping past the flat-headed rise of the old Roman fort, which had for two millennia watched silently over the settlement below. The village green was dotted all over with large, dark puddles, their surfaces alive as the rain slammed down into them like bullets, droplets bouncing up and out in a dance.

Hawes, and its sister village of Gayle, were only a few miles away now, and Harry was irritated that instead of looking forward to arriving at his new home, he was instead thinking about all the possible bad reasons why Detective Superintendent Walker was waiting for him. The mean part of him hoped she was standing outside his new front door getting absolutely drenched; seemed only fair.

Harry 's phone rang.

'Grimm,' he shouted, never sure that the hands-free was going to work well enough for him to be heard.

'Just to let you know that we're back at the office,' Jadyn said. 'What with the weather being so wet.'

'I don't want to be at the office,' Harry said, aware of just how grumpy he sounded, and not really caring right then, either. 'I'm moving house, remember? That's what's happening, so that's where Walker can meet me, like I said.'

'She's brought food, Boss,' Jadyn said. 'Like, for the whole team.'

'So what?'

'There's a lot of it,' Jadyn explained. 'And she said she would really like to meet you here, if at all possible. She also said that it would be the most secure place in which to speak to you.'

'Secure?'

'Yes.'

Harry sucked in a deep breath and held it just long enough to have Jadyn ask, 'You still there, Boss?'

'Yes,' Harry answered. 'We're just the other side of the turn-off to Burtersett. We'll be there in five.'

'There's not much parking,' Jadyn said. 'Town's properly busy now.'

'Best you nip out and make sure there is, then, hadn't you?' Harry said, then hung up.

'Whatever it is, it's not Jadyn's fault,' Grace said.

'I know.'

'Then don't be such an old grouch. He'd throw himself in front of a bus if you asked him to. You know that, don't you?'

'I'd never ask him to do that,' Harry said. 'Think of the mess. And I'd have to clean it up.'

'You're missing the point. On purpose, too, which makes it worse.'

Harry squeezed the steering wheel, making his knuckles turn white.

'Whatever this is about, I'm sure it'll be fine,' Grace said. 'And even if it isn't, it will be because of that team you've been lucky enough to find yourself in charge of.'

Harry knew that Grace was right. He reached out his left hand and squeezed her leg.

'Thanks,' he said.

A few minutes later, they arrived in Hawes. And, as Jadyn had said, the place really was busy. Saturdays always were, but when the rain hit, everyone arrived in their cars, so the place soon snarled up. In the marketplace, however, Harry spotted a parking place with a police sign smack-bang in the middle of it. Standing beside it, and looking like a bedraggled rat, was Jadyn. He waved as Harry indicated right, gesturing to the parking space. Amazingly, he was smiling, Harry noticed. He drove in and Jadyn moved the sign, then dashed over to the driver's side of the vehicle.

'I moved mine,' he said, as Harry climbed out into the wet, 'so you could park here. And I thought I'd just keep an eye on it, didn't want someone trying to nick it. Oh, and Jen's on her way over to Leyburn, to check up on that break-in.'

'You're soaked,' Grace said, calling over from the other side of the vehicle.

'Come on,' Harry said, smiling at Jadyn, thinking about what Grace had said about the constable. 'Let's all get inside, shall we?'

Grace pulled Harry to one side, seemingly oblivious to the rain.

'Whatever this is, it's work,' she said. 'So, I'll leave you to it and head back to the flat. There's still plenty to be done, so I may as well get on with it.'

'You can go and see what the house is like if you want,' Harry said and held out the set of keys Brian the personality vacuum had given him.

Grace shook her head.

'Not a chance of it. It's yours, so you need to be the one to open that door. Oh, and we still haven't talked about that housewarming party you're having.'

'That would be because I'm not having one.'

'Well, seeing as you have that reunion this week,' Grace said, reminding Harry again of something else he didn't want to think about, 'and assuming it all goes okay and you don't just turn up and spend the whole time frowning, you could maybe invite them all up here, couldn't you?'

'No.'

'Wrong answer.'

'You're not going to give up on either the party or the reunion, are you?' said Harry .

'Of course I'm not,' Grace replied. Then, not giving Harry a chance to respond, she brushed a kiss against the rough scars on his face and headed off through the rain.

Turning to make his way over to the community centre, Harry caught sight of a tall, thin man rushing through the rain towards him. It was the journalist, Anderson, a man Harry held as much warmth and regard for as he did wasps. He held up a hand to stop him before he got any closer.

'No,' he said, walking off. 'Whatever it is, that's your answer.'

The man came alongside, keeping pace with Harry .

'Just a few questions,' he said.

Harry kept on walking.

'Just wondering if the police have any measures in place to deal with Mischief Night,' the man asked. 'Or is it a tradition you're happy to endorse?'

Harry stopped, turned to face the man, and raised a finger at him. The man stopped talking. Harry noticed that Anderson looked more than a little bedraggled, his clothes creased, eyes sunk.

'That's the second time today someone's mentioned Mischief Night,' he said. 'My advice to you is not to mention it again.'

'Why?'

Harry stepped in close.

'You look like you've had a rough night,' he said. 'Let's not make tonight even worse you being thrown in a cell, what do you say?'

Anderson's eyes widened.

'You can't threaten me.'

Harry narrowed his eyes and smiled.

'Oh, believe me, I never threaten.'

Anderson went to speak but Harry turned his back on him and walked off at a brisk jog.

In the office, the first thing he noticed was that the team was clearly on good form, the bright sound of their chatter bouncing around the room with gay abandon. The second thing he noticed was that standing among them was someone new, who broke off from a conversation with Liz and turned to walk over and meet him.

'DCI Grimm, I'm Detective Superintendent Walker,' the woman said.

'Well, I didn't think you were here dressed early for Halloween,' said Harry .

Walker cocked her head to one side just enough to let Harry know she was going to let that slide, but that he'd also best wind his neck in a little.

'Hungry?' she asked.

Harry 's eyes caught sight of the table against the wall, which was holding various plates of cakes and other tasty treats.

'I didn't think I was but seeing that lot has made me change my mind,' Harry said. 'Very generous.'

'Your Detective Sergeant advised that I visit Crockett's Butchers. Somewhat enthusiastically, I might add.'

'It's Cockett's,' Harry corrected, a little too sharply. 'And yes, I bet he did. I'm actually surprised he didn't volunteer to go for you himself.'

'Actually, I did,' Matt said, who was standing just a step away, and holding a decent slab of cake close to his mouth. 'But she insisted on going herself.'

'I'll warn you,' Harry said to Walker, 'buying their affection with food will only work really well and ensure their undying loyalty. I made that mistake myself.'

'That's the idea.'

'I see you've done this before.'

'A few times, yes.'

Harry was struck then by the fact that not only was the person he was talking to Swift's replacement, she also seemed to be, well, human, and he regretted his Halloween dig earlier. He remembered then that Swift's initial glacial-like coldness towards him had eventually thawed, at least enough for them to work together and understand each other, if perhaps not necessarily to always see eye-to-eye. Walker, though, had clearly read a completely different manual on management.

Walker led Harry over to the table.

'Your DS was particularly keen to point out that if I was to provide a few treats, I should also include this.' She pointed at a slab of creamy white cheese on a plate. 'For the cake. I simply can't even begin to understand why, and never have been able to either, I hasten to add. Seems a bit early in the day for me to be eating cheese, but that doesn't appear to be the case for some.'

Harry saw that Matt was munching down a good chunk of the stuff.

'I'm with you on that,' Harry said. 'They've finally won me over with it, but even I have to draw a line somewhere. And cheese and cake before eleven in the morning is that line.' He paused then, looking to move the conversation away from food to the real reason they were standing together in the office on a day he was supposed to be doing something a little more exciting. 'Anyway, nice though this all is ...'

Harry allowed his voice to fade, the unspoken question more than clear.

'Yes, to business,' Walker said. 'You have an interview room, I believe?'

'We do,' Harry said. 'We also have the local library on the other side of the entrance hall if you want to join. They've all the Herriot books, so I hear, and a cracking range of audiobooks. Lovely staff, too; very helpful.'

'Another time, maybe.'

'Come on, then,' he said. 'This way.'

In the small interview room, Harry waited for Walker to sit down before doing so himself. When he did, he got straight to the point.

'Well, ma'am, I'll be honest, I can't say I'm pleased to see you. I'm going to assume that whatever's brought you here isn't good, is it?'

Walker shook her head.

'I'm afraid not, no.'

'Thought as much. What is it, then? Some case I was involved with years ago has come back to bite me on the arse, is that it? You'll be spoiled for choice with that, I shouldn't guess.'

'No, it's not that,' Walker said. 'It's about your father.'

Harry sat up with a jolt. His blood turned cold, and he was fairly sure his heart stopped just long enough to have him worried it might not start again.

'That bastard?' he spat, teeth clenched. 'What about him?'

The man was in prison, Harry knew that for sure. The case against him—cases, actually—was huge, and both the defence and prosecution were still busy preparing for everything to go to court. He wasn't fully up to speed with what was going on, but he assumed everything was still going along as well as anyone could expect. The law was a huge machine, and the cogs turned slowly, yes, but they turned, and that was the important thing.

Walker went to speak, then paused.

'Best you say what you've come to say,' Harry said, growing impatient. 'Rip off that plaster, if you know what I mean.'

'He's escaped,' Walker said.

And Harry roared.

CHAPTER SEVEN

Harry was out of his chair so quickly that he kicked the thing backwards and into the wall hard enough to leave a dent in the plaster. Not that he cared, and he didn't even bother picking it up as it clattered to the floor.

'Escaped? What the bloody hell do you mean, he's escaped? How can he have? What on earth happened? Prisoners don't just escape, do they?'

Walker said nothing, just sat calmly at the table.

Harry turned back to the fallen chair, picked it up, went to put it back on its legs, paused, and then hurled it against the wall. 'Shit!'

The word hissed out of Harry through gritted teeth, and the chair bounced off the wall, narrowly missing his own head, and landed behind him in the shadows.

Harry had to force himself to not reach for the chair again and batter it into a twisted lump against the wall and the floor, maybe even kick down the door as well, just for the fun of it.

'DCI Grimm,' Walker said.

Harry rounded on her, rage burning through him, his eyes wide with it as though soon the flames would shine behind them, and he needed her to feel the heat. She was still sitting in her chair, calm and relaxed.

Harry made no move to join her.

'Harry ...'

Hearing his name caught Harry by surprise, not just because he hadn't expected it, but because it was spoken with seemingly genuine warmth and concern. But when he replied, his voice was a snarl of rage caught in a snare of disbelief.

'He can't have just escaped. It's impossible. A mistake. No one just walks out of prison without anyone noticing. We both know that. This isn't the nineteenth century; prisoners don't just tie sheets together and shimmy over the walls.'

Walker said nothing, clearly waiting for him to sit back down.

Harry finally obliged, collecting his chair and placing it back on its legs. They wobbled a little as he sat down; he'd bend them back into place another time. Either that or just rip them off completely, depending on how the rest of this conversation went.

'Better?' Walker asked.

'Not really, no,' Harry said. 'The door was next.'

'It had a lucky escape, then.'

'Oh, there's still time yet for me to kick it in, trust me.'

There was a knock at the door.

Harry barked a gruff, 'What?' at the interruption.

The door opened and Matt slipped into the room. Harry saw concern in the man's eyes.

'Well, what is it, Detective Sergeant?' he asked, his voice biting at his words.

The look on Matt's face was enough to tell Harry that his argument with the chair hadn't gone unnoticed.

'Just checking everything's okay, that's all,' Matt said. 'And wondered if you needed anything to help with whatever it is you're, er, discussing. Tea, perhaps?'

'No, I don't want any bloo—'

'That would be very much appreciated, thank you,' Walker

said, cutting Harry off. 'And if there's any cake or whatever left, could you bring some of that through as well?'

'Of course, not a problem at all,' Matt said, then reversed out of the room.

In the silence left by the DS, Harry sighed and sank a little in his chair. Finding himself almost immediately uncomfortable, he sat back up and leaned forward, his elbows resting on the table, his head momentarily in his hands as he rubbed his face, as though trying to scrub off the awful news he'd just been given.

'How are you doing over there, Detective?' asked Walker.

Harry dropped his hands to the table. For once in his life, he didn't know what to say.

'How did he do it, then?' he asked. 'How did he escape?'

'The *when* is just as important,' Walker said.

Another knock at the door and this time Matt didn't wait to be called in, pushing through the door with a flourish.

'Here you go,' he said, resting a well-stocked tray on the table. 'Pot of tea, two mugs, milk and sugar, and enough cake to keep you going, I think.'

The plate, Harry noticed, was barely visible beneath all of the cake.

'There's only two of us,' he said.

Matt turned serious and rubbed his chin thoughtfully.

'Fair point,' he said. 'You know what? I'll fetch some more. Oh, and I forgot the cheese ...'

Harry held up a hand to stop him.

'No, we're good, thanks,' he said. 'This is plenty.'

'Thank you, Detective Sergeant,' said Walker.

'If you need anything else, just knock on the wall,' Matt said, a smile creasing his face as he looked at Harry . 'Doesn't need to be so loud next time, though, okay?'

'Understood.'

Matt made to leave the room, then paused and added, 'Maybe we should think about getting a trolley? It would make it a lot easier, wouldn't it? We'd be able to carry more, and it'd add an air of class that's definitely missing right now.'

The DS didn't wait for a response and closed the door behind him.

Harry saw that Walker was smiling.

'He means well,' he said, pouring the tea. 'Unconventional, I suppose, in the way he helps manage the team, but it works, because he knows them and the area better than anyone.'

'You've a good team here,' said Walker, reaching for some cake. 'Local knowledge is everything, particularly somewhere like this. I'm already impressed.'

Harry gave a short laugh.

'I wasn't, not when I first arrived, anyway. More me than them, though. Wasn't sure what to expect. And they're nothing like anyone I've worked with before. Took a while for us to get used to each other.'

'Bristol, right?'

'Mainly, yes.'

'It's certainly very different round here than what you're used to.'

Harry handed Walker her tea.

'Where are you from yourself, then?' he asked.

'I've moved around a fair bit, actually,' Walker said. 'Not really sure I'm from anywhere. Hard to say where I'd call home now, if that makes sense.'

'And Swift's replacement is ill?'

Walker gave a nod.

'Came on rather suddenly, apparently. I don't have any details.'

'Do you know how Swift is?' Harry asked.

Swift had been quiet for a while, and Harry was a little concerned. He'd heard plenty from him during the last big case, which had involved the D-Sup carrying out an arrest at Leeds airport. But after that, not much at all, and not a thing for the last two or three weeks.

Walker shook her head.

'No, I don't, I'm afraid,' she said.

'No news is good news, though,' said Harry . 'Sometimes, anyway.'

They both sipped their tea.

'So ...' said Harry , looking to get back to the elephant in the room.

'Your father was in hospital,' Walker said, placing her tea down in front of her. 'As I understand it, he had a very bad fall in prison, bad enough to break his arm quite seriously, ended up with concussion as well, and by all accounts was in a pretty bad way.'

Harry shook his head, rolled his eyes, but said nothing. He didn't need to.

'You don't believe me?'

'Oh, I believe you alright,' Harry said. 'I just don't believe him. But keep going ...'

'He was taken to the hospital. And yes, before you ask, he was kept under guard.'

'So, what happened, then?'

'We're not exactly sure.'

Harry laughed, but the sound was about as warm as a blast from a walk-in freezer.

'Well, that's bollocks, isn't it?'

'I'm sorry?'

'Someone knows. It's just that they're not saying. Last thing anyone wants is for this to get out, am I right? Though surely he's regarded as a danger to the public?'

'Not necessarily,' said Walker.

'And what does that mean?'

'It means that although there's a truckload of stuff going to be dumped on him from a very high height once he gets to court, he currently doesn't have much pinned to him, does he? It's not like he's wanted for a dozen or more murders and is solely responsible for the crack epidemic sweeping the country.'

'That bastard murdered my mother,' said Harry , his voice

quiet, but no less menacing because of it. 'And I'm sure there are bodies buried in unmarked graves that he's responsible for.'

'But your mother's death is the only one we're certain of,' Walker said. 'Yes, the case against him is huge, and he can be linked to a hell of a lot of stuff, but not enough to put out a public statement.' Walker leaned in then and Harry saw her eyes narrow, her jaw harden. 'He's caused untold pain to thousands, and he will pay for it, Harry . You can be sure of that.'

Harry really couldn't believe what he was hearing. After all this time, so many years looking for his father, to finally have him behind bars, and then to have this happen? It was almost laughable.

'So, you have a man with a broken arm, and supposedly a serious concussion, and he just ups and walks himself out of hospital, like he's off on his holidays. Is that what you're telling me?'

Walker said, 'It does seem like that. However, we do think that he had help. My understanding is that a fire alarm went off, and that was the distraction for his escape.'

'A fire alarm? There has to be more to it than that.'

'I'm telling you all that I know.'

'It's not enough,' Harry said. 'And who is this royal *we* you keep using? Because you sure as hell aren't including me in it. Not yet anyway, if I'm reading this right.'

'You are reading it right,' Walker said. 'There's a team looking into it.'

Harry fell silent for a moment, mulling over what Walker had told him. He then remembered something else that Walker had said just before Matt had entered the room carrying the tray.

'You mentioned something about the "when" being important.'

'It is.'

'So, I'm going to assume the reason you're here, then, is because this has only just happened and you want to know if he's been in touch.'

'Yes, and also no,' Walker said. 'Actually, it's no and yes.'

'What?'

'No, it hasn't just happened, and yes, I've been told to ask if your father has been in touch.'

It was right there, in that moment, that Harry knew his day had just got a whole lot worse. Which was saying something considering how bad things had turned since he and Walker had entered the interview room just a few minutes ago, the air almost souring with every passing second and the more he learned.

'Wait a minute,' Harry said, lifting a finger to point at Walker. 'Are you telling me that he's been on the run for ...' He paused, leaned back, stared at the ceiling, shook his head, swore, dropped his gaze back down to stare at the Detective Superintendent. 'When?' he asked. 'When did this happen? When did he escape custody? How long has he been out?'

'It was two weeks ago,' Walker replied.

Harry shook his head in disbelief.

'Two weeks? You're having a bloody laugh, aren't you? Two weeks?'

'I'm deadly serious.'

And she was, Harry could hear it in her voice.

'Then why the bloody hell am I only hearing about this now? What the—'

Walker raised a hand as though to calm Harry .

'I was only informed late yesterday myself. Which is why I thought it pertinent to come over here first thing today.'

'Pertinent? Really? I'll tell you what would've been pertinent, making sure that bastard's legs were broken as well as his arm! And if I get my hands on him ...'

'It was an accident ...'

Harry leaned back and laughed, but the sound was cold and hard.

'Of course it wasn't a bloody accident! If he had help, which you seem to be suggesting is the case, and I'd be inclined to agree with you on that by the way, then breaking his arm was a part of it, wasn't it? That was the plan.'

Walker went to speak, but Harry didn't give her the chance.

'You know as well as I do that getting hold of a phone in prison, if you're someone like my father, is easy, isn't it? Every prison has a bent warden or two. A few phone calls and somehow he's sorted out a nice little plan to bolt; it's that simple. My guess is that he charmed his way just enough to not be a problem. Then he stages an accident, breaks his arm—I'd be checking he didn't have someone do that for him, by the way, because my guess is he did—fakes a concussion and the story behind the break, and ends up in hospital. Then all that's needed is a distraction or two, and off he walks.'

'You make it sound easy.'

'That's because it obviously was, otherwise, you wouldn't be here now telling me this, would you?'

'No.'

'Exactly.' Harry paused for a moment to calm down. 'So, what now? What exactly do you want from me, if anything?'

'Has he been in touch?'

'You're not asking me that in all seriousness, are you?'

'I have to,' said Walker.

'Well, he hasn't, and I can assure you that if he had, I'd have reported it.'

'What about your brother? Ben, isn't it?'

'What about him?'

'Could your father have contacted him instead of you?'

Harry said, 'Firstly, the only reason that man would have to contact either of us is out of spite and revenge. Probably a little bit of smugness, too, just to rub it in our faces that he was out again and free to do whatever the hell he wants.'

'What are you getting at?'

'Right now, he's still on the run, isn't he? And he's got more than enough sense to not come after us yet, even if he wanted to. That would just be asking for trouble, wouldn't it? I mean, you're here, checking up on it all, aren't you? And he would know that. So, no, he hasn't been in touch. And I'd know if he had contacted Ben, I promise you that.'

'Why?'

'Because he's my brother.'

'And that's reason enough?'

'More than.'

There was a pause in the conversation, both Harry and Walker just sitting, thinking about what had been said so far.

'Look,' Walker said, 'I truly am sorry to be the bearer of this news. When I was told, my reaction was very similar to your own, though perhaps without the furniture rearrangement.'

'Sometimes, it's necessary.'

'You must go through a lot.'

'I buy cheap.'

Walker smiled at that.

'You have my word that I am looking into this personally. I know I'm only acting temporarily as your detective superintendent, but that does not mean you are any less of a priority than anyone else I'm responsible for. Right now, this is top of the list. You have my word on that. It is vital that your father is brought to justice.'

Harry actually found himself believing her.

'So, now what?' he asked.

'My suggestion, Detective, is that you carry on with your life as planned for the next few days. You're moving house, I understand, yes?'

Harry gave a nod.

'Bought a place up here. And I'm as surprised as anyone by that, if I'm honest.'

'You must like it here an awful lot, then.'

'It grows on you,' Harry said, unable to hide the smile. 'Or in you. Maybe both. Kind of gets a hold of you and won't let go. There's just something about it.'

'There is,' Walker said. 'So, do not let what I've just told you ruin your day. I suspect that is exactly what your father would like to happen, which is why he may well be in touch sooner rather than later. If he is, you know where I am.'

'I do,' Harry said.

Walker rose to her feet and held out a hand.

'Very good to meet you,' she said. 'I only wish it had been under different circumstances.'

'I second that,' Harry said. 'I appreciate you coming over.'

'I'll leave you to it, then.'

Walker made her way to the door. Harry followed and opened it, then allowed her through. At the main door out of the community centre, she stared out into the day beyond.

'Looks like it's still raining,' she said.

'Lovely, isn't it?' Harry said.

Walker looked up at him, an eyebrow raised.

'Is it?'

'After the rain, the air here smells like ...' Harry thought for a moment, searching for a way to describe what he meant, what it was like to head outside and take a stroll across wet fields beneath glistening fells. 'Like the world's just alive,' he said. 'Like every bit of it is breathing.'

Walker smiled.

'You really do love it here, don't you?'

'Like I said, there's just something about it.'

'I envy you,' Walker said, then pushed out into the rain.

CHAPTER EIGHT

Harry stepped back into the office. Gordy and Matt came over, barring his way.

'Anything we need to talk about?' Gordy asked.

'Yes and no,' Harry said, thinking that there was no need as yet to let anyone know what Walker had told him. It was a personal matter, and right now it didn't impact the team. If there came a time when it would, then he'd tell them.

'You sure about that?' Matt said, folding his arms across his chest.

'It can wait.'

'Then best you just turn back out that door and get back to what you're supposed to be doing.'

'Are you kicking me out, Sergeant?'

Matt shook his head.

'I think you'll find that what I'm actually doing is simply enforcing our policy on annual leave.'

Despite everything that he'd just been told by Walker and the dark clouds he could feel gathering inside his head, Harry felt a smile ease its way onto his face.

'I'd be surprised if you knew where that was, never mind read it.'

'I'm full of surprises,' said Matt.

'He's got a point though,' said Gordy. 'This is a big day for you. Whatever Walker was here for, unless we need to all be on it right now, my advice is to forget it and just get on with your plans.'

'Unless you need to throw around a few more chairs, that is,' Matt said with a faint smile. 'I can always go and find a few extra as well, if you think that would help.'

Harry hesitated. He knew they were both right, but it was still hard to peel himself away from the job, even on a day like this.

'The break-in over in Leyburn,' he said.

'Is none of your concern right now, is it?' said Matt. 'I'll be in touch with Jen in a while, see what's what. Nowt we can't handle ourselves, I'm sure. Hardly something for you to be worrying about.'

'You'll call me if you need to, though?'

'If we have a sudden hostage crisis, yes,' said Gordy. 'Or if a zombie biker gang swoops into town to raise hell.'

'Zombie biker gang?' said Harry , raising an eyebrow.

Gordy laughed.

'It is Halloween after all, isn't it? And Anna's a horror movie fan, would you believe it?'

'But she's a vicar,' said Harry , picturing Gordy's partner in his mind.

'And she's happy to point out that a lot of horror tropes stem from the Bible. Apparently, of all the genres, it's the most theologically interesting. Or something.'

'Well, I'll take yours, or Anna's word for it.'

Gordy pointed at the door.

'Anyway, enough dillydallying; be off with you, man! Go!'

With one last look at the team, Harry turned and made his way out of the community centre to be welcomed by the rain. Walking down the lane, his collar up against the weather, he remembered something and turned to head back to the community centre, only to see Matt now at the door.

'You just keep walking, now, you hear?' he called out, pointing away past Harry . 'Go on.'

'I am,' Harry said, 'but I've just remembered something.'

'Of course you have.'

'Anderson's knocking about,' Harry said. 'He caught me earlier just as I turned up.'

'That'll be Mischief Night, then,' said Matt.

'It was. Looks rough as well, like he was out a little too late last night, if you know what I mean.'

Matt said, 'He didn't do anything about it last year but seems like he's back on it again. Bit of a personal mission I think, that one. Certainly seems to be.'

'Not sure I'm following,' said Harry .

'He likes to use it as a stick to poke us with, that's all,' said Matt. 'Seems to think it's an example of how ineffective we are, how society has gone to the dogs, that kind of thing.'

'Must be a slow news day, then.'

'Something like that, no doubt, but I'll keep an eye out, just in case. Now, off you go, then.'

'You don't have to watch me to make sure that I do.'

Matt folded his arms and stared; he wasn't going anywhere. Harry wouldn't put it past the man to follow him a little either, just to make sure.

A few minutes later, and arriving at the flat, Harry was drenched.

Grace met him at the door.

'Dad's here,' she said.

Harry wiped the rain from his face with his bare hands, flicking the water to the floor.

'What? Why?'

'That was exactly what I said when he turned up.'

'What about the dogs?'

'Best you come in,' Grace said. 'And get yourself out of those clothes.'

Harry raised a cheeky eyebrow.

'Not sure we've time for any of that, do you?' he said.

Grace laughed and pulled him inside.

'Everything okay with the new boss?'

'I'll tell you all about it later,' Harry said. 'How are things here, then?'

'Come and see for yourself.'

Grace led Harry through to the living area, where he was greeted with a handshake from Arthur, Grace's dad. Behind Arthur, lying on the floor in a tangled heap, were three dogs.

'Now then, Harry ,' Arthur said.

'Arthur,' Harry said. 'Thought you were staying home to look after the dogs?'

Harry glanced over at Smudge. She looked up at him from where she was snuggled up with Jess and old Molly, who belonged to Grace and Arthur respectively. Smudge's tail wagged, but not enough to imply she was about to get up from her prime position of cosy warmth to say hello.

'I was,' Arthur replied. 'But your Smudge wouldn't stop whining. Then the other two joined in, and beyond shooting the daft buggers, I didn't know what else to do.'

'Well, this is better than that option, I suppose,' Harry said.

'They'll be no bother, I'm sure,' Arthur said. 'And I'll get on with cleaning and tidying here while you and Grace move in. How's that sound?'

Grace stepped in and said, 'That's very kind, Dad.'

Arthur rubbed his chin.

'Just out of interest, though, what are you doing about furniture? All of this is staying here, if I'm right, isn't it?'

'You are, and it is,' Harry said. 'I have a van turning up with a load of stuff later today.'

'And he's had so much fun buying it all, haven't you?'

'No, I haven't.'

Arthur laughed.

'Well, if that's what's happening, best you get on,' he said, and plonked himself down on the sofa.

'Thought you said you were here to help?' said Harry , staring at Arthur as he made himself comfortable.

'And right now, I'm staying out of your way,' Arthur said.

Harry left the old man to relax and headed back through the kitchen, then down the hall to the front door, Grace following him.

'Come on,' he said. 'Let's go see this new house of mine before anyone else comes along to try and bugger things up.'

'You sure you don't want to change?'

'I'm only going to get soaked again when moving everything, aren't I?' Harry said. 'So, what's the point? Come on ...'

Harry didn't wait for Grace to reply and opened the front door.

A few minutes later, and after a very short drive out of Hawes, then past the primary school and up the hill to Gayle, Harry was standing outside the front door of his new home, keys in his hand. He'd parked up just away from the house, the place itself having no parking. That had been the one thing which had caused him a little worry, but as Grace had pointed out, there was more than enough parking on the roads and lanes around and about, and it wasn't like the village was ever so busy as to never be able to find a space.

'And anyway,' she'd said, looking out through the kitchen window, 'I'd sacrifice a little bit of convenience with parking for that view, wouldn't you?'

Grace's voice pulled Harry from his thoughts.

'You have to actually put one of those in the door for it to work.'

'An expert on keys, are you?' Harry replied. He remembered then what had happened over in Leyburn, that he'd need a new lock for the front door. Looking at it, he wasn't overly concerned; a replacement would be easy to find and install himself.

Grace reached out and grabbed the hand Harry was holding the keys in. Then the key was in the door.

'And you also have to turn it for it to work,' Grace added.

Harry turned the key, opened the door, and stepped inside.

'Welcome home,' Grace said, stepping in behind him.

'Thanks,' Harry replied, moving further into the house.

Harry was struck by just how much his life had changed. Here he was, stepping into a house he had bought, in an area he now classed as home, and with him was a woman who, when he was brave enough to admit it—and then only to himself—was becoming more and more important to him with each passing day.

'Everything okay?' Grace asked.

'Yes, absolutely,' Harry said.

The air in the house was still, and it seemed to Harry that the building had been waiting for him, almost as though it had something secret to show only him.

'Come on, then,' Grace said. 'Don't you want to have a look around, get a feel for the place before we start bringing in the boxes? Actually, that reminds me ... just a minute ...'

Grace turned round and dashed back outside to the Rav4, a moment later returning with an old biscuit tin and a kettle.

'And what's that?' Harry asked.

Grace opened the tin.

Inside, Harry saw tea bags, a small bottle of milk, two mugs, and a packet of gingernut biscuits.

Grace said, 'You can't move into a new house without christening the place, now, can you?'

Harry laughed.

'To be honest, I had something else in mind,' he said with a wink.

Grace's eyes widened.

'We've no time for those shenanigans,' she said. 'Come on.'

Harry followed Grace along the hallway to the kitchen, passing the door to the lounge. He was tempted to have a look inside, but he also fancied a mug of hot tea, the cold from the rain having seeped into his bones.

In the kitchen, Grace put the kettle on, and Harry opened the biscuits. A little window over the sink looked out onto a small garden and Harry saw that Grace had been more than right about forgoing the parking for what lay in front of him.

The garden was small, not quite a postage stamp, but not far off. A shared access path crossed in front of the row of cottages, of which Harry 's was a part. Laid to lawn, with flower borders on each side, a small footpath of worn flagstones threaded its way down the middle. And at the end was Gayle Beck.

Harry leaned over and opened the window. Wind blew in and with it came not just a few drops of rain, but the joyous gurgle and splosh of the beck, its deepening waters dashing down towards Hawes and beyond, and turning a deep golden brown with the peat washed down off the fells in the rain.

'You were right about the view,' Harry said, as Grace handed him a mug of tea and a biscuit.

'I know,' Grace replied and lifted her mug to his. 'Cheers.'

Harry clinked his mug against hers.

'Shall we have a look around, then?' he said.

Grace didn't wait for an answer and turned on her heel, back into the hall.

'Let's start upstairs,' she said. 'That way you can imagine what it'll be like to wake up tomorrow and know that all of this is yours.'

'I don't need to imagine it,' Harry said. 'I know that it's mine, don't I?'

Grace, however, wasn't listening and was already halfway up the stairs.

At the top, they checked out the bedrooms, Harry deciding which was to be his and which was to be the spare. It wasn't a difficult decision, as the largest also overlooked the beck, and he rather liked the idea of waking in the morning to the gossip of the river.

'Bathroom will need a clean,' Grace said. 'We can bring all the cleaning stuff up with the next trip.'

'Then let's make that sooner rather than later,' Harry said, looking at his watch. Midday was closing in on them faster than he'd realised. 'That delivery of furniture will be arriving in a couple of hours, and I'd rather have most of my stuff in before it does.'

With that said, Harry led the way back downstairs and made for the front door.

'Wait a minute,' Grace said. 'What about the lounge?'

'What about it?'

'You've not been in it yet.'

Harry was keen to get on, but he stepped back into the house.

'Come on, then,' he said and pushed through into the final room.

Inside, on a blood-spattered plastic sheet rolled out across the floor, was a body.

CHAPTER NINE

THE QUIETLY GRUESOME SCENE CAUGHT HARRY OFF GUARD, but not so much that he responded to it with any degree of shock. Instead, the sight of it was so unexpected, so incongruous with where he and Grace were, that the first feeling that swept through him was one of absolute bemusement.

As Halloween's went, this one was really turning out to be a corker, he thought. And considering that fact, that this was the one day of the year dedicated to all things spooky and terrifying, he briefly wondered if perhaps this was some kind of prank, the body a fake. But he could see very well that it wasn't; there was something inherently obvious about a dead body and faking one was, to Harry 's mind, impossible. Plus, there was also the smell, the sickly tang of decaying flesh, though he noticed something else behind it, like an old barbeque left out in the rain.

'Grace,' Harry said, snapping around to face her, immediately barring her way into the room. 'You're not to come in here. Stay right there.'

Grace was still in the hall and hadn't yet stepped into the room. She had no idea what he'd just discovered and Harry wanted it to stay that way; hearing about it would be enough, seeing it would only haunt her, and for how long, he couldn't even guess.

'Why? What's up?' Grace asked. 'The previous owner left a load of junk or something? That happened to me when I moved in, you know? The dirty buggers, they just left a pile of rubbish bags in the kitchen. Not nice.' Her face screwed up, and she gagged. 'Wait ... just what the hell is that smell? Hell, Harry , that stinks. Is it rats?'

'Not yet, it isn't, no,' Harry said, his answer a little more cryptic than he'd have liked.

'What do you mean, not yet? That doesn't make any sense at all.'

Grace moved to push past, but Harry made sure she could go no further, broadening his shoulders and pushing out his chest to make him seem even more imposing than usual.

'Harry ...'

'Trust me,' Harry said, 'you do not want to see what's in there.'

'Why? What is it?'

'I need to call the team,' Harry said. 'Right now.'

'You can't be serious ...' Harry watched Grace's expression turn grave. 'Bloody hell, you are, aren't you?'

Harry pulled out his phone and then stepped back out of the room into the hall, swishing the door shut behind him and making absolutely sure that it was shut and wasn't about to get pushed open again by a sudden huff of air from outside pushing through the front door.

'I don't understand,' Grace said, worry in her voice. 'What's going on?'

Harry didn't respond as Gordy then answered his call.

'If you're calling me to check up on how Jen's doing over in Leyburn, I'm going to have to come round there and smack your feet,' Gordy said.

'My feet?' Harry said. 'What?'

'Something my mother used to say when we were kids. I think it's because she used to chase us up the stairs, slapping them with her hands to hurry us a long.'

'I need someone to call forensics,' Harry said, walking away from the lounge and towards the front door, at the same time making sure that Grace was with him.

'Forensics?' Harry heard the confusion in the DI's voice. 'Why? Are you not at your house, then? What's going on? What's happened?'

'Yes, I'm at my house,' Harry said, aware that Grace was staring at him. 'And yes, I need Sowerby here ASAP.'

'You never say ASAP.'

'And I'd prefer it if you never mentioned that again.' Harry looked at Grace, then said to Gordy, 'Look, we're at the house, and I know this is going to sound bizarre in the extreme, but there's a body in the lounge.'

'Slow down, Harry , you're not making any sense.'

Harry wasn't about to slow down.

'We've been here a while, and it was the last room we checked. No idea how long it's been there. I've not had a chance to have a closer look yet; thought it prudent to call you first and get things moving.'

'If you're pulling my leg, I'm not laughing,' said Gordy.

'Neither am I,' Harry replied. 'This isn't exactly the kind of housewarming gift I was expecting, that's for sure.'

'A body, though? And you're sure that's what it is?'

'I may not be Sherlock bloody Holmes, but I'm pretty sure I know what a body looks like.'

'I'm calling Sowerby now,' Gordy said. 'I'll send you a text when I know more.'

'Thank you. Who else is with you?'

'Jen's out to Leyburn, as you know,' Gordy said. 'And Matt's had a call in from someone on the local bonfire committee. Liz has—'

'The what now?' Harry asked. 'There's a bonfire committee?'

'There is,' Gordy said. 'Not sure what's happened, but Matt certainly rushed off at quite a pace. He can't half move when he wants to. Anyway, as I was saying, Liz had to dash off over to White Scar Caverns, I think, so that leaves Jim, Jadyn, and myself.'

'Send them both over,' Harry said. 'Now.' And hung up.

Harry saw Grace turn her gaze from him to the closed lounge door, then back to him once again. All colour had drained from her face and her eyes were wide with disbelief.

'A body? In there?'

Harry nodded.

'As in dead?'

Another nod.

'Who is it?'

Harry scratched his head.

'Not a clue.'

'But why would they be here, Harry , whoever they are?'

'That's a question I'm already asking myself. Doesn't make much sense right now, that's all I know for sure.'

Grace shook her head, then laughed, but there was no humour in it.

'This is a joke, isn't it? I mean, it's Halloween! This is a prank, Harry . It has to be. You know, I bet it was Matt. He'd do something like this, I'm sure of it. Call him now.'

'Grace, I can assure you that this is no prank,' Harry said. 'And funny though Matt is, a body in the lounge is stretching it. Anyway, you can smell it just as I can, can't you? And that's a smell you never forget, believe me. It's also one that you can't fake.'

'It's like roadkill that's been out in the sun,' Grace said.

'I don't want it to be a body, and I'd love this to be Matt trying to be funny, but it is what it is and that's all there is to it.'

'But Harry ...'

Harry reached out to hold Grace's hands. When he spoke next, his voice was calm and quiet.

'I need you to go and sit in the car, okay? This is a crime scene now. I need to have a look around. Jim and Jadyn are on their way, and it won't be long before the circus arrives, so I need you out of the way.'

'The circus?'

'Forensics,' Harry explained. 'Big white vans, people dressed head to toe in PPE. The kind of thing that makes conspiracy nuts think we've found another UFO. Which, frankly, I'd prefer to any of this, that's for damned sure.'

That comment garnered a flicker of a smile from Grace.

'Another UFO?' she said. 'How many have you found, then?'

Harry leaned in and whispered, 'I'm not at liberty to say.'

Grace reached out and rested a hand on Harry 's arm.

'Are you okay?'

'No, I'm bloody well not,' Harry said through gritted teeth, his voice filled with darkness. 'Not by a long shot.'

Grace made to leave, then turned to stare at him.

'What?' Harry asked, seeing a question in her eyes.

'You think someone did this on purpose, don't you? I mean, obviously they did, because this can't be a random event, but you already think there's more to it.'

'Why do you say that?'

'You've that look.'

'What look?'

Grace pulled her phone out of a pocket, pointed it at Harry , then turned it around so he could see the screen. Staring back at him was his own scarred face. He could see that his jaws were set, his eyes dark and narrowed, deep furrows ploughing ridges across his forehead.

'That one,' she said.

'I always look like that.'

'No, you don't,' Grace said, shaking her head. 'I'll admit that you have variations on stern and terrifying, but right now, it's something else.'

'What?'

'Fury,' Grace said. 'You hide it well, but it's there. I can sense it as well as see it. Actually, I can feel it coming off you like heat. And the only reason you'd be feeling that at all isn't just because there's a body in your house on the day that you're moving in. No, it's because you already suspect there's more to this than happenstance; you suspect intent.'

Harry said, ‘I’ll be out in a bit.’
Grace headed outside.

CHAPTER TEN

Alone now, Harry turned back to the lounge door. Even though this was a day off, he was still able to reach into a pocket and pull out some PPE. He quickly covered his shoes, then slipped on a facemask and some disposable gloves. He also had a little pot of vapour rub and dabbed some under his nose. It wouldn't completely disguise the smell of the corpse, because that smell had already crawled inside his nose, but it would mask it enough to make his time close to it a little more bearable.

With a shove, the lounge door slipped open. Harry stepped inside. The room was gloomy, the grey light falling in from the window doing little to reveal much beyond the outline of the figure on the floor.

Harry flicked on the light switch, and the room was flooded with a brightness so sudden it was momentarily painful. The bulb had no shade to dampen the light, and it glared out, cold and stark. Harry blinked, then slowly opened his eyes, giving them time to adjust. Then the bulb popped, and the room shot back into the gloomy half-light.

The body was in the middle of the room, lying on its back. From where Harry was standing, he could see by the build that it was a man. Whoever he was, he was dressed in blue jeans, a black jacket of some kind, buttoned up the front. He was wearing cheap trainers, white socks.

Harry cast his eyes around the room, looking for clues, looking for something that was out of place.

How the body had got to where it was in the first place was the first thing he tried to figure out. Carrying someone unconscious or dead was no easy task, the human body was heavy and unwieldy when lifted. It required strength and a little technique. The fireman's lift was easy enough if the person you were carrying was able to climb up onto your shoulders. If they weren't, you were faced with lifting a dead weight from the floor, which was a task in itself. And whoever this was on the floor in front of him, they were no lightweight. Not fat, but not thin either. He'd put them at between thirteen and fourteen stone, and Harry knew even he would struggle to heft someone like that off the ground.

They could've been dragged in, Harry thought. And if so, whether they had been dead at the time, or unconscious, that would be something for forensics to establish. If dragged in, then Harry would suspect that this had been done by one person working alone. Had there been two, they could've carried the body into the room instead.

The plastic sheet was large and had been rolled out almost to the edges of the room. Why protect the carpet underneath, unless of course, the plastic sheet had been used to bring the body into the house? That made some sense, Harry thought; it would maybe be easier to slide it in on the sheet than physically handle the body itself, dragging it by its arms or legs. The sheet was slick with blood, which filled the room with its sickly scent of meat left in the sun, and rust.

Sticking close to the wall, Harry turned to his right to make his way around the room, doing his best to stay away from any blood spatter, his eyes on his surprise visitor. He spotted some muddy footprints on his way, partly covered with blood. He stayed away from them; forensics would want them as untouched as everything else.

Harry was now able to see the face, and immediately wished that he couldn't. It was so badly burned that its features were unrecognisable in the dim shadows laying across the floor.

That explained the barbeque smell I noticed earlier, Harry thought, and kept moving on round, but he stopped and looked back at the face.

Almost as though they were working independently of him, Harry noticed then that his fingers were scratching his cheek, his own scars itching just enough to make him rub his face. Memories of the day he'd received them tried to push their way to the front of his mind, but Harry forced them back. Now was not the time. Now was never the time. Another reason he was none too keen on the reunion. Joining the police had been a good excuse to get away from what had happened, and he just wasn't sure he wanted to be reminded of it again, not after all this time. But there was no space in his mind right now to be worrying about that, not right now with what was lying in front of him.

Harry moved on around the body. Looking closer, he saw that the jacket wasn't actually black at all, but dark blue, with darker patches across it where something from inside was leaking through. He could just make out the collar of a white T-shirt underneath. He suspected the patches were blood and other fluids, none of them nice.

Having done a full circuit of the room, Harry was back to the lounge door when he heard someone enter the house.

'Hello? Boss? We're here.'

Harry quickly stepped out of the room to see Jadyn and Jim standing in the hall. He slipped off his facemask, pulled off his gloves.

'You took your time,' he grumbled, immediately aware that he was simply taking his frustrations out on the two young officers. Sometimes, his grouchiness annoyed even himself.

'We came here straight away,' Jadyn said.

'It's true, we did,' agreed Jim.

'I know,' said Harry with a firm nod, his voice a little warmer. 'Thank you. I'm just a bit grouchy, that's all.'

'Not like you,' said Jim under his breath.

Harry ignored him, but knew that the PCSO had a point.

'Finding a body in my lounge isn't the best way to put me in a good mood. So, if either of you are responsible, I'm going to be very annoyed.'

Jadyn said, 'Forensics is on their way. And Sowerby said she'll be here in about twenty minutes. Her mum will be with her as well.'

Despite the circumstances, that news made Harry smile.

'Quite the double act they make as well, don't you think?' he said.

'This is a lovely little place, Boss,' Jim said, looking around the small entrance hall.

'If it wasn't for the small matter of the corpse in the lounge,' said Harry .

He almost laughed then, struck by just how strange and ridiculous the whole thing was.

'No, you're right, there is that,' Jim said. 'Not my idea of soft furnishings.'

'You both know what to do,' Harry said, putting his trust in Jadyn and Jim. 'Cordon the place off. Decide which one of you is going to be the Scene Guard. As for the other, I'd like them to just pop around to the neighbours and give them a heads up. Don't tell them exactly what's going on; they'll find that out soon enough, so best to keep the panic at a low heat for now. Just inform them that the police are looking into something and it'll be a little busy for a while, that's all. Nothing to worry about, that kind of thing. And, while you're at it, see if anyone heard anything last night or saw anything.'

'It's not easy to sneak a body into a house without someone noticing something,' Jadyn said.

Jim said, 'I'll do that, Boss. I know a few of the folk who live round and about.'

'Of course you do,' Harry smiled. 'Can't beat a good bit of local knowledge.'

Jadyn set himself to the side of the door.

'I've the clipboard ready,' he said, waving it in the air for Harry to see. 'I'll get everyone's details down and keep you updated with what's going on.'

'I'm not going anywhere,' Harry said.

'Actually, you are,' Jim said. 'The DI told us to tell you to head back to the flat for now.'

'Did she, now? And at what point in the proceedings was our wonderful DI put in charge?'

'You're on leave,' Jim said. 'So, she's the commanding officer, isn't she?'

'I'm needed here.'

'She said you'd say that,' said Jadyn. 'Which is why she also said she would follow us up here in a few minutes to oversee everything.'

Harry said, 'You do all remember that I'm the DCI, don't you? Which means I'm the one in charge. That's the whole point of those letters before my name.'

'Of course we do,' replied Jim. 'You're the boss. But regardless of that, best you get going before she arrives. Unless, of course, you want to wait around and speak to her yourself?'

Harry shoved his hands in his pockets, glanced back at the lounge door, thought for a moment about what was lying on the floor on the other side of it.

'You know, any other day I would,' he said. 'But right now, I think I'll just go with the flow.'

'That's a very sensible decision,' said Jim. 'The DI will be very happy to find you not here.'

'That's true,' said Jadyn. 'She'll be over the moon to not have to tell you all of this herself.'

Harry headed outside and climbed into the driver's seat of the Rav4.

'Everything okay?' asked Grace.

'There's someone dead in the lounge of the house I've just bought,' Harry said.

'Bound to put a bit of a dent in your day.'

'Feels a little more like someone's lobbed a grenade at it then driven a tank through it to make absolutely sure it's ruined.'

'So, what now?'

Harry wanted to go back into the house. Not to be a part of the investigation, but to get on with the only reason he was there in the first place, to move in and claim it as his own. Except that wasn't going to happen, was it? And with the house now a crime scene, he wouldn't be doing so for a good while yet, either.

'You hungry?' he asked.

'Is it that time already?'

'It is,' Harry said, and instead of waiting for an answer, he pulled away from the kerb. The Fountain Inn in Hawes was calling, and he was in the mood for ham and eggs. But there was something else he needed to do first, something that he should've done immediately after his chat with Walker. So lunch would have to wait a while longer.

CHAPTER ELEVEN

Mike the mechanic came out to meet Harry as he walked over from where he'd parked up at the garage just on the outskirts of Hawes. After leaving his house in Gayle in the capable hands of Jim and Jadyn, Harry had dropped Grace off back at the flat and told her he'd be back soon to then head out with her dad for some lunch.

'Dropping it off for a check over, are you?' Mike said, wiping hands already marred with black oil stains, and nodding at Harry 's Rav4. 'Could probably do with a service, what with winter knocking at the door.'

Harry shook his head.

'Is Ben around at all?' he asked. 'Said he'd be in to do some overtime.'

'Inside, putting a brew on,' Mike replied. 'Too keen, that young brother of yours, not that I'm complaining.' Again, he glanced over at the Rav4. 'You'll be thinking of replacing it soon though, like, won't you? It was only meant to be a stop-gap if I remember.'

'Was it?'

'Well, maybe not a stop-gap, no, but it's old and you could do with something a little more appropriate, I'm sure.'

'Appropriate how, exactly?' Harry asked. 'And would I be right in thinking that what you actually mean is more expensive?'

Mike laughed.

'Well, you just have a think,' he said, leading Harry into his garage. 'And if you decide that you need to swap it out, I'm sure I can find something suitable.'

In the garage, Harry made his way past a Land Rover Defender up in the air on a vehicle lift.

'Like that, you mean?' Harry said, gesturing up at the vehicle.

'Maybe,' Mike said.

Further on, Harry entered a small office to find Ben over by a small kitchen unit pouring water into a couple of mugs. He saw Harry , smiled, then frowned.

'Something up with the Rav?' he asked. 'Mike and I have been saying how you should think of replacing it, sooner rather than later as well.'

'Funnily enough, that's what Mike said; those exact words.'

'Great minds, and all that.'

Harry looked back over to Mike and said, 'You mind giving us a few minutes?'

'Not a problem,' Mike said, and he grabbed a steaming mug from Ben, then headed back out to get to work on the Defender.

Harry turned back to Ben.

'Something's up, isn't it?' Ben said.

'You could say that, yes,' said Harry . 'Best you grab yourself a seat for this.'

'I'm fine standing.'

'Sit.'

Harry dropped himself into a chair and nodded at another opposite.

Ben sat down, but his eyes didn't leave Harry 's.

'Is it Grace? Has something happened? Has there been an accident? Is she pregnant? She's okay, isn't she? Look, if there's anything you need me to do, then—'

'It's not Grace,' Harry said, deciding to not go into any of what

Ben had just run through. 'This is a little closer to home, I'm afraid. I was going to come and tell you about it a bit later, maybe over a pint or something, but with how my day's going, I thought it best to just come and get it over and done with now.'

'You're rambling.'

'I'm getting to the point.'

'By way of a detour.'

'Journeys with detours give the best views.'

'Not this one.'

Harry sucked in a hard breath through his nose, then let it out, trying to relax himself.

'He's escaped, Ben.'

Confusion creased Ben's face.

'Who did? What are you talking about? Who's escaped?'

Harry 's glare drilled into Ben's eyes.

'That bastard we're both unfortunate enough to have as a father.'

Ben quietly snorted.

'Don't talk bollocks, Harry . He's in prison. He can't have escaped.'

'Not something I'm in the habit of doing, if I'm honest,' Harry said.

Ben stood up, turned his back on his brother, raised his hands to his head as though he was trying to stop it from exploding. He started pacing around the room.

'But he can't have done, Harry ! He's in prison! Prisoners don't escape! That's the whole bloody point of being in prison!'

'Sorry to burst your bubble of absolute confidence in our excellent and infallible justice system, but I'm afraid to say that they do, actually,' Harry said. 'Not just a couple here and there, either.'

Ben stopped pacing and turned round to look down at Harry .

'How many?'

'Does it matter?'

Ben repeated the question.

'I don't have exact figures to hand, obviously, but over the past five years, a few hundred at least would be my guess.'

Ben's eyes widened.

'A few hundred? You're having a laugh, right?'

'Again, something I'm not in the habit of doing.'

Ben paced around the room once again.

'So, what you're telling me, is that murders and rapists escape from prison on a regular basis, and that one of these escapees happens to be the man who killed Mum?'

'Probably best you sit yourself back down, Ben,' Harry said.

Ben kept pacing, ignoring Harry 's instruction.

'Where is he, Harry ? Why did he escape? And how, exactly? Tell me. I want to know.'

'I'd be telling you right now if I knew myself. All I do know is that there was an accident in prison and because of it, he was then sent to hospital. It's from there that he managed to escape custody.'

Ben shook his head and exhaled through his nose, the sound of an animal angry and ready to strike out.

'That doesn't just happen, Harry . You know that as well as I do. Someone helped him, didn't they?'

'Right now, I have no further information. The new detective superintendent came over today just to tell me.'

'So, this has only just happened, is that what you're saying? Which means they'll catch him, doesn't it, and that's why she was over, to tell you that, right?'

'Those two things aren't connected. And no, it hasn't just happened.'

Harry saw a new wave of shock slam into his younger brother and he dropped into a chair, his face suddenly pale.

'You mean he's been out there for ... Bloody hell, Harry , how long has he actually been on the run?'

'Two weeks,' Harry said. 'Or so I've been told. The detective superintendent only just found out herself, which was why she came straight over. Sounded shocked herself, if I'm honest.'

Ben was on his feet once again.

'Two weeks?'

'You need to try and stay calm,' Harry said.

'He could be here, Harry ! He could be up here, couldn't he? Just biding his time, waiting to come and—'

Ben's voice crashed and burned, and his shoulders fell.

'You need to understand that he's on the run, Ben,' Harry said, keeping his voice calm and quiet. 'He knows people will be looking for him, and not just the police either, if you ask me. There's plenty of others who I'm guessing want to have a little chat with him. And if they learn he's out, well, that might not go too well for him, if you know what I mean.'

'I don't.'

'He's been in custody long enough for anyone who knows him to be getting worried that he might have let a few things slip,' Harry explained. 'Maybe given over a few names, that kind of thing, to try and soften things up a bit for when it all ends up in court.'

'That's suicide, isn't it? He'd never be a grass.'

'It's self-preservation is what it is,' said Harry . 'He's not an idiot. He'll be wanting to make sure he's okay, no matter what happens. Right now, though, he'll have gone to ground. The last thing he'll be thinking of is coming here.'

'You don't know that.'

'I do. He'll be staying away from anywhere that he knows the police will be keeping an extra eye on. Right now, we have nothing to worry about.'

Ben shook his head and breathed out sharply through his nose.

'You really expect me to believe that?'

'He's not coming after us,' Harry said, leaning forward, elbows on knees, his voice calm, caring almost, but still firm. 'His one thought right now will be survival. He's looking after number one. Wherever he is, it's a very long way away from here, that's for sure. My guess is he's already abroad somewhere, and it won't be much of a holiday, either.'

With nothing left to say, Harry leaned back and allowed Ben some time to take it all in. Harry wasn't about to say it, but his concern wasn't so much that their dad was making a beeline to Hawes to take his revenge on him, but instead, it was for Ben, and that this news didn't send him spiralling.

Harry had seen it before, Ben's fragile shell broken by news that would have him looking for ways out, most of them illegal. His brother had made so much progress since joining him in the Dales and Harry was keen to make sure that whatever their father was up to, it didn't cause Ben to fall back into his old ways. He had a life here, now; a job, a girlfriend, and that was more precious to Harry than anything else on earth.

'You going to be okay?' he asked.

Ben looked up.

'Yes,' he said with a slight nod. 'You don't need to worry. And yes, I know you are. I can see it in your eyes.'

Harry didn't want to say anything, but Ben had a history of falling back on certain things to help him cope. Booze had never been his first port of call, and he'd always gone for something harder, more capable of taking the pain and reality away.

'You need to explain this all to Liz when you get home tonight,' Harry said.

'I will.'

'I can come over as well if you need me to.'

'No, I'll be fine with it.'

Harry clenched and unclenched his hands, then looked at Ben again.

'And you're absolutely sure you'll be okay?'

'Harry , if you're worried I'm going to head out to get my hands on something illegal, that just isn't going to happen. I'm fine. I promise. Actually, it gives me something to talk about this afternoon, doesn't it, in counselling?'

'I suppose it does,' Harry agreed. 'I'll leave you to it, then. I've got plenty to be getting on with.'

'How's the move going?' Ben asked, standing up to lead Harry out of the garage.

'Too many bloody boxes.'

'I can come over later this afternoon if you need me.'

'Don't you worry yourself about that for now,' Harry replied. 'You'll have a lot to talk about with Liz, as well as that counsellor this afternoon.'

'I can still pop in, though. It's no bother at all.'

'No,' Harry said, his voice a little too sharp. 'Not today. I'll give you a call.'

Harry saw the confusion on Ben's face.

'You okay, Harry ?'

Harry reached out and rested a hand on Ben's shoulder, gave it a gentle squeeze.

'It's all just a lot to take in, really, isn't it?' he said, then made his way back to his vehicle and drove back into town.

CHAPTER TWELVE

Following Harry 's instructions, Jim had headed out to knock on a few doors to let people know what was going on and to not worry. The DCI's house sat huddled in a quaint terrace, staring out over Gayle Beck and up onto Wether Fell beyond the village. He could hear the water bouncing along, its music a gentle serenade to the wind dancing in the trees.

The house to the left was occupied by a middle-aged couple on holiday from somewhere in the US. They had met Jim at the door dressed up in all the right gear for a day tramping across the moors. For some reason, after Jim had spoken with them, they had then wanted a selfie with 'a local bobby' and before he'd realised what was going on, or had time to say no, the photo had been taken. Then they'd headed off at a fair pace, across the bridge over Gayle Beck, seeming unfazed by the weather, a waterproof map held out in front of them like a compass.

The house on the other side of Harry 's cottage was quiet, and no answer came to his knock at the door, so Jim made his way around various others. More often than not he ended up having a chat with someone either he knew well, or his parents did.

Hawes was like that, he thought, a place where nearly everyone knew everyone else.

He knew that some would find that claustrophobic, the fear that too many people would know your business. But it wasn't really like that. It was more that everyone looked out for everyone else. This was a community, one born long ago and still going strong. A lot of houses were holiday cottages, that was true, but the small market town still managed to maintain a local population that went back generations.

When he came back around to Harry 's new place, Gordy had arrived, but she and Jadyn were still waiting for the arrival of the forensics team, the pathologist Rebecca Sowerby, and her mum, the district surgeon. So, on the off-chance that someone was now in, Jim rapped his knuckles on the door of the house adjacent to Harry 's, the one where there had been no answer. This time, however, he heard a shuffle from behind the door. Then the latch clicked, and the door was pulled inward.

Jim went to speak, but from the darkness on the other side, a voice shot out with a sharp, 'What is it, then?'

Jim tried to peer into the shadows and was able to make out a small figure leaning on a stick. They stepped forward, and he found himself being stared at by a woman dressed in a novelty apron, which would probably give him nightmares for months.

Jim introduced himself and said, 'I'm just letting you know what's going on next door. Don't want you getting worried when you see the police going in and out of the place.'

'Why would I be worried?'

'I'm sorry, I didn't catch your name,' said Jim. He was trying to place her face, but right now was at a loss.

'Didn't give it, now, did I?' the woman said. 'Though I'm surprised you don't remember.'

Jim waited.

'It's Mary,' the woman said. 'Mary Iveson. Surely you remember, James?' Jim, a little taken aback to hear his name, saw a smile edge its way onto Mary's face. 'You're one of mine, after all, you know.'

Jim was still lost, even more so now that he knew Mary recognised him.

'I should be getting back next door,' he said.

'Quickly now,' Mary said and reached out to pull Jim inside, then before he knew where he was, she marched him into a small lounge and sat him down on a soft armchair.

'Thank you,' Jim said, not really sure why.

Mary sat down opposite. Jim saw a twinkle in her eye, and she gave him a sly wink.

'How's your father, then? He was a good-looking man back in the day, you know. Still is.'

And then he knew; Mary was an old flame of his dad's from way back when the man had been a teenager. His dad had mentioned her a few times, and Jim had seen her around and about over the years. But then everyone had. She kept herself to herself now mostly, but she had spent most of her life as a maternity nurse and helped with the births of half the Dale by all accounts, including his.

'He's fine, thank you,' Jim said.

'And you've turned out well, by the looks of things,' Mary said, leaning forward to pinch Jim's uniform between her slim fingers. 'Look at you, in all your finery. Makes me right proud.'

Jim couldn't help but smile.

'Anyway,' Mary said, leaning back and getting herself comfortable, resting her stick against the wall. 'You were saying something about next door.'

'I was,' said Jim, and explained again, giving a little more detail this time, but not too much. 'So, there's nowt to worry about.'

'If there was nowt to worry about, you wouldn't be round here telling me there was nowt to worry about, would you?' Mary said, narrowing her eyes.

Jim wasn't quite sure what to say to that. Which was a good job, really, because Mary was still speaking.

'I've that Grimm chap moving next door, your boss, and now here you are popping round on the day he moves in to tell me not to worry about all the police that'll be turning up. Doesn't sit right, that, does it, Jim?'

'I'm afraid I can't give you any more details,' Jim said. 'I'm just here to reassure you, that's all. I'm sure further information will come out as and when.'

'Does it have anything to do with last night?'

Jim sat up.

'Last night?'

'I heard something,' Mary said. 'Woke me up. I remember, because I was thinking to myself that your Mr Grimm wasn't due to move in till today, so what was he doing around in the middle of the night? That's what I wanted to know. I'm not nosy, I just like to know what's going on, if that makes sense.'

Jim pulled out his notebook.

'Do you know what time this was, Mary?'

'Just gone one in the morning, I think,' she said. 'At first, I thought it was the sheep that woke me up. They were properly going off on one last night, somewhere up on the hills. Anyway, I heard sort of a thump or a bang or something from outside and then I was awake. Not much I could do about that, really, so, I had a look out of my window, but didn't see anyone outside the house, just some poor sod heading up the road towards the bridge, stumbling all over the place, and a vehicle parked just up by the bridge. Off home after a late night, I would think, if you know what I mean, whistling and singing as they went. Looked like they were carrying a barrel of the stuff home with them!'

'And you heard a thump?'

Mary reached for her stick and tapped it on the floor.

'Not like that though,' she said. 'More of a bang, maybe? Not really sure.'

Jim thought about the body in Harry 's house.

'Was there anything else? Voices, perhaps? Did you hear anyone talking?'

Mary paused, tapping her chin with a finger as she thought for a moment.

'I may have done,' she said. 'But they were muffled. There was something else, too. I remember now. Burning.'

'Burning?'

'Yes,' Mary said. 'You see, I came downstairs to go to the toilet. Always happens in the night anyway, so seeing as I was awake, I thought I'd kill two birds, if you know what I mean. Anyway, as I went back to bed, I noticed the smell of burning, coming through the window at the top of the stairs. I always have it open. Don't like the house to be too hot, certainly not upstairs, otherwise I can't sleep.'

'Any idea what it was?' Jim asked.

'I thought it might be your Grimm chap lighting a fire next door, to warm the place up, get rid of the damp, that kind of thing. There's been no one in there for a while now, and you know how these old dales houses get if they're left to their own devices for too long.'

Jim did indeed; the cold could seep in, bringing with it a dampness that would set in for days and chill you even with a fire roaring in the grate.

Jim asked if there was anything else.

'Also thought I smelled meat,' Mary said. 'Like something in the oven, but that was it.' She looked thoughtful for a moment, then added, 'You can let that boss of yours know that I'll be keeping an eye on that garden of his. I've spent a good many hours making sure my little patch is the way it is, so he'd better not be thinking about bringing my side down.'

'I'm sure he won't,' said Jim.

'He's a gardener then, is he?'

Jim laughed.

'I'll take that as a no.'

'To be honest, I don't know,' Jim said, though the idea of Harry fussing around some pretty rose bushes couldn't help but make him smile.

'Not everyone has green fingers,' said Mary. 'I'll be happy to teach him a thing or two.'

'I'm sure he'd appreciate it.'

At the door, Mary stopped Jim for a moment before he headed off.

'I mean what I said, you know that, don't you?' she said, her voice quiet. 'I'm proud of you, James.'

Jim stood there as Mary reached up and gave him a gentle pat on his cheek. Then she stepped back into her house and closed the door.

Back round at Harry 's, and now standing with Jadyn and Gordy at the door, Jim saw two women striding towards the house. They both waved.

'Right then, where is it?' said the first, arriving to stand in front of the three of them, clad in an old waxed jacket.

Gordy stepped forward and led them both into the house. As she did so, Jadyn let out a gasp and ducked behind a bush in Harry 's garden.

Jim stared at the constable, somewhat confused.

'Everything alright, there?' he asked.

Jadyn peered out from where he was hiding.

'What? Yes. I mean, of course. Just thought I saw something, that's all. A clue, maybe.'

'A clue ...'

'Yes. But it wasn't. A clue, I mean. It was just a ... thing.'

Jim noticed that Jadyn, along with talking rubbish, was looking nervously down the road. He followed his line of sight and saw an expensive BMW heading down towards Hawes.

'Someone you know?'

'What?'

'In that car,' Jim asked, then remembered what Matt had said earlier about something being not quite right with Jadyn. And hadn't he mentioned something about his family, right before that new detective superintendent had turned up?

'What car?' Jadyn said.

Jim waited for Jadyn to come back out into the open.

'So, are you going to tell me what's going on, or are you going to be spending the rest of the day ducking behind bushes every time a smart car rolls past?'

Jadyn let out a sigh.

'Best you just get whatever it is off your chest,' Jim said.

'They're staying just over the bridge,' Jadyn said. 'Didn't tell me either, not until like two days ago. Apparently, they thought it would be a nice surprise.'

Jim was no clearer as to what Jadyn was talking about.

'Who's staying?' he asked.

Jadyn turned to face Jim.

'My parents,' he said. 'And my younger sister.'

CHAPTER THIRTEEN

Following lunch with Grace and Arthur, during which he had consumed a generously sized plate of home-baked ham, with two eggs and a very large portion of chips, Harry was now fighting the urge to just go back to the flat for a nap. Instead, however, he was making his way back to Gayle, on foot this time, to clear his head. It wasn't a long walk. The rain had eased, and the fresh air was already pinching his skin. Cars swished past, casting thin waves of greasy water as they went, and Harry had to stand on the far side of the pavement as he walked, to stop from getting soaked.

Despite the turn in the weather, the visitor centre at the creamery was busy, the car park full. Harry had heard good things about the food there, and Grace had dropped a few hints about maybe grabbing a hamper for Christmas. He'd still not visited, but perhaps, once he'd settled into his new home, he would.

His new home ...

Harry found himself shaking his head and laughing at the events of the day. A dark sense of humour had been a survival mechanism in the Parachute Regiment. It was no different in the police. Yes, there was a body on the lounge floor of the house he'd just bought, and that was awful, but the funny side of it, the timing, the sheer insanity of the whole thing couldn't be ignored.

At the top of the hill, Gayle laid itself out in front of Harry and he headed along the road, which dipped just a little, before heading back up again into the village itself. He passed the footpath on his left, which led over fields and back into Hawes, down by the church. That was a favourite haunt of his, to take a stroll along the flagstone path, usually in the early morning with Smudge, to see the mist lying quietly in the fields above, and to listen to the song and call of birds and sheep far off.

When he arrived at his house, Harry was met by Jadyn and Jim.

'Gordy won't be happy,' Jadyn said.

'She'll get over it,' Harry replied. 'How are we all getting on, then?'

Jim told Harry about his little excursion around the houses nearby, and then explained what Mary Iveson, Harry 's new neighbour, had told him.

'What time was this?'

'She says a bang woke her up around one in the morning, and that she heard someone coming back from the pub.'

'Anything else?'

'Said she could smell burning.'

That caught Harry 's attention.

'And that was around the same time?'

Jim nodded. 'I got the impression she thought it was you round there early warming the place up.'

'Well, it wasn't, was it?' Harry said.

'Like I said, I think she just thought it was you.'

'No sign of the Scene of Crime team, then?' Harry asked.

Jadyn said, 'The pathologist and district surgeon are here. No one else as yet.'

A voice called Harry 's name, and he looked over behind Jadyn and Jim to see Gordy staring at him.

'Well, you stayed away longer than I expected,' she said. 'Almost feel like I should applaud.'

'Don't.'

Gordy raised her hands as though she was about to clap, but dropped them again.

'They're inside, then?' said Harry .

'They are.'

Harry pushed past Jadyn and Jim and made his way into his house. Gordy held up a hand to stop him.

'You can't stop me from going into my own house,' Harry said, 'crime scene or not.'

'I'm not,' Gordy said. 'I just want to say that I'm really sorry this has happened. Seems more than a little unfair.'

'More unfair on whoever that is in there on the floor,' Harry said.

Gordy gave a nod, but Harry caught something behind it, other thoughts rolling around the DI's mind.

'You're thinking the same as me, then?' he said.

'And what's that?'

'That this isn't a random event.'

'You think it's personal?'

Harry gave a non-committal shrug.

'I think saying it's personal is maybe pushing it a bit. And my ego isn't big enough to assume someone out there wants to get to me so bad they'd do this. But it is odd, I'll give it that.'

'You don't think the date's relevant?'

'Halloween? God, I hope not,' Harry said.

Gordy said nothing else, which was more than enough, Harry thought and he moved past her and into the house.

The smell was still there from the lounge, but there was enough fresh air moving through the house now to have taken the edge off a little. Regardless, he dabbed more vapour rub under his nose and donned the necessary PPE, including a facemask.

'There he is.'

The voice came from the district surgeon who was standing in the lounge doorway.

'Afternoon, Margaret,' Harry said.

Margaret Shaw came over to stand in front of him. She was smaller than Harry , smaller than most people, actually, but what she lacked in height she made up for in personality. She was a force of nature and Harry had warmed to her immediately, having first met her a good while ago now, while investigating a farm accident which had turned out to be anything but.

'Either you have friends with a very sick sense of humour when it comes to housewarming gifts, or ...' Margaret looked thoughtful for a moment. 'To be honest,' she continued, 'I don't have an *or*, because this is just plain odd, isn't it? But with an added smattering of absolutely horrendous.'

'It is that,' said Harry . 'What've we got, then?'

'A body in your lounge is what we've got, Harry ,' said Margaret. 'Nice place, by the way,' she added. 'Well, it would be if it wasn't for you-know-what. And this may sound monstrously out of place right now, but I really do hope you're happy here. You know, eventually, once this is all cleared up. And assuming you still want to live in a house where a body was found in the lounge. Most people wouldn't, but then you're not most people, are you, Harry ?'

Harry couldn't help but smile.

'I'll take that as a compliment.'

'As well you should because that's how it was meant.'

'Not like I've anywhere else to move to, anyway, is it?' Harry glanced over Margaret's shoulder, into the house. 'Now, tell me about the body in the lounge.'

'Male,' Margaret said. 'Mid to late sixties and definitely dead. I'm very sure of that.'

'I guessed that bit.'

'Nothing gets past you, does it, Detective?'

'All part of the training, spotting when folk are dead.'

'Nice to know all those years we both spent learning our respective trades weren't wasted, then.'

Harry asked, 'How long?'

'Time of death, you mean?'

'Was he killed here?'

Margaret gave a nod.

'I'm afraid so,' she said. 'Which, for some reason makes this seem even worse, doesn't it? I'll have to leave all the icky details to Rebecca, though.'

'Icky? Is that a technical term, then?'

'One of many.'

'Anything else?'

Margaret frowned for a moment, then pulled off a glove and reached up to Harry 's face. Before he could do anything, she wiped something from the corner of his mouth with a finger.

'Egg,' she said.

'You could've just told me.'

Margaret gave Harry a cheeky little wink.

'What? And waste an opportunity to stroke that wonderfully rugged face of yours? Not a chance of it.'

Harry looked over Margaret's shoulder to see Rebecca crouching by the body.

Margaret moved to one side to allow Harry past, before heading out of the house.

Walking into the lounge, Harry hung back by the door, keen to not get in the way of someone and their work. He was struck once again by the blood on the plastic sheet.

'Hello, Harry ,' the pathologist said.

'Hello, Rebecca,' Harry replied.

Rebecca Sowerby looked over her shoulder and up at Harry . He noticed that the jacket the deceased was wearing was now unbuttoned and loose.

'People usually send flowers or chocolates or a bottle of wine.'

'All of those would've been much preferred to this, I can assure you.'

Sowerby reached out and took a corner of the plastic sheet between her fingers.

'Can't say I rate the gift wrapping.'

'No card, either,' Harry said. 'What's the world coming to?'

Rising to her feet, Sowerby came and stood next to Harry .

'How are you doing?'

'Probably best not to ask,' Harry replied. 'What can you tell me?'

'Not much more than what my mum has just said. And I'm not about to go poking around much yet, not until we've had the photographer in. Should be here in five minutes or so.'

Harry moved away from Sowerby, sweeping slowly round the body till he was standing over the head.

'Your mum says he died here, in this room. Any idea how?'

'Right now, not exactly, no.'

'Not exactly? That doesn't sound good.'

'None of this sounds good, because it isn't. Look ...'

Sowerby moved to the body's face and eased open the jaw. Harry saw that the dark space inside the mouth was filled with some kind of material.

'Gagged?'

'He could scream all he wanted with that in his mouth and no one would hear him in the next room, never mind next door.'

'What about the burning?'

'It's fresh,' Sowerby said. 'Done last night. My guess is that whoever's responsible made good use of one of those handheld burners you can use in the kitchen.'

Harry had no idea what Sowerby was talking about, and his look clearly communicated that.

'You know,' Sowerby said, trying to explain further, 'to crisp up the sugar on a crème brulé, something like that.'

Despite where they were standing, and what was lying in front of them, Harry laughed.

'Oh, right, one of those handheld burners,' he said. 'Of course, how could I forget? I mean, I'm forever getting mine out to crisp up the old crème brulé there. Just you try and stop me.'

'Sarcasm doesn't suit you.'

'And neither would anything as ridiculously pointless as a handheld burner in my kitchen.'

Sowerby asked, 'You have any idea who this is?'

'Why would I?' Harry replied. 'Anyway, all that burning, it's kind of ruined his face, hasn't it? The poor bastard.'

'True. Even so, though.'

'Even so, what, exactly?'

Sowerby came round to stand beside Harry .

'Why would anyone do this?' she asked. 'It doesn't make any sense.'

'Oh, I'm sure it does,' said Harry . 'Just not to us. There's purpose behind it.'

'But here, though, in your house? They were tortured to death, Harry . And that's not the worst of it.'

Harry frowned as Sowerby dropped back down to the floor.

'How do you mean?' he asked. 'How can any of this not be the worst of it? He had his face burned off while he was conscious and I'm going to guess that wasn't the best experience he ever had.'

Sowerby reached out and gently eased the jacket open.

Harry stared down at what was revealed.

'Good God ...'

'Something like that, yes,' said Sowerby.

Harry wanted to turn his head away from what he was staring at. But he couldn't, and he wouldn't.

Beneath the jacket, the white T-shirt had been snipped, top to tail. And, underneath it, so had the dead man's stomach. The line of the incision was cleanly cut rather than hacked.

'This was done post-mortem,' explained Sowerby, pointing at the incision with the tip of a finger. 'A small mercy, I suppose. Once the heart's stopped and lividity sets in, blood doesn't really flow, it oozes. His blood will have pooled in the lower areas, the buttocks, that kind of thing. That's why it hasn't sprayed everywhere, covering the walls and the ceiling.'

Harry dropped down next to her.

'As modus operandi go, this one's certainly original, isn't it?'

Sowerby gave a nod and said, 'I've not had a chance to look over the rest of the body, the legs and whatnot. Feel free to stay if you want.'

'There were some footprints,' said Harry .

'Yes, we've taken samples. The soil from the tread marks may tell us something, it may not.'

Voices tumbled in from outside and Harry looked over to the lounge door, immediately concerned about who was out there with his team, not least because he'd seen Anderson earlier.

'Can't be the press, can it?' he said.

'Already?' said Sowerby. 'God, I hope not.'

Harry left the room and headed outside, but before he'd even got two steps away from the door, someone rushed towards him and threw their arms around him.

'Mr Grimm! I cannot say how happy I am to finally meet you! We've heard so much about you. Are you free this evening? For dinner? We have so much to discuss!'

Harry managed to peel himself from the grip of whoever it was that had accosted him. He stepped back to see a well-dressed black woman standing in front of him. Harry guessed that she was probably a few years older than him, early fifties perhaps.

'I'm sorry, ma'am,' Harry began, but then Jadyn stepped in front of him. 'If this is your view of being a good Scene Guard, Constable, then—'

'Boss,' Jadyn said.

'What?'

Jadyn opened his mouth to speak, but nothing came out. The woman was still staring at him and had now been joined by a man, also early fifties, and a young woman.

'Out with it, Constable,' Harry said. 'Or are you now blessed with the skill of telepathy and wish to tell me what the hell is going on with nothing but the power of your mind?'

Behind Jadyn, Gordy looked over to Harry and mouthed the word, *Sorry*.

'I'd like you to meet my family,' Jadyn said.

CHAPTER FOURTEEN

'Mrs Okri?' Harry said, his eyes flicking from Jadyn to the woman.

'Ginika,' the woman said, clearly introducing herself. 'And this is Samuel, my husband, and Isioma, our daughter. My other two are far too busy with their careers to be joining us, I'm afraid.'

Mr Okri held out a hand and Harry shook it without thinking, feeling for a moment like his brain had short-circuited. Barely a minute ago, he had been staring at a mutilated corpse. Now he was at what appeared to be some impromptu family gathering. Mr Okri was tall and slim with a bright, warm smile and kind eyes. Isioma, Jadyn's sister, seemed to be doing a very good impression of someone who didn't want to be there at all, hiding behind her hair and her phone.

'Pleased to meet you,' Harry said, immediately aware that his tone wasn't entirely convincing. 'However, I'll have to ask you to move away, please. As you can see, this is a crime scene, and it's going to get rather busy.'

Almost on cue, two large white vans pulled up opposite, quickly followed by a black estate car. First out was the photographer. The man waved over at Harry like they were old friends. They most certainly weren't. Harry held up a hand to stop him and the rest of the Scene of Crime team from heading over while he sorted out whatever this was that was happening right in front of him. Then, climbing out of the estate, he saw Anderson the journalist, trying to ruin his day. With a quick nod to Gordy, she headed on over to meet them, and he was pleased to note how irritated Anderson looked to have his route blocked.

'Please,' Harry said, gesturing to Jadyn's family to follow him into the small garden in front of the house and to allow the forensics team through. It also meant they were out of the view of the beady eyes of the journalist. 'If you wouldn't mind?'

'We won't get in the way, I promise,' Mr Okri said, staying right where he was. 'A crime scene, is it? How interesting. Is Jadyn in charge? I'm assuming so.'

'He must be,' said Mrs Okri. 'He's a wonderful boy. Very talented. Why he joined the police, we have no idea.'

Harry caught the barbs in the comment, but realised they weren't meant for him as Jadyn jumped in and said, 'Mum, you need to do as he said. You can't just walk around a crime scene.'

Mrs Okri smiled at her son, and reached out to hold his face between her hands.

'If you say so, you handsome boy.'

Harry looked at Jadyn, who rolled his eyes and shook his head, clearly embarrassed.

'I'm sorry,' the constable mouthed, then he turned to his parents. 'Mum,' he said again, his voice firm, 'move.' Then he added a more friendly, 'Please?'

After a little more hesitation, Mrs Okri followed Harry , and Jadyn shooed his father and sister along to join them in the garden. Jim stayed over by the house.

Harry looked over at Gordy and gave a wave. She was talking to Anderson. Jadyn then headed back to where Jim was standing to continue his duty as Scene Guard.

'He's directing things then, is he?' Mr Okri said. 'That's good to see. A natural manager.'

'Like his father,' added Mrs Okri. 'We had hopes for him to go into finance like his brother, you know, but he insisted on the police.'

'It's a good career,' Harry said. 'And he's a good police officer.'

'I'm sure he'll get it all out of his system soon, though,' said Mr Okri. 'Now, what is it he is doing, exactly?'

'He's the Scene Guard,' Harry explained. 'He's making sure we know exactly who's on-site and why. It's an important job. We can't have just anyone walking in and out due to the sensitive nature of what we do.'

'Like I said, directing things.'

Mrs Okri asked, 'Who's that going in now, then?'

'The photographer,' said Harry . 'We already have—' He caught himself before he said too much about who exactly was on-site and what they were doing. '—a good number of specialists carrying out the investigation.'

'And what crime is it that they're investigating, exactly?'

'I'm afraid I'm not able to go into any details at this time.'

'I bet it's a murder.'

This was from Jadyn's sister. It was the first time she had spoken since Harry had met the family, her attention focused utterly on the screen of her phone.

'A murder? Really?' said Mrs Okri. 'Is that what this is, Mr Grimm? How exciting!'

Harry was starting to wish he'd stayed inside his house with the body and the pathologist.

'Well, it's certainly been lovely to meet you,' he said, stepping away from the gathering, 'but I am going to have to ask you to leave now. We're very busy, as you can see.'

'Yes, with the murder,' said Mrs Okri.

'Crime scene,' corrected Harry , but Mrs Okri wasn't listening.

'And who is that man over there?' she asked.

Harry looked to see where she was staring and caught sight of Anderson. He was now on the other side of the river and staring at them through a small pair of binoculars.

'Ignore him,' Harry said.

'He's not ignoring us, is he?'

Harry explained who Anderson was.

'Would you like me to have a word with him?' Mr Okri asked, puffing out his chest a little.

'No, we can handle things just fine,' Harry said, jumping in before the man headed off. 'They're a necessary evil, I suppose, journalists, aren't they? I'm just not sure how necessary sometimes. Anyway, I'm sure you have plans for the day and I wouldn't want to go holding you up. There's certainly plenty to see and do around here. It's a beautiful place.'

'Oh, those can wait,' said Mr Okri. 'We're here to see Jadyn anyway. I'm sure he could deal with that journalist for you.'

'Well, he's on duty right now,' Harry explained, 'and I've often found that the best way to deal with the press is to ignore them.'

'He looks so smart as well, doesn't he?' Mrs Okri said.

Harry heard a snort of laughter from Jadyn's sister.

'Yes, he—' he said, only just managing to stop himself. 'Anyway, I need to get on. Thank you for stopping by. Lovely to meet you.'

'Oh, we're around all week,' Mrs Okri said. 'We've heard so much about Jadyn's life up here that we thought we would come and see it for ourselves.'

'We used to holiday over in the Bedale area,' said Mr Okri. 'We're even thinking of buying a cottage around here, a little escape to the country for us, that kind of thing.'

'Well, it's nice if you can afford it,' Harry said, growing a little frustrated now with the Okri family outstaying their welcome more than a little.

Before Harry could do anything to stop her, Mrs Okri walked over to Jadyn and gave him a hug and a kiss. Then she was back with her husband and daughter.

'Dinner this evening, then?' she said, looking up at Harry , eyes expectant.

'I'm sorry, what?'

'Dinner,' Mrs Okri said. 'Jadyn can give you the address. Samuel's a superb cook.'

'I'm afraid I'm busy this evening,' Harry said. 'But that's a very kind offer.'

'Well, we will have to arrange something else, then. I'm sure you have so much to tell us about Jadyn and all the work he does.'

Harry watched as Jadyn's parents and sister crossed the road and climbed into their car. He kept his eyes on them, watching as Jadyn's sister climbed back out again and headed off down towards Hawes on her own. Probably just wanting a bit of time on her own, he thought, which was fair enough.

As Jadyn's parents drove off, overtaking their daughter, she pulled out her phone, then popped something blue into her mouth, before posing for a selfie. A moment later, a thick, white plume of vapour enveloped her head, only to be quickly dispersed by the wind. Harry saw Jadyn, who was busy dealing with the SOC team, glance over at his sister as the sweet scent of the vapour swept past.

Gordy came over to stand at Harry 's side.

'Sorry about that,' she said. 'Entertaining though, I think you'll agree.'

'Will I?'

'No.'

'Why didn't Jadyn mention they were visiting?'

'I think he only found out at the last minute that they were coming,' Gordy said. 'He's as surprised as the rest of us.'

Harry rubbed his eyes, weariness from the day already gathering behind them.

'Anderson is being a right pain in the arse today, isn't he?'

'His usual nosy self, that's all,' Gordy said. 'Ignore him; he hates that more than anything. Smells a bit, too, if you get close to him. Not good. Anyway, I know what'll cheer you up.'

Harry didn't like the sound of that at all.

'I don't need cheering up,' he grumbled, but the DI was already jogging over to her vehicle. When she returned, Harry was, for once, at a loss for words.

'Ta-dah!'

Harry stared at what Gordy had retrieved from her car and was now holding in front of him. 'Ta-dah? At what point does any of whatever this is require a ta-dah?'

The DI presented the chocolates, Prosecco, and helium balloon to Harry , who didn't so much as move a finger.

'You shouldn't have,' he said. 'By which I mean, you really, really shouldn't have. And if you think I'm going to take those off you, you've another thing coming.'

'But you have to I'm afraid; these are your housewarming gifts, from Anna and me.'

Harry looked at the heart-shaped balloon. The wind caught it, causing it to twist on its ribbon, then thunk Gordy on her scalp.

'No, I don't.'

Gordy's hands didn't move. Harry finally gave up and relieved her of the gifts.

'Thank you,' he said. 'Certainly better than what someone else left for me, I suppose.'

'Remember, it's the thought that counts,' said Gordy.

Harry glanced back at the house. 'That's what worries me,' he said. Then he turned back to Gordy and added, 'And I really have to keep this balloon?'

'Of course you do. That's the best part! Who doesn't love a balloon?'

Harry saw the photographer emerge from the house and he swiftly handed the wine, chocolates, and balloon back to Gordy, then pulled out his car keys and gave them to her as well.

'Drop them in the Rav for me,' he said, then before she had time to argue, he jogged over to catch up with the photographer.

'Hold up,' Harry called out.

The photographer stopped halfway across the road. A car came around the bend to their right, from the bridge over the beck, and the driver beeped its horn at the figure now in front of it.

Harry waved the car on, glaring at the driver as they rolled past.

'Nice balloon,' the photographer said, then looked over at the crime scene. 'It's a gruesome one, isn't it?'

'It is,' Harry agreed. 'How did you get on?'

'Why do you ask? Something you're looking for specifically?'

Harry shook his head, not sure why he'd asked the question.

'Just wasn't really expecting this on moving day, that's all,' he said.

The photographer's eyes widened.

'Moving day? On Halloween? You mean ... you ... no way!'

'I'm afraid so,' Harry said.

'Classic!'

Harry was trying to think of an appropriate response to the photographer's very obvious amusement at the situation that didn't involve smacking him hard to the ground with an open palm, when he heard his name being called. He looked back to the house to see Jadyn waving him over. He walked over and ducked under the cordon tape.

'It's Sowerby. She wants to talk to you,' Jadyn said.

Harry stepped back into his house. It was already full of visitors, all of them dressed head to toe in white paper PPE suits.

'In here ...'

Harry followed the voice back through to the lounge. Sowerby was standing on the opposite side of the room, the body still on the floor between them.

'What is it?'

'I think we need to talk in private,' Sowerby said.

'Why?'

Sowerby walked around the room, then led Harry across the hall and into the kitchen, making sure they were out of earshot. She pulled down her facemask.

'I found something.'

'If it's anything occult, I'm going to be very upset,' said Harry . 'I'm already going off Halloween as it is.'

'It's not occult. However, it is, well, it's odd, is what it is. Which is why I wanted you to see it first, before it goes off to be analysed.'

Sowerby lifted a small plastic evidence bag. Inside, Harry saw a white feather, matted somewhat with dark blood.

'Why are you showing me that?'

'Because I found it, that's why.'

Harry had dealt with a case in the Dales before in which feathers had been a clue left by the killer. And that made him more than a little nervous.

'Can't be a copycat,' he said.

That case had been someone meting out revenge for the very sad death of his sister at the hands of some local bullies when they were only children. It had been as tragic and sad as it had been disturbing.

'You think that, too, then,' Sowerby said. 'Thought you might. It was found inside the deceased's mouth as well, which is another coincidence.'

'I don't believe in coincidences.'

'Doesn't mean they don't happen.'

'This is different, though,' Harry said. 'In that other case, they were eagle feathers, I think. And I'm pretty sure what you have there isn't.'

'I'm not sure what bird it's from,' Sowerby said, 'but I'd be inclined to agree with you, yes.'

'Need more than just a single white feather to link it to what happened with that, though,' Harry said, as a call from outside interrupted them.

He looked up to see Jim standing in the open lounge door.

'What?' Harry said.

'There's a truck,' Jim said. 'It's just pulled up outside, like.'

'Well, tell it to move on, then,' Harry replied. 'Bloody hell, Jim. Do I need to tell you how to do everything?'

Jim's face dropped. Harry was about to apologise for snapping, when Jim spoke again.

'The driver asked for you,' he said. 'That's all.'

'What? Why?' Then Harry remembered. 'Bollocks,' he said. 'My furniture's arrived.'

CHAPTER FIFTEEN

When evening came round, Harry was physically and mentally exhausted. Having managed to sweet talk the landlord of the flat, he at least had somewhere to store all the new furniture he had ordered, as well as his belongings, which were now in boxes.

'Well, you're not sleeping here; you know that don't you?' Grace said.

'And neither am I going to impose on you,' said Harry .

'Such a gentleman,' Grace smiled. 'Though a bit presumptuous to assume I'd even be offering you my sofa.'

'I'll have you know that it's a very comfortable sofa.'

Grace laughed and Harry found himself dragged out of the flat and into the evening. The rain had eventually stopped, but only after Harry , and the driver who had turned up with all of his new furniture, had got completely soaked unloading everything that he had ordered and stacked up inside the flat.

The air was rich and bright with the scent of peat and fern and bracken, blown down from the fells by a cool breeze swirling its way through Hawes.

The drive over to Grace's house in Carperby was carried out in silence. Sowerby's revelation at the crime scene had forced its way to the front of Harry 's mind, but he had kept the information to himself for now. Until the body's identity was confirmed, he saw no point in telling anyone about the feather. If he and Sowerby had made the connection to it being a possible copycat, then others would, too, and he needed them focused, not getting caught up in anything like that. He had also given strict instructions to Sowerby to keep the discovery confidential; it was just the kind of juicy detail that the press would devour hungrily, and he was in no mood to be dealing with any of that. Even though he had no doubt that a run-in with the press would be very cathartic, dealing with Anderson and anyone else who turned up with a sack of questions and attitude didn't fill him with joy.

Grace let them into the house, where they were met by a barrage of fur as Smudge launched herself at Harry .

'Get down, you daft mutt,' he said, his voice grumpy, but the dog didn't care, and followed Harry through into the house, tail wagging hard as she tried to push in front of him to get his attention.

Arthur was there to meet them, with his own dog, Molly, and Jess.

'She was fine early on,' he said, 'but she's been moping around all afternoon.'

Harry sat down on the sofa in Grace's lounge and Smudge dropped her head hard onto his knees. The room was warm and cosy thanks to the deep, red glow from the embers in the wood-burning stove in front of him. Smudge stared up at him, her big, brown eyes tucked under long, dark eyelashes.

'Soft bugger,' said Grace.

'She is that,' said Harry , and scratched the dog's head.

'I wasn't talking about the dog.'

Arthur said, 'I'll be leaving you to it, then. There's cottage pie in the oven, nice and warm. Made it this afternoon. Thought you might appreciate it, what with everything that's been going on.'

'You shouldn't have,' said Harry .

'Really? Well, I'll just take it home, then, shall I?'

'No, I'm sure we'll find a use for it.' Harry laughed.

"Come on, Molly," Arthur said, and headed off, his dog at his heels.

Grace walked him to the door. When she returned, Harry was deep in thought.

'How are you doing?'

'I've had better days,' Harry said.

'You have,' said Grace. 'But there's something else, isn't there?'

'Is there?'

Grace dropped herself down next to Harry .

'What is it? What's going on in that head of yours?'

'You mean other than the fact that a body was found in my house, which is now a crime scene, so I can't actually move in yet?'

Grace leaned back. Smudge moved her attention from Harry to her, and Grace stroked the dog under her chin. Jess pushed in for a bit of the action as well, and soon both dogs were nuzzled in, their eyes focused only on their owners.

'Something happened,' Grace said. 'When you headed back to the house after lunch. I can see it, even now, hiding behind those eyes of yours.'

Harry rested a hand on Grace's knee.

'It's probably nothing,' he said.

'Then it probably won't hurt to talk about it, will it? Unless you can't, of course.'

Harry was silent for a moment. Then he sat forward, his hands clasped together as though in prayer. He was about to speak when there was a knock at the door.

Grace went to answer it and then called back to Harry .

'There's someone at the door for you.'

Harry 's first thought was that it was Anderson and he pulled himself to his feet and headed through to see who was disturbing their evening.

At the front door, Grace was staring down at three very small, and very cute, vampires.

'They've found us,' Grace said, grabbing hold of Harry in fear. 'There's no escape. We're doomed!'

Harry , a smile on his face, crouched down, his eyes on the smallest of the undead, a girl no older than eight, he guessed. 'You are very, very scary,' he said, pointing a finger at her tiny nose. 'I don't think I've ever been so terrified of anyone in my entire life.'

The girl grinned, baring plastic vampire teeth, which seemed to glow in the dark a little. A nice touch, Harry thought.

'You see that, Grace?' he said, looking up at her over his shoulder. 'Looks like we're done for. We don't stand a chance.'

Grace let out a dramatic gasp, her hands clamped over her mouth in mock terror.

The girl laughed, as did her two friends, a boy and a girl who looked around the same age.

Behind them, a young woman laughed. Harry looked up at her and gave her a wink. He didn't know her name, but he'd seen her working behind the counter in the local Spar.

'Any ideas to save us before they turn us into one of their slaves?'

'I've heard chocolate works well,' the woman said.

Harry reached into his pocket and pulled out a handful of chocolate bars he'd picked up on his way over from the office. He held them out to the vampires.

'If I give you these, do you promise to not drink our blood?'

The girl cocked her head slightly.

'Maybe,' she said.

Grace said, 'Actually, I'm not sure that these are even real vampires. I need proof.'

Harry rubbed his chin.

'She has a point, you know,' he said. 'How do we know you're really vampires? You could be pretending, just to get free chocolate. Just how scary can you be?'

'Very scary,' the girl said.

'Yes, really scary,' her two friends agreed. 'The scariest of scary.'

Harry stood up.

'Right then, I need to see your scariest faces,' he said. 'I want to be so scared that I won't be able to sleep tonight. Terrify me!'

The three little vampires giggled.

'On a count of three ... One ... Two ... Three!'

Harry watched as the three children pulled the least scary faces he had ever seen, baring plastic teeth in wide mouths, their fingers out like puppy paws rather than claws.

'What do you think?' he asked, turning to Grace.

'I don't think I'll sleep again,' she said.

Harry ducked down again and handed over the chocolate.

'Well done,' he said. 'Now off you go, back to the graveyard with you.'

With a wave to the young woman chaperoning them, Harry closed the door. Back in the lounge, he sat down, Grace beside him.

'You were going to say something,' Grace said. 'Before Hammer House turned up at the door.'

Harry said, 'Remember the new DSup?'

'Is there a problem?'

'Not with her, no. In fact, she seems great, which is quite a surprise. It's more to do with what she told me.'

'And what was that?'

Harry explained to Grace what Walker had told him about his father's escape from custody.

'Ben didn't take it too well,' he said. Seeing the shock and worry in Grace's eyes, he added, 'But he'll be okay.'

'Bloody hell, Harry , why didn't you say anything?'

'Because I just wanted to get on with moving into the house rather than have to worry about that as well. Then, well, you know what happened next, so my mind was elsewhere.'

'Even so,' Grace said.

'Anyway, the thing is, there's been a development with my unwanted house guest.'

Grace frowned.

'Harry , I know as well as anyone that "*there's been a develop-*

ment" is police code for something bad is going on. What's happened?'

'There was this case, a few months after I arrived here,' Harry said. 'The victims were found with white feathers.'

'So?'

'So,' Harry said, 'the body in my lounge was also found with a feather.'

'Not sure I understand.'

'You know me and coincidences,' Harry said.

Grace's eyes widened.

'You think it's the same person?'

Harry shook his head.

'Not a chance of it. This is completely different, plus he was convicted.' He rubbed his eyes, trying to avoid remembering the case, but unable to ignore the memories, not least the god-awful sadness of the killer's father at what his son had done.

'Then what?'

Harry gave a shrug.

'To be honest, I don't know. It's just caught me off guard, I think. It's probably nothing. Still, it is strange.'

'You think it means something?' Grace asked.

Harry had been thinking about that ever since Sowerby had shown him what she'd found. Feathers are one thing, but white feathers? They meant something else.

'Cowardice,' Harry said.

'What?'

'There are lots of examples in history of a white feather being given to those who were regarded as cowards,' Harry explained.

'Really?'

'In the First World War, white feathers were given to men to publicly shame them into signing up.'

'That's a bit unpleasant.'

'War has that reputation.'

'Don't see how that's got anything to do with this, though,' said Grace.

'And right now, neither do I,' said Harry . 'I need some tea.'

He stood up then, shooing Smudge away to go and lay beside Jess, before walking out of the lounge and into the kitchen. On the way, with Grace following, he caught sight of his reflection in a mirror by the front door. He looked tired.

Wondering how Ben was doing, he went to pull his phone from his pocket to send him a text, but as he moved away from the mirror, a thought forced him to stay right where he was. He leaned towards the mirror, bringing himself within millimetres of his own ruined reflection. The thought refused to shift, only growing stronger as he stared himself down, exploring the awful scars on his face with his hand.

'Itching again, are they?' Grace asked, coming round to stand beside Harry .

Harry remained where he was, his frown becoming heavier on his forehead as he thought back to the body in his house. Whoever it was, why had the murderer burned the man's face? There had to be a reason. Was it a message? If so, what the hell did it mean? And just what the hell was the white feather about?

Harry stepped away from the mirror.

'I'm fine,' he said and walked through to the kitchen.

Kettle on, he sent a message through to Ben, then grabbed a pair of oven gloves and pulled out the cottage pie Arthur had made. Steam rose from the crispy potato topping as Harry rested it on top of the oven.

'Smells good, doesn't it?' said Grace.

'I've changed my mind about the tea,' said Harry , and pointed at the cottage pie. 'That needs beer. And, as it happens, so do I. You could say that it's been one of those days.'

Grace pulled two bottles of Wensleydale Gold from the fridge and popped the tin caps off before handing one to Harry .

'You have a lot of those,' she said.

Harry took a sip of the beer. God, it's good, he thought.

His phone pinged.

'Ben,' he said, checking the message. 'I sent a message just to see how he's doing.'

'And?'

'Says he's fine,' said Harry , putting his phone away, and taking another, deeper, sip of the beer.

'He's with Liz, so of course he is,' said Grace.

'He's doing okay with that counselling as well.'

'That's good to hear. It's not easy talking about stuff, but it helps.'

'It does.'

'TV dinner, then?'

With the food served up, Harry followed Grace back through to the lounge. His reflection glanced over his shoulder at him from the mirror again, but he ignored it; whatever it was trying to tell him, right now he wasn't interested and was too tired to care. There was always tomorrow.

In the lounge, Grace took a sip of her own beer.

'Sorry we're not having these in your new place,' she said.

'These things happen.'

'No, they really don't; people generally don't find that someone's left a body for them on move-in day.'

'No, you're right, they don't,' Harry said, then clinked the neck of his bottle against the one in Grace's hand. 'But it'll certainly be something to remember, won't it? Cheers anyway.'

Grace replied in kind.

'One good thing about all this, though,' Harry said. 'We won't need to be talking about a housewarming party for a good while, will we?'

Grace shook her head in mock disbelief.

'You can put a positive spin on anything, can't you?'

'Everything except that, yes,' Harry said.

'There's still the reunion.'

'Well, I doubt I'll be able to go now,' Harry said. 'What with all this going on. Shame really, but there you go.'

'It might be exactly what you need.'

Harry lifted his bottle of beer.

'This is exactly what I need,' he said, taking another sip, before leaning over to kiss Grace. 'And that.'

Later that night, when mental and physical exhaustion finally rolled them into bed, the only thing Harry could see when he closed his eyes was the burned face of the body he'd found on his lounge floor. Only now, it was staring out at him from the mirror by the door.

CHAPTER SIXTEEN

Harry could have very easily come up with a list of at least a dozen things he would rather have been doing on a Sunday than standing in the mortuary with the pathologist, Rebecca Sowerby. It didn't help that for this Sunday in particular he'd had plans. Not just unpacking, either.

Even though he had moaned about not wanting a housewarming party, he'd decided in the end to make a minor concession and had put together a small party for just himself, Grace, and Smudge. It wasn't going to be much; just a takeaway, a bottle of wine, and a little something he'd bought her to say thanks for putting up with his unavoidable bad mood when it came to all things moving house, but now even that small affair wasn't happening. And all because of whoever it was now lying under a white sheet on the stainless steel slab in front of him.

Having called him first thing that morning, Sowerby had met Harry outside the hospital, and then led him through a network of corridors to the mortuary itself. The walk through the building made Harry feel like a rat in a maze, albeit one where medical staff seemed to rush out at him from all directions carrying clipboards, pushing trolleys and beds and wheelchairs, eyes wide with an alertness achieved only through too much caffeine, nicotine, and stress.

They were both wearing the required PPE. To the side of the table sat a trolley, laden with various surgical tools, all of which seemed to Harry to have been designed in the Middle Ages, their only nod to modern-day being the surgical steel they were made from. They glinted meanly in the bright light from the bulbs above, and all around them the white walls of the room were almost dazzling.

'You certainly know how to make a bad day worse,' Harry said. 'And it's not even lunchtime. Well, not for another ten minutes, anyway.'

'I know,' Sowerby replied. 'Sorry about that. Just thought it best to have you over now rather than later. It's certainly been a Halloween to remember, hasn't it?'

'It's already one I'm doing my best to forget.'

The air was sharp, filled with all the smells that only a hospital could mix together in some oddly disconcerting brew, as though to smell it was to be given just a hint of all the bad things that could happen to the human body, even death. And that other smell was there, too, wasn't it, Harry thought, right at the back of it all? It was a smell he knew very well, because it was impossible to hide and even more impossible to ever forget when he'd been so close to it so many times, felt its hot breath on his neck in the thick of battle, down amongst death in the bullets and blood.

'It's okay,' Harry said. 'You made up for it with the tea and biscuits.'

'Can't beat a Hobnob.'

'Or a Rich Tea, as you well know,' Harry said. 'Though I am partial to a Caramel Wafer.'

Sowerby laughed at that.

'Something funny?'

'Everything you just said,' Sowerby replied. 'But particularly the use of the word *partial*.'

'I'll bring some over next time you invite me,' Harry said. 'Tunnock's are the best, though. And I'm pretty sure Police Scotland is fuelled by them.'

'Up there a lot, then, are you?'

'Last time it was a flying visit,' Harry said, remembering another case some time ago involving a missing girl and the briefest of meetings with the DCI who had been lead on the case over the border, a large man who made even his own gruff, scarred face seem almost approachable. 'And I didn't have time to go shopping, which was a shame.'

Sowerby yawned.

When she had met him outside, Harry had noticed a weariness in her eyes. Walking through the mortuary and seeing that the single bed in the office had been slept in, had told him why.

'You sleep here much, then?' he asked.

'It's usually a rota thing,' Sowerby replied. 'But with this, I just decided to stay.'

'It's no more important than any other case.'

'You try telling Matt or any of the rest of your team that.'

'Well, none of them know what you found on the body yet, so they'd have been none the wiser.'

Sowerby frowned.

'You've not told anyone, then? About the feather, I mean.'

Harry shook his head.

'Not on the team, no. I mentioned it to Grace, which I probably shouldn't have done, I know, but sometimes you have to share a little with those closest to you, don't you?'

'You're not worried about a conflict of interest, then?'

'Because this might be a copycat?' Harry shook his head. 'Not in the slightest. Even if it was, even if it's some mad bastard thinking that linking whatever the hell this is to me is some kind of game, it's not a conflict.' He gritted his teeth, breathed deep, then exhaled slowly. 'Right now, as far as I'm concerned anyway, someone decided to leave a body in my house and I'm here for you to confirm who the hell it is and to tell me what you've found out, simple as that.'

Sowerby seemed to hesitate, as though she was unsure as to whether calling him over had actually been the right decision.

'Something the matter?'

Sowerby went to say something, took a breath.

'Possibly,' she said. 'Might make you change your mind about the whole conflict of interest thing, as well.'

'Well, are you going to tell me, then, or make me guess?'

Another pause. 'It's just that there's something else I found and …'

Harry didn't like mysteries. Which was perhaps a little odd, he supposed, being as he was a detective and all.

'Look, it'll be easier if I just get on, I think,' Sowerby said.

'You know best.'

'When I know anything. You want to see anything else first?'

'Like what?'

'X-rays, reports on body fluids, the internal examination, that kind of thing?'

'Thrilling though all of that sounds, not really, no,' Harry said.

'If you're sure?'

'More so now that I know there's something you're not telling me.'

Sowerby reached over and pulled back the white sheet between them to reveal just the head. She then raised her eyes to look up at Harry over the top of her face mask.

'It's not that I'm not telling you.' Sowerby breathed in and out slowly, as though preparing herself for something. 'It's just that this is … well, I'm not sure how we approach this now. What I'm about to show you, what I'm about to tell you, it changes everything.'

'How? You're not making any sense.'

Harry stood there under the power of Sowerby's stare, waiting for her to explain.

'The thing is, we've been able to confirm his identity,' she eventually said.

As far as Harry was concerned, that was good news, so why did she look so worried? What the hell was going on?

'So, we know who this is, then?' he said. 'That's a hell of a start. Well done. I'm impressed.'

Harry noticed then that Sowerby was holding out her hand.

'What've you got there, then?'

'We found this in his clothing, Harry ,' she said. 'And what we've learned confirms what this tells us.'

Harry saw clasped in her fingers an evidence bag. Inside the bag, he saw an ID card, about the size of a credit card. He noticed then that Sowerby was looking even more serious than usual. And considering he couldn't actually see most of her face thanks to the mask, that was saying something.

'What's wrong?' he asked.

'Please, just have a closer look, Harry ,' Sowerby said. She held the bag up a little higher for Harry to see the card inside. 'You need to. It's better that way, I think, than me saying anything.'

Harry leaned in, his eyes narrowed. The evidence bag was obscuring the card inside a little, and he couldn't quite make out the words, or the passport-sized photo.

'I'm not sure I—' Then he saw it. 'That's a prison ID.'

'I was going to call you, but I thought it best to speak to you in person, get you over here to confirm things. I mean, something like this, it's not best talked about over the phone anyway, is it?'

Harry wasn't really listening, the revelation impossible to take in.

'But it can't be. I mean, there's no way that what you're suggesting is—'

'Obviously, we'll have to run through various other checks to confirm it,' Sowerby said, cutting in. 'Double check those medical records, match them to what we've found with the autopsy, that kind of thing, and we're already in touch with the prison. They're not too happy about this coming back to them either. Sounds like there's a hornet's nest there that keeps getting kicked.'

'But this doesn't make sense,' said Harry , screwing his face up, shaking his head, trying to dislodge the information now taking root in his mind.

'I just wanted to tell you face-to-face. I thought it was for the best. That card is also why I worked on this through the night. I needed to be certain, to be absolutely sure, before I told you.'

Harry stared at the body, at the card in the evidence bag, his mind a maelstrom of confusion and such wild emotion that he didn't know whether to laugh or roar.

'There's not a chance in hell that it's him. It can't be. It's impossible.'

'Harry ,' Sowerby said. 'I'm pretty sure— No, I'm actually dead certain that this is ...'

The pathologist's voice died on the words she was trying to say.

Harry was staring again at the ID, at the name, the face in the photo staring back at him. Then, before he knew what he was doing, he snatched the evidence bag from Sowerby's hand, and stared at Sowerby.

'Harry ...'

'Right arm,' Harry said. 'Just above the elbow.'

'What?'

Harry reached out to grab the deceased's arm.

'Don't,' said Sowerby, reaching over before Harry could interfere. 'Just tell me, okay? Whatever it is, just say.'

'There's a scar,' Harry said. 'Just past the elbow.'

Sowerby reached out and turned the arm over for a closer look.

Harry stared down at the pale flesh. There, etched into skin the colour of an old pastry, was a ragged scar, lined with dots.

'You're right,' he said. 'See that scar? It's from a fight. He was outside a pub, drinking with some of his friends. He was supposed to be home. He tried to push me up against a wall, give me a good leathering.'

'What happened?'

Harry turned his eyes to Sowerby.

'I was back from my training, having a little celebration with Mum and Ben. Then he turned up with a couple of his pals.'

'I'm going to assume it didn't end well.'

'Not really, no,' Harry said. 'I ended up throwing him through the lounge window.'

Sowerby shook her head.

'I'm sure that really helped,' she said.

'Made me feel better, so yes, it did rather.'

'What about his mates?'

'One followed him soon after, the other took a hefty boot to the bollocks and just managed to crawl out of the house before throwing up.'

'Bloody hell, Harry ...' Sowerby glanced down at the body, then back up at Harry . 'You believe me now, then?'

'Oh, I'd put money on it,' Harry said and handed back the ID card. 'That's him. That's my father.'

CHAPTER SEVENTEEN

'Mr Peter Grimm,' Sowerby said, then rattled off facts Harry knew but had long forgotten or cared about; where the man was born and when, a potted medical history.

Harry noticed then that Sowerby was no longer speaking. He looked up to see her staring at him over the top of her face mask.

'You okay over there?' she asked.

Harry glanced back down at his father's dead face, the burns he had suffered. His skin was grey and pale, like putty, and he hadn't had a shave in a few days, his chin rough with short, dark bristles. The man looked older than Harry remembered, as though death had aged him by at least a decade or two, the callous, self-centred life he'd led having kept him looking unnaturally young.

'I'm fine, honestly,' Harry said.

Usually, Harry made a point of trying to make a connection with a victim of a crime, particularly when it came to murder, which he was assuming this was, judging by the evidence so far. They had lived lives rudely snatched from them, usually violently, often without cause, and it was important to him that they knew, even in death, that he would do everything he could to bring them justice. Not just for them, either, but their family, their friends.

Because the impact of a murder was far-reaching, its thin claws reaching out to cut and scratch and maim on a scale few really ever knew or understood unless touched by such an awful event personally.

But for once, Harry not only had no need, he had no desire at all, to connect with the dead thing in front of him. The man had lived a life dedicated to causing others pain. That he was now gone was only a good thing. The world was better off without him. No, he had no need to connect with the victim of the crime.

As to the person who'd perpetrated it, though, Harry thought, that was someone he was very keen to find indeed. Whether his father had deserved to die or not wasn't his concern; that the killer knew where he lived and had invaded his life so personally and horrifically absolutely was.

Sowerby said, 'Look, this isn't pretty.'

'Then there's no point putting it off, is there?' Harry replied.

'The face is really only the start of it.'

Sowerby rolled the white sheet further down the body with a gentleness Harry thought his father did not deserve, pausing just below his waist. The man's dignity had been spent a long time ago, but seeing him as he was now, a sallow-skinned corpse naked on a metal slab, hollowed out and cut up by knife and saw, if there had been any left, it had been utterly removed.

'Bloody hell,' said Harry .

'I did warn you.'

'I know, but ...'

'He's lucky he was dead for most of it, that's all I can say,' Sowerby said. 'Not this bit, actually; he was alive for what was done to his face, and some of the other stuff. Whoever did this, they certainly had an imagination.'

'Some of the other stuff?'

'We'll get to that.'

The burns on the face had been rough to look at, but now, with the full scale of what had been done to the body, Harry was almost inclined to agree, though a very dark part of him briefly imagined the screams his father would have made had he not had that gag stuffed in his mouth at the time.

'So, he wasn't alive for it all?'

Sowerby shook her head.

'And you're sure about that? I mean, if whoever did this decided to crack on with torturing him, I'm assuming they wanted him alive for the whole concert rather than just the opening song.'

'Very sure,' Sowerby said. 'I could go into the technical side of things if you want?'

'You mean lividity and oozing blood?'

'Yes, but there's more to it than that.'

'No doubt,' Harry said. 'Happy to take your word for it, though.'

Sowerby pointed at the damage, notably the cut to the stomach Harry had seen the day before.

'Like I just said, we know that at least some of this was done post-mortem, so it's obviously deliberate, but I think there's more to it than that.'

'In what sense?'

Sowerby pointed at the burns to the face.

'This just doesn't look random to me. I don't think whoever did this set to it with the burner just for the hell of it. This was all done with a purpose. I know that this sounds weird, but it's almost as though whoever did it was following a design.'

Harry took a moment to digest what he'd just heard.

'You can't be serious.'

'I don't mean that they did this with some sort of artistic endeavour in mind, more that they had decided on, and knew exactly what they were going to do. It just doesn't strike me as random. It's too deliberate, too thought out.' She pointed to the left arm, which was still touching the metal slab. Harry noticed marks on the wrist, that the hand was missing a couple of fingers.

'Looks like he was tied,' he said.

Sowerby gave a nod.

'Wrists and ankles, to stop him moving too much while all of this was done to him. The fingers were snipped off; found those in one of his pockets. The ropes were removed, I'm assuming, once the killer was finished. We've found some threads in the wounds. Nothing special. Just some green, lightweight nylon rope, that's all. Oh, and there's a couple of fractured ribs, too.'

'Whoever's responsible really went to town, didn't they?'

'My guess is that whoever did this, they straddled him to keep him pinned to the floor.'

Harry turned his attention to the wound he had been shown the day before. It had been reopened and was now a part of the considerably larger Y-shaped incision bisecting his father's torso, which had been cut by Sowerby as part of the autopsy.

'What about this, then?' he asked.

'Yes, that …' Sowerby said, somewhat reticently, as though she wasn't too happy to be discussing it.

'Something the matter?'

'That was definitely done post-mortem,' Sowerby said, not answering Harry 's question. 'I'm guessing that's why the plastic sheet was put down in your lounge, because of the mess from doing something like this, the contents of the stomach making a bid for freedom, that kind of thing. I'm amazed the stink of the place wasn't more ferocious. You're lucky, because that can soak into the walls and be impossible to remove.'

Harry shook his head, then rubbed his eyes hard enough to push them out the back of his skull.

'Yes,' he said, staring at Sowerby over the mutilated body of his father, 'when I think about all of this in a few years, I'll definitely see that as the lucky part.'

Sowerby gave an apologetic shrug.

'Sorry, mortuary humour.'

Harry asked, 'Why do any of it, though? What's the actual sodding point of any of it?'

Sowerby didn't answer, not right away.

'The cut went all the way through,' she said eventually. 'Whoever did this, they just kept on going and had a good old rummage around inside.'

'You make it sound like they were looking for something.'

'They were.'

Harry did a double take.

'They cut him open to look for something? It's hardly Lucky Dip in there, is it?'

Sowerby said nothing.

'So what were they looking for, then?' Harry asked.

'The stomach.'

Harry 's world swam. What was this, a horror movie? 'What do you mean they were looking for the stomach?'

Harry needed a moment alone to get his head around it all, but that was a luxury he couldn't afford.

Sowerby held up two plastic evidence bags. Inside one, and flattened out, was a sheet of paper. Harry could make out writing on it and lots of folds. The writing was spidery and confused, and the paper was dotted with spots of blood and bloody fingerprints. In the other was another plastic bag and an elastic band.

'This,' she said, shaking the bag containing the sheet of paper, 'was found inside this smaller bag, here.' She lifted the other bag up and shook that, too. 'They cut through to find the stomach so that they could stuff these inside it.'

Harry rubbed his eyes, the weariness of dealing with what he was learning already beginning to take its toll.

'And the bag protected the sheet of paper from the contents of the stomach,' he said.

'Exactly. Planned and deliberate, all of it.'

This is becoming increasingly disturbing, Harry thought, if that's at all possible

'What is it, then?' he asked. 'What's written on that piece of paper?'

Sowerby placed the two plastic evidence bags on the trolley

and then handed Harry another sheet of paper, this one clean and fresh.

'I copied it out for you,' she said.

Harry read the document with a growing sense of disbelief. He saw words like sorry and regret, and fell through sentences expressing remorse, a catalogue of the awful things his father had done.

'This is ... Well, it's horseshit, isn't it?'

'That's not for me to say,' Sowerby said. 'I'm just showing you what I found.'

Harry jabbed a finger in the direction of the body.

'But a confession? From this bastard?'

'That's how it reads, yes.'

'He'd never write this, not unless he was under considerable duress.'

'Funny you should say that,' said Sowerby. 'Because if you think what you've seen so far is bad, I suggest you prepare yourself.'

A shiver scraped sharp claws down Harry 's spine.

Harry counted off the damage to the body in his mind; the burns to the face, the ragged cut to the gut to find the stomach, the snipped fingers.

'It gets worse?'

Sowerby gave a shallow, slow nod.

'What else did you find?'

Sowerby reached for the white sheet and pulled it down to reveal the genitalia, or what was left of them.

'He was castrated,' Sowerby said. 'Cleanly done, too, I might add. But there's more. Well, less actually, if you see what I mean.'

'I don't.'

'You will. His testicles were found in his stomach, though I'll refrain from showing you those, I think. And then there's this ...'

Sowerby rolled the white sheet down the rest of the way to reveal the legs.

For a moment, Harry wasn't entirely sure what she was showing him. Yes, there were two legs in front of him, and they looked bloody for sure, so there was damage, but what kind, he couldn't quite make out. The flesh looked strangely loose, though, he thought. No, not loose, more sort of unsupported, if that made any sense, which it didn't, not until Sowerby told him why.

'He's been deboned,' she said. 'Both legs below the knee. And that, I can assure you, was done while he was alive.'

CHAPTER EIGHTEEN

Nausea wasn't something Harry was generally a victim of, but after what Sowerby had just shown him, he was pleasantly surprised to have not been violently reintroduced to his breakfast.

It was true that he had never liked his dad. The man was and always had been a violent and abusive bastard. When pushed, Harry would say that his only redeeming feature had been his absence, because he had been out of their lives more than in. The problem had always been, though, that when he did turn up, it was akin to having someone throw a live grenade into a crowded lift: there was no escape, and the damage was always horrific.

What Harry was having trouble dealing with now was that no matter how awful a human being his father was, what had been done to him was equally horrific, if not more so. That someone had done such things to him made Harry 's skin crawl. His superb, well-practised skill of being able to just lock things securely away in the back of his mind was failing him right now. If he closed his eyes, all he could see was the terrible mess the killer had made, playing out in slow motion, but with a soundtrack his subconscious insisted on conjuring up of his father screaming as the terrible surgery was carried out. The pain, Harry thought, would've been unthinkable.

'How are you doing over there?'

Harry heard Sowerby's voice, but he didn't respond.

'Harry ?'

Who would do this, and why? It didn't make sense. He'd seen revenge killings, organised crime groups taking out members from either side, sometimes throwing in a little bit of kidnapping and torture of their own. And they could get quite imaginative with it all as well, in the worst kind of ways. But he'd never seen this. Ever.

'Do you need to sit down?'

Harry shook his head, looked over at Sowerby.

'What?'

She repeated the question.

'No, I'm fine,' Harry said.

'You went quiet there, even a little pale.'

Harry stepped away from the body for a moment, trying to gather his thoughts. When he turned back, he did so with far too many questions that needed to be answered. One, though, pushed to the front.

'Did you find anything else?' he asked. 'What about those footprints I saw?'

'Still being analysed,' said Sowerby. 'Hopefully I'll have the details for my report. If not, I'll send that on after.'

Harry stared down at the awful remains of his father.

'So, how did he actually die, then? And I know the answer is right in front of me, but something pushed him over the edge, didn't it? And I'm assuming it wasn't just blood loss. What part of all this was the killing blow?'

'I don't think it was any one thing, to be honest,' Sowerby said. 'More a case of everything working together to bring on sudden cardiac death.'

'A heart attack, you mean?'

'The only conspicuous post-mortem finding, other than all the very obvious stuff we can see in front of us right now, is that your father suffered from chronic atherosclerosis.'

'I'm assuming you don't expect me to know what that is.'

'It's where the arteries narrow thanks to a build-up of a sort of plaque-like substance made from fats, cholesterols, that kind of thing,' Sowerby explained. 'That causes the arteries to narrow, sometimes even burst. I think the pressure of what he was put through was just too much and everything sort of went pop.'

'Pop? You're saying he wasn't meant to die?'

Sowerby shook her head.

'No, I'm just telling you what I've found,' she said. 'But I'm inclined to think that yes, he was meant to die, just not exactly when he did. You don't do this to someone and expect them to survive, do you? That's not really the point. This is to make someone's last moments absolutely horrific. It's beyond imagining.'

Harry frowned as he tried to push through the horror of it all and see something—anything at all—clearly.

What he knew so far, not just from Sowerby, either, but from what Walker had told him, and what he'd seen at the crime scene, was that someone had helped his father escape from hospital, perhaps even been instrumental in the original plan to have him transferred from prison to a medical facility from which he could then do a runner. Then, between that event and Harry himself finding his father dead the day before, someone had taken him to his house, tortured and killed him, for reasons as yet unknown.

Had it been the same someone who had helped him escape? Did such a thing even make any sense? Harry wasn't sure that it did, but he wasn't about to rule it out. Right now, he wasn't ruling anything out. And was it in any way linked to that other case with the feathers? Harry needed to lie down in a dark room, but then a thought struck him.

'What you're saying then, and what I'm hearing and seeing, is that the killer probably wanted him to be alive for every bit of what was done to him.'

'What a happy thought.'

'It isn't, is it?'

'Not really, no, but go on.'

Harry did exactly that.

'It's like I said earlier, isn't it? The killer wanted him alive to experience the whole menu of pain, rather than just a few choice courses.'

Harry saw Sowerby's eyes widen.

'Menu of pain?' she said. 'A few choice courses? What is with you today? That's two off-the-cuff metaphors about the same thing in just a few minutes.'

Harry shrugged.

'Probably something I read.'

'You read? You're full of surprises.'

'Anything else?' Harry asked.

'We found a fair amount of amphetamine sulphate in his system. And tranexamic acid.'

'Speed,' Harry said matter-of-factly, drawing on years of dealing with drug crime. 'To keep him awake and alert by the killer as they went to town on him.'

Sowerby nodded.

'The tranexamic acid would have slowed down his bleeding.'

'Makes sense. They wouldn't want him bleeding out halfway through everything they had planned.'

'Must've been disappointed when he died on them, then.'

'And yet, they still finished what they'd started, didn't they?' Harry said. 'Trouble is, though, I've no idea why they started any of it in the first place, and in my bloody house, as well.'

'Maybe it was to get that confession,' Sowerby suggested.

'All of this, for that?'

'It's possible.'

'And who, exactly, would get him to confess?' Harry continued. 'What's the point of it? Who's benefiting here? Because I tell you right now, it's not me.'

Sowerby said, 'We also found psilocybin.'

'Magic mushrooms?' Harry shook his head. 'With all that going on in his system, I'd be amazed if he had a clue what was going on at all.'

'Some people call it hippy flipping,' said Sowerby. 'Mixing

MDMA and psilocybin. Personally, I think it's much more to the point to just call it absolutely bloody idiotic.'

'Magic mushrooms, though?' Harry said. 'You've got to know what you're doing, haven't you, if you go looking for them?'

Sowerby raised an eyebrow and a faint smirk played at the corner of her mouth.

'Speaking from experience, are we?'

'God, no,' said Harry . 'Not my idea of fun playing Russian roulette with mushrooms. Pick the wrong ones and the best that'll happen is nothing at all. The worst? You poison yourself and die vomiting blood. The season's right, though. How was it ingested?'

'We found nothing in the stomach to suggest he'd eaten them.'

'Drank it, then?'

'Looks that way, yes. With all of that in his system, you could get him to walk off a cliff and he'd have had no idea he was doing it.'

Harry turned his attention back to the confession and read it through once more.

'I don't buy it,' he said.

'Why?'

Harry lifted the confession and started to read.

'To all those I've ever hurt and caused pain, I am truly sorry. And that's just the first sentence.'

'So?'

'So, that's not how he spoke, is it?'

'I wouldn't know.'

'Well, I would,' Harry said. 'Plus, I wouldn't have put it past this bastard to refuse to confess, no matter what was being done to him. But that's not what's really bothering me.'

'Really? Then what is?'

'That paper you pulled out of his stomach, the writing on it?'

'What about it?'

'There's something off about the writing,' Harry said.

'How do you mean?'

Harry gave a shrug, scratched his forehead.

'It just doesn't look right.'

'He was probably being tortured at the time,' Sowerby said. 'Which I'm guessing would make anyone's writing look a little off.'

'I get that,' Harry said. 'But it's more than that. It's been a good while since I've seen his writing—years, I'm guessing—so I could be wrong.'

'You think it's fake, then?'

'I'm not sure. But then why would someone go to all this trouble to then fake his confession? That doesn't make any sense at all.'

'The fingerprints on the original are his,' Sowerby said.

Harry moved away from the body. Sowerby reached for the sheet and covered up the horror of what had been done. As the sheet swept up the body until it was completely hidden, Harry was momentarily struck by the thought that he would never see his dad's face again. That was it, the last time, gone. He searched then for some semblance of grief, a hint of heartache deep down for the loss of the man who had been his father. But there was nothing there, not even a cold emptiness, to reach out and grab. He had never missed the man when he was alive. He was dead now, so what was the difference, really?

Back in the small office, Sowerby made them both another mug of tea.

'So, what are you going to do?' she asked, handing Harry the hot drink.

Harry held up the mug.

'Other than grab a biscuit to dunk in this, you mean?'

Sowerby held out the packet of Hobnobs.

'Right now, I don't know,' Harry said, dipping the edge of the biscuit in his tea. 'I didn't like the man. Everyone knew that, especially him, but someone killed him and then left him in my house. There's also a good chance they helped him escape prison in the first place, and my guess would be it was so they could do this to him once he was out.'

'Like I said, it all seems very planned and organised.'

'It does, doesn't it?' Harry said. 'Anyway, I'm just thinking out loud right now.'

Sowerby took a sip from her own mug, then eyeballed Harry through the steam.

'I guess what I meant was, what are you going to do about the fact that the victim is your dad?'

'This isn't personal.'

Sowerby laughed.

'Just because you hated the ground he walked on and the air he breathed, absolutely does not mean that this isn't personal. Also, *isn't* personal is different to *wasn't*, don't you think?'

'Doesn't matter,' said Harry . 'This is a case that needs investigating, so that's what I'm going to do; investigate it. Detective, remember?'

Sowerby fell quiet and sat back in her chair.

'Something bothering you?' Harry asked.

Sowerby leaned forward then, resting her elbows on her knees, mug clasped between her hands. Harry saw just how weary she was as she stifled a yawn.

'What about the conflict of interest?'

'We've been over that,' Harry said. 'A possible link to another case doesn't count.'

'But what you're suggesting now, leading an investigation into the murder of your own father, very much does. And you're not worried by that at all?'

'No,' Harry said, voice firm. 'I'm not.'

Sowerby sat up.

'Trouble is, though,' she said, 'someone will be, won't they?'

CHAPTER NINETEEN

Finished with Sowerby and the remains of his father, Harry headed away from Harrogate and back to Grace's. He would've liked to have enough time to pop into Betty's, a tearoom Matt had mentioned more than a couple of times, if only to find out what on earth a Fat Rascal was. Every time he'd asked the DS to describe it, the only answer he'd received was a wide-eyed, 'Delicious!' which wasn't much to go on, really. Anyway, Grace wasn't with him, so even if he'd have had time to spare, he'd have driven on.

He'd considered heading straight back to Grace's in Carperby, but his mind was too busy with what was swirling around in it, in no small way thanks to what he'd seen in the mortuary. He decided then that what he needed was a bit of space in his mind to work it all through as best he could, and the place to do that was his new house, the crime scene.

Harry gave Grace a call on the way, just to let her know what he was up to, and to check that she was okay looking after Smudge a while longer. But there were no problems there. As their original plans for the day had been so completely scuppered, she was making good use of the time by attempting a little bit of training with the dog, and that was going as well as could be expected.

'She's an idiot,' Harry said, swinging his vehicle up Old Gayle Lane to arrive from the opposite direction, instead of through Hawes and up the hill.

'She's actually showing a lot of potential,' Grace replied.

'Yes, but at what, exactly? Running around like her tail's on fire? Rolling in sheep shit?'

'One day, she'll surprise you, I promise. Just you wait and see.'

'That's exactly what I'm doing.'

Conversation over, Harry pulled over to park up and clambered out into a bright, brisk day, somewhat different to the day before. The air had teeth, and he hunched up his shoulders as he headed over to his house, ducking under the cordon tape to get to the front door. It didn't exactly make him feel welcome.

The key slipped into the lock easily, at which point Harry swore under his breath as a he remembered it would need to be replaced sooner rather than later. Which was when another thought struck him, and he almost kicked himself for not thinking of it earlier. He pulled out his phone and rang the office.

Jadyn answered.

'The break-in at the estate agents' in Leyburn,' Harry said. 'Has Jen got her report in on that yet?'

'I'll have a look now,' Jadyn said.

'How's the family?'

Jadyn was quiet, then said, 'Sorry about that, Boss. I didn't know they'd just turn up.'

'Well, they're certainly friendly.'

'I guess.'

There was a pause, then Jadyn said, 'I've found it, Jen's report. There's not much in it, but it's been done.'

'Not really a surprise,' Harry said. 'Can you run it over to me?'

'Sure, where are you? At Grace's, still?'

'I'm at my place, the house I mean, not the flat.'

Harry heard a very audible gasp.

'You're not moving in, are you?'

'Well, seeing as it's still a crime scene, no, I'm not. Just having another look around, that's all.'

'I'll send it up with the Sarge,' Jadyn said.

'Will you? Why?'

Harry heard a scuffle at the end of the line, then another voice spoke to him. It was Matt.

'Someone's only gone and nicked all the bloody fireworks,' the DS said, forgoing any kind of greeting. 'Can you believe that? They belong to the community, don't they? Folk raised money to buy them. And some selfish little sod has only gone and broken in and taken them. Makes my blood boil. I'm proper mad about this. I only put them down there yesterday.'

'What fireworks?' Harry asked, already confused. 'Put them where? What are you talking about?'

'All of them, that's what I'm talking about!' Matt said. 'No thought at all to the kids who'll have been looking forward to seeing them and now can't. Obviously, there's the bonfire and the jacket potatoes as well, but it's the fireworks, isn't it? That's why they go. That's why anyone goes.'

'Matt ...'

'Who nicks fireworks, anyway? I mean, I can kind of understand wanting to nick something that's worth a bit of cash, a car or whatever, and I'm not condoning that at all, obviously, but this is just lazy and selfish, isn't it? Properly stupid.'

Harry allowed Matt the time to continue with his rant.

'Whoever they are, they probably just decided that rather than buy a few things that go bang themselves, they'd rather break into a shed and steal from the kids, haven't they? That'll be it, I'm sure of it. And that's what's really got me about this, Boss, that the kids will be so disappointed. So, we've got to do something about that, haven't we? I'm not about to have the little ones all sad on Bonfire Night, that's for sure.'

'Well, you'll be on it, I'm sure,' Harry said.

'On it? I'm all over it,' Matt replied. 'Been out there gathering evidence this morning, and I was about to head out again, ask around, that kind of thing. And I'll be keeping the Bonfire Committee up to date as well. But we're going to need to raise some more money, I think. Can't see us getting them back in time.'

'That's all very good to hear.'

Matt then asked, 'Anyway, how are you doing, yourself, like?'

'Well, I've had better weekends,' Harry said.

'I'm sure you have. What are you on with now, then?'

Harry was surprised then to hear a rare note of suspicion in Matt's voice, like the man knew something but wasn't about to say exactly what quite yet.

'You do know that you've still got today down as leave, right?' Matt said. 'And right now there's not much else we can do until we get the forensics report in, and the photographs. Then we can go through it all with the team tomorrow morning. Make sure it's all done proper.'

'We always do things properly,' Harry said, growing increasingly confused.

'We do, yes we do,' said Matt. 'So, how were things over at the mortuary?'

'How did you know?'

'Sowerby just called the office, and she told me that you'd been over. That's why I just mentioned the forensics report. She's going to try and get it to us by the end of the day.'

'That's good,' Harry said, wondering why Sowerby hadn't just called him instead.

'And you're up at the house again, right?'

'Just having a look around, trying to get things into order in my head, maybe spot something that's been missed.'

'So, definitely not treating this as a day off, then?'

'No, because it isn't, not now, anyway.'

'I'll be joining you, then.'

'There's really no need.'

'See you in five.'

Harry went to say something else, but Jadyn was already back on the phone.

'He's on his way, Boss. He's got Jen's report with him.'

Matt arrived barely ten minutes later.

'Stopped off on my way,' he said, handing Harry a white paper bag and a folder. 'Penny Garth Café was open. Thought you might be hungry. Actually, I know you are because tea and biscuits in a mortuary do not a lunch make, do they, now?'

Harry hadn't realised that he was in need of a bite to eat until Matt had mentioned it. He'd headed over to Harrogate straight after breakfast, and lunchtime had been and gone by the time he'd finished with Sowerby.

'What is it?'

'Sausage, red onion chutney, and cheese panini. Oh, and some potato wedges as well.'

Harry stared at the DS.

'You've gone a bit upmarket, haven't you?'

'Posh nosh for a Sunday,' Matt said. 'Enjoy. Oh, and that's Jen's report from the break-in yesterday. A thrilling read.'

As Harry and Matt munched on their food in silence, Harry wondered what he'd see inside his new house that he could have missed the day before. Probably nothing. But it was worth a look anyway.

'How's Joan and the apple of your eye?' Harry asked as he had a quick scan of Jen's report. She'd taken samples of some dirt she'd found inside the estate agents' from some very faint footprint marks on the carpet, and a few photos. The dirt was now with Sowerby's team. All in all, sod all, Harry thought. But as he wasn't one for coincidences, he had a feeling that whoever had carried out the break-in had done so to then get access into his house. It would be good to have that confirmed.

'They're both good,' Matt said. 'We still don't get much sleep, but that's all part of being a new parent, isn't it? But she's properly lovely, she is. Beautiful. And Joan is the best mother anyone could wish for.'

'Enjoying fatherhood then?'

'I am indeed,' said Matt, wiping a crumb from the corner of his mouth. 'Anyway, how about you? Yesterday wasn't quite what you were expecting or had planned, was it? As move-ins go, it's one to remember. Or not, I suppose.'

'Hard to forget, even if I want to.'

'Mind if I ask why you're back over here today? And while you're at it, you can tell me why, on a day off, you're here at all.'

'Not like I've much else to be on with,' Harry said. 'Everything I own is either in a box or in a bag. And I'd only be kicking my heels, getting in Grace's way, if I wasn't over here.'

'And what about the trip to the mortuary, then?'

'Sowerby called me over.'

'Did she, now ...'

'Actually yes, she did,' Harry said, hearing a questioning tone in Matt's voice.

'Any particular reason?'

'Just wanted to go through a few things, that's all.'

'And these things couldn't wait or be put in her report for us to go through together tomorrow, then.'

Harry stopped eating and turned to look at Matt.

'I'm noting a tone,' he said.

'There's no tone,' Matt replied.

'Oh, there's a tone alright. So, why don't you tell me what's bothering you, Detective Sergeant, so we can have it all out in the open?'

Matt finished off his last potato wedge, then brushed the crumbs from his palms.

'You're not being honest with me,' he said at last. 'No, maybe it's not that. More that you're not telling me everything, and that's not how we work, now, is it?'

'I've told you everything that I need to,' said Harry .

'And yet here I am,' said Matt, and he jabbed a finger over towards Harry 's house, 'knowing that it was your own father that you found over there, right? And it's not you that's told me that, is it?' Matt turned to face Harry head-on, his eyes wide. 'No, don't answer that, because it bloody well wasn't, was it? It was Sowerby.'

Harry searched for a response, a little stunned by the tone of hurt and anger in Matt's voice.

'It's a private matter,' he said, and realised how lame an answer that was as soon as the words fell from his lips.

Matt laughed, but there was no humour in the sound, just irritation.

'Now that's some ripe old bollocks, right there, isn't it?' he said. 'What the hell do you take me for? And just who the hell do you think you're speaking to anyway?'

'My detective sergeant, that's who,' Harry said, his own voice rising now.

'Really? Is that all I am? Well, is it?'

Harry gave the shrug of a petulant teenager.

Matt, however, wasn't finished.

'Well, I hate to break it to you, Harry , but I'm not just that, am I? I'm your friend, too, aren't I, you bloody idiot! Honestly, I could shake you hard enough to rattle your head off your shoulders sometimes, you know that, don't you?'

For a split second, Harry thought Matt might slap one of his great meaty palms across his face. Which, Harry had to admit, would've been an odd way to support what he'd just said, but he wouldn't have put it past him.

'If you're worried about how I'm dealing with the fact that it was my father, there's no need,' he said.

Harry really didn't want to have this conversation, but he had a feeling there wasn't going to be any escaping it.

'Oh, I think there is a need,' Matt said. 'I think I've every right to be worried about how this is affecting you, even though I know you'll swear blind that it isn't, and why you're keeping it all to yourself.'

'I only just found out,' Harry said.

'And here you are, nosing around the crime scene.'

'I am allowed,' Harry said. 'DCI, remember?'

Harry heard Matt suck in deeply through his nose, then exhaled slowly, as though working to stay calm.

'Look,' Matt said, 'from whatever angle you look at this, there's a conflict of interest, isn't there? You can't escape that, I promise you. And I'm not going to let you, either.'

Harry said nothing. Didn't see the point.

'You can't go investigating the murder of your own father,' Matt continued. 'You just can't. It's not right.'

'This is different.'

Matt shook his head in disbelief.

'Different? How, exactly? Because you're the great Harry Grimm and the rules don't apply? Is that it?'

'Of course it's not like that!'

'Well, it bloody well sounds like it to me, like, that's for sure.'

Harry was growing increasingly frustrated at the interrogation by his DS.

'It's not like I'll be investigating the death of someone I care about, is it?' he said.

'Not sure exactly what that has to do with the price of eggs.' Matt shrugged.

'Eggs? What?'

'Eggs,' said Matt. 'Fish, take your pick. Your point is irrelevant. Or, as you would say, horseshit nonsense.'

'I'll bloody well investigate whatever the hell I want to investigate,' Harry mumbled under his breath.

'You're already not seeing things clearly,' Matt said. 'And that's a problem, isn't it? Surely even you, the most stubborn arse of a man I've ever known, can see that.'

'How exactly am I not seeing things clearly?'

'Ben, for a start,' Matt said.

'Ben? What about him?'

'Does he know, Harry ? Have you told him that his dad's dead? Well, have you?'

Matt rarely used Harry 's first name.

'No, not yet—'

'Not yet? Why the hell not? What's wrong with you? Don't you think he's got as much right to know as you?'

'The man was a bastard.'

'I don't care if he was Satan's own brother and ate babies for breakfast,' Matt said. 'Ben still needs to know!'

Harry wasn't sure if he'd ever heard Matt raise his voice like this at him before. His gut reaction was to just turn around and tell the DS to sod off and mind his own business, but what Matt had said earlier was stopping him; that Matt genuinely cared and saw himself not just as a colleague but as a friend was something Harry wasn't used to.

'I've not told Grace either,' he said.

'Then it looks like you've got a busy few hours ahead of you, doesn't it?' Matt replied, shaking his head.

Harry waited for a moment before turning to leave. He took a couple of paces, then stopped and looked back at Matt.

'In case you're wondering, I'm not happy that this happened, you know. Not by a long shot.'

'I wasn't, and I'd be worried if you were,' Matt replied.

'Really? Why?'

Matt came over, his hands shoved deep in his pockets.

'Because you were only ever interested in justice,' Matt said. 'And what happened in that house of yours Friday night? Well, that's revenge, isn't it? No other word for it.'

'But revenge for what?' Harry said. 'That's what I want to know.' Then he turned and headed back to his vehicle. Climbing in, he pulled out his phone and made a call.

Grace answered.

'Hi,' he said. 'I'm just heading over to Ben's, but there's something I need to tell you first before I do ...'

CHAPTER TWENTY

Monday had arrived on the back of an emotional and late Sunday afternoon with Ben and Liz. It was now early afternoon, and the team had been busy with various tasks from the action book, as well as catching up on what had happened over the weekend, checking when the forensics report and photographs would be in, and anything else pressing for the week ahead.

Following his somewhat heated chat with Matt, Grace had driven over to be with him, with Smudge and Jess coming along for the ride, to be with Harry as he shared the news about their father with Ben. And though he wouldn't necessarily admit it in public, having the two dogs around actually helped, as they had provided a furry and friendly distraction from the awfulness of what they all now knew.

Ben had taken the news well enough, Harry thought, and with Liz at his side, he was fairly confident his brother would be okay. The shock, however, had still written itself into his brother's eyes as he'd sat there listening to Harry , taking it all in.

Obviously, Harry hadn't shared everything, the manner of death, the torture, and he'd asked Grace to not say anything about the feather either, or indeed anything she had seen or even smelled at the house herself. All Ben needed to know was that his father was dead, someone had killed him, and now a police investigation was underway.

'And you're sure it's him?'

'Absolutely,' Harry said. 'I wouldn't be here telling you any of this if I wasn't, I promise you that.'

'But why kill him? I mean, I know why, don't I? But why do it in your house? What's that about? And who the hell did it?'

'Haven't the faintest idea how to answer any of that,' Harry said. 'But we'll be doing everything we can to find out. My gut tells me the man had a long list of people who'd be happier with him dead.'

'Including us,' Ben muttered.

Harry understood his brother's response and said, 'There's a stark difference between wanting someone out of your life for good and wanting them dead and acting on it. Neither of us would jump into a river to save him from drowning, but neither would we hold his head under the water until he was gone.'

Though he didn't generally approve of adding alcohol to situations as serious as this, Harry had also grabbed a couple of bottles of red on the way over to Ben's. A glass or two, like the dogs, served to distract, and had provided another focus away from what they were talking about.

When he and Grace had finally headed home, Ben had, at the very last minute, walked over to Harry and given him a tight, almost desperate hug.

'I'm sorry you had to see that,' he said.

Harry had returned the hug.

'I've seen worse,' he said. 'You'll be okay, won't you?'

Ben stepped back.

'I will.'

'And I'll make sure of it,' Liz added from behind, stepping close to put her arms around Ben.

'For now, I'd prefer it if you kept this to yourselves, though,' Harry said, and everyone agreed.

Monday morning hadn't brought with it any clarity as to what had happened, however, and Harry had headed to work bleary-eyed from a restless night. Having read Jen's report on the break-in, he'd concluded that whoever had let themselves into his house with his father had also broken into the estate agents' for the keys. He'd also checked in with Sowerby, who had confirmed that the footprints at the two sites matched. All of this added to the growing unease inside him that this was not only very well planned but also directed at him. Why though, he just couldn't figure out, not yet, anyway.

Finding out where he was moving to wouldn't have been all that difficult. He was the local DCI, this was Wensleydale, so the only way he would ever have been able to keep where he lived and was moving to a secret would be to live out of the Dales under a completely different identity.

The previous night, his dreams had been dark, twisting nightmares, and lying awake to stare into the darkness had done nothing to purge his mind of all that his dad had suffered. Yes, he'd hated the man with every ounce of his being and had on numerous occasions wanted to kill him himself, but he'd still never have wished for him to go through what he had endured in those last god-awful hours of his mean life.

Harry noticed that Jadyn was already at the board, pens at the ready.

'Right then,' he said, clapping his hands together, the sound like a gun going off. 'Let's get on then, shall we? What have we got in the action book for the week?'

Gordy said, 'This week, other than what happened up in Gayle, our focus is Mischief Night on Wednesday, and Bonfire Night.'

'And we've had a report in of someone spotted doing a bit of wild camping.'

'Not much of a crime, really, is it?' said Harry .

'It is when wild camping is actually parking up illegally in someone's field and making a proper mess of it with your tyres.'

'Ah, right,' said Harry . 'A busy one, then. And it just got a little busier, thanks to my noticeably buggered up moving day.'

Jen jumped out of her chair.

'Damn it!'

'Something the matter?' Harry asked.

'We forgot!' she said.

'Forgot what?'

Jen dashed out of the office and then returned carrying some parcels neatly wrapped in brown paper. She presented them to Harry .

'We can keep them,' she said. 'If you don't want them yet. You might not, what with everything going on. Might be more appropriate when you're actually in. Assuming you still go ahead with it all, like.'

'They're your housewarming presents,' Liz explained.

'You shouldn't have,' Harry said. 'I do appreciate it, don't get me wrong—I just don't need housewarming presents.'

'Need has nowt to do with it,' said Jen.

'Well, it's all very kind, but right now, I'm sort of lacking in a house to warm, aren't I?'

'That's what I wondered,' Jen said, and sat back down, shoving the parcels under her chair. 'We'll keep them then, until you're in properly.'

Matt, Harry noticed, had a hand raised, so he looked over and waited for him to speak.

'There's also the theft of the fireworks,' Matt said. 'Best put that in the book as well. Total value is only around a grand or so, but that's not the point. Whoever took them has done their best to ruin a nice night out for the kids, and I'm not going to let that be the end of it, you mark my words.'

'Any leads, then?' Harry asked.

'I took the fireworks over to the barn at the end of the footpath that heads over from Hawes to the bottom of Gayle,' he said. 'That was Saturday, around the time everything was kicking off up at your place. It's not exactly a major crime, I know, but I've cordoned the area off and will be heading over there again for another look around. There's some tyre marks and a few footprints. Looks like someone popped in for a nosy first, then headed off and came back with a vehicle to take it all.'

'Witnesses?'

Matt shook his head.

'What was the security like?'

'It's a barn at the end of a field,' Matt said. 'No matter how many locks you put on a place like that, you could probably still squeeze in through a gap in the wall.'

Jim laughed at that.

Harry asked, 'Who knew the fireworks were being kept there?'

'As far as I'm aware, it was hardly a closely guarded secret. This is the Dales, after all, and secrets here are as rare as unicorn shite.'

Harry thought about the location.

'Not a very secure place to store them, though, was it? And I don't just mean because it's a barn; it's a very public place.'

Matt said, 'I don't think the bonfire committee thought anyone would even think about nicking it all. It's only a few fireworks after all; hardly worth the effort really.'

'And yet, here we are,' Harry frowned.

'Anyway,' Matt said, 'keeping a secret in a community like ours is pretty bloody difficult.'

'Doesn't sound like a crime of opportunity though, does it?' said Jadyn. 'A barnful of fireworks isn't something you just stumble on, is it?' 'Barnful is stretching it, I think,' said Matt. 'A few boxes, that's all. Metal ones, mind. Nice and safe. Except from the hands of selfish gits, that is. Regardless, I'm looking into it. I've also had a call on the way to work from someone over in Appersett this morning. Last night, someone threw a few fireworks into their garden. Could be a coincidence, or it could be whoever took them did so just to play silly buggers this week and cause mischief.'

'Something to keep an eye on, then,' said Harry .

'The main problem we have, though,' continued Matt, 'is that we probably won't find the fireworks till after Bonfire Night, will we? And you know what that means, don't you?'

'No fireworks?' Harry shrugged.

'Exactly,' nodded Matt. 'Which means we'll be having to buy some more.'

Harry saw every member of his team snap their heads round at this to stare at Matt.

'What? How?' asked Jim. 'I've not got the cash to go replacing all of those.'

'I don't think any of us have,' said Liz.

Matt tapped the side of his nose.

'Don't any of you go worrying about that,' he said. 'Just you leave that with me for now. But I'm going to assume here and now that I can count on the support of everyone in this room, like, yes?'

'Sounds a little ominous,' said Gordy.

'Well, can I?' Matt repeated.

'Just so long as it doesn't involve emptying my already thin wallet,' said Jim.

A murmur of agreement rippled through the room. Harry took that as a sign to move on with things, namely what had happened up in Gayle.

'Ready, Constable Okri?'

'Always,' Jadyn replied.

A cough interrupted before Harry could continue. Gordy was staring at him.

'So, have you officially cancelled your leave, then?' she asked.

'Well, seeing as a crime scene doesn't really make for the easiest of houses to move into, then yes. Is that a problem?'

'Not at all,' Gordy said. 'You've filled out the necessary form, then?'

Harry frowned, narrowed his eyes at the DS.

'There's a necessary form?'

Jadyn leaned in and whispered, 'I'm afraid to say, Boss, that there's always a necessary form.'

'I'll do that after this, then.'

'Make sure that you do,' said Gordy.

Harry tried to move things on with a quick rundown of events.

'Quick recap of what's been going on and what we know so far,' he said. 'Approximately two weeks ago, and following an accident in prison, an individual awaiting trial was transferred to a hospital for treatment and in the process escaped from custody. Two days ago, a body was found in a property in Gayle.'

The pen Jadyn was using on the board seemed squeakier than usual. Harry tried to ignore it.

'Forensics have now established that the body and the escapee are the same individual.'

The pen squeaked some more.

'We have the forensics report in already, thanks to the pathologist working to get it to us nice and early. The photographs of the crime scene will be with us later today. There was also a further crime scene in Leyburn that looks as though it is linked to what happened in Gayle. And, just to warn you, what I'm about to tell you, and what you will see from the photographs, isn't pretty.'

Matt's arm was raised once more.

'Yes, Detective Sergeant?'

'Just wondering if there's any other detail you've missed there, that's all.'

Harry shook his head.

'Not that I'm aware of.'

'And you're sure of that now, are you?'

Harry knew exactly what Matt was getting at, but he wanted the team to just focus on the facts of the case, rather than the fact that the deceased was his father. Yes, the identity of the body was also a fact, but it was also a distraction.

'For now, yes.'

Harry watched as Matt folded his arms and said no more, just stared. He also saw confusion writ large on Liz's face.

The office was strangely silent, Harry noticed, guessing that the team had picked up the strange hint of tension now in the air.

'Anyway,' he said, moving things along as best he could, 'what we do know is that the individual died at the scene.' He then explained as concisely as he could, and without the additional gory details, what had been done to the victim, and also mentioned the feather found in the deceased's mouth.

At this, Jim said, 'Feathers? Again?'

'That's exactly what I thought,' said Harry . 'But the one found on the body is small and white, rather than one from something like an eagle.'

Jadyn asked, 'Was that the first case I was involved in over here? I think it was, wasn't it? Is this a copycat, then?'

Harry said, 'If you don't mind, I'd like to nip that thought in the bud immediately. I don't think this is a copycat. Also, I don't want even a hint of that as an idea or a fleeting thought getting into the hands of the press, because it's just the kind of thing they love.'

'And by they, you mean Anderson,' said Jim.

'It's a consideration, though, isn't it?' asked Jen.

'We'll put it on the board, but we'll keep it to ourselves,' Harry suggested.

'Why a white feather, though?' Jadyn asked. 'What does it even mean?'

'Historically, it means cowardice,' Harry said, remembering his chat with Grace a couple of nights ago. 'But let's move on from that for now. We need to get out there and knock on some doors. Also, we have the details of the hospital, so we'll need someone to go and chat with the staff there. It'll mean a bit of a trip out as well.'

'Me, I'll go, I'll do that.'

Harry looked at Jadyn.

'That was a bit keen, Constable.'

'I'd just like to go, that's all,' Jadyn said.

'Isn't your family up here to visit?'

'Exactly,' Jadyn said. 'I mean, well, what I meant is, they're not just here to see me. I've a job to do, haven't I? And visiting a hospital would be a very important part of that job.'

Harry could see the flicker of desperation in the young constable's eyes.

'I'm assuming the reason they've visited, though, is to see you at work, hear all about what you get up to, see you in action, that kind of thing?'

'Yes, but—'

'So, if you ended up not doing much while they were here, they wouldn't be best pleased, would they?'

'No, probably not.'

Harry looked over to Jen.

'DC Blades,' he said, 'do you have anything planned for tomorrow? I doubt a visit today is on, after all.'

Jen shook her head.

'But I just volunteered,' said Jadyn. 'Honestly, it's fine. I don't mind going. I'd really like to.' He turned to Jen and added, 'What about Steve? What if you're late or delayed or something happens?'

'Like what?'

Jadyn shrugged. 'I don't know,' he said. 'Something. Could be anything.'

'Doesn't matter anyway,' Jen said. 'Steve's fine. He looks after himself.'

I'm sure he does, Harry thought, remembering his encounter with Jen's huge pet monitor lizard some time ago.

Harry looked at Jadyn and Jen. 'Well, I'm sending you both. DC Blades will lead on this, and you will be there as support. Give the hospital a call when we're done.'

Jadyn's face lit up.

Harry turned his attention to Matt.

'I'll need the team knocking on doors. Considering what happened, I can't see how someone didn't notice something going on. Also, I think we should have a look at that other case with the feathers, just to rule it out. DI Haig?'

'I'll contact the prison, see what I can find out from that side of things,' Gordy said. 'There's bound to be a list of names of those whose own criminal dealings with the victim might lead us to various suspects, though obviously anyone who's capable of carrying out a murder like this is also more than capable of getting away with it and leaving no trail to follow. I'll also chase up the photos, see if forensics has anything else for us, contact next of kin, that kind of thing. Oh, and I'll find you that form I mentioned.'

'Lucky me,' said Harry , then noticed that Matt once again had his hand raised.

Jen then said, 'And I'll need the victim's ID when I contact the hospital.'

Matt raised his hand and said, 'That mention of next of kin, there.'

'What about it?'

Harry 's patience was almost worn through by Matt's pointed, loaded approach to questioning, but Jen's point was fair enough. Time to bite the bullet, he thought, and to get that final detail out in the open, particularly with what Gordy had just said. It wasn't something he could keep a secret or would even want to; he'd just been putting it off till the end of the meeting so that he wouldn't have to spend the rest of the time talking about it.

With a pointed glance over at Matt and then at Liz, Harry said, 'On that, what I'm about to tell you is for this room only.'

He noticed everyone lean forward just a little, the bait of his words hooking them in.

'As I've said, it has been confirmed that the identity of the victim at the crime scene over the weekend, and of the individual who escaped from custody two weeks ago, are one and the same. A prison ID card was found on his body and was checked by the pathologist.' He paused, reading the words in his mind before saying them. 'The victim's name is Peter Grimm.'

Harry allowed his words to settle on his team, watching as realisation dawned on their faces.

'And to be absolutely clear on this, Peter Grimm is, or was, my father.'

More silence, thicker this time, expectant.

Jadyn was first to break it.

'Bloody hell, Boss,' he said, his voice quiet and sombre.

'Yeah, something like that,' Harry replied.

For a moment or two, no one else said another word. Thinking the shocked silence had gone on long enough, Harry went to speak, but Matt took to his feet.

'Right then,' he said, 'now that we've got that out of the way, who's free tonight?'

As one, the team turned to look at the DS.

'What? Why?' asked Liz.

Matt grinned.

'Remember what I said about being able to count on everyone's support vis-à-vis the missing fireworks?'

'I already don't like this,' said Jim.

Matt's grin, Harry noticed, grew even wider.

'I know it's no longer Halloween, but in the name of a good cause, who's up for a bit of fancy dress?'

CHAPTER TWENTY-ONE

WITH THE NEWS ABOUT HIS FATHER NOW OUT IN THE OPEN, Harry was surprised to feel rather relieved more than anything. He'd wanted to keep the whole issue a secret, ignoring the fact that such a thing was impossible. Now, with everyone aware of the situation, he could relax.

Also, with Matt focused on raising money to replace the missing fireworks, and the team now set to with various tasks in relation to what had happened in Gayle, there had been no further mention of anything to do with his continued involvement being a conflict of interest. Well, there hadn't been until Detective Superintendent Walker had called.

'Of course, in light of this new information, and I'm sure you can understand why, not just personally but professionally as well, you will no longer be involved in the case.'

Harry had tried to protest.

'With respect, I think I can be a real asset to the investigation.'

'So do I,' Walker said, 'by staying the hell away from it. If you're required, if your input is needed, then you will be involved accordingly. I'm sure that Detective Inspector Haig can lead on this now. And I'm available should my services be required. You will be kept up-to-date with any developments, any suspects, I'm sure.'

And that had been the end of the matter, conversation over, no room for argument. Harry was off the case and was now staring at a week ahead that he wasn't really sure what to do with.

Come the evening, Harry was already wondering what to do with himself. Even though it was very early days and little would have been done or progress made, the temptation to call Matt or Gordy, or indeed anyone on the team, to find out what was happening with the case was almost too much. So, to keep his mind off it, and to stop himself thinking of the now-impending trip south for the reunion, he was back at the flat in Hawes, and once again sorting through boxes. Plus, he now had an extra day to do nothing, the reunion not being till Wednesday. And Harry wasn't exactly good with free time, which is why he generally tried to ignore it.

'Have I told you what Matt's up to, tonight?' he said.

Grace shook her head.

Harry then explained about the fireworks and Matt's plan to do a bit of fundraising himself, with the help of the team.

'You're not joining in, then?'

Harry shook his head.

'Not a fan of fancy dress if I'm honest.'

'You sure about that?'

Harry stared at Grace.

'I saw you Saturday night,' she said. 'Even with everything that had happened, you were a proper softy with those tiny vampires.'

'That's different.'

'How?'

'They were real vampires, and I had to save us both from being bitten.'

Grace laughed and crouched down beside him.

'I'm not sure there's much left to throw out,' she said, as Harry started to shuffle through the contents of another box.

Smudge and Jess were with them, both curled up together on the floor, a big ball of warm, snoring fur.

'Can't hurt to look though, can it?' Harry said, pulling out a pile of magazines. 'I mean, I don't need these, for a start, do I?'

'What are they?'

'Police magazines.'

'What?'

Harry handed Grace what was in his hand.

'I thought you were joking,' she said, staring at the magazine on top of the pile.

'Hard to joke about something that dull.'

'Then why do you still have them?'

Harry shook his head.

'Not sure. There's useful stuff in there sometimes. Maybe.'

'You read them, then?'

'No.'

'Then how do you know?'

'Which is why I think I should chuck them in the bin.'

Harry stuffed his head back in the box, then lifted his head and looked over at Grace.

'What is it?' she asked, worry in her eyes. 'What's wrong?'

Harry lifted an envelope from the box and opened it.

'These,' he said, and slipped out a small collection of photographs. He shuffled through them, shaking his head. 'Bloody hell ... just look at us ...'

Grace sidled up beside him to peer over his shoulder.

'When were they taken?'

'Too long ago, that's when,' Harry said. 'There's more somewhere, I'm sure of it, from when I was doing my basic training, P Company, that kind of thing. These, though, are from when I was on tour.'

'Afghanistan?'

Harry gave a nod and lifted a photo showing six soldiers armed to the teeth, all of them smiling.

'That's us,' he said. 'I'm the handsome one in the middle.'

'Looks like a photo for Soldier of Fortune magazine,' Grace said.

Harry laughed at that.

'Full of piss and vinegar, that's what we were.'

'What a delightful phrase.'

Harry smiled.

'Not sure where I heard it, but it's pretty accurate. Thought we were invincible.'

'You look it.'

'We weren't, though.'

Harry slipped the photos back into the envelope and dropped them into the box.

'You should take them with you, to the reunion,' Grace said. 'Seeing as you're going now.'

Thanks to Walker's intervention, Harry had been left with no more excuses to duck out of going. And Grace was clearly going to make sure that he went. That would mean a very long drive, but he'd worry about that later.

'That would be a nice thing to do,' Grace said, interrupting Harry 's thoughts. 'Don't you think?'

Harry wasn't so sure.

'I'll see,' he said. 'You hungry?'

Grace punched Harry softly on the arm.

'Subtle change of subject, there.'

'Doesn't answer the question.'

About a quarter of an hour later, they were down at the public bar at the Fountain Inn, both dogs with them, and already curled up at their feet under the table. Harry ordered their food, two portions of scampi and chips, a pint of Gamekeeper Bitter each, from the Wensleydale Brewery, and they sat down in a corner.

The bar was just busy enough, Harry thought, with enough chatter in the air to make the place feel alive.

'It'll all work out, I'm sure,' Grace said, resting her hand on Harry 's.

'I know it will,' Harry said, though he wasn't so sure. Leaving the investigation in the hands of his team wasn't the issue, not really. It was more what the end result would be; someone had done terrible things to his father, but it was the why, above all else, which bothered him.

Harry took a deep draught from his glass.

'I'll drive,' Grace said. 'Back to mine, I mean. It's not like we'll be staying at yours, is it? And I think you could probably use another pint after that one, seeing as you've already nearly finished it.'

Just then, as Harry picked up his knife and fork to tuck in, the door to the bar opened, and in walked a huge man dressed as Frankenstein's monster. Following behind him came a sight straight out of a horror movie, as three zombies shuffled in.

'Evening all,' the man bellowed, striding into the centre of the bar. 'Now, who's up for a scare?'

'Bloody hell, that's Dave Calvert,' Harry said, staring up at the monster now standing directly in front of him.

Frankenstein's monster stared down at Harry , eyes wide with menace, but the grin on his face ruined any chance of being scary.

Stuck to each side of the man's neck were two plastic bolts. Dave's face, neck, and hands were green and decorated with various fake scars. He was wearing a black donkey jacket, ripped jeans, and a pair of black Wellington boots. To Harry , Dave looked like the farming version of Frankenstein's monster, an undead stockman about to head out onto the hills to bring in a flock of zombie sheep. Not a bad idea for a movie, that, he thought.

'Harry !' Dave said, his green skin making his teeth seem bright white. 'Good to see you and Grace out. I hear things haven't gone so well with the move. Nowt to worry about, I'm sure it'll be sorted.'

'What the hell are you doing?' Harry asked.

'What does it look like I'm doing?'

Harry shook his head.

'Not a clue,' he said.

One of the zombies stepped forward.

'Now then, Boss,' it said.

Harry did a double-take.

'Matt?'

'Remember what I was on about earlier?' Matt said. 'Well, here we are, out raising money to replace those missing fireworks. I managed to persuade this lot to join in.'

The other two zombies stepped forward and waved. It was Jim and Liz.

'What about Jadyn and Jen? And where's Gordy?' Harry asked.

'Jadyn's out with his family, Jen's on duty, and Gordy will be taking over from her later on.'

'You've certainly put some effort into your outfits,' Grace said, munching on a piece of golden scampi.

'Got to put the effort in, otherwise, what's the point?' Matt said. 'Anyway, Joan loves a bit of fancy dress herself, so she helped me knock this up earlier.'

'Didn't fancy joining in herself, then?'

'No,' said Matt, shaking his head. 'She's at home with the little one. Still a worry with the asthma, like. Though it's probably a bit late to be out with her, anyway.'

Dave leaned over and said, 'By the way, I've some news of my own; I'm giving up the offshore life and taking a few months out, maybe even a year, have to see. Might not bother to go back. Bit tired of it, if I'm honest. Time for a change.'

'Sounds good,' said Harry .

'It does indeed. Can't wait, actually. I tell you, all these years living in two places, it's knackering. It'll be good to stop and take stock.'

'What'll you do next, then?' Harry asked.

Dave looked thoughtful for a second or two.

'You know what? I've not the faintest idea! How mad is that?'

As the big man laughed at his life decisions, Harry turned his attention to Jim and Liz.

'How did he rope you both into this, then?'

'Not just us, Ben, too,' said Liz. 'Didn't you know?'

Harry shook his head, smiling at the thought of Ben dressed up like Liz and Jim.

'He's joining us in a bit. Said he was going to give you a call.'

Harry frowned.

'Why?'

'Not sure. And I'm guessing by the look on your face, he hasn't.'

'No, he hasn't.' Harry frowned and stood up.

'Where are you going?' Grace asked.

Harry pulled out his phone.

'If he was meant to call and hasn't yet, I want to know why.'

'It's probably nothing.'

'I'd prefer to make sure it's exactly that.'

Leaving Grace and the two dogs with the impromptu horror movie set in the bar, Harry made his way outside into the chill night air. The sky was starless and seemed as though it was pressing down somehow, intent on suffocating the land below.

Phone to his ear, Harry called Ben, but there was no answer.

'Harry ?'

Ben's voice was decidedly closer and less electronic than Harry had been expecting and he stared at his phone, confused. Then he saw another zombie approach from across the road. The zombie waved as it came to stand in front of him.

'Ben?'

'Liz and the others inside?'

'They are,' Harry replied.

'What are you doing out here?' Ben asked. 'Thought you were at Grace's.'

Harry explained, and then told Ben what Liz had said to him a couple of minutes ago.

'That? Oh, it's probably nothing,' Ben said.

Harry had left his coat inside the bar and the evening was cold, but he hardly noticed.

'What, exactly, is probably nothing?' he asked.

Ben didn't immediately reply, and Harry watched a frown crease his brother's Halloween makeup.

'When we were leaving to meet up with Matt and the others, I thought I saw something.'

'Define something,' said Harry , unable to disguise the concern in his voice.

'I honestly don't know. I heard a noise, thought I saw movement over behind a car outside the house, and there was a flash, but that was probably just a car rolling past I guess.'

Harry breathed through his nose like a bull.

'You're sure you didn't see anyone, though?'

'I'm just a bit paranoid, I think,' said Ben. 'What happened over the weekend, it's just made me jumpy, that's all. I had a nosy around, found the food recycling bin on its side.'

'Fox?'

'Reckon so.'

Harry wasn't sure what to do. Even though it sounded like what had happened really was nothing more than a hungry animal sniffing around for a free meal, part of him still wanted to jump in his car and head over to Liz and Ben's place in Middleham to check things over.

'You know, it sounds just like that,' Harry said eventually, realising there was no sense in having Ben any more spooked. 'Understandable to be unnerved though. No bad thing, either. Always best to be alert.'

'By which you mean paranoid.'

Harry nodded at the door back into the pub. 'After you.'

Back inside the bar, Harry sat down with Grace, while Ben wandered over to join Dave and the others, who were still chatting and collecting money.

Harry picked up a chip from his plate and used it to point at Frankenstein's monster and his gaggle of zombie friends.

'They raised much yet?'

'Seem to be doing okay with it,' Grace said. 'Everything okay?'

'Half of my team is dressed up as extras from a Hammer Horror movie,' Harry said. 'I'm not sure that can ever be described as okay.'

'You know what I mean.'

Harry thought about what Ben had told him, which wasn't much. Still, it would play on his mind, regardless. He'd send a message to Matt later, though, just in case.

'Honestly, it's nothing,' he said. 'Now, where were we?'

Grace picked up another piece of scampi.

'Eating our last meal before the zombie apocalypse.'

'Sounds fun.'

'It's certainly tasty,' she said. 'And we've tomorrow to plan, haven't we?'

'We have?' Harry said.

'Well, if the reunion's not till Wednesday, and you're not at work, then yes, we have.'

'Any suggestions?'

Grace thought for a moment.

'You've not been to Aysgarth Falls yet, have you?' she asked.

'I've driven past, that's all.'

'That's decided then,' she said. 'The weather we've had, they'll be spectacular.'

Harry reached for his beer and raised it to Grace.

'I can't wait,' he said, and the surprising thing, he realised then, was that he truly couldn't. The Dales had him, hook, line and sinker, and he wasn't about to let even the death of his own father ruin it for him.

CHAPTER TWENTY-TWO

Jadyn didn't like hospitals. He'd volunteered to go because he was happy to grab any opportunity to not be under the watchful eye of his family. But now, as they headed to where the hospital was located over in Harrogate, he wasn't so sure, memories of his last visit to one still very much raw and bleeding.

It had been bad enough last night, sitting round the table in the cottage they'd rented out, spending the entire time trying to justify his existence to his parents. Okay, so they had never really understood why he'd gone into the police force in the first place, but surely, at some point, they'd just get used to it? He had to hope so, because there was only so much he could take. He loved his parents dearly, but that sense that they were more than a little disappointed with his decision was hard to deal with. All he wanted was their blessing, that was all, and he figured that wasn't too much to ask.

He was actually pleased to have his sister Isioma there, not least because in the few moments she dragged her face away from her phone, she would back him up. Though she'd eventually left him alone with them, heading out into Hawes on her own. She'd always had that knack of walking into a room of strangers and turning them into friends, so no doubt the same would happen again. He'd always admired that about her and been a little jealous. He'd have joined her, too, but with the day he had ahead of him now, he'd instead headed home to get his head down.

On the drive over from Hawes, Jen at the wheel, Jadyn did his best to try and ignore the growing knot in his gut, but as they drew ever closer, the knot only tightened.

'Everything okay?'

Jen's question sat unanswered in the car between them.

'Jadyn?'

'Yes?'

'I asked—'

'I'm fine,' Jadyn said. 'Sorry, just not a fan of hospitals, that's all.'

'No one likes hospitals,' replied Jen. 'I don't think they're designed with that in mind.'

'I know, it's just that ever since ...'

Jadyn's voice faded.

'Ever since what?'

Jadyn rubbed his neck unaware he was even doing it.

'Oh God, of course,' said Jen.

Like people crowding into a lift, the memories pushed into Jadyn's mind, quickly filling it to bursting point, taking him back to when he'd been snatched off the streets of Leyburn by a group of hard-right racists. They'd taken him to a remote barn, strung him up, all because of the colour of his skin.

He squeezed his eyes shut, tried to force the memories back into the darkness. The rope around his neck, being hoisted up and up and up, the burning in his chest as his lungs tried to suck in air that just wouldn't come, the darkness of death crushing everything to dust, the pain ...

'I'll be okay,' he said. 'It's ages ago now, isn't it? Mad that it still affects me.'

'No, it isn't,' said Jen. 'I still have flashbacks of when I was kidnapped. It wasn't for long, but the terror, it's still with me. Pretty sure it always will be, too. I just grow better at dealing with it, I guess.'

Jadyn remembered what had happened to Jen, how she'd been taken by a killer who seemed happy to blame the entire female population for his own inadequacy and inability to score a date. They'd only just got to her in time, up on the moors behind Gunnerside in Swaledale. Harry had taken the killer down with a full-body tackle that would've snapped the spine of a horse.

'I didn't realise,' Jadyn said.

'I don't talk about it much,' said Jen.

'Same.'

'Maybe we should,' Jen suggested. 'And, before you worry that I'm saying we both head off to therapy, I'm not.'

'Thank God,' Jadyn laughed.

'Yeah, we've probably both had more than our fair share of that, right?'

Jadyn gave a nod.

'But we could always go for a chat over a pint sometime, if you wanted to.'

'I'll maybe take you up on that.'

'Do.'

Jadyn took a deep breath and exhaled slowly.

'So, what do you think about this being Harry 's dad?' he asked.

'Right now, I don't know,' Jen replied. 'Must be strange for him and Ben, though. It's not like they liked the bloke, is it?'

'Not much to like, by all accounts. Still, though, this is all a bit odd, isn't it?'

'It is, but all we can and should do is our job. No point overthinking it. We'll just go in, find out what we can, then report back.'

Jadyn still felt unsure.

'Not having Harry on the case, though,' he said. 'I know it makes sense, but it doesn't feel right.'

'Gordy will keep him up to date on things,' said Jen. 'And if we need his input, I'm sure that's not a problem either.'

A few minutes later, they pulled into the car park at the hospital.

'Come on,' Jadyn said, opening his door. 'Let's get this done.'

Inside the hospital, Jadyn's senses were immediately overloaded by the sights, the sounds, the smells. The hospital entrance was also a café, but the rich aroma of coffee did nothing to disguise the medical tang of the air.

'Where do we go, then?' he asked.

Jen pulled out a notebook, checked a page, then walked over to a map of the hospital hanging on the wall.

'There,' she said, dropping a finger onto the map, then off she strode, and Jadyn had to hurry to catch up.

They walked through numerous doors and along such a network of tunnels that Jadyn quickly lost all sense of direction. The deeper they went into the hospital, the worse the smells and the sounds became. Then, when they rounded a corner to be almost smashed into the wall by an occupied hospital gurney being pushed by a gang of medical staff, the knot in Jadyn's stomach made him almost double over.

'I remember that,' he said. 'I remember what it's like being pushed through corridors like this.'

'It's something you're unlikely to forget anytime soon.'

'I've tried.'

'You can go back to the car,' Jen said, and Jadyn saw genuine concern in her eyes.

'No, I'm good. Honestly, I'll be fine.'

Jen pointed ahead. 'We're nearly there. Next corridor on our left, I think.'

Jadyn followed, and soon they were at the glass-surrounded reception to a ward.

Jen went over and spoke with the receptionist. A moment later, a woman in a smart navy suit approached them and introduced herself.

'Mrs Evans,' she said. 'I'm one of the senior hospital managers.'

Jen introduced herself and Jadyn.

'Probably best if we talk in my office,' Evans said, then without waiting for confirmation from either Jadyn or Jen, she turned on her heel and walked over to a blue door.

Jen led the way and Jadyn followed, finding himself inside a small, neat office, which overlooked a little courtyard filled with various plants and a bench or two.

'Thank you for seeing us,' Jen said, as they all took a seat.

'I hope I can be of some help,' Evans replied, now sitting at a very clear desk. 'We've never had anything like this happen before.'

'I'm sure,' Jen said.

'The prisoner, I mean the offender, a Mr Peter Grimm, wasn't it?'

'Yes,' Jadyn said, deciding to be a part of proceedings, if only to help keep his mind focused on something other than his last experience of being in a hospital and the fact that they were there inquiring after Harry 's father. 'He was here under guard after breaking his arm while in custody.'

'I have the medical file here,' Evans said, opening a drawer and pulling one out. She opened it. 'Compound fracture to the arm.'

'Ouch,' said Jadyn.

'I should say so,' Evans agreed. 'That's why he was brought in; the medical team at the prison just didn't have access to the required facilities and resources to deal with it. He was rushed in, operated on, then kept in for observation. All standard practice.'

'So, what actually happened?' Jadyn asked.

Evans leaned back into her chair.

'Fire alarm,' she said. 'We have drills for them, obviously. Regular as clockwork. This one wasn't a drill. And no matter how many times you practise for just such an event, when it happens in real-time? People panic, don't they?'

'More often than not, yes,' said Jen.

'This was worse, though,' continued Evans. 'Lots of smoke in one of the corridors. That sent a lot of people over the edge.'

'So, it was an actual fire, then?' asked Jadyn.

Evans shook her head.

'Fire Service found some smoke canisters. Someone clearly thought it would be funny to let them off. I assure you, it wasn't. You would be amazed at some of the things people will do in a hospital.'

'I'm sure,' said Jen.

Evans leaned forward.

'We've had streakers, dirty protests, guns. Someone even brought in a barbecue once.'

'A barbecue?' said Jadyn.

'Hard to believe, I know, but true none the less. It was someone's birthday, and they always had a barbeque. Set it up right outside there, actually, in that little patch of garden. They couldn't understand the problem at all. Did smell good, though.'

'The canisters, what happened to them?' Jen asked.

Evans shook her head.

'Not a clue. Probably thrown away, unless the fire service kept them. Maybe they handed them to the police we had in soon after.'

'That's a little unfortunate,' Jen said. 'But we'll follow that up for sure.'

'I've got photos of them, though,' Evans said, pulling out her phone. 'Took a couple of pics for reference, just to educate the staff, in case they see anything similar again. You never know. Here you go ...'

She flipped the phone round and Jadyn saw an image of a green canister with white lettering on it.

'They look military to me,' he said. 'Can we have a copy of that, please?' He looked at Jen and said, 'The boss would know more about that, wouldn't he?'

'I'll send it to you once we're done,' Evans said.

'So, there was smoke and a fire alarm,' Jen said, carrying the discussion forward.

'And a fair amount of panic,' Evans said. 'You can't just evacuate a hospital. There are strict procedures. And because this wasn't a drill, and because of all the smoke, you can imagine what it was like; the wards aren't exactly full of people who can walk unaided, plus there were any number of operations going on at the time.'

'What happened with Peter Grimm?' Jadyn asked.

'I wish I could say,' said Evans. 'I've looked at the CCTV, interviewed staff, and you're not the only police we've had in either. But we've nothing at all to go on. Though my money is on whoever set off those smoke canisters. Too much of a coincidence otherwise, isn't it?'

Jadyn said nothing, but if there was one thing he'd learned from DCI Grimm, it was to not believe in coincidences.

'You mean no one saw what happened to him? Not even the police officers stationed to guard him?'

'Apparently not,' Evans said. 'I think they were as surprised by the fire alarm and the smoke as anyone. It doesn't take much to be distracted in a situation like that, does it?'

'Even so,' said Jadyn, finding it hard to believe that two police officers would lose sight of their charge.

'The problem is that it was like a stampede,' Evans explained. 'I think they were just overwhelmed by the weight of people. They were pushed away from the door for only a few moments, but that was enough. And with the corridor full of smoke, people coughing and spluttering and choking and running into each other.'

'Was anyone hurt?'

'Thankfully, no,' Evans said. 'Which is a small mercy, I suppose.'

Jadyn didn't want to think about the huge bollocking the officers who'd been guarding Harry 's father must have received.

'What about the injury?' asked Jen.

'There's no way it was an accident,' Evans said.

'How do you mean?'

'The break, it just didn't make sense. It takes a lot to break a bone. They're seriously strong, they have to be. This break, I'd expect to see it after a workplace accident, a building site maybe, or perhaps someone was doing some DIY at home, fell off a ladder. That kind of thing. Even then, it's rare.'

'Not sure I follow,' said Jadyn.

Evans looked at him.

'How did he break his arm like that in prison? We were told that he fell. From what, exactly? No, it wasn't an accident. It was deliberate. How he did it, and how he dealt with the pain of it, I just don't know, but no, I don't believe he fell. Not in the slightest.'

Jen jotted down a few notes, then asked if there was anything else Evans thought she might be able to tell them.

Evans shook her head.

'No, sorry, that's it, I'm afraid. I really wish I could be of more help. I'm assuming you've not found him, then? That's why you're here, I mean.'

'It's an ongoing investigation,' said Jadyn. 'We're just checking up on a few details.'

Meeting over, Evans led them out of her office.

'Don't hesitate to contact me again if you need to ask any more questions,' she said. 'I doubt I'll have any more answers, but you never know.'

Back out in the car, Jadyn clipped in his seatbelt.

'So, what do you think?' Jen asked.

'I think I'm pleased to be out of there,' Jadyn answered. 'I also think whoever set off those smoke canisters helped with the escape.'

'Same,' said Jen. 'But ...'

Jadyn turned to look at her.

'But what?'

It was a moment or two before Jen spoke.

'It looks like Harry 's dad had his arm broken deliberately so that he would end up here, right? And the only reason he'd do that is to escape.'

'That's what I'm seeing, too,' said Jadyn. 'Which means whoever threw the canister was a part of the plan.'

'So, how does he go from escaping from hospital, to then ending up dead in Harry 's house? It just doesn't make sense.'

'Maybe something went wrong,' Jadyn suggested. 'Maybe word

got out that he'd done a runner, and a rival found out and had him killed.'

'He wasn't just killed though, he was tortured,' said Jen. 'Plus, why do any of that at Harry 's place?'

Jadyn stared through the windscreen at the hospital car park as his mind did its best to shuffle everything from the past few days into some sort of order.

'It's like all of this is meant to look like one thing, but it's actually something else,' he said.

'How do you mean?'

'I'm not sure,' said Jadyn. 'But my gut's telling me there's something bigger here.'

'And you listen to your gut often, do you?' said Jen. 'Harry would be impressed.'

She started the engine and checked her watch.

'It's going to be late when we get back,' she said.

'Steve won't be happy,' said Jadyn.

'Fancy going for that drink?'

Jadyn said yes quicker than he'd expected.

CHAPTER TWENTY-THREE

'YOU'RE GOING.'

'I know.'

'Then to do that, you actually need to leave the house, get in that knackered old car of yours, and drive there. That's how going somewhere works.'

'It's not knackered.'

'What?'

'The Rav. It's not knackered.'

'And that's what you'd like to focus on right now, is it?'

Harry huffed.

'I don't like reunions.'

Grace folded her arms and stared.

'Been to a lot then, have you?'

'No.'

'Then how do you know?'

'Intuition.'

Harry stared at Grace as she handed him his car keys, plonking them into his upturned palm. He was standing in the hallway of her house and dithering. Not something he did much, so he'd just gone with standing in one place and checking his jacket pockets a few too many times. In one of them was the small collection of photographs he'd found on Monday night. He'd tried to leave them behind, only to find that Grace had slipped them back into his jacket.

'You'll enjoy it,' Grace said, gently pushing him towards her front door. 'When was the last time you saw any of them?'

'Years ago. You saw the photos. Just before I joined the police.'

'Then it's been too long, hasn't it? You'll be amazed at how little any of you have changed. It'll be just like old times, I promise.'

'I'll hold you to that,' grumbled Harry . 'And anyway, it won't. In those old times we were a bunch of twenty-something lads, either armed to the teeth and out in theatre, or back here and training. None of us are that now, are we?'

Grace gave a smile.

'That's probably a good thing,' she said. 'Have you packed everything?'

'I'm only away for one night. It's not like I need much.'

'Everyone forgets their toothbrush,' Grace said.

'Packed.'

'What about that Kindle I bought you?'

Harry laughed at this, and the mood lightened a little.

'That, too.'

Grace had her own and Harry had found himself picking it up and kind of just staring at it, then reading bits and pieces of whatever book Grace had on the go. In the end, she'd become so fed up with finding that he had lost her place, or opened a new book, that she had just bought him one to use himself. Initially, he'd thought it to be a waste of money, because he didn't have time to read. 'Then make time,' Grace had said, and he had.

Now he found himself carrying it around with him most days, and if he had a spare minute or two, dipping into whatever it was he was reading at the time. Right now, that just so happened to be Goldfinger, by Ian Fleming. It was another thing about him that had changed, because in his previous life he'd never had much time for books. Now, though? Well, it wasn't that he had any more time, just that he used that time differently. And those Bond books were definitely better than the movies.

Thinking back to when the invite to the reunion had arrived, Harry had at first considered not mentioning it to Grace at all. That way, he wouldn't have even had to bother thinking about it, never mind consider actually going. But with everything that had happened over the weekend, it had actually come in rather useful as a solid reason to not be around. He still wasn't all that keen on going, though, even more so after the day they'd spent together yesterday at Aysgarth Falls.

He'd never regarded himself as much of a romantic, but really, that's what the day had been all about; just being the two of them and their dogs, strolling through the woods, taking photos, gazing at the terrifying beauty and power of the falls themselves. They'd even taken in the café overlooking the falls, not just for coffee either, but a decent lunch. He hadn't wanted it to end because it was what his life was now, and the promise of it was almost impossible to grasp. His life had changed beyond anything he could have imagined, and he felt more strongly than ever that travelling back into the past wasn't going to do anyone any good, because it rarely did.

Harry was a firm believer in leaving the past where it was. Trying to relive it, even as a memory shared among friends, was not his idea of fun. However, there was also something else bothering him, and it had disturbed his sleep enough the past three nights to be on his mind now. And that was the injuries inflicted on his father, the ones to the man's face, which reminded Harry so much of his own. And although he was no longer a part of the investigation, he didn't think it would hurt anyone if he scratched a certain itch, which was the idea that maybe there was a connection to his past. He couldn't see how there was, but there would be no harm in finding out. And it allowed him to justify going in his own mind, regardless of his own feelings on it all.

Gordy and the team would be busy checking out various leads, most of which would be criminal associates of his father who Harry had no doubt would have watertight alibis. Deep down, he suspected that whoever was responsible would never be found, and that didn't just go for the person who carried out the killing, but whoever set the whole thing in motion and ordered it.

Grace leaned past Harry and opened the front door. At their feet, Smudge and Jess stared up at him, though Harry wasn't entirely convinced either dog was all that bothered about him leaving.

'You've the address of the hotel where you're staying?' Grace asked.

'I have.'

'And you'll call me when you get there?'

'I will.'

'Just to let me know you've arrived.'

'Of course.'

Grace smiled.

'These emotional farewells are just too much sometimes.'

A kiss goodbye and Harry headed over to his vehicle. The journey ahead was going to take at least six hours, if not more. The satnav said just under five, but he was allowing for rest breaks and crappy traffic.

He slipped the key into the ignition and at exactly that moment, his phone rang. Harry was tempted to ignore it but couldn't.

'Grimm,' he said.

'You've not left, then?'

Gordy's question made Harry 's stomach clench, because he knew there was only one reason for her to ask it.

'If this is about the fact that tonight is Mischief Night, then—'

'You've a visitor,' Gordy said, interrupting.

'A visitor? Then tell them I'm busy. Which I am, so it's not exactly a lie. Week off, remember? Plus, there's that whole conflict of interest thing.'

'I think you'll want to speak to him,' Gordy said.

Harry rubbed his eyes, then caught sight of Grace staring at him from her front door, concern in her eyes.

'Who is it and why?' Harry asked.

'A certain DCI Drake,' Gordy said. 'He's here about your father.'

'Bollocks,' Harry said.

'Thought you might say that.'

Harry took a moment. He wasn't part of the investigation anymore, that was true, and he had a hell of a long journey ahead, but if he just drove off, he'd spend the rest of the day trying to stop himself from just turning around to find out what this Drake actually wanted, or what he had to say.

'I'll be there in twenty,' he said.

'Sorry,' Gordy replied.

Harry hung up and Grace was at his window, which was open to the day and the cool air rushing in.

'Something's up, isn't it?'

Harry explained.

Grace leaned in and gave him the gentlest of kisses on his scarred face.

'Remember to call me when you arrive,' she said, then headed back into her house, closing the door behind her.

The journey over to Hawes seemed to be over before it had even begun, and Harry parked up in the marketplace with little to no recollection of it. He'd driven over on autopilot, wishing the miles away, the glory of the Dales rushing past unnoticed.

Gordy met him at the door and apologised once more.

'It's not your fault,' Harry said. 'Unless of course it is, and you and I are about to have a serious falling out. How's the rest of the team?'

Gordy quickly went through what everyone had been up to the day before, and even though Harry was keen to hear about Jadyn and Jen's trip to the hospital, and if there had been any progress on the missing fireworks, he didn't really take any of it in; his mind was already on the road ahead and he wanted to get going.

Following Gordy into the community centre, Harry found the visitor waiting for him outside the office. He was a smallish man with a neat beard, dressed in jeans, a brown knitted jumper that looked homemade, and a waxed jacket. He was leaning on a folding metal walking stick, and had several large brown folders under his arm.

The man handed over a small wallet from his jacket pocket, which Harry flipped open and inside found an ID staring back at him. He handed it back, barely giving it even a cursory glance.

'DCI Drake,' the man said. 'Don't suppose you'd mind if we had a little chat now, would you, Mr Grimm?'

CHAPTER TWENTY-FOUR

A FEW MINUTES LATER, AND HAVING AVOIDED POPPING INTO the office itself to talk to the team, Harry was with his visitor and sitting in the interview room. He poured out two mugs of tea, then reached for a biscuit. Taking a sip, he took a moment to look over the lip of his mug at the man opposite him.

Drake's beard was well maintained, Harry noticed, unable to think of a better description for the smartly trimmed, greying hedge which adorned the other DCI's face. Harry had never worn a beard himself. The stubble that sprouted from his face, ready for a shave in the morning, was about as attractive as a patch of scorched scrub in a nuclear wasteland.

When they'd entered the interview room, Drake had folded up his walking stick before removing his jacket to hang it over the back of his chair, and dropping the pile of brown folders and his car keys onto the table in the process. The jacket was well cared for, the wax coating deeply ingrained in the dark green cotton. The brown jumper beneath, homemade or not, was of thickly spun wool and Harry suspected was as warm to wear as any modern fleece or down jacket. Leather patches adorned the elbows and shoulders, much like the military pattern jumpers Harry had worn back in the day.

Drake had reminded Harry of someone when he'd first met him, but it was only now, as they sat opposite each other, that he realised who, and the memory made him smile.

'Jameson,' Harry said, 'that was it.'

'Jameson was what?' Drake asked over the top of his own mug. 'And who's Jameson, anyway?'

'You remind me of him, that's all,' Harry said. 'A DCI who helped me a fair bit when I started out in the police.'

'An old friend, then?'

'We lost touch. He moved away, I think. Can't remember where to, exactly.' Harry placed his mug back down on the table. 'So, how can I help you, Mr Drake?'

Drake placed his own mug on the table as well, and raised his eyes to meet Harry 's. 'Rumour has it that you've had a busy weekend,' he said, stretching out his left leg and knocking into Harry 's foot in the process. 'Sorry about that. My leg gets a bit stiff thanks to a nice bit of arthritis coming along a little too early.'

Harry frowned, leaned back a little.

'Does it, now? Well, I've never been a fan of rumour. Can't trust it. Often no better than its evil twin, that being gossip, if you know what I mean.'

Drake smiled warmly and Harry found himself relaxing a little, his initial suspicions of any detective just waltzing in through his door dissipating not exactly like oil on water, but not far off.

'The fact that I know this at all is probably quite the surprise, I should think.'

The man, Harry noticed, didn't really have an accent. If he was to try and describe it, he'd have said *general English*, an accent that was really from anywhere and could probably just mould into place wherever Drake happened to be. It wasn't posh or city, that was something he was pretty sure of. It was rough, the kind of accent Harry would have imagined archers and blacksmiths to have had down the centuries. It reminded him of the way soldiers talked, their accents mingling together into one all of its own. There was a natural cheeriness to it as well, a voice made for telling stories, he thought, because it was one you just wanted to listen to.

'Well, I suppose it would be, yes,' Harry said, 'if I knew exactly what it was you were referring to.'

Drake took another gulp of tea.

'Can't beat a proper cuppa, can you?' he said, lifting the mug up to stare at it. 'Anyway, the thing is, when I first heard about what had happened, that's what had me thinking. I mean, it happens more frequently than people realise, doesn't it? But not with someone like this. Not very often at all, actually.'

Drake spoke in a relaxed and calm manner that Harry wasn't used to, not in the police, anyway. Harry had a sense that the man could have you just talking about anything, even if you didn't want to. A very useful skill in the police force, that was for sure, especially so in an interview room. He decided it was probably best if he kept himself a little on guard and didn't give too much away.

'Strikes me that you've been taking lessons in beating around the bush,' he said.

'I'm here about your father,' Drake said.

Harry decided it was time for him to do some slow and deliberate tea-drinking, so he reached once again for his own mug.

'What about him?'

'For a start, I know he escaped just over two weeks ago now,' Drake said. 'Nothing has been leaked to the press, which says just enough I think about who and what your father was.'

'Should I ask how you know this?'

Drake gave a shrug.

'You can, but there's little to tell. Us detectives, we can't help keeping an eye on things, can we? Like yourself, I'm sure, I'm always poking around in things, even if they have nothing strictly to do with me. Past cases, unsolved crimes, the usual. You never know, do you?'

'And what might I never know?'

Drake leaned forward, elbows on the table.

'It's all about connections, isn't it?' he said, drawing a line across the table with a finger and tapping it three times on the way. 'That's what this job is, really, when you think about it; joining up the dots to see a picture few others can. And I think we can help each other with this one, work together a little.'

'I like that,' said Harry . 'A very good description, indeed. But it doesn't really answer my question. Plus, there's the fact that I'm not actually a part of the investigation, for obvious reasons.'

'Conflict of interest.'

'Exactly.'

Drake said, 'News of your father's escape was kept quiet for too long, as you know. When it got out, it spread like wildfire; everyone knew, because everyone wanted to find him. I made a few calls, spoke with a few of the team working with your detective superintendent, did a bit more digging yesterday, then jumped in my car this morning, and here I am.'

Drake leaned back and from a pocket in his coat removed a pipe and a tobacco tin. He opened the tin, filling the room with a sweet, earthy, almost mushroomy aroma. He then proceeded to pinch the tobacco and stuff it into the pipe, almost nonchalantly, Harry noticed, like he wasn't even aware of what he was doing. Harry couldn't help but laugh.

'Now that is something I remember about Jameson,' he said. 'Someone bought him a pipe and slippers for his fiftieth.'

'That someone wouldn't happen to have been you, then?'

'Took to carrying it around with him,' Harry said, refraining from answering the question. 'Even smoked it now and again. Some cherry-flavoured stuff, I think.'

Drake finished with his pipe and slipped the tin back into his pocket. 'There's a case I've been working on for a good few years now, and I'm here to see if I can join up a few more of those dots I mentioned.'

Harry was now trying to work out the man's age but couldn't quite pin it down, putting him anywhere between mid-fifties and mid-sixties.

When Drake spoke again, the cheery tone of his voice had

fallen away, replaced with an edge as keen and hard as sharpened steel. The pipe was now an extension of his hand, a conductor's baton, waved in the air to dance between his words.

'Someone like your dad doesn't just walk out of prison on a whim, now does he?' he said. 'Don't worry, I'll answer that one for you. No, he bloody well doesn't. So, he must have had a little help, wouldn't you think?'

'I would,' Harry agreed.

'So, someone helped him escape, but why? That's the question, isn't it? What's the reason behind it?'

Harry leaned back and folded his hands in his lap.

'There's more than one, I'm sure,' Harry said. 'For a start, I wouldn't be surprised if he had enough cash stashed away to pay for an escape plan, a little box buried deep in a wood somewhere.'

'Possibly. But if that's the only reason someone helped him, then why are we both sitting here now, in this room?'

'Not sure I understand.'

Drake leaned back in his chair, arms folded.

'When someone like your father manages to break out of prison, it's to get away, isn't it? To go to ground, stay safely out of sight for a year or two, before coming back out of the shadows to play silly buggers again, right?'

'Why else?'

'Exactly,' Drake said. 'Why else, indeed?'

Harry frowned.

'Not sure I follow.'

'The fact is, I don't think there is a why else,' explained Drake. 'Which makes his death even more mysterious, wouldn't you think?'

Harry couldn't hide his shock at Drake's words. So far, they'd been chatting about his father escaping prison, but now they were onto what had happened five nights ago in Gayle.

'Where are you going with this, exactly?' he asked.

'The escape of your father is one thing,' Drake said, 'but what happened to him afterwards, well, that doesn't make much sense at all, now does it?'

Harry wasn't a fan of kicking unanswered questions around the room like a beach ball.

'How about you get to the point?' he said.

'The point,' Drake said, pointing at Harry with the mouthpiece of his pipe, 'is that my guess is your father expected to disappear, but not so permanently, if you get my meaning. And that means someone either caught him before he could go to ground—'

'Or the whole thing was a trap from the off.'

'Exactly,' Drake said, his face lighting up at Harry 's statement.

Harry found himself enjoying talking to another DCI. Drake had an air about him that made Harry feel they could just have easily been in a pub talking over a pint, as in an interview room.

'But why would they do that?' he asked.

'You mean motive?'

Harry shook his head.

'He collected enemies like some people collect stamps.'

Drake reached for the stack of brown folders he'd brought with him and slid it over into the middle of the table. Opening the first, he removed a small map of England and an envelope, along with various notebooks. The notebooks he stacked to one side. The envelope he opened and from within removed a small pile of photographs.

He lifted the first photo to show Harry the chubby face of a man with very little hair.

'This is, or perhaps I should say was, a certain Mr Nightingale. Drugs, mainly, but dabbled in a bit of people smuggling. Not a nice man by any measure you'd care to use. Disappeared five months ago, then turned up a few days later in a disused caravan in Cornwall, dead as can be.'

He moved on to the next photo, another man, skinnier than the first, with mean eyes sunk in shadow.

'This here is a Mr Philips. Started out selling the kind of home movies no one should ever see or be a part of. Naturally progressed into people smuggling. No drugs, though; apparently that was against his moral code, would you believe it? Disappeared four years ago. His body was later found inside the hull of an abandoned canal boat somewhere in Warwickshire.'

'Where are you going with this?' Harry asked.

Drake revealed photo number three. It showed a woman, mid-thirties Harry guessed, though it was hard to tell due to how she looked, her gaunt, dark hair cut in a bob, set around the hard eyes of a wolf.

'This is Ms Church. A little bit of burglary to feed a drug habit and before you know it, she's running county lines and making a fortune from kids as young as nine who she would often pay in drugs rather than cash. Disappeared two years ago, her body was discovered later in the cellar of a recently closed pub in the Fens in Lincolnshire.'

Drake then spread the remaining photographs out on the table.

Harry stared at the rogues' gallery in front of him. He reached over for the files, Drake doing nothing to stop him, and looked through records of evidence on a case he had grown used to seeing throughout his time in the police.

Drake presented another photograph. Harry saw his father's face staring back at him.

'Peter Grimm, disappeared two weeks ago.'

'So I've heard.'

'And his body was discovered Saturday just gone, barely a mile from where we are now sitting and having this lovely little chat.'

Harry wasn't really sure how he was expected to respond. Drake hadn't as yet divulged the actual reason for his visit, so Harry wasn't about to be helpful. So, instead, he continued to look through the files. He found photographs of various crime scenes, more than he was used to seeing, if he was honest, but that was no bad thing. Every detail seemed to have been captured, the victims in gloriously gory close-up, every inch of the locations covered. Whoever the photographer was, Harry wouldn't mind getting their number.

'There's a connection?'

'There is.'

'I'm just seeing photos of people the world is seemingly better off without, all of them dead,' Harry said, shoving the evidence back into the files.

Drake took another glug from his mug, then pointed at each photograph in turn.

'These,' he said. 'Their deaths. They are all connected. They are the dots.'

'How's that, then?'

Drake sat back, said nothing, giving Harry time to come up with his own theory, though it was one he almost laughed aloud at.

'You can't be serious?'

Still, Drake said nothing.

'You mean you're suggesting that someone is out there going around killing criminals? And that they've now added my father to their list?'

'This is no suggestion,' Drake said. 'Each of these people in my files was killed by one person, someone who somehow managed to wriggle their way into their respective lives. And I have reason to believe that your father is potentially victim number eleven.'

'Eleven?' Harry was stunned by the number. 'Bloody hell, Drake, you've been watching too many late-night movies.'

'I doubt that,' Drake replied. 'The last movie I watched was back in the seventies. Something about spaceships. More of a book person, really. Would love to be able to write myself, if you know what I mean. I'm always coming up with characters, but writing them down, that's where I trip up. They say everyone's got a novel in them, don't they?'

'Doesn't mean they should all have a go at writing them, though,' Harry said. 'Anyway, you've not really given me much in the way of these supposed dots, have you? Other than the fact that they're all criminals and they're all dead, what's actually linking them together?'

Drake reached a hand once again into the folder.

'What else have you got in there?' Harry asked. 'A kitchen sink?'

'This,' Drake said, and handed Harry a sheet of paper.

The paper was a copy of a handwritten note, the writing scrawled and difficult to read.

'What is it?'

'That,' Drake said, 'is a confession found in the gut of Mr Nightingale. I could show you nine others, but I don't think that's necessary, do you?'

Harry lifted his eyes from the paper to find himself caught in the hard stare of a man with eyes as grey as a winter's moon.

'Tell me, Mr Grimm,' Drake said. 'Did you find one, too?'

CHAPTER TWENTY-FIVE

HARRY STARED AT THE NOTE IN HIS HAND, CAUGHT A FEW sentences as he scanned it. He thought back to his father's body, what the man had suffered on the floor of his house.

'And this is Nightingale's writing?'

Drake gave a nod.

'As far as I can tell, yes,' he said. 'I've done a comparison with various other samples I was able to get a hold of and they match. Why do you ask?'

'The note we found on my father's body,' Harry said, 'there's something not right about it.'

'How do you mean?'

'I'm not sure that he wrote it. I can't say for sure, but it doesn't look like his writing. Not to me, anyway.'

'You sure about that?' Drake asked. 'I thought the same of Nightingale's and all the others. But of course, the confessions were put down in the last few moments before death. Stress can have a surprisingly debilitating effect on someone's ability to write even their own name.'

'I get that,' said Harry , handing the note back to Drake. 'I may have hated the bastard, but I knew his writing.'

Drake picked up the note and slipped it back into the folder.

'I'm assuming this is where I ask how I can help?' Harry asked.

'Actually, it's me who has come here to ask you that very question,' said Drake. 'I'll need to speak with whoever is leading the investigation.'

'Well, it's not me,' Harry replied with a shrug.

Drake let out a long, calm sigh, then sat forward again, his hands playing with the pipe he'd filled earlier.

'Difficult for you, I'm sure, but it's the right decision. You can't be a part of this investigation, Grimm. You just can't, and you know that. I mean, there's conflict of interest, and then there's this.'

'I want to find who did this to him as much as anyone else, believe me.'

'Oh, I do,' said Drake. 'But there's already too much emotion in how you just said that. Being objective would be a challenge.'

That comment annoyed Harry . Maybe it was meant to, though, he thought.

'I'm always objective.'

Drake laughed, but Harry couldn't help but notice a cold edge to it.

'We all think that, don't we?' Drake said. 'Remain apart from what we're investigating, keep that distance. Remind me how you ended up in the Dales in the first place?'

'Been reading up on me, then?'

'Let's just say I'm thorough when it comes to my research, if you know what I mean. I like to really know a person before I meet them.'

'You say thorough. I say nosy bastard.'

Harry could feel his irritation growing. As they'd talked, he'd started to like Drake, to warm to him. Now, though, as with all but a very select few who he found himself growing fond of, Harry suddenly was going off the man. He'd already thrown a chair across the room in the past couple of days; he had a horrible feeling he was growing close to doing so once again. But that wasn't going to get either of them anywhere. If Drake was here to help, then he had to give him the benefit of the doubt.

For a moment, neither detective spoke. It was Harry who finally broke the silence, having had a little chat with himself.

'Sorry about that,' he said. 'My blood boils easily, some days. And this is one of those days. One of those weeks, actually, if I'm honest.'

'Water off a duck's back,' Drake said, smiling again. 'Quite literally, too, actually.'

'You mean you're a duck? The beard's a disguise, then?'

Drake laughed, the warmth there once more, and Harry 's sudden dislike faded again.

'It can be, yes,' he said. 'My name, it has two meanings, and one of them, would you believe, is duck.'

'Not quite as on the nose as mine, then,' Harry said.

'It also means dragon, well, snake dragon or snake monster, if you want to be really accurate. I did a bit of research into the family tree a few years ago. Thought it might be a nice little hobby.'

'And was it?'

'No idea,' Drake said. 'No time for hobbies with this job, right? And what am I going to do with *snake monster* other than get a tattoo?'

'And did you?'

'Goodness, no. Not one for needles. Anyway, where were we?'

'I'd just called you a nosy bastard.'

Drake packed away the photographs into the folder.

'I'm not in a position to tell you what to do, and neither do I want to,' he said, now holding the closed folders on his lap. 'I'm not your superior officer and I'm not here to take over this investigation either; I'm here to help.'

'Then my advice is to speak with my DI, Gordanian Haig. She's leading things now.'

'There's also another point that I'm not sure you've considered as yet,' Drake added.

'And what's that?' Harry asked.

'There's a chance, Grimm, that you're potentially a suspect.'

Harry 's laugh was as immediate as it was loud.

'Am I bollocks a suspect. I admit, there are many times I wanted to kill the man, but that doesn't mean I'd actually do it.'

'Look, I'm sure you've got a watertight alibi—'

'Too bloody right I have,' Harry said, and told Drake exactly where he'd been Friday night and with whom.

'Regardless,' Drake said, 'you know as well as I do that close family members are often responsible. I'm not saying that you are, I'm just saying that you're right there, aren't you, in the firing line? I'm also fairly sure you don't need me to tell you what the press will think when they find out. And they will find out, Grimm. You can bet on it.'

Harry pushed his chair out from under the table and stood up, shoving his hands in his pockets as he started to pace slowly around the room.

'My problem is doing nothing, though,' he said. 'I will, but it's not easy. Not by a long shot.'

'Well, you'll have to, if you want this case solved.'

Harry sat down again, slumping a little in his chair. Drake, he was beginning to realise, was making a lot of sense. He was also treating him with a level of kind, thoughtful professionalism that was rare in the world in which they both worked.

'Look,' Drake said, 'I promise you, I've not driven all the way up here from Somerset just to ruin your day. I just thought it would be best to speak to you first, before doing anything else.'

Harry paused at this.

'Somerset?'

'I set off in the early hours to miss the traffic,' Drake said. 'I'll probably pass out with tiredness in a couple of hours, but hopefully coffee will stave that off long enough for me to find somewhere to stay for a few nights while I work on all this.'

'Whereabouts?' Harry asked. 'In Somerset, I mean.'

'Over Glastonbury way.'

'There was a chance of a job for me there, you know?' Harry said, then added with a laugh, 'Too many hippies and wizards, though, for my liking. There's even a magic well, you know.'

'What magic well?'

'Something to do with the holy grail, I think,' said Harry . 'I'm surprised you've not heard of it.'

Drake laughed.

'Too distracted by the aforementioned hippies and wizards. I notice your accent hasn't left you.'

Harry shook his head.

'Part of my DNA, I think.'

Drake placed his pipe in his mouth for the first time since filling it.

'You're not going to smoke that in here, are you?'

'I only light it when I come to the end of something,' Drake said, shaking his head. 'A little celebration, if you will, chasing the leaf with a couple of matches. Like this, I find it helps me to think. You should try it sometime.'

Harry roared at that.

'Me? A pipe?'

Drake asked, 'So, if you're not on the investigation now, what are you going to do with yourself?'

Harry mulled things over for a few moments, tumbling everything around in his head like washing in a dryer. This was a lot to take in. He wanted to find out who had killed his father, but he had to leave it in the hands of others. He'd already decided on that, and perhaps now, with this Drake involved, it would all be sorted a little more quickly.

'I'm actually on leave now, anyway, what with the house move and everything. So, that's made it easier to step back.'

'That's good,' Drake said. 'You've the perfect excuse to not be around, haven't you? Get yourself moved into your house, then come back to work next week.'

'Not sure I have, actually,' Harry said, 'seeing as the house is going to be a crime scene for a while yet. It'll need a hell of a clean-up after what was done to my dad in the lounge. A new carpet, that's for sure. Plus a new lock on the front door.'

Harry saw Drake's eyes widen at this.

'I'm sorry, what?'

'You didn't know?'

'Didn't know what?'

'That's where it happened,' Harry explained. 'I found his body in the lounge on the day I was supposed to be moving in.'

Drake shook his head.

'Bloody hell, Grimm ... I've a location, that's all. No mention of you being the owner.'

'Not what you expect to find on the day you move in,' said Harry . 'First house I've ever bought in my life as well. As signs go, it doesn't bode well, does it?'

Drake, Harry noticed, seemed stumped.

'So, whoever killed your father knows where you live?' he said.

'It's a bit of a puzzler, isn't it?'

'Masterful understatement, I should say,' said Drake. 'None of these other cases have the victim in a location like that.'

'How do you mean?'

'A location that's connected to the victim or their family.' Drake fell quiet for a moment, deep in thought. 'Hearing that, I think it's even more important that you step away as soon as you can, by which I mean today, Grimm, if that's at all possible. The further away you are from things, and the sooner, the better. I'll work with the team and we'll see how we do. Obviously, this could all be a horrible coincidence, but you never know, do you?'

'Coincidence? No such thing,' Harry said. 'He was left there on purpose. Why, though, that's the issue, isn't it? And if it is the same person who murdered all those other victims in your files, then why suddenly change?'

'I'll keep you up to date on things,' Drake said. 'So, probably best if you make sure you're easy to contact.'

'I'm heading down south,' Harry explained. 'Aldershot way. The team has my number if you need it.'

'Aldershot?'

'A few old army mates are getting together.'

Harry wondered then about mentioning the possible connection between what had been done to his father and his own scarred face, but decided to keep it to himself for now. It was a long shot anyway, and he didn't want anyone stepping in to tell him he couldn't do a little bit of digging.

Harry led Drake out of the interview room and into the main office. He then instructed Gordy to take the DCI through everything they had on the case and to put him in touch with Sowerby.

'Anything else?' Gordy asked.

'I bloody well hope not,' Harry said, and turned on his heels to head back outside.

CHAPTER TWENTY-SIX

Having pushed out of the office, Harry realised that Drake had followed him.

'Just want to say well done for making the decision to stand back,' he said, stepping in alongside Harry and leaning on his walking stick. 'Hard though it is. And at least you'll be busy for a day or two; that'll help.'

'Well, talking to you has at least helped me see it's the right thing to do,' Harry replied.

'Oh, it was nothing.'

'You should go into counselling.'

Drake laughed at that.

'Anyway, I'll leave you to it,' he said. 'I'll be in touch if I need to, and I hope that the reunion goes well.'

Harry went to say goodbye when he heard another voice calling him. He stopped, stared, clenched his teeth, and wondered if the world was conspiring to ensure he never actually made it to this blasted reunion that he didn't even want to go to in the first place.

'Mr Grimm ...'

'No,' Harry said, holding a finger up to stop the man right where he was. 'Not now, not today. No. In fact, not ever.'

The man ignored Harry 's finger and continued walking over towards him. He was tall and slim and wore his clothes about as well as a garden cane in a plastic bag.

'Who's this, then?' Drake asked.

'This here is Mr Anderson,' said Harry , noticing then that the journalist looked even rougher than he had on Saturday. Whatever lifestyle he was living, it certainly wasn't healthy, he thought. 'He's our very own local journalist with a knack for popping up at the worst of times.'

Not that Harry could actually think of any time that wasn't made worse by a journalist turning up. He had no time for them. He was fairly sure that out there somewhere were one or two who were okay, did their job well, and were in it for the right reasons, but he'd just never met them.

'Just a few questions, Mr Grimm, that's all,' Anderson said, holding out a card to Drake. 'Contact details,' he said.

Drake laughed.

'Journalists, you're all the same. You know that, don't you?'

'How do you mean?' Anderson said, eyes flickering between Harry and Drake.

'Desperate for a story,' said Drake. 'How desperate, though? That's the question, isn't it?'

'Not sure I understand what you're getting at.'

'Not getting at anything,' Drake said. Then he looked at Harry and added, 'I'll head back inside, see what's what, see how I can help.'

'Probably for the best,' Harry replied, his eyes back on Anderson. 'Wouldn't want to get any blood on you, now, would we?'

Harry had his hand on the Rav4's door handle and watched as Drake headed back to the community centre, limping a little on his stiff leg. Once he was out of earshot, Harry turned his attention back to Anderson.

'For your information, it's my day off,' he said. 'And just in case you were wondering, I'm not about to waste any of it on you.'

'I hear there's been a theft,' Anderson said. 'Do you have a comment on that?'

That caught Harry 's attention. He'd been expecting to hear mention of the grisly goings-on up at his house, something about his father's escape from custody, not this, not a theft.

'Do you, now?' he said, opening his door. 'A theft, is it? Well, if you leave a message with my team, perhaps we can arrange a proper chat when I'm back. Or not at all, maybe, which would be my personal preference.'

'You said it was a day off.'

'It is.'

'So, you'll be back tomorrow.'

Harry shook his head.

'I'm afraid not. You see, that's my day off as well.'

'But—'

Harry sat down in the driver's seat.

'And the rest of the week, actually. Just throwing caution to the wind, aren't I?'

'The crime scene, though,' Anderson said. 'Are you able to give me any details as to what occurred? People are asking questions. Don't you think they deserve answers?'

'All in good time,' Harry said. 'That time not being now.'

'What about those fireworks, then?'

Harry frowned.

'And what fireworks would those be?' he asked.

'The stolen ones.'

'Not that I am able to comment at this moment in time, but how would you know about such a thing in the first place?'

'I'm a journalist,' Anderson said, a little too proudly, Harry thought. 'I have my sources.'

'Don't suppose you'd care to share them?'

'They're confidential.'

'And so is any information relating to any current, or indeed any, case that we may or may not be investigating,' Harry said.

Anderson, though, was clearly not about to back down.

'A crime scene in Gayle and a large quantity of explosives goes missing and you're taking the day off?'

'Explosives?' Harry said. 'Fireworks aren't exactly a few kilos of C4, now are they?'

'C4?'

'Semtex,' Harry explained. 'It goes boom.'

'So, it's your belief, then, that the public have no need to know about the possibility of this deadly material being—'

'Deadly material?' Harry laughed.

'What do you think people will have to say about you not taking this danger to the public seriously?'

Before Harry could stop himself, he was back out of the car and eyeballing Anderson.

'If you're implying that I'm neglecting my duty, then I suggest you retract that statement,' he said. 'And quickly.'

'I'm just saying what I see,' Anderson said. 'And I'm fairly sure people will be very concerned that such a large quantity of explosives has gone missing and that their DCI is taking a holiday.'

'It is not a holiday and a few rockets and a roman candle or two is hardly a large quantity of explosives, is it?' Harry said, raising his voice just enough to make a woman walking past stare.

Anderson grinned.

'So, you confirm, then, that they have been stolen. That's correct, yes?'

Harry breathed through his nose to calm himself down, the sound that of a bull about to attack.

'The team,' he said, 'is more than capable of getting on with things in my absence. Plus, we will have another detective who has been brought in to support them while I'm away.'

'That's a little strange, isn't it? Why would another detective be called in for a simple theft?'

Harry wanted to strangle Anderson.

'He hasn't been called in for a theft.'

'So, there's something bigger going on, is there? Can you tell me what?'

Harry opened his mouth but closed it again before something he would immediately regret fell out of it. Though I probably wouldn't regret it that much, he thought.

He climbed back into the Rav.

'Mind I don't catch you in the door.'

He slammed the door.

Anderson knocked against the window.

Harry ignored him, reversed out of his parking space, then headed off on his long journey to Aldershot. In his rearview mirror, he saw Anderson turn to head to the community centre. He quickly put a call through to the office and Matt answered.

'It's Grimm,' he said. 'That weasel Anderson is nosing around again. He just ambushed me at my car, and now he's heading your way.'

'What the hell does he want? He can't have got wind of what happened at your place, surely? Not yet.'

'Thankfully no, he hasn't,' said Harry . 'But those missing fireworks you mentioned? He's poking his nose into that for some reason.'

'Doesn't strike me as something the press would be fussed about. Must be desperate for a story.'

'That's exactly what Drake said. And I reckon, given the chance, he could easily turn a few boxes of missing fireworks into a terrorist plot or something equally idiotic.'

'Thanks for the heads-up,' Matt said. 'Oh, look, there he is now. This should be fun ...'

Harry hung up and didn't look back. His mind was racing, bouncing between his original conclusion that whoever had killed his father was most likely an old criminal associate, and the notion that there was a slim chance that this was all somehow connected to his own past. And with Drake turning up and suggesting that there might be someone out there working their way through the criminal underground with more than a little success, it was enough to not just give him a headache, but put him in a coma for weeks.

Harry forced himself to stop trying to think of it all at once because that wasn't going to get him anywhere other than running around in circles. In front of him, Wensleydale called him on. But then, as the boundary of Hawes came up to greet him, he decided with all that was going on that a different route was needed, if only to give his mind time to adjust. It would add a good half an hour at the very least to his journey, but right now, he just didn't care.

Slowing down, he turned around at the end of Old Gayle Lane and headed back into town. Just past the rope maker's, he turned right, and a couple of minutes later, rolled over the bridge spanning the Ure, the river rushing underneath. The road followed the river along, and ahead, the fells rose to meet the sky, rich, lush green touching the grey.

Harry pointed the Rav up towards Buttertubs Pass. The road was a favourite, not just of his, but of many in the Dales. As he glided over the top of the moors, then down on into Swaledale on the other side, he found himself wondering if perhaps a few days off was actually a good idea after all. Yes, there was this reunion he was heading to, but the rest of the week was now open to him. He could explore a bit, he thought, head off further afield in the Dales, just tramp around the place, not as DCI Grimm, but instead, as just plain old Harry .

Driving on, the tops of the fells calling him, the darkness of the last few days faded a little, and Harry couldn't help but smile. Because, no matter how bad things were, or could get, he was here, now, wasn't he? And the Dales, he knew deep down, were becoming more and more like home.

CHAPTER TWENTY-SEVEN

Back in Hawes and outside the community centre, Matt stood and stared as Anderson approached, confidence in every step, his jacket creased, his shoes wet and muddy.

'How do,' he said.

Anderson was whistling nervously, Matt noticed, the sound immediately becoming one of the most irritating things he had ever heard. The notes seemed to want to have nothing to do with each other, unable to agree on any kind of tune at all. They bounced around in the air with violent abandon. It was, in every way, an unpleasant sound that set his teeth on edge.

Anderson came up to Matt, stopped whistling, and smiled, his mouth thin, making Matt feel as though he was now under the glare of a lizard who hadn't eaten in too long. His teeth were the faint yellow of a pub ceiling, back when smoking had been allowed in public spaces. And his breath suggested he probably chain-smoked his way through most days.

'Officer—?'

'Dinsdale,' Matt said. 'Detective Sergeant, as it happens.'

'Yes, of course,' Anderson said, writing something down in a little notebook. 'I wonder if you would be able to spare me just a minute or two? I have a few questions about something.'

Anderson was attempting to be charming, Matt thought, but it wasn't very convincing. The man reminded Matt of the worst kind of door-to-door salesman, all smarm and charm, desperate to sound as though they were only there to help, whereas the opposite was more often than not the case.

'Then fire away,' answered Matt, clapping his hands together enthusiastically. 'I'm all ears, like.'

'Really?'

Matt enjoyed how surprised Anderson looked. This was going to be fun.

'Oh, absolutely,' he said. 'Why, we may even be able to help each other. How about that for an idea? So, what's this about, then?'

Anderson looked at a notebook clasped in one of his skeletal hands, the skin stretched across the bone like paper on a kite. Then he yawned, his mouth stretching open as though he would at any moment try and swallow Matt's head.

'Keeping you up, are we?' Matt said.

Anderson ignored Matt. 'I understand we have two crime scenes. One, I still have no information on, the other is to do with a theft of fireworks.'

'And you're here because you have information about it, I assume, is that right? Because that would be very helpful.'

'So, you're confirming it, then?'

'We have a number of ongoing investigations,' Matt said. 'As I'm sure you understand. This is one of them. Busy, busy, busy, that's us.'

'But about the fireworks specifically, I mean. I understand they were stored in a local barn? Is that correct? And if so, do you know how they were removed?'

'Seems to me that you understand quite a lot,' said Matt. 'Not sure why you need to be talking to me at all, if that's the case. Unless, of course, you know something we don't. In which case, it would be my professional advice to share it.'

'Do you have any leads?' Anderson asked. 'I'm sure I don't

need to remind you that fireworks are dangerous. Personally, I'm all for banning them. And is there a connection between the two events? Your DCI Grimm didn't deny that there wasn't.'

'My guess is that DCI Grimm said nothing about anything,' said Matt. 'As for fireworks, a lot of people feel like that about them, which is understandable. They are, as you just said, very dangerous indeed. Not the kind of thing anyone should be playing with if you ask me.'

Anderson was busy jotting down notes in his notebook. About what exactly, Matt really didn't know. It wasn't like he was telling him anything.

Anderson asked, 'Do you think it's a local job or could someone out of town have taken them?'

'Yes,' said Matt. 'Exactly.'

'Yes, what?'

'Could be local, could be someone out of town. Hard to say until we find them, really, but definitely one of those two.' Matt leaned in, narrowing his eyes at Anderson. 'Anyway, how is it that you know about this in the first place?'

'I'm a journalist,' Anderson said, bristling a little. 'It's my job to know.'

'So, you do have some information yourself then, yes?'

'Pardon?'

'You said it's your job to know and that you're here about the fireworks. If you do have some information that you think might be useful, I'd be very grateful to hear it.'

Anderson coughed into his hand, clearly trying to gather his thoughts.

'You know the worst of it?' Matt said. 'The fact that the children won't get to see all those lovely fireworks on Bonfire Night. Wouldn't you agree?'

'I would.'

'Which is why we're raising money to buy some more. I doubt we'll be able to provide much, but it's worth a try, isn't it?'

'Admirable,' said Anderson.

Matt closed the distance between himself and the reporter with a single, swift step.

'So, if there is anything you can give to help, it would be hugely appreciated.'

Matt watched Anderson's face drop.

'Pardon?'

'I assume you'd like to donate,' Matt continued. 'To help us buy fireworks for the kids. You're obviously concerned about the theft and I'm sure that you would like to set an example for everyone else and help out.

'Well, to be honest, I don't generally donate.'

'It's good for you though,' said Matt. 'Trust me. You'll feel so much better about yourself if you do. And while you're thinking of how much to give, you can also think about telling me how you found out about the missing fireworks in the first place.'

That caught his attention, thought Matt.

'And give away my source?'

Matt waited.

'No, I can't do that. I'd be breaking my word. That's not how things are done.'

'You'd be withholding information is what you'd be doing. And that's something the police don't look too kindly on, I'm afraid. But then, you know that, don't you?'

Anderson then asked, 'What if a group of local teenagers took those fireworks and decided to go around terrorising people with them? Have you thought about that?'

'This time of year, there's always an idiot or two who thinks it's funny to mess around with fireworks. Fewer than there used to be, thankfully.'

'What about the victim in this, though?' Anderson said.

'Victim?' Matt said. 'What victim are we talking about here?'

Anderson gave a shrug.

'I'm just saying that it would be terrifying to have someone use fireworks to scare you or something. And we need to be aware of that, don't we? And can you tell me if there is a connection between this theft and the other crime scene?'

Matt stared a little harder at the journalist, chewing on the words the man had just said.

'You're right, it would be pretty scary, wouldn't it? Particularly if the victim was in their eighties and living on their own. There they are, trying to sleep, when BOOM!'

Matt's roar made Anderson jump.

'What the hell was that for?'

Matt didn't answer and instead said, 'Now, is there anything else, or are we done?'

Anderson handed over a business card.

'This has my contact details on it,' he said. 'I would really appreciate it if you were able to keep me up to date on this.'

'Really?' Matt said, staring at the card. 'It's just fireworks. It's hardly the crime of the century, is it?'

'I'm sure the public will see things a little differently,' Anderson replied.

'Of course you are.' Matt turned back towards the community centre. 'Well, I'd best be off. This has been a surprisingly useful conversation, to be honest with you, so thanks for that.'

Matt saw worry write itself a little too clearly across Anderson's face.

'Has it?'

'Oh yes, very much so,' Matt replied. Then, before he headed back into the community centre, he turned back and held out a hand.

Anderson stared at it, clearly confused.

'I'm sorry, I'm not sure I—'

'Your donation,' Matt said. 'Towards the fireworks. To replace the ones that have been stolen. Remember?'

'Ah, yes, that,' Anderson said. 'No cash, I'm afraid. Never carry it. I won't keep you, though.'

And with that, he turned on his heel and headed back up the lane, then turned right into town.

Matt headed back into the community centre and on into the office to find Jim on his way out.

'Where you off to, then?'

'Had a call in from Hardraw. Something to do with a couple skinny-dipping in the pool at the bottom of the Force. Apparently another visitor didn't take too kindly to seeing them bobbing about in the buff as it were. They're all waiting for someone to go over and have a chat.'

Matt shuddered.

'I threw myself in there once, when I was a lot younger. Freezing.'

Jim's eyes widened.

'You skinny-dipped at Hardraw Force?'

'Good God, no, I'm not a complete idiot. Harry did that a while back, though, didn't he? Though I'm fairly sure the only reason he did it was because Grace was there in her swimsuit.' Matt rubbed his chin thoughtfully. 'You said these skinny dippers are waiting for you, right? So, they're not going anywhere?'

'They've popped into the Green Dragon for a pint and some food I think,' said Jim. 'Why do you ask?'

Matt leaned in close.

'How do you fancy doing little bit of surveillance before you head on over?'

'Sounds fun. Who?'

'Anderson.'

'The journalist?'

Matt took Jim outside and to the end of the lane, to look out on the marketplace.

'Where is he?' Jim asked.

Matt scanned the crowd, spotting the gangly form of Anderson just about to walk past the market hall.

'There,' he said, jabbing a finger over the heads of the crowds.

Jim headed off, but Matt called after him.

'And if you lose sight of him, just follow that god-awful whistle of his.'

With Jim gone, Matt headed back inside the community centre. There was a murder investigation to be on with, true enough, plus those missing fireworks. And he'd still not managed to speak with that farmer about some idiot making a mess by wild camping or whatever it was they'd been up to in their field, but first things first: tea.

CHAPTER TWENTY-EIGHT

Following Matt's instructions, Jim had set off at a pace to stay on the heels of Anderson. He didn't know the man well, none of them did, but he had a habit of turning up without warning now and again, seemingly to just get in the way. Jim knew him well enough though to be fairly sure that having him around was never good. Anderson had never really caused any trouble, true, but there was just something about him that set Jim's teeth on edge. And if Anderson was up to something, whatever it was, it was best they knew what it was.

Anderson had headed off through town, walking along the main street and towards the primary school at the top of the hill, lighting a cigarette on the way. Jim had jogged away from Matt to catch up. Before reaching the school, however, Anderson had turned into a small car park, just before the chippy. From there, he had then followed a short footpath tucked around behind the school which led to another car park.

Jim had done a good job of tracking the man, while also either staying out of sight or looking otherwise engaged, which wasn't exactly easy to do in a place where everyone knew who you were and folk liked to have a chat.

In the second car park, Jim wondered if Anderson was about to jump in a car and scoot off somewhere, but instead, he slipped between the cars, to then head on up to Gayle.

Following, Jim thought that if it had been him, he would have taken the little flagstone path, which threaded its way out behind the church and up through the fields, silently tethering Hawes and Gayle together, as it had done for centuries. That way was considerably prettier, though the fences lining the sides of the path had certainly put a few noses out of joint.

Jim noticed then a thin whine of a sound and remembered what Matt had said about the man's whistling; it wasn't good and reminded him of the sound a balloon makes when the air screeches out of it. Not that he had needed it to follow him, thanks to the smell of cigarette smoke trailing behind him.

On past the creamery, Anderson paused for a moment at the footpath heading back to Hawes, looking at the small barn where the fireworks had been stored, the place now shut behind some cordon tape. Then he was off again and soon they were drawing close to Harry 's new house, which was still skulking just down from the bridge over the beck, and behind the cordon tape they'd put out at the weekend. Jim couldn't help but feel for Harry , but he knew the DCI would soon push past it and get on with things. Though he had no doubt that being taken off the case was driving his boss a little crazy.

Anderson stopped walking, looked up from his phone, then crossed over the road. He stopped by the bridge and crouched down, checking the wall for something, then carried on towards Harry 's.

Jim stayed back, quietly observing.

With his phone out in front of him, Anderson snapped a few photos of Harry 's house and the tape.

Did he know the house was Harry 's? Or was he just being a nosy git? Jim suspected both.

Anderson ducked under the tape and slunk across to the house. He leaned in, looking through the windows, then tried the front door.

Jim was about to head over and ask just what the hell he was doing when Anderson took off again, walking down a narrow lane. Jim followed, but as he did so, he stopped where Anderson had checked the wall. He saw marks in the stone, scratches that looked like a car had scraped its bumper against it, something that happened all too often on the narrow lanes and bridges in the Dales.

Still, he took a couple of photos, then chased after the journalist. If Anderson had a car, then the lanes in this part of Gayle weren't exactly the best of places to park up, not unless he had deliberately set out to really annoy the locals and block the way. Not that Jim would put it past him. Of course, he could also be parked up on the other side of Gayle Beck, over the ford. It was a slightly more direct route, going this way, Jim thought, but not by much, especially if you were on foot. Anyway, no one would be foolish enough to try and walk across it; that was just suicidal.

Jim stayed on Anderson's heels, sure that there was no way the man would be daft enough to try and navigate his way across the ford. Except, he was, and Jim found himself pulling out his phone to get whatever was about to happen on video.

Hanging back just far enough to stay out of sight, Jim watched as Anderson made his way towards the edge of the beck. He hesitated, staring down at the brown water, which was a little deeper than usual because of the rain, and certainly fast-flowing. Jim knew that if the weather turned bad again, the ford would easily be impassable, not just on foot, but by vehicle as well. The thing was, though, even when there was barely a trickle running through, the ford was always impassable by foot, something the locals just took for granted.

Anderson took a step forward into the water. Jim noticed that he was wearing sturdy boots, so that was something, at least. Not that it would help him. Nothing would, other than turning back, and it was obvious that he wasn't about to do that, not yet anyway.

Another step, and another. The going was certainly slow, but so far, so good, and Jim was impressed; luck was on Anderson's side so far.

Still, though, Jim kept recording; he knew what was to come. It was only a matter of time.

Anderson took another step, and this time wasn't so surefooted. He stretched out his arms to maintain his balance.

Just a few steps more, Jim thought.

Anderson was now not so much walking as shuffling. He was about a quarter of the way across; the water was deeper, and it was building into tiny eddies around his ankles.

Anderson roared as water splashed up over his boots. That's about to be the least of his troubles, thought Jim, smiling to himself.

Another step, and another.

He was doing well, Jim thought. Better than most managed, anyway.

Anderson's yell cracked the moment like a brick through a window. In one smooth motion, almost as though he had been practising it to perfect it, Anderson's shuffle turned into a fall, both feet swooping up in front of him, legs in the air, and he crashed down into the beck on his backside.

The beck, though, had only just started to have its fun.

Quickly trying to regain his feet, Anderson turned over onto all fours and tried to push himself back up. He managed to climb back onto his feet, only to have them kicked away by the water once again. This time, he landed on his side, then the water took him, pushing him along like a boulder caught in a flood.

'Now then, Jim. What's going on here, then?'

The voice was that of Alan Hogg, the father of one of Jim's old school friends, Neil.

'Nowt much,' Jim said, trying to think only of Neil as his best friend of old, rather than a young man who had been murdered. Alan must have seen what was going on and come over to watch as well, he thought.

'Doesn't look like nothing to me. In a bit of a pickle, isn't he?'

Jim laughed.

'You could say that.'

'He's done well to get that far, though.'

'Further than I expected, actually.'

Alan gave Jim a lock of amused shock.

'Now then, you've not been here just watching him, have you?'

'He was making his way across when I arrived,' Jim said. 'There's no way he'd hear me above the water, anyway.'

'Shouldn't you be helping him get out of there?'

Alan had a point, but not much of one.

'Nothing I can do,' said Jim.

Anderson was now on all fours and slowly crawling his way through the water. His language was painting the air with colours lurid and violent.

'We could call someone,' Alan suggested, somewhat insincerely, Jim thought.

'No, he'll be fine,' Jim said. 'It's a lesson learned, isn't it? I'll go and meet him round the other side, make sure he's okay.'

'I'll leave you to it, then,' Alan said and headed off. But as he did so, he turned back and said, 'You doing okay, Jim?'

Jim gave a shrug.

'Not too bad.'

Neil's death was a while ago now. It had hit his parents understandably hard. But they'd coped well with it, and also helped Jim come to terms with the loss.

'You've not been around lately. Helen would love to see you. Any excuse to fill that biscuit tin.'

Jim smiled.

He had visited them fairly regularly after what had happened to Neil, to talk about him over a fresh pot of tea and the amazing home baking of his mum. Work and life had got in the way this past while, though.

'I'll pop in next week,' Jim said. 'How's that sound?'

'Grand,' Alan said. 'I've been looking through some old photos and found some crackers of you and our Neil at primary school.

And some from Halloween, the two of you out trick-or-treating. We'll get those out when you come over.'

'I'll give you a call.'

'No need,' said Alan. 'We're always in.'

With a final farewell, Alan headed off.

With Alan gone, Jim watched Anderson for a couple more minutes, then turned and headed back the way he had come, taking a right up the main road, over the bridge, then round to where Anderson was making his painfully slow and no doubt very cold progress.

When Jim arrived at the other side of the ford, Anderson had somehow managed to scramble out of the water.

Jim waved.

'Now then,' he said, walking over. 'Anything I can do to help?'

Anderson was soaked and muddy, and Jim could only imagine how cold he was.

'What the hell do you want?'

'I saw that you were having a bit of trouble there,' Jim said. 'Thought I'd see if you needed a hand.'

'A bit bloody late, aren't you?' Anderson snapped. 'Look at me! I'm soaked, I'm filthy, and I'm freezing!'

'What happened?' Jim asked, working hard to maintain an air of ignorance about the events of the past few minutes.

Anderson's face, Jim noticed, was growing redder by the second. At least the beck had stopped his whistling.

'What the hell do you think happened? I walked across the ford, that's what bloody well happened. And I've a good mind to sue the town council for this. That thing is lethal. It's a danger to the public.'

Jim stared at Anderson, then at the ford across the beck, then back at Anderson.

'You didn't try and cross it on foot, did you?'

'No, I floated across on this invisible canoe I've got with me right here, but unfortunately, I capsized halfway across and had to swim the rest of the way.'

'Really?' Jim said. 'That's unfortunate.'

Anderson was now shaking, not just with the cold either, but with barely contained rage.

'What? Unfortunate? Of course I walked across. How the hell else do you think I got here?'

'Why didn't you go round? It's much safer.'

'Because my phone told me this was quicker, that's why.'

'Can't have done.'

Anderson paused, pursed his lips.

'Well, the signal froze, and it looked quicker, so that's the way I went. But what does it matter? Needs a warning sign if you ask me. Dangerous doesn't even come close to describing it.'

'No one walks across the ford, not even when it's dry,' Jim said. 'It's like glass.'

Anderson stared at Jim for a moment, then turned and squelched off to the car park just on the other side of where they were standing, making his way over to a nondescript black estate car.

Jim walked along behind him.

'You don't need to follow me,' Anderson said, quickening his pace and lighting a cigarette. 'I'm absolutely fine, I promise you.'

At the car, Jim asked, 'Been driving across the fields, have you?'

'What?'

Jim pointed at the car. It was covered in mud, great splats of it splashed down the side, the wheels thick with the stuff.

'This is the Dales and it's coming up to winter,' Anderson said, walking round to the rear of the car. 'Everyone's car looks like that.' He then pulled off his jacket and opened the boot, only to slam it shut again almost immediately.

Jim asked if there was a problem, surprised by Anderson's behaviour.

'No, no problem at all,' Anderson replied, opening the rear passenger door to throw in his jacket. 'Forgot it was full, that's all.'

He opened the driver's door and dropped into the seat, then started the engine.

Jim walked over and rapped a knuckle on the window.

Anderson dropped the window into the door.

'What?'

'The mud—,' Jim said.

'What about it?' Anderson said, cutting Jim off.

'I was just going to say that you want to watch yourself driving with that much of it on your wheels, that's all,' Jim said. 'It'll be worse than walking across the beck.'

'Thanks for the advice,' said Anderson. 'No, really, thank you, so very, very much.'

He slammed the door.

Jim watched as Anderson reversed out of where he was parked and then drove off.

Well, that was entertaining, he thought, not really sure what he'd managed to gather from following the man, other than a fun video to show the team.

Jim was about to head back through Gayle when he stopped and turned back to where Anderson had been parked. The mud on the car was easily explained to a degree, but there was no denying that the man had behaved oddly when he'd opened the boot of his car. And he'd not been too happy with being followed either, had he?

Jim crouched down to look at the tyre marks in the dirt. Ever suspicious, he took a few photos of them, then headed back into town. On the way, he stopped at the barn at the end of the footpath to Hawes and took a few more photos. Then he called Matt and explained what he'd been up to.

'Call me suspicious,' he said, 'but I think we need to keep an eye on Anderson.'

'Fair enough,' Matt said.

'He was acting very suspiciously around his car,' Jim explained. 'And he looks rough as hell. I don't know what's going on with him, but something isn't right.'

'He was probably a bit dazed and more than a little cold and grumpy; we need more than acting suspiciously.'

'I know,' Jim said, as a faint memory floated through his mind, something he'd heard, or something someone else had heard or seen, he wasn't sure, but the more he tried to grab onto the thought, the fainter it became. Then it was gone, and he had nothing.

'I'll have a think,' he said, and wandered back into town.

CHAPTER TWENTY-NINE

HARRY CHECKED HIS WATCH AND WAS PLEASED TO SEE THAT despite his rather unnecessary and out-of-the-way detour, he would still most likely arrive at his hotel in time for a nap and a shower before heading off to the reunion. Of course, there was always the off chance that he wouldn't make it in time and would miss the party. But spending a night on his own in a bland hotel didn't exactly excite him, so he kept his foot down and sped on. Not that the old Rav4 sped anywhere exactly, but it certainly had a good old go.

The journey was uneventful, the traffic flowing fine, even the weather staying dry, and Harry stopped halfway at a motorway service area for a coffee and a stretch. He was managing to keep his mind off everything that was going on back in Hawes, but it wasn't easy. It wasn't really that his father was dead or how the man had died that was bothering him, more that there was some connection there to him, perhaps even his past, and he had no idea what it was.

But his team was on it, and he was at least busy. Plus, by happy chance, he was also going to be able to check up on his old army mates. The similarity between what had been done to his father's face and his own scars bothered him.

It could be a coincidence, but when was that ever the case? he thought. Though why someone would try and connect his past to his father's murder, he had no idea. It just made no sense, which was why he'd kept any such thoughts along those lines to himself.

He checked his phone.

Just heard from Grace. Housewarming a great idea. Will make sure I'm home for it. Dave

Well, that was that, then, Harry thought, Grace had already sent word out to Dave Calvert. And if Dave knew, then the team knew, and that meant, at the very least, an overly excited Matt.

A walk around the service area had Harry dodging litter and trying not to walk into people strolling around staring at their phones.

Back in the Rav4, he started the engine, switched on the satnav once again, and turned on the radio. He'd not heard anything from the team yet and he was telling himself that was fine and nothing to worry about, that they were busy, that no news was good news. Trouble was, he wasn't listening to himself and was fighting the urge to punch in a call to Gordy.

What I really need, Harry thought, is a radio station with no news bulletins. Because the last thing he needed was to be reminded every fifteen minutes about how bad things were in the world. If it wasn't the icecaps melting or war erupting, it was criminals running around doing what they do best, ruining people's lives and causing misery.

So, in the middle of a brief report on something awful happening somewhere he'd never heard of, Harry turned the knob on the Rav4's old radio. After a few minutes, and getting increasingly frustrated with what he was listening to, he finally gave up and switched the damned thing off, deciding that driving in silence was the best option by far. He then reached over to put his phone in the glove compartment, but it buzzed in his hand, another message making itself known. He was tempted to ignore it, but curiosity got the better of him and he pulled off the motorway.

There were two messages, not one.

Hope journey is okay. We're both looking forward to seeing you. It's been too long! Amy and Ant x

Harry tried to remember what Amy looked like, but gave up. Her husband, Anthony, though, he would remember for the rest of his life, which was perhaps one of the reasons he was none too keen to set off on the second half of the journey. As far as Harry was concerned, some memories were best left undisturbed, no matter what any of the therapists and counsellors had told him.

The second message was much shorter and read:

See you later, Shithead. Ed

Harry laughed at that, then locked his phone away before finally making his way back onto the road. Which was when the skies darkened, and the rain fell.

When he arrived at his hotel, his nerves stretched thin from driving through the rain on busy roads, Harry sent a text to Grace to let her know he'd arrived and to wish her luck for Mischief Night, though neither of them expected much to happen out in Carperby. He then asked the receptionist to book him a taxi for later and headed straight to his room. He was almost tempted to try out all of the various pillows the hotel had provided, to really see if there was any difference at all between them, but in the end he was just too tired, so he passed out for half an hour on the one already placed on the bed. It was good enough.

Nap done, and now showered and wearing what felt like was his Sunday best, Harry left the hotel and climbed into the rear of a nondescript silver saloon car parked outside.

'Let me guess,' said the driver, a man who had managed to fill the car with a nauseating mix of air freshener and deodorant, 'ex-Para, right?'

'Right,' Harry said, keeping his answer short, hoping for a quiet journey.

'Thought so. It's obvious.'

'It is?'

'Usually it's a reunion, or a visit to the cemetery, that kind of thing,' the driver said. 'When were you in?'

'Long enough ago to forget most of it,' Harry lied, because he could remember all of it, and some of it in far too much detail. Those particular memories he'd dealt with as best as he could, by locking them away, leaving them behind, or both.

The driver rambled on for a while, taking Harry on a guided tour of people he didn't know or have any interest in, but who had also served in the military. Harry offered the occasional murmur or nod, to give the impression he was listening. Then, when the journey was over, he left the driver a tip.

'Word of advice,' he said. 'Learn to read your audience.' Then he climbed out of the car and walked off without looking back.

As the taxi pulled away, Harry turned his attention to the house in front of him. It was a semi-detached with a front garden laid to paving, a black SUV parked up in front of it with spots of rust visible bubbling up through the paintwork. There were a few scratches here and there, mainly to the bumpers; Obviously, the vehicle was not all that easy for the driver to park.

Harry walked over to the house and reached out to give the front door a sharp knock. It opened with the creak of hinges begging for a little oil.

A woman somewhat smaller than Harry was standing in the doorway. She stared up at him with wide eyes set beneath a dark ponytail flecked with grey. She looked both tired and also strangely alert, as though she spent a lot of time keeping herself awake with copious amounts of caffeine. She was wearing a weary smile and, unless it was a trick of the light from the lampposts in the street behind him, she was smaller than Harry remembered.

The smart, black dress she was wearing for the night ahead hung a little too loosely on her, Harry thought, as though she'd bought the size out of habit, unaware of the fact she'd shrunk a little. The open door she was standing in only added to the impression that in the years which had passed since they'd last met, few, if any, had been easy. Her arms were covered in long black gloves, which sparkled a little. If he was going to describe them at all, Harry would have said that they were chic, but he wasn't, not least because he hadn't the faintest idea what that word actually meant.

'Hello, Harry ,' Amy said.

Harry attempted a smile.

'Hello, Amy,' he replied.

CHAPTER THIRTY

Everyone was on duty, but that didn't make Jadyn feel any better about it. He had little experience with Mischief Night, but judging by what he'd heard, it had the potential to be about as much fun as ramming pins in his eyes. Still, it meant that he'd had a good excuse to not be sitting down to another evening meal with his well-meaning parents, listening to them suggest numerous careers he could choose other than the police.

The evening was a cold one, the wind blowing through Hawes laced with just enough ice to suggest that the morning could bring with it a frost. His breath clouded in front of him, ghostly plumes fading in fear of what the night held. So far, though, that fear seemed unwarranted.

Hawes was quiet, the streets, lanes and alleyways empty of all but shadow. Isioma was out again, apparently having made friends already, just as he'd expected. The rest of the team was doing their best to keep an eye on things across the Dales, an impossible task really; there were too few of them to cover such a vast area, but he hoped the cold of the night would play to their advantage and keep anyone with a thought of mischief behind closed doors and in front of a fire.

Gordy was patrolling Leyburn, and Jen the various other

villages up the dale, including Middleham, Carperby, and Redmire. So far they had reported in with only a handful of incidents, most of which involved kids out past their bedtime knocking on doors and running away.

Matt was making his presence known further on, rolling around Aysgarth, Askrigg, and Bainbridge. He'd had a bit of a fright thanks to what at first he'd thought was someone playing silly buggers in the stocks on Bainbridge green. He'd headed over to see what was what, expecting someone more than a little drunk, only to find a dummy without its head, the neck covered in a good amount of fake blood. The photos he'd sent through had made Jadyn laugh, particularly the one of Matt with his head where the dummy's should have been.

Liz was out and about on her motorbike, taking in the smaller villages and hamlets where she could, and Jim, like Jadyn himself, was walking around Hawes and Gayle. With the events of the past few days, it had been decided that it made sense to have both of them visible. He wasn't sure how much of a deterrent they were, but as there had been no incidents so far, he allowed himself to think it was down to them as much as it was the chill in the air.

Strolling through the marketplace, Jadyn remembered that there was that DCI Drake as well. He wasn't a permanent member of the team, so had nothing to do with the night's activities. Instead, he was enjoying an evening staying in a local bed and breakfast.

He seems like a decent bloke, Jadyn thought as he walked past the Fountain Inn, easy to talk to, and clearly as keen as any of them to find out who was responsible for what had happened up at Harry 's new place.

Through the windows of the pub, Jadyn saw that the bar was busy, people enjoying a few pints and a game of darts. He didn't see Isioma in there, but there were plenty of other pubs around for her to be enjoying, and he doubted he'd see her until the following day.

Walking on, a call came in on his radio from Jim.

'How's things in town?'

'A riot of absolutely nothing happening,' Jadyn said. 'You?'

'Gayle's about the same,' Jim replied. 'Someone egged a door, then tried to egg me when I chased after them.'

'Did you catch them?'

'No. But I know who it was, and I'm off round there now.'

Jadyn laughed.

'I hope you're ready with your *I'm not angry, I'm very disappointed* face.'

'I've been practising it all day. Where you heading to now?'

Jadyn was about to say he'd be making his way along the cobbles, past Cockett's, when a bright light burst in the street followed by a boom which he felt right down to his feet.

'What the hell was that?'

Jadyn didn't answer right away, his ears still ringing. Then came another flash, only this one zipped past him at speed to explode a second or two later up by the Penny Garth café.

'Jadyn? You alright?'

'I'm fine,' Jadyn said, his heart thumping out a rapid tattoo. 'Fireworks.'

'Right,' said Jim, 'I'm on my way.'

'No, you've that egg thing to follow up.'

'Fireworks trump eggs,' replied Jim. 'I'll be there in five.'

With Jim now on the way, Jadyn shook his head in some attempt to stop his ears from ringing. He looked up and down the marketplace, but saw nothing. The place was deadly quiet, the only sound that of the wind whispering to itself as it ducked and dived between the hostelry and home.

A movement caught Jadyn's eye. At the end of the marketplace, where the tarmac road gave way to cobbles, he saw a shadow dash down an alleyway. He gave a shout and made to run, only to be faced once again by another flash, this one heading straight for him.

Instinct took over and Jadyn ducked, dropping to the ground as a rocket sped over his head, before suddenly skipping upwards to explode high above. The blast lit the marketplace with a rainbow of glittering colour.

A shout in the dark had Jadyn on his feet. He saw a group exiting the Fountain Inn, one of whom broke away and headed over towards him.

'You alright down there, lad?'

Jadyn looked up into the burly face of a man in a chequered shirt and jeans, his head home to a small number of tenacious grey hairs still clinging to life.

Jadyn was about to answer when another figure joined them.

'That looked close,' said Jim, helping Jadyn to his feet with a strong heave.

'It was,' Jadyn replied, brushing himself down.

The man in the chequered shirt pointed over to where Jadyn had seen the movement in the shadows.

'Came from over there,' he said. 'Saw it from where I was sitting in the window.'

'I've just come from over there,' said Jim. 'It was the quickest way over from Gayle. I didn't see anyone, so they must've ducked out of sight just in time.'

The man swore under his breath.

'Mischief Night,' he said. 'You'd think people would have better things to do with their time, wouldn't you?'

With that, he turned and headed back into the bar, along with the others who'd come out to see what all the fuss was about.

Jadyn stood facing Jim.

'Is it always like this?'

'It can be,' Jim replied.

Jadyn asked, 'Are you thinking what I'm thinking?'

'And what's that?'

'The fireworks; what if they're the ones that went missing?'

'If they are, then there's more where that came from, isn't there?'

Jadyn gave a nod.

'Come on, then,' he said, pointing over to where the rocket had been fired from. 'That's the way they went.'

'They'll be long gone by now, though,' Jim said.

'Or hiding,' said Jadyn. 'Which is where these come in useful.'

He pulled out his torch and flicked it on. Jim did the same, and they both headed over to the other side of the road.

Standing in the alleyway, Jadyn was struck then by just how thick darkness could get. It was almost as though he had to physically push through it as they edged forward, their torches barely able to make a dent.

He noticed a faint scent in the air, something he recognised, but wasn't really sure why. The smell was hard to place, hidden as it was behind the nostalgic aroma of fireworks freshly lit.

'See anything?' Jim asked.

'Not a thing,' said Jadyn.

'There's the graveyard just ahead. After that, it's the path over the fields to Gayle.'

'Maybe whoever it is, is hiding there,' Jadyn suggested.

The path ahead was narrow, the flagstones slick beneath their feet. To their left rose the black edifice of the church, rising into the oozing gloom above. Then just ahead, Jadyn saw the graveyard. It was small, and overgrown, and the night seemed to twist itself in and around the ancient gravestones.

Jim stopped dead.

'What is it?' Jadyn asked.

Jim pointed ahead.

'Movement,' he said.

Jadyn strained his eyes to try and pierce the darkness, again noticing that familiar smell.

'You think it's them?'

'Could be,' Jim said, his voice a barely hushed whisper. 'Could also be a cat or a badger, even a deer.'

Jadyn spotted a flicker of light in the far corner of the graveyard.

'There,' he said.

'I see it,' said Jim. Striding forward into the graveyard itself, he shone his torch on where the light had come from. 'Come on,' he said. 'Out. Whoever you are, we know you're there.'

Laughter.

'We've got the only entrance into this place covered,' Jadyn said, joining in with Jim. 'So best you give yourselves up now before someone gets hurt with those fireworks you're playing with.'

Then the graveyard exploded, or at least that was how it seemed. The small light Jadyn had spotted earlier blossomed into such a raging blast of colour and flame that he threw himself behind the nearest gravestone. He saw Jim do the same as the sky erupted and around them dozens of whizzing, whirring, whooshing beads of light filled the air, exploding around them in a hail of sparks, the concussion of each crack and boom slamming into him and Jim like mines on a battlefield.

When it was finally all over, Jadyn peered around the edge of the gravestone.

'Well, that's one way to cover your escape,' he said.

Jim stood up, casting his torch all around.

'Yeah, they've gone,' he said. 'There's no one here now except us.'

Jadyn joined Jim, and they made their way to the top corner of the graveyard. There they found a large metal box, lid open, its contents still smouldering.

'Glad it wasn't me who lit that lot,' said Jim. 'And it looks like we've found our missing fireworks.'

'I'd be happier if we'd caught whoever nicked them and set them off in the first place,' said Jadyn. 'That rocket nearly took my head off.'

'Yeah, you did look a little surprised by that,' laughed Jim.

The air was rich now with the smell of burning, the pungent note of the propellant and explosive in the fireworks filling the air as wisps of smoke curled upwards still from the metal box.

'Do you smell that?' Jadyn asked.

'Of course I do,' Jim replied. 'Fireworks.'

Jadyn shook his head.

'No, there's something else behind it. I'm sure there is. I smelled it earlier, back in the alleyway.'

Jim sniffed the air.

'Smells like pear drops,' he said. 'Weird.'

'You don't recognise it from anywhere?'

'Not that I can think of, no,' said Jim.

Jadyn tried to place it but still couldn't.

'So, what do we do with this lot, then?' he asked.

'You're the constable, you tell me,' Jim replied through a smile.

Jadyn reached for his radio and called Matt.

'Yeah, that's them alright,' Matt said. 'They got away, then?'

'They did,' Jadyn said. 'Used the cover of the fireworks to make a break for it.'

'It'll be kids then. They'll be hiding somewhere, out of breath, half terrified, half buzzing with the excitement of it all. And they set the whole lot off?'

'They're lucky they didn't do themselves some damage, looking at it all,' said Jadyn. 'What shall we do with it, the box, I mean?'

Matt was quiet for a moment, then said, 'Clear it up. Don't want to be leaving it all behind, littering the place. That's the least we can do, isn't it?'

Call over, Jadyn looked at the mess of burned-out fireworks at their feet.

'We'll need bin bags,' he said.

'We've some at the office,' Jim said. 'I'll go fetch them.'

With Jim gone, Jadyn had a quick look around the site. He doubted that he'd find anything that would give them a clue as to who the culprits were, but it was worth a look regardless. Just as he was about to give it up as a hopeless cause, something caught his eye in the grass; a pale blue disposable vape pen. That would explain the sweet smell, he thought. He pulled out an evidence bag, picked it up, sealed it, then dropped it in a pocket.

When Jim returned, they quickly cleared everything away, then headed back to the office, the metal box carried between them, filled with the burned-out carcasses of the fireworks.

'Well, that was exciting, wasn't it?' Jim said as they walked across the marketplace.

'That's one word to describe it,' said Jadyn. 'So, what do we do for the rest of the night, then?'

'Hope that there's not another box like this out there somewhere, I think,' said Jim.

Later, when Jadyn headed home, he pulled out the vape pen and stared at it. Jim had described the smell as pear drops. Jadyn knew that he recognised it from somewhere, but when he finally arrived home and headed for bed, he was still none the wiser, and the thought of it kept him awake for longer than it had any right to.

CHAPTER THIRTY-ONE

For a moment, neither Harry nor Amy spoke. Eventually, Harry broke the silence.

'It's been a while.'

'You'd need two pairs of hands to count the years, probably more.'

'True.'

Harry waited to be invited in, stifling a yawn. The final part of the journey had been long, and the nap hadn't quite dealt with his tiredness. The roads had turned busier the further south he'd travelled, with the first sodden breath of winter chasing travellers up and down the A1 with the Harry ing urgency of a mother shooing children into shelter from a storm. Around him, the darkness seemed to close in, and he shoved his hands deeper into his pockets. In one of them, his hand brushed up against the reason he was here in the first place: the invite, which had been light on words but heavy in meaning.

Amy stepped back from the door.

'In you come, then.'

Harry gave a nod and stepped into the house.

'We won't be long, but I'll take your coat, anyway.'

'Thank you,' said Harry , and slipped off the waterproof jacket he had bought in Hawes back in the early days of his time there. The jacket was worn and faded now, but it still did its job, protecting his smarter attire beneath it from the worsening weather. He had no doubt, though, that sooner or later someone on the team would comment on it and tell him it needed to be replaced.

As Amy took the coat, lifting it up to hang on a row of hooks beneath the stairs, something fell out of one of the pockets. She knelt to retrieve it from where it had fallen beside a packed suitcase, then held it up between them, a frown creasing her brow.

'A dog biscuit, Harry ?'

Harry laughed, but the sound seemed lonely in the house, as though the place had heard nothing like it in a long time.

'They're surprisingly nutritious,' he said.

'You have a dog?'

'I do.'

Smudge was probably being spoiled rotten by Grace, Harry thought. He envied them both.

Amy stuffed the biscuit back into Harry 's jacket.

Harry nodded at the suitcase.

'Going away or just returned?'

'My job involves a bit of travel,' she said. 'I'm a private English tutor now. Did my degree, eventually went freelance to give me flexibility with caring for Ant.'

'Fair enough.'

'We've a nurse who helps out when I'm away, and he comes in most weeks as well. Wish he could come in more sometimes; it's not easy.'

'I'm sure,' said Harry .

Amy then turned around to prod him in the arm with a slender finger. 'Just checking,' she said.

'What, exactly?'

'That you're real and not an imposter.'

'Surely this proves I'm not,' Harry said, pointing at his face.

'Amazing things can be done with makeup.'

'I wouldn't know,' Harry said. 'Though I'm going to assume, based on personal experience, that an IED is a little more painful.'

Amy led Harry across a small hallway to pause at a closed door.

'Coffee?'

'Tea, actually,' Harry said.

'Still like a brew, then?'

'Once a soldier, right?'

'Yeah, that's true enough.'

Amy hesitated, caught between pushing through the door in front of them and heading along to the kitchen, which he could see just a couple of steps away from where they now were.

'He's ... he's in there,' Amy said, gesturing to the closed door to Harry 's right. 'With the nurse.'

Harry put out a hand to the door to push on through, but Amy reached out to stop him, her hand tiny, almost childlike, compared with his own, and pulled him along into the kitchen and busied herself by the sink. Above it, a window stared out onto the garden, a patch of green held in by high wooden fencing, a lawn, and little else, not even a tree.

Harry saw empty jars on the draining board.

'Jam,' Amy said. 'The jars, I mean. They're for jam.'

'What? Oh, right, yes. You make a lot, then, do you?'

'An attempt at a hobby. Haven't done very well. Just a few canes out the back, that's all. For raspberries. Have to try these things, though, don't you?'

Harry had never in his life considered making jam.

Amy said, 'He's not who he was. Anthony, I mean.'

'I know.'

Amy shook her head.

'No, Harry , you don't. You can't. No one does. The others haven't seen him yet. That's why I wanted you to come here first, to help me get him to the pub.'

'How are they all, then?' Harry asked.

'Ed's Ed,' Amy said. 'He doesn't change. And Andrew's found God, in case you didn't know, so make of that what you will.'

Harry wasn't as surprised by that as he would have expected. But then, war makes people look for answers in lots of places. And answers were, as often as not, little more than escape routes. But to each their own.

'God? Really? I didn't even know he'd been out looking for him.'

'No atheists in foxholes, right?'

'There are all types in foxholes, Amy,' Harry said, perhaps more gravely than he should have, so he quickly moved on. 'You said Anthony isn't like he was; last I heard, he was doing okay, all things considered.'

'That was twenty years ago, Harry , give or take.'

Twenty years? Harry thought. Had it really been that long?

'Even so ...'

When Amy spoke again, her voice broke on her words, like the smallest of waves on a rocky shore, and Harry saw uncertainty in her eyes.

'It's not just the injuries. The constant pain, it's ... Well, you'll see.' She went to turn away from Harry , but paused, then looked up at him again. 'This whole reunion ... everything, it ... Look, I'm sorry. You should go, leave him here.' She reached out and tried to push him back out into the hall. 'Please ...'

Harry didn't move, his eyes still on Amy. She kept pushing, but he wasn't about to budge. He knew what she'd had to deal with over the years, how the young husband returning home from a war zone so long ago had changed her life in ways she could have never imagined. None of them could.

'Amy ...'

'I mean it, Harry . This was a mistake. It's all a mistake. I'm sorry. Please, just go. It's too late. I can't do this. I can't!'

Harry reached out to gently remove Amy's gloved arm from his own and she winced a little.

'Sorry,' Harry said, pulling his hand away.

'No, it's fine,' Amy said, now rubbing her wrist. 'Caught myself on the corner of a cabinet in the kitchen earlier, that's all.' She lifted her hands and waved them like a jazz singer. 'Luckily, I had these in the wardrobe.'

An awkward silence sat between them for a moment.

'We all lost touch,' Harry said, unable to bear it any longer, the silence worse than any awkward conversation. 'And I should've made the effort, not allowed life to get in the way. The others came, so I'm here, too. The reunion, it'll be fine. It may even help.'

'Yes, but—'

Harry ignored the interruption and kept talking.

'What happened over there, in Afghanistan, it was impossible for any of us to come back unchanged. You know that, Amy, we all do. So, maybe now's the time?'

Amy said nothing, just staring off to the side, focusing on nothing.

'Anyway,' Harry added, 'I didn't just come for him or you or the others. I came for myself as well. I know that's hard to believe, but it's true.'

Amy lifted her face to look up at Harry .

'Really?'

Harry wasn't about to tell her the real reason he was there, but he could tell Amy needed some reassurance.

'It's like you said in the invite.'

'To be honest, I don't remember what I wrote.'

Harry pulled the letter from his pocket, opened it.

'Right here,' he said, and dropped one of his thick fingers onto the page.

Amy leaned in for a closer look and read out the words in front of her.

'"Don't be a dick, Harry , just come."'

'So here I am,' said Harry , holding out his arms as though presenting himself to an audience. 'Not being a dick, as you so clearly and concisely instructed.'

Amy smiled, and Harry saw an echo of warmth in her eyes.

'Don't think I put that in the other invites.'

'Less chance of them being a dick?'

'Maybe. Though with Ed, I'm not so sure. How's it going for you so far?'

'Okay, I think.' Harry looked along towards the door to the lounge. 'Now, about that tea, before we head off?' he said, and didn't give Amy time to answer. Instead, he walked along to the door and pushed on through into the room beyond.

The lounge was cramped rather than small, due in no small part to the bed which occupied a large area directly in front of him. The space between him and it was taken up by an armchair covered in a worn, patchwork quilt. Behind the head of the bed, the curtains were pulled across the window. Harry noticed dust on the folds; the curtains looked as though they had been that way for a long time, rather than only since the night had drawn in earlier that evening.

A simple gas fire sat in the far wall, a sofa to Harry 's left, then another armchair, half of which contained two small piles, one of books, the other of magazines. The air was stale with the woody aroma of hand-rolled cigarettes. An ashtray sat on the mantelpiece above the fire. Leaning against the wall, a prosthetic leg stood alone. He saw a mirror lying on the floor, pushed into a corner, a faint covering of white dust and a store card lying on its surface.

In a corner of the room, Harry spied a pile of old army kit of fatigues, a bergen, even a mess tin. It was as though Amy had put the stuff there to remind Anthony of who he had been, and not just a soldier, either, but a paratrooper, his maroon beret perched on top for all to see.

A large flatscreen television loomed over the room from the far corner and was spilling out the colourful sights and sounds of a darts tournament. That made Harry smile, and not just because of the games he had played with the team in the public bar of the Fountain Inn back in Hawes, either.

On the screen, a dart thwacked into the board, the crowd roared, and a memory long forgotten stirred in Harry 's mind of Ant's love for the game. It, along with his enthusiasm for a particular way of breaching a locked door, had been the source material for the nickname he'd been known by. They'd even had a darts shirt made for him, though Harry guessed that was long gone by now or forgotten in a box somewhere in a dark recess of the loft.

The walls were hung with numerous photographs, many of them showing younger men, fitter and full of life and ready to take on the world. He saw dress uniforms and fatigues, red berets and weaponry. And he saw amongst them all, not only the faces of old friends staring back, some of which he had even buried, but his own as well. He didn't recognise it at first, the untouched skin almost alien.

From the bed, one of the faces turned towards him.

CHAPTER THIRTY-TWO

Anthony Stratton was a shell. If Harry had not seen so much horror in his own life already, then the shock of it would have ripped across his face as fast as the shrapnel had on that day so long ago. The events of the previous weekend fizzed away to nothing in his mind as his past raced up to meet him in all its lurid violence.

Harry knew the injuries Anthony had suffered. He had personally dragged the man from the wreckage of a WMIK Land Rover when they'd been trying to escape an ambush on that awful day. Even so, what lay in front of him now was beyond the worst even his own dark imagination could conjure.

Anthony was skin and bone beneath a clean striped shirt and dark tracksuit bottoms, and Harry found it almost impossible to match the man in front of him to the hulking brute he had known so well in their younger days. Anthony had been someone Harry had drunk with, laughed with, fought alongside.

How could this be the same man, with grey skin and sunken cheeks, the flesh of his face little more than a thin mask over a barely disguised skull, and eyes lost in hollows as deep and dark as a mine? Harry wondered.

Between Harry and the man on the bed was a middle-aged

man wearing a white buttoned top usually seen in hospitals and pulling on a black duffle coat. He picked up a small bag from the floor.

'I'm just going,' he said. 'He's all ready to go, aren't you, Anthony? A quick wash, clean clothes, and ready to take on the world.'

'You're the nurse, then,' Harry said.

'What gave it away?' the man replied with a smile.

'How is he?'

'Up and down. There's only so much anyone can do really. He has to be a part of his own recovery if he's to recover properly. Hopefully, this reunion will spark something in him. It needs to.'

Harry stepped back as the nurse made his way to the lounge door, catching a sense of urgency in those last few words.

'I didn't catch your name,' he said.

The nurse handed Harry a card with his name on it and plenty of letters after.

'It'll do him good to see you and the others,' he said. 'Don't expect too much, though. But just by being here, you're doing him good, I'm sure of it.'

The nurse left the room.

Harry turned his attention to his old comrade-in-arms.

'Now then, Shotgun,' he said, ignoring the vision of horror before him and instead attempting to focus on the man somewhere inside it. He was briefly aware of how easily the northern greeting rolled off his tongue.

Anthony said nothing. Harry held the man's stare.

'Thought I'd pop in for a visit,' Harry continued, pulling something from a trouser pocket. 'It's been a while. I bought you this.' He held out a bottle of Tabasco sauce, which he'd picked up on his journey down. They'd all come to depend on it, a magic splash of the stuff vital to make the boil-in-the-bag meals they'd lived on at least almost edible. 'I'm guessing Amy's cooking hasn't improved much, right? Thought it might come in useful.'

Anthony said nothing.

Harry reached over and placed the bottle of Tabasco on a cupboard pushed up against the wall, managing to find just enough space in between numerous boxes of medication.

Harry sat down in the armchair at Anthony's side. He then leaned over to the books and magazines, trying to work out what to say next, what to talk about. Nothing helped, the books little more than airport thrillers, the magazines little more than celebrity gossip and true crime.

He spotted a small pouch of tobacco and some cigarette papers on the bed. Saying nothing more, he took the tobacco and pulled out one of the cigarette papers. Though he'd never been a smoker himself, it was something that, like a good number of soldiers, he'd found himself taking up while on tour, but had given up as soon as he had returned home. Cigarettes helped to take the mind off the patrols, the firefights, the lack of sleep and the ration packs. And they gave soldiers something else to bond over. A 'bine and a brew', Harry remembered with a smile, as his fingers worked by muscle memory alone and soon enough, the cigarette was rolled.

Harry lifted the cigarette and placed it between Antony's lips.

'Lighter?'

Anthony didn't respond. Harry glanced over at the ashtray, saw a lighter close by. He reached for it, rested the ashtray on the bed, then lit the cigarette.

Anthony sucked on the tobacco with a stuttering, shallow breath, the end of the cigarette glowing a vibrant orange. The scent of it whisked Harry back to days holed up in Forward Operating Bases, nights on stag keeping watch while the others slept, the sounds and the smells and the sights of war never far away and often too close for comfort.

With thick plumes of smoke slowly settling into thin layers floating in the centre of the room, Harry waited for Anthony to reach up with his left hand to take the cigarette from his mouth and tap off the ash.

He had no right hand, no right arm.

He didn't move.

Harry gave it a moment longer, then reached up and did it himself, remembering as he did so of trying to find that missing arm on the battlefield. He'd scrabbled briefly but desperately around in the dirt and the chaos, then given up as the rounds zipped in all around them after they'd rolled into an ambush.

Harry searched for something to say. No words came. Twenty years had been and gone. He wondered why he was there, what good this was supposed to do. But Amy had asked, and he had answered, with a not-so-gentle nudge or two from Grace.

The lounge door opened. Amy walked in carrying a heavy tray and a heavier smile.

Harry rose to his feet and took the tray, noticing it held only two mugs.

'Here, let me,' he said, and placed the tray on a coffee table in front of the sofa.

'Couldn't remember if you take sugar or not,' Amy said.

'I don't.'

'I brought it anyway. And biscuits. Fig rolls, too.' She looked over at her husband. 'You used to love those, didn't you? Remember?'

Harry saw how his old friend stared over at his wife, eyes empty, the only answer given another draw on the cigarette.

'I only let him smoke if someone's in here with him,' Amy said, her words falling out of her, tumbling into one another. Her hands shook as she poured the tea and some of it spilled onto the tray. 'What if I was out and there was a fire? The nurse is only here for a few hours each day. We have friends who pop round to help when I'm away. Which isn't often, but I still have to go, you know? We need money from somewhere, don't we? And it's all down to me, all of it. It's not like he'd be able to do anything about it. The fire, I mean. And then what?'

It was at this comment that Harry found his eyes turning back to Anthony and, for the briefest of moments, glancing at the space where the man's legs should have been, both lost in the blast that had also taken his arm.

A stifled sob brought his attention back to Amy.

Harry sipped his tea, leaned forward, and rested his elbows on his knees to stare at her over the rim of his mug.

He spoke, his voice quiet.

'What's going on, Amy? A reunion is one thing, I understand that. But what is it you're not telling me? And don't even think about saying everything's fine. Detective, remember? I know something's up.'

Amy opened an orange Club biscuit, dipped it in her tea, took a bite, then pointed at her husband with the nibbled end.

'I'd tell you to ask him yourself, but there's no point. Is there, Ant?'

Harry looked over at Anthony, then back at Amy.

'Not sure I understand.'

'He's not spoken in years,' she said. 'Selective mutism. That's what I've been told, anyway. Hard to believe, really. Used to be a time he'd never shut up.'

Harry was sure he hadn't heard right.

'Years? How's that even possible?'

'Trust me, it is.'

'How many?'

'At least ten. Maybe more. Can you imagine living with that?'

'No, not really,' Harry said, unsure if that question was about Anthony, herself, or them both.

'PTSD is hell,' Amy continued.

'I know.'

Amy barked the smallest of laughs, and it rolled across the room like a marble in a metal tin.

'No, Harry , you don't. You can't. None of you can, not like this.'

Harry allowed a moment of silence to sit between them. Not so much because he had nothing to say, but because it was down to Amy to explain further. He could see that things were tough, that Anthony was in a bad way, worse than he had expected, but the reason for him being asked to visit still hadn't been made clear.

Movement caught his eye and Harry turned to see the cigarette fall from Anthony's lips. He lunged, and the stub landed in his palm. He crushed it, the moment of pain from the burning tobacco gone in a second.

'Amy ...' Harry said, gently pushing her to talk.

Amy lifted her eyes to her husband, then turned them on Harry , sweeping round to bear down on him like the beam from a searchlight.

'He ... He's ...'

Whatever she was about to say caught in her throat as Harry 's attention was pulled away by another sound. He turned to see Anthony's shoulders shaking. At first, he thought his old friend was laughing, but he soon realised the opposite was true.

'He's what, Amy?' Harry asked.

'Dying,' Amy said.

CHAPTER THIRTY-THREE

Harry shuddered as the air in the room turned to ice.

'Dying? How? What do you mean? I don't understand.'

And he really didn't. How could he?

'I said that you weren't ready for this, didn't I?' Amy said.

Harry knew as well as anyone that Anthony's injuries had been horrendous, life-changing in the extreme, but the man had survived, fought the battle to survive despite the odds. So how the hell could he be dying? Okay, so they'd all lost touch, but Harry had received enough news in the early days to be sure that things were going as well as could be expected. This just made no sense at all. Between what was going on at home and this shocking news, Harry felt a headache coming on. Rubbing his temples, he was suddenly back in the lounge of his new home, staring at the body of his father. Then the scene shifted, and he was standing with Sowerby, his father's ruined body on the stainless steel slab, those injuries that had been inflicted upon him raw, except that they were bleeding as he stared at them, the wounds fresh, the blood cherry red and slick.

Amy rose to her feet, pulling Harry from his thoughts. She made her way over to the mirror he had seen on the floor, only to stop, as though changing her mind, and turn back to where she'd been sitting to roll herself a cigarette.

'You never used to smoke.'

'There are lots of things I never used to do, Harry . And lots of things that *we* used to do, but don't anymore, if you know what I mean. And no, I don't just mean sex, either, in case that's what you were thinking.'

'I wasn't,' Harry said, noticing the sharp edge to Amy's voice, his eyes flicking over to that mirror again; drugs had never been his thing, but he knew the paraphernalia as well as anyone on the force. He thought back to her eyes when she had opened the door. Perhaps she's not just using caffeine to keep herself awake, he thought.

Amy lit the cigarette, drew deep, but still stood facing away.

'He stopped talking a few years ago. Can't remember exactly when. The nightmares had returned, the flashbacks. He started counselling again, therapy, but then something happened. Don't know what, if I'm honest. He just ... fell silent.'

'That must've been difficult.'

'A little.'

Masterful understatement by us both, Harry thought.

'He gave up on going out. The prosthetics? He just stopped using them, wouldn't even touch them, like they were a reminder of what he'd lost, rather than something that would help him get back out there and live. He just stayed in bed more and more. It's hard to argue with someone who won't respond. Then he started to waste away. I think he just gave up.'

'That doesn't sound like Anthony.'

Amy pointed at her husband.

'That's because that isn't Anthony, not anymore, Harry . Not by a long shot.'

Harry was usually confident in most situations, stress somehow working to sharpen his mind. But right now, he was floundering. Not least because he couldn't see how they were ever going to get

Anthony to the reunion, or why they would even want to. But that wasn't going to stop him from trying.

'You can't mean that,' he said, his eyes on what remained of the man he had stood beside in battle more times than he would ever be able to fully remember.

Amy turned around, sucked on the cigarette, and breathed out a grey cloud.

'He's also starving himself,' she said.

'What?'

'Refusing to eat,' Amy explained. 'He's lost so much weight now I could probably lift him out of that bed all by myself if I wanted to.'

Harry found himself shaking his head in an attempt to dislodge what Amy had just told him.

'You mean he's dying on purpose? Because he wants to?'

Amy nodded.

'I've tried, you know, but I can't exactly force him to eat, can I?'

'Yes, you bloody well can!' Harry said, unable to disguise the faint tone of anger at the situation. But it wasn't aimed at Amy, more at Anthony, for giving up. 'What about the nurse? He can help. That's what he's for.'

'There's only so much he can do.'

'What about your doctor? Can't you get him seen? Surely you can have Ant admitted to hospital, maybe get a feeding tube?'

'He'd be sectioned, Harry ,' Amy said.

'You don't know that.'

Amy ignored him.

'Can you imagine what that would be like for us?' she asked.

'He's killing himself, Amy,' said Harry . 'He's killing himself and you're ... You're just letting him do it.'

Harry knew immediately that he'd gone too far then, but he wasn't about to apologise.

'Probably best you don't start quoting the Mental Health Act at me, Harry .'

'I wasn't going to, but if this is what you're saying it is, then he needs help. You both do. And more than a sodding reunion, that's for sure.'

'You think I don't know that?'

Harry heard the tension in Amy snap like a guitar string.

'I'm not suggesting you don't,' Harry said.

Amy rounded on him then, fire in her eyes.

'Look at him, Harry ! Just look at him! How can that be my husband? You don't think I've tried to do everything for him, to save him from himself? It's destroyed me! I'm dead inside, Harry , you hear me? Dead! And what use would a padded room be, anyway? Can you tell me that?'

Harry didn't respond to the spit of venom in Amy's voice.

'They'd keep him alive, yes, but then what? What if there's just nothing left of him in there at all? What if all of that was smashed apart and left in the desert, and the little of him you brought back had already just withered and died? You ever thought of that? Well, have you?'

Harry resisted the urge to stand up, to take control of the situation. Instead, he remained seated, focusing on keeping his voice calm. He didn't want Amy to feel threatened in any way.

'I'm not a doctor, Amy. I can hardly be the best person you know to talk about getting help. I doubt Ed and Andy are either.'

'You're the best we've got.'

'No, we're not.'

'I'm not asking you to talk to him about getting help!' Amy's voice was a cry, raw and desperate. 'You *are* the help, Harry ! You and Ed and Andy! You're it! His last chance. No, you're *our* last chance. That's the whole point of it all. Can't you see that, even now? Bloody hell, how thick can you be?'

Harry was confused.

'What? I don't understand ...'

The slap came out of nowhere, and with such speed and fury that the shock of it stung Harry as much as the strike itself.

'Talk to him, Harry ! Say something! Make him snap out of it, because I'm done trying. I've nothing left, I'm empty, I can't go on, not anymore. He'll listen to you, won't he? Get him out of here and in that pub. Talk about old times, whatever crazy shit you all used to get up to; anything, okay? Just snap him out of it before I lose my mind completely and do something else I regret!'

'Something else? What do you mean by that?'

Amy jabbed a finger into Harry as she screamed at him, as though doing so would force her words to take root in his flesh. 'He listened to you when you told him to stay alive, didn't he? When you dragged him out of that vehicle in pieces, bits of him hanging off all over the place? It's your fault he's here at all, so take some responsibility for it. You're the reason he's still alive, after all!'

'I'm not, Amy, you know that, I know you do.'

'Yes, you bloody well are! Of course, you are, so own that for once, please! If it wasn't for you, he'd be dead, Harry ! Dead! And who's to say that wouldn't have been better than this?'

Harry was stunned by that, and could hardly believe Amy had said it.

'You don't mean that. You can't.'

'Guess again, Harry ,' Amy replied, her voice impossibly loud, especially considering her size. It was as though right there, in that moment, all those years of anger and pain and worry were all coming out at the same time, fuelling a fire that now burned white-hot deep inside her.

'That day, we all saved each other,' Harry said. 'It wasn't just me. Ant played his own part in it. Ed, Andy, we all got out of there together.'

There had been six of them on that patrol, three in each vehicle, clearing a number of buildings in a remote compound, following reports of insurgent activity in the area.

'You were in command,' Amy said, jabbing a sharp finger into Harry with each point she made. 'You led the patrol, you held them together, you got them out of there!'

'Amy, we were a team.'

'You were their goddamn leader, Harry . You can't escape that, even though we all know you've tried your best to do exactly that.'

Those words stung, probably because there was some truth in it, Harry thought. He'd joined the police for a number of reasons, and Amy had just nailed one of them to the floor.

'What did Ed and Andy say when you told them?'

'You mean you haven't spoken to them?'

Harry said nothing.

Amy sighed, her shoulders slumping.

'No, wait, don't answer that. I know you haven't. Doesn't matter anyway; they said nothing, really. No bloody use.'

'Doesn't sound like them.'

'People change.'

'Not that much.'

Amy's face was a rictus of disbelief as she shook her head, then pointed at her husband.

'Look at him and say that to me again, Harry , I dare you. Tell me he hasn't changed.'

She had a point, Harry thought.

'I still think you need medical help here, Amy,' Harry said. 'A nurse isn't enough. If Ant's not listening to you, he's not going to listen to me or any of us, is he?'

Amy stepped in close and glared at Harry .

'You know what, Harry ? You're probably right,' she said, her voice quiet now, strangely calm. 'But the least you can do is try, don't you think? That's all I'm asking from any of you, his supposed oldest mates; to meet him in a pub and just see if you can't bring him back. Because if you can't, Harry , then no one can, and after that, just what the hell is the point of anything?'

Without another word, Amy turned and left the room, heaving the door shut behind her.

CHAPTER THIRTY-FOUR

For a moment or two, Harry didn't move. What Amy had said, it was a lot to take in, perhaps too much. But he was here, so better to try than not. The case involving his father, everything that had happened back in the Dales, faded from his mind, and all that mattered was trying to help an old friend.

Getting up out of the chair, he moved over to sit himself down on the bed.

Anthony barely registered his presence.

'I'll be honest, Ant,' Harry said. 'I'm not quite sure what Amy thinks I can do here. You always were a stubborn old bastard, weren't you?'

Harry waited for some response from Anthony, some sign that he was listening, but there was nothing.

'This whole not-eating thing, though? Well, that's not you at all, is it? You're not the giving-up type. Never were.'

Still nothing from Anthony, just the thousand-yard stare of a Para fresh out of combat. Was the man still so haunted by that day?

'You can't do this to yourself. You can't just give up. You didn't then, did you? Refused to, if I remember rightly. All that blood and the pain and you were busy looking for your rifle, spotting muzzle flash.'

Harry spotted a flicker of movement and Anthony slowly turned his head to face him.

'So, you are still in there, then?'

Anthony's eyes widened a little. He gave a nod, though the stare was still there.

'Pub it is, then,' Harry said, and quickly glanced around the room for a wheelchair, assuming that there was one in the first place. Then he saw it, against the far wall, behind another chair, folded up and covered in a blanket.

He walked over and pulled it out into the centre of the room.

'Amy?' Harry called, but there was no answer, so he smiled down at Antony and said, 'Looks like it's just you and me then, mate.'

With surprising gentleness, Harry bent over and slipped an arm behind Anthony's back, another under his legs, then lifted him. The soldier had gone from mountain to mouse, Harry thought, alarmed and horrified by the ease with which he held him. Amy had been right when she had said she could've lifted him on her own.

Harry lowered Antony into the wheelchair.

Amy entered the room.

'Harry , I think you should—'

'Leave?' Harry said, noticing how her mouth had fallen open at the sight in front of her. 'No chance, Amy. I didn't drive all this way just to bloody well turn round again and go back home.'

And the Dales really was home, wasn't it? he thought. He was already missing the place, the people, Grace and Smudge. That place had changed him.

'He's not been in that thing for God knows how long,' said Amy, interrupting Harry 's thoughts.

'Well, he's in it now,' said Harry , then he turned to Anthony. 'Right then, Shotgun, pub?'

Harry didn't wait for an answer, just nodded at the lounge door. Amy opened it and Harry pushed Anthony out into the hallway. Amy dodged past and pulled open the front door. Outside, the weather was all howling winds whipping at the world with dark strands of rain.

'I'll get the car open,' Amy said and dashed out.

Harry followed soon after, quickly placing Anthony in the passenger seat, then stowing away the wheelchair in the boot. He climbed in behind Anthony.

'How far's this pub, then?'

'A couple of miles or so,' Amy replied, starting the engine. 'I'm driving us there. I've booked a taxi for after.'

Harry saw her glance at her husband as she turned the car around in the drive and headed off towards their destination. There was hope there, he thought, just a flicker of it. At least he hoped that's what he saw and not despair.

The pub sat all alone on a lane more pothole than tarmac. The roof was thatched, and glowing windows stared out from beneath it like eyes under a heavy fringe.

Amy pulled them into the car park out front. Harry jumped out and soon had Anthony in the wheelchair. To enter the pub, he turned around and pulled the wheelchair in backwards, swinging Anthony back around once they were inside.

The first thing Harry noticed was the change in the air. The biting, metallic tang of the wet and dark world of the night outside, was swamped by a warm blast of comfort, thick with chatter and the malty notes of ale, and behind it the heavy scent of burning wood. The second thing was how the chatter dropped to a muted muttering as the door slipped shut behind them.

People stared at them from behind beer glasses, eyes narrowing on the edges of paused conversations.

'Evening, all,' he said, his voice deliberately loud as he caught the eyes of a few of the gawkers. He then walked over to the bar. Amy came over to stand beside him. Harry looked at her and asked, 'So, where are they, then?'

'They'll be in the snug,' Amy said. 'I reserved it for us for the evening.'

A barmaid with dark hair and a lot of piercings pointed Harry in the right direction.

Harry pushed Anthony along and soon heard voices he recognised but hadn't heard in so long now that it was as though he was walking into the last moments of a barely remembered dream. And then, there they were, two men from those long-ago days, sitting in a cosy alcove.

For Harry , time stood still.

'Well, you're uglier than I remember,' said the man on Harry 's left, who stood up to greet him, with an extended arm and an enormous smile. He was dressed in a tweed jacket and blue jeans, dark hair cut with a side parting.

'At least I can blame an IED,' Harry said, shaking the man's hand, noticing faint, white scars stretching up beneath his cuff, the two missing fingers taken off by a round that had come too close. 'What's your excuse, Ed?'

The other man, who was to Harry 's right, also rose to his feet. He was shorter than Harry and wearing a mottled green, knitted jumper, and brown corduroy trousers.

'It's been a long bloody time, Harry ,' he said.

'You're not wrong,' Harry replied, and shook his hand as well. 'Good to see you, Andy.'

Harry saw Ed look past him to Amy and then Anthony. He then came out from behind the table and gave Amy a hug before doing the same to Anthony.

'We should've done this years ago,' he said.

'I wish you had,' said Amy. 'And so does Anthony, I'm sure.'

Harry saw Anthony's eyes flicker around the group, but that was the only sign that his old friend was listening in.

Ed and Andy sat back down, with Ed shoving himself along to the end of the table, Harry taking his place. Amy eased Anthony up to the table, then asked what everyone was drinking and popped back to the bar.

For a moment, no one spoke. Ed and Andy lifted their half-drunk pints, Ed sinking his in a gulp, Andy somewhat more cautious.

'Thirsty, then?' Harry asked, looking at Ed.

'And hungry,' Ed replied, tapping his stomach, which Harry noticed had grown a fair bit since they'd last met, the man's shirt and jacket barely able to hold itself back from bursting the buttons. 'Here.'

Ed slid a menu over to Harry , who stared at it without reading a word.

'Prices have gone up a bit since we last did this,' Harry said.

'Prices rising, hair receding, stomachs expanding.' Ed laughed, resting his empty glass back on the table, then tapping his tummy affectionately. 'Age doesn't take any prisoners, does it?'

Andy said, 'So, still in the police then, Harry , is that right?'

'It is.'

'Took us all by surprise when you jumped ship.'

'Had my reasons.'

'That'll be that bastard of a dad of yours, then,' said Ed.

And everything else, Harry thought, acutely aware of the memories that meeting his old friends had forced to the surface.

'I needed a change,' he said. 'He gave me a good excuse.'

For a moment, Harry was back in his new house, walking into the lounge, seeing the body, smelling it. He'd still heard nothing from the team, from Drake, not even a text, and he had to take that as a sign that they were just getting on with things. He'd send a message to Matt and Gordy later, see how things were.

'How's Ben?' asked Andy.

'He's well, actually,' said Harry , and quickly explained how his brother was doing. The truth was, though, that he wasn't entirely sure. He'd taken the news about their dad as well as could be expected, and he'd been out having fun raising money with Matt and the others, but Harry couldn't help worrying that it was just the kind of event that would knock his brother back. How far, though, that was the question?

Amy arrived with a tray of drinks.

'Pork scratchings as well?' said Ed, seeing the packet lying next to the glasses. 'Nice one, Amy. Beats any fancy starter, right?'

'Personally, I'd prefer a little bit of paté on toast,' said Andy, 'or a tomato and mozzarella salad, but whatever floats your boat.'

'When did you turn posh?' Ed asked, and opened the scratchings.

Harry looked over his drink at his two old friends.

'So, what are you both up to now, then?'

He realised he knew nothing at all about what Ed had been up to for the last twenty years. As for Andy being a vicar? Well, he thought, the man no doubt had his reasons.

'Truck driver,' said Ed. 'Well, I used to be, anyway. Long-distance stuff, all across the UK and Europe, that kind of thing. Now it's just van work, really; delivering parcels all over.'

'Sounds good.'

'No, it doesn't. It sounds shit because that's what it is, mate. But it's a job, right, and you have to take what you can get sometimes, don't you?'

Harry wasn't sure how to answer that, noting a raw edge to Ed's voice.

'You don't enjoy it, then?'

'I've been driving for nigh on fifteen years,' said Ed. 'It's lasted longer than my marriage did, and I get to eat in all the best roadside cafes. Not that great for the figure, but who's watching?'

Harry turned his attention to Andy.

'Amy tells me you're in the church now.'

'Hard to believe, right?'

Harry shook his head.

'Not sure why it should be. So long as you're happy in what you do, that's what matters. How is it?'

'Tough,' Andy replied. 'And lonely at times. The vicarage is huge, and I'm on my own. The place gets cold as well. But the church community, they've been really good. Very supportive and understanding.'

Of what? Harry wondered.

'Ever get married?'

Andy shook his head.

'No, I've not been with anyone since ...' A flicker of pain crossed the man's face, as though he was suddenly remembering everything all at once. 'I'm better off alone, I think. Not much I can do about it anyway, is there?'

'You both still live in the area, then?' Harry asked.

'Never left,' said Ed, then he glanced over at Anthony. 'Good to see you as well, mate,' he said. 'You're looking well.'

The lie was said with genuine warmth, thought Harry , but the words fell on cold, hard, unfertile ground.

'What do you get up to these days, then?' Ed continued, clearly undeterred. 'You were a tough old bastard, you know? And what was it we called you? Bloody hell, my memory ...'

'Shotgun,' Harry said.

Ed laughed.

'That was it!'

'On account of the way he used to blast through doors with that shotgun,' Andy added, then he rubbed his forehead and frowned. 'Was that really us back then? Seems so long ago. I can hardly believe it.'

'You're not the only one,' said Harry . 'Look ...'

He pulled from his pocket the old photographs he'd found back at the flat.

'Holy shit!'

'Not sure that's language becoming of a man of the cloth,' said Ed, looking over at Andy. 'But you make a fair point. Look at us!'

For the next few minutes, Harry found himself lost to a world of laughter, which threaded itself through memories of the better times, times when the only way to get through the day with any sense of their sanity and humanity intact was to laugh. Their humour had been dark, their day job often darker, with death's shadow always a little too close. They even took a few photos to compare with their younger selves, and almost wished that they hadn't.

Ed held up a photo.

'Love this one,' he said.

Harry leaned in to see six men leaning against a WMIK Land Rover.

'Look at Ricky,' Andy said.

Harry 's eyes fell on a slim soldier at the right of the photograph. Ricky Harris had been a quiet lad, generally spending his free time climbing or running. But in battle, he had been ferocious.

'And there's Tak,' said Ed, pointing at the sixth soldier in the group. 'As always, acting like an idiot.'

Taksh Chowdhury was in the middle of the photo and, for reasons Harry could no longer remember, was doing a handstand.

'Not so much acting like an idiot as showing off, if you ask me,' he said.

Ed raised a glass.

'To old friends,' he said.

Harry and Andy raised their own glasses, and for a moment everyone fell quiet.

The silence was broken when a young man wearing a simple waiter's uniform of a white shirt and black trousers came to stand at their table.

'Ready to order?' he asked, his hands holding a small notebook and pencil.

'My guess is three ribeyes,' said Ed.

'And that's just for you,' said Harry , collecting the photos and putting them back in his pocket.

'Three ribeye steaks, then,' the waiter said.

'Medium rare for me,' said Ed. 'Get that fat melting, but keep the meat good and pink.'

Harry and Andy asked for theirs the same way, and Amy ordered salmon.

'What about you, then, Anthony?' Andy asked.

'I'm afraid he can't, not at the moment,' Amy said. 'He's on a special diet.'

Harry caught Andy's eye and shook his head to tell him not to ask any questions.

The waiter left the table.

'Is it the meds, then?' Ed asked, looking at Anthony and Amy. 'That's tough, mate. You used to eat enough on your own to feed a whole troop.'

Anthony coughed then, and Amy snatched up a napkin to cover his mouth.

'Christ alive …' said Ed under his breath and reached for his drink, shaking his head.

Harry was quiet for a moment, then leaned over the table, and said, 'Lads, a word …'

Andy and Ed looked over at him, clearly confused.

Harry felt Amy's hand reach out to grab his wrist.

'Please, Harry , don't,' she said.

Harry ignored her and stood up, his eyes on the other two.

'Move,' he said.

'We're none of us soldiers now, Harry ,' Andy said, and Harry saw a bleak hardness in the man's eyes. 'We don't follow orders, not anymore.'

'Once a soldier, always a soldier,' Harry replied, and walked away from the table.

CHAPTER THIRTY-FIVE

Outside, and sheltering under the porch, Harry was joined by Andy and Ed.

'So, what's going on, Harry ?' Ed asked.

Harry explained as quickly and calmly as he could everything he'd heard and seen back at Amy and Ant's house.

'So, he won't talk and he's also starving himself? Why would anyone want to do that?' Ed said. 'Doesn't make any sense.'

'Maybe he's just had enough,' said Andy, pulling a large hipflask from a pocket and offering it around. Harry and Ed declined, but he took a deep slug of whatever it contained. 'It happens. I've dealt with parishioners who, for whatever reason, have just given up hope; illness, losing a partner, even the death of a pet. You'd be amazed at what can tip someone over the edge.'

'No one's going to starve themselves because their dog's died,' said Ed, his words riding a mean laugh.

'It's nothing to mock, I assure you,' said Andy.

Harry jumped in, keen to prevent these two old friends from falling out.

'Look,' he said, 'Amy's got us three here to help try and get through to Anthony. I don't know how or even if that's possible, but we owe it to them both to try. Amy, she's in a real state, never seen someone so close to the edge.'

'How, though?' said Ed. 'Sounds like he needs professional help.'

'Amy's either too scared or just too exhausted, I think, to take him. Perhaps both. However, if we can get him to at least respond, that would be something and maybe give her a bit of hope.'

'It's clearly been hard for them both,' said Andy. 'I can understand that.'

'If you ask me, it's self-indulgent and ungrateful,' said Ed. 'You saved his life, Harry .'

'*We* saved his life,' Harry said. 'We all saved each other that day. Remember?'

Andy said, 'I try not to.'

'Well, you should. We got out of there as a team.'

'Not exactly in one piece, though, not any of us,' he countered. 'And not all of us, either.'

Ed laughed, the sound as welcome as it was inappropriate.

'It's not funny,' said Andy, and judging by the look on his face, he still found it impossible to even smirk about what had happened.

'Of course it's funny,' Ed said, then held up his hand. 'I lost a couple of fingers that day, but you lost a bollock. That's always going to be funny. Nothing you can do about that, I'm afraid.'

Dark humour had helped them all survive in the desert, but laughing about that day was pushing it, Harry thought. Six men were now four, one killed in battle, one lost to PTSD when they'd returned home, and the rest of them carrying scars and injuries for the rest of their lives from what had happened, with Anthony the worst affected by a country mile. Harry had learned to live with his, embraced them even. Though he somehow managed to laugh about the loss of his fingers, Ed had also nearly lost his arm, and Harry had spotted the lurid white of the scars when they'd shaken hands. Andy's wound was out of sight for obvious reasons, but the impact of it was obviously still raw.

Harry wondered if that was why the man had never met anyone, never settled down.

Andy said, 'Think I lost my sense of humour that day as well. Glad to be alive though. How we got out of there, I'll never really know.'

Ed gestured at Harry with a nod of his head.

'Because of this ugly bastard, that's how, and I'll always be grateful. Which is why I think Ant should be, too.'

'We fought our way out as a team,' Harry said, but Ed was focussed on Andy.

'I'm pretty sure I remember Harry hoofing me out of the way of the flames with a well-aimed boot.'

'I needed to get your attention,' Harry said. 'A boot up the arse seemed the best option at the time.'

'It worked,' said Ed. 'But it wasn't my arse, was it? You broke a couple of ribs.'

Harry needed to move them on from reliving those blood-soaked memories, not least because they all remembered it differently, and no matter what any of them thought, they'd been lucky to get out at all. He needed them both to be with him when it came to helping Anthony and Amy.

He also wanted to try and ask a few questions linked to what had happened to his father back up in Hawes. He'd not mentioned it yet, not really had the chance. Had they noticed anything strange, someone following them perhaps, just a change to their normal every day which seemed out of place? He didn't expect much, if anything at all, but he'd sleep better knowing more than he did right now.

'My view is we don't mention anything about Anthony's condition. Instead, we just go in there and treat this like a normal night back in the day, if you know what I mean.'

Ed's grin widened. 'You mean ten pints each and a fight with a few Royal Marines?'

Harry couldn't help but laugh at that.

'Did you order some in?'

'Sorry, no,' said Ed. 'My bad.'

'What I mean is that we just crack on like nothing's changed,' Harry said. 'All we have to do is have a few drinks, laugh, tell old stories, see if we can get through to Anthony with that. Unless you have a better idea, that is?'

Neither Ed nor Andy offered one.

'That's decided then,' said Harry . 'So, let's keep things light, and see if we can get Amy laughing, and then who knows, maybe Anthony will join in.'

Harry led them back into the pub and over to the snug. The food was waiting for them, the air rich with the delicious aroma of charred meat.

'That smells bloody wonderful,' Andy said, dropping himself down in his seat. Harry had to agree and reached for the mustard, before handing it round the table. He then lifted his pint glass.

'Well, here's to old times and even older faces,' he said.

Andy, Ed, and Amy clinked their glasses against his.

'Seems a bit unfair to describe what you have as a face,' said Ed. 'I think it's an improvement on what you had before, though.'

'I asked them to make me look more like you,' Harry replied.

Andy then chipped in and said, 'The likeness is uncanny.'

For a good while, as the meal was devoured and the drinks flowed, Harry found himself relaxing into the whole affair. He'd not wanted to come along at all, always believing that moving on is better than looking back. What had happened over the weekend seemed distant, far enough away to be of no concern.

Sometimes, he thought, you just drifted away from people. It was a natural part of life. And yet, here they all were, friends who'd not seen each other in over two decades, getting along as though no time had passed.

But it had, and Harry couldn't shift that fact, even as Andy and Ed arm wrestled across the table, Ed accusing Andy of cheating, because he apparently had God on his side. Then, just as they'd ordered desserts, Andy looked at Harry and asked, 'So, what actually happened with your dad in the end?'

'How do you mean?' answered Harry .

'Did you ever get him for what he did to your mum and Ben?'

'I wasn't out for revenge.'

Ed laughed.

'Like bollocks you weren't,' he said. 'Anyway, it's not like he didn't have it coming, is it?'

Harry finished what was left in his glass.

'He's dead,' he said.

'And I'll raise a glass to that right here,' said Ed, doing exactly that.

Andy raised his own, but Harry kept his empty glass in his hand on the table.

'Something up?' Ed asked.

Harry looked at his old army friends, at Amy, and thought once again about the weekend. How could any of that be linked to them? It didn't make sense. Whoever had killed his father had done so for their own reasons. That it had happened in Harry 's own house made him wonder if that was little more than a message to the rest of the criminal fraternity, a way of letting them know that this could just as easily happen to them, on their own home turf. Which meant that whoever had done it was so beyond the reach of the law as to be untouchable. Even so, he needed to make sure that these people were safe.

'He was murdered,' Harry explained. 'Happened at the weekend actually.'

Shock slammed a fist into the faces staring at him.

'You're not serious,' said Andy.

'As I remember, he's rarely anything else,' said Amy.

'I'll spare you the details,' said Harry .

'You know who did it?' asked Ed.

Harry shook his head.

'He pissed off a lot of people in his time. My guess is that one of them, maybe a whole group of them, decided to get rid of him permanently. I found him.'

More shock ricocheted through the group, their eyes even wider than before.

'What? How?' asked Ed.

'I was supposed to be moving into my new house on Saturday. Turns out someone had left me a little moving-in present, namely the body of my murdered father.'

The air lit with swearing and gasps.

Harry was about to tell them more, but decided against it. The more he thought about it, the more it struck him as madness that what had happened could be linked to his own past, or that any of those in front of him could be at risk. It just didn't make sense.

'That's horrendous,' Andy said.

'I know you hated the bastard,' said Ed, 'but even you wouldn't be mad enough to off him on your own territory.'

Harry had nothing else to say and for a while, it seemed that no one else did either. Then the desserts arrived and Amy stood up to excuse herself, stumbling just enough to tumble backwards onto the floor with a surprised giggle.

Harry stood up to help her back onto her feet, but she pushed him away.

'I'm fine,' she said, her words slurring a little. 'Don't need a man to help me, not anymore, let me tell you, Mr Detective Man.'

Harry stayed where he was as Amy swayed in front of him.

'We'll maybe make this the last drink and call it a night,' he said, looking over at Ed and Andy, hoping for some support.

'My round,' Amy said, leaning across the table now and ignoring Harry . 'Same again?'

'Sounds good,' said Ed.

'Why not?' agreed Andy.

'Come on then, Harry ?' Amy asked. 'Your dad's dead, right? Someone did you a favour and you're free of him at last! Time to celebrate, I think, so what'll it be?'

Harry could feel the effects of the booze just in the background of his mind, but Amy's stumble had sobered him up enough to make him realise he'd had enough.

'I'm good,' he said.

But Amy wasn't listening. She was leaning on the table and staring at her husband.

'What about you, Love?' she asked. 'A pint? You remember what a pint tastes like, don't you? Or maybe something stronger? You always liked bourbon. Shall I see what they've got behind the bar?'

Harry reached over to pull Amy gently away and back to her chair.

'Come on, Amy,' he said. 'Think about what you're saying now.'

Amy slapped his hand away.

'He's not said a bloody word all evening, Harry ! Not one! The very least he can do, is have a drink, don't you think? I mean, how difficult can it be? It's just liquid, isn't it? All he has to do is swallow. Doesn't even have to chew!'

Harry had a sense then of the evening suddenly unravelling in front of his eyes as Amy turned back to her husband.

'Why won't you speak? Why stop eating? Why do this to yourself? It doesn't make any bloody sense, does it?' Her voice was cut through with pain as tears fell.

Andy leaned over and tried to get Amy to calm down, but she shooed him away. Harry noticed how the group sitting at the table opposite them had fallen quiet. Ed, on the other hand, had sunk deep into his chair as though he was trying to pull the shadows over him to hide beneath them like a kid under a blanket.

Amy hadn't finished.

'After everything I've done for you, the years I've given of my life, and for what, for you to just die on me?' Her voice was shrill, ripped and torn, the frustration and pain of years pouring out of her. 'You don't get to just decide what's best for both of us, you hear me? None of this is up to you! It's not up to you, you bastard!'

Amy slapped Anthony across his face, the sound echoing around the alcove.

Someone appeared in front of them—the landlord.

'I need to ask you to keep it down,' he said.

'Oh, just fuck off, will you?' Amy screamed. 'Just fuck off and mind your own fucking business!'

Amy's language and the venom in it lit a fire in the air and Harry felt the eyes of everyone in the pub staring at them.

'And now I need to ask you to leave.'

Amy wasn't listening.

'Who the hell do you think you are? We're paying customers!' she said. 'And I'm not leaving until I see this husband of mine have at least one drink, you hear?'

The landlord looked over at Harry , clearly beckoning him to help.

'We have a taxi booked,' Harry said, 'but it's not due for a while yet.'

'I'll see if I can sort one out for you,' the landlord replied. Then he looked at Ed and Andy and added, 'Make that two.'

'No, you won't,' Amy said. 'We're not going anywhere, because we're staying, aren't we, my love?'

Then she dropped herself down onto her husband's lap.

Anthony's arm shot out and he clamped his hand onto Harry 's wrist. Harry noticed that the man's flesh was clammy and damp, but the grip, though weak, was still firm enough to make him take notice.

Harry stared now at his friend as Amy sobbed into the crook of her husband's neck.

'What is it?' Harry asked.

Harry felt Anthony's grip tighten, saw the man's eyes widen even further.

'What is it, mate?' Harry said. 'I'm not telepathic. None of us are. But we are here to help.'

Anthony's mouth started to move, his lips parting. Harry was sure words would soon follow.

'That's it,' Andy said, seeing what was happening and clearly trying to encourage. 'Come on, Anthony ...'

Amy leaned back, her arms outstretched around his neck.

'Anthony?'

Anthony's lips drew further apart to show brown teeth. His breath slipped out, stale and fetid.

'Please, Love,' Amy said. 'Please ...'

Then, as though the effort was just too much, Anthony slumped back in his wheelchair, arching his back, as a moan crawled out of him laced with animal-like pain.

Tears welled and fell.

Amy pushed herself up onto her feet.

Harry had expected her to scream or yell or throw something. Instead, she just stood there, calm and still.

'Makes you wonder, doesn't it?' she eventually said.

'What does?' said Harry .

'Everything you did over there. If it was all actually worth it in the end.' She stared at Anthony and sighed. 'If *this* was worth it ...'

Ed broke his silence. 'We won, though,' he said.

'Did we? How, exactly?'

Andy reached a hand over to rest it on Amy's shoulder, but she shook it off.

'I'm sorry,' he said. 'I wish we could do more. We all do.'

'So do I,' said Amy. 'So do I. But you can't, can you? No one can. What's done is done. And he's already decided, hasn't he? A coward's way out.'

A few minutes later, the bill settled, Harry saw Ed and Andy to their taxi.

'I'm sorry we lost touch,' Ed said. 'And I know this is very late in the day, Harry , but thank you. For what you did, I mean, getting me out of there.'

'Me too,' Andy added, leaning across Ed from the other side of the car. Harry noticed that he had the hipflask in his hand again.

Harry had nothing he could say to the two men in front of him, nothing at all, so he was thankful when Ed spoke again.

'You around tomorrow?'

'I'm heading back home,' Harry said.

'We should go to the cemetery tomorrow,' Ed said. 'See Ricky and Tak. You got time for that?'

'I do,' he said.

'I'll text you tomorrow, then.'

With that agreed, Harry waved them on their way, then went back to help get Anthony and Amy into the taxi.

'What about you?' Amy asked. 'How will you get back?'

'I'll sort something,' Harry said. Even if it means walking, he thought. 'He needs help, Amy. You both do.'

Amy reached out to grab the door handle.

'Can't help a coward,' she said, then slammed the door shut.

As Harry watched them go, he was so deep in thought that he didn't even notice the rain.

CHAPTER THIRTY-SIX

Harry woke up in the hotel to the sound of his phone buzzing nearly as loudly as his own head, even though he'd not set an alarm. He grabbed it and answered.

'What?' he said, rubbing tiredness from his eyes, and saw that the morning had only just slipped past nine AM.

'DCI Grimm?'

Harry didn't place the voice immediately.

'Yes, who is—' Then he remembered. 'Drake?'

'How was the reunion?'

'Fine,' Harry said, now sitting up to swing his legs out of bed. 'Yeah, it was fine. I'll go with that. But you're not calling me about that, though, clearly.'

'No, I'm not,' Drake said. 'When will you be back?'

'Late afternoon. Why? What's happened?'

Harry noticed a pause in the conversation. It wasn't much, but it was enough to have him concerned.

'Nothing has happened. Not as such, anyway. Just thought it would be sensible to have a chat, go through a few things.'

'As such? What does that mean? You have some suspects?'

'It means I could do with talking through the case with you, if that's possible. When you get back, I mean, not now. Face-to-face would be better, I think.'

Harry wasn't so sure. Waiting, putting something off, just wasn't his style. If you're going to pull the plaster off, better to do it in one go rather than prolong the pain.

'I'm still on leave, remember?' he said. 'Not sure you should even be speaking to me.'

'I will be speaking to you as a person of importance, that's all. And I can do that.'

'Makes me sound like I'm a suspect still,' said Harry through a yawn. He had a long journey ahead of him and wanted to get cracking. 'Is there anything I need to know? I'd rather have some idea of what we're going to talk about.'

Drake paused just a little too long.

'I'm an impatient man,' Harry said.

'Everyone knows you're not a suspect,' Drake said.

'There's a *however* at the end of that, isn't there?'

'There is. It's the press.'

'What is? You don't mean Anderson, do you? He was nosing around about the fireworks, that's all.'

'Well, he's nosing around about this now, too. Not in a good way, either. My worry is he's going to try and push a narrative that'll boost his own profile, if you know what I mean.'

Harry did, all too well.

'How do you know?'

'One of your PCSOs saw him up by your place. Said he took photos, even tried the front door.'

'Did he, now ...'

'I'm not saying he knows anything yet, but I have my suspicions, and you need to be aware that he's sniffing around.'

'He's always sniffing around. It's what he does,' Harry said.

He stood up and walked over to the window of his hotel room. Pulling back the curtain a little, he saw a grey sky resting low. With a stretch, he then walked through to the small bathroom and turned on the shower. Steam was soon billowing out into the bedroom like a cheap special effect from a late-night horror movie. The thought reminded him of Matt and the others on Monday night and he wondered how they'd got on, how much money they'd raised.

'Well, thank you for calling,' Harry said.

'You don't mean that.'

'You're right, I don't. But I'm glad you did.'

'We'll talk when you get back,' Drake said. 'Safe journey, Grimm.'

Harry threw his phone across the room to land on the bed. Then he headed through to the bathroom. He stripped off and almost fell into the shower to stand under the thundering storm of hot water.

As the heat soaked into him, Harry 's mind played back over the evening before, not just seeing Anthony as he now was, but Ed and Andy, too, and Amy.

It had been an odd experience, he thought. Amy was clearly under incredible strain, and he wondered if the travel she did with her job was only really necessary just so she could escape for a while. He couldn't blame her for it; her life had been dramatically changed by what had happened to her husband. That they were still together said a lot, though the stress of it all was written in her eyes, the strain in her voice keenly edged with pain.

Though the stress wasn't all he'd seen in her eyes, was it? he thought. There was that mirror on the floor as well. Harry knew people would turn to anything to get them through if things got bad enough, and it was easier than most people realised to get your hands on substances that would help dull the pain.

As for Ed and Andy, Harry wasn't so sure. Ed seemed to be running from something, the long-distance driving something he could blame for his failed marriage. Andy's crutch wasn't just religion, but that hipflask he'd brought out a couple of times; Harry wondered how much of a crutch it had become.

Reluctantly shutting off the shower, Harry went to stand at the sink and brush his teeth. He reached out to the mirror and wiped away the steam. He stared at his reflection, remembering things he had tried to forget. He reached a hand up to touch the scars, recalling once again when he'd caught his reflection in the mirror back at Grace's. Something had struck him then, hadn't it? But he'd not known what, and it was playing on his mind once again, even more so after last night.

Harry leaned closer to the mirror, his fingers tracing the terrible grooves cut into his flesh in jagged lines, which still itched after all these years. At least Andy's wounds were hidden, he thought, whereas his, Ant's, and Ed's were there for all to see.

Phone ringing, Harry dashed out of the bathroom, and answered without thinking.

'What?'

'Harry ? It's Ed.'

'Is it? Why? What's happened? Are you okay?'

'The cemetery, remember?' Ed said. 'Last night, we talked about going. Ricky and Tak, remember?'

Harry swore under his breath.

'I'm guessing you'd forgotten.'

'No,' Harry lied. 'I'm actually just getting ready. Something's come up though ...'

'You okay to pick me up?' Ed asked, clearly not listening to what Harry had said. 'I'll call Andy as well and we can grab him on the way.'

'I'm not sure I can,' Harry said. 'I got a call, and—'

'You owe them this, Harry ,' Ed said. 'Whatever's going on, a few minutes of showing them a bit of respect won't hurt, will it?'

Harry was fifty-fifty about just fobbing Ed off. He needed to get back north, to speak with Drake, with the team. But he also knew that Ed had a point.

'Send me your address,' he said, knowing deep down this was something he couldn't and shouldn't try to get out of. 'I'll be round as soon as I'm done here.'

CHAPTER THIRTY-SEVEN

Harry quickly got himself dried, dressed, and out the door. About twenty minutes later, when he arrived at Ed's address, he found him standing at the side of the road in front of a three-storey building of small flats, their balconies a Technicolor explosion of washing out to dry, numerous different plants, and in some cases, elaborate examples of bunting. He really wanted to head back up north, but he had to trust in both Drake and his team. Neither was he about to go back on his word to Ed.

Ed climbed into the passenger seat.

'Andy's meeting us there,' he said, clipping in the seat belt. 'You remember where it is?'

'It's not a place you ever really forget,' Harry said.

The journey from Ed's to the cemetery was carried out in silence. Harry wondered if Ed was doing the same as him, thinking back to times and events they'd both worked so hard to forget.

Arriving at the cemetery, they parked up and Harry allowed Ed to lead the way.

The graveyard was quiet, and Harry was very aware of the sound of his footfalls as they made their way along narrow paths to their destination. All around, grey-white gravestones stood in regimental rows. The air was still, just a soft breeze joining them, almost pulling them along as they walked.

This is a place of ghosts, Harry thought, not just of people either, but of the lives ruined by their loss. Sorrow had soaked into the very ground on which they walked.

When they arrived at the graves of their fallen friends, Harry came to a dead stop.

'Any idea where Andy is?' he asked.

'He should be here,' Ed replied, checking his phone. 'He said he would be. There's no message though.'

Now that they were there, Harry wasn't entirely sure what they were supposed to do. He had no speech prepared, nothing he really wanted to say. And yet, deep down, something told him that just being here was perhaps enough.

'You know, I've not talked about that day with anyone,' Ed said. 'Not since it happened. Not really.'

'What's there to say?' said Harry .

'I went to counselling, the usual,' continued Ed. 'All that bollocks about decompressing or whatever, but I never really touched on the reality of it. How could I? I sort of said just enough to tick all the boxes and be signed off as fit, I think. Head down and crack on, if you know what I mean.'

'I do,' said Harry . 'And it's not just that day, though, is it? It's the whole experience; being on tour, wondering if you'll survive the next twenty-four hours, never mind ever see home again.'

'And they didn't, did they?' said Ed, staring at the quiet sods of earth at their feet. 'Well, Tak did, but not sure that counts.' Ed shook his head, swore under his breath. 'PTSD is a bitch, isn't it?'

'It is,' Harry said, his voice quiet.

Like all of them, Tak had been haunted by what he'd experienced, only it had become too much in the end.

'Could've been me.'

'Could've been any of us.'

Neither of them said anything else for a few minutes, trapped in their own thoughts.

Ed broke the silence.

'I can still smell it, you know?' he said. 'Never would've thought that was a thing, that the reek of a place could be so intense that it never leaves you. But it doesn't, does it? It's always there, at the back of my throat.'

Harry heard Ed swear then, spitting the words out into the morning air.

'It's a long time ago,' Harry said. 'No, it never leaves you, but I think you have to leave it, if that makes sense. Probably doesn't. If you don't, if you keep hold of it, it'll drive you mad.'

'You say that like it's easy to do.'

'No, I don't,' said Harry . 'It's the hardest thing to do. And I'm not saying forget it either, because that's different, just that you have to move on, otherwise you get stuck.'

Harry noticed Ed turn to face him. When he looked up, he saw tears in the eyes of his old friend.

'Sometimes, I wish ... No, I can't say it ...'

'Say what?' Harry said, concerned now.

'It's just that after seeing Ant, it all came rushing back. I didn't think it would, but it did, Harry . I didn't sleep; I couldn't. Not a wink.'

Harry kept quiet, giving Ed the space to say what he needed to.

'I thought life would get back to normal, that once I came back, healed a bit, that I'd be able to get on with things. But that's not how it is, is it? I mean, just look at Tak.'

'It's not easy for anyone,' said Harry .

Ed turned from Harry then and walked away a few paces. Harry didn't follow. Ed crouched down, picked up some stones from the path, and threw them.

'I drank,' he said. 'Heavily. That's why she left me. Tina, I mean. You never met her. She was lovely. Really helped me turn things around, but I couldn't hold it together. Then ... Then one night I ...'

Harry walked over to stand with Ed.

'What happened?' he asked.

'The flashbacks,' Ed said, tears streaming down his face now. 'They never went away. I thought they had, but they came back. The drink, it helped to dull them, but I'd still get these nightmares, wake up screaming in the night. It was too much for her.'

'Not everyone can handle it,' Harry said.

Ed turned to face him and before Harry could react, the old soldier had his hands around his neck.

'This is how I woke one night, Harry , just like this, my hands around her neck, squeezing.'

Harry grabbed Ed's wrists, tried to gently prise them apart. He wasn't being strangled quite yet, so there was no need for a more violent response. He hoped there wouldn't be, either.

'Ed ...'

'She was just staring up at me, Harry , like she didn't recognise me. I can still see it now. The fear in her eyes, the knowledge that I was going to kill her, that she didn't stand a chance.'

Ed's hands started to squeeze.

Harry tightened his grip on Ed's wrists.

'Ed, you need to stop. You need to let go. Now.'

'That's what it did to me, Harry , don't you see? It turned me into the kind of person who can wake up in the night trying to kill his girlfriend. And for what? What the hell was it all for? Why did we even bother coming back if that's what we are now?'

'Ed ...'

'You should've left me there, Harry . You should have left us all there. Can't you see that? You have to see that. You have to!'

Ed's hands squeezed harder. Harry was choking now, stars bursting at the edge of his vision.

'You have to see, Harry ! You did this to me, to all of us! It's your fault, all of it, damn you!'

The soldier in Harry reacted. He grabbed Ed's hands and yanked them backwards, pulling Ed towards him. At the same time, he arched his own back and lifted his knee to send it hard into Ed's stomach, his foot crashing into his bollocks. Harry gave no time for Ed to react, instead pushing the man away with as much force as he could muster, sending him sprawling on the ground.

Harry stared down at his old friend, his heart rate through the roof. His fists were clenched, up and ready for attack.

Ed just lay there on the ground, flat out on his back.

'Bloody hell, Harry ...' He coughed.

Harry said nothing, kept his distance, his guard up.

Ed rolled onto his side, spat, then climbed slowly to his feet. He turned to stare at Harry .

'You see?'

'No, I don't see,' said Harry . 'What the hell was that all about?'

'This is who we still are,' Ed said. 'We never really left that day, or Afghanistan, behind; we brought it home with us instead, Harry .'

Harry relaxed a little, but still kept his distance.

Still coughing, Ed headed back to the graves of their fallen friends.

'You know what?' he said, as Harry joined him. 'They're the lucky ones. It's done for them, isn't it? They're gone. Us, though? We're still here, aren't we? Reliving it all the sodding time. Every day, the echo of it, the stink, it's there. And it never goes away.'

'I'd rather be alive,' Harry said.

'Last night, I said I was grateful for what you did,' said Ed, turning to stare dead eyes at Harry . 'Truth is, Harry , and I'm sorry I have to say this, but not a day goes by where I don't hate you for it.'

Ed walked away, heading back up to where Harry had parked. Harry gave him a moment, then followed on. When they arrived at his car, Ed walked straight past.

'Ed ...' Harry called.

Ed didn't reply, just kept on walking.

Harry headed home.

CHAPTER THIRTY-EIGHT

When Harry turned off the A1, to make his way through Bedale and on towards Wensleydale, he noticed an odd feeling start to crowd into his already busy mind.

The journey had been long, his stops few and short, and he had fuelled himself on a diet of energy drinks and fast food. With every bite of the burger he'd pushed into his face at the halfway point, he had heard Jen admonishing him for it, pestering him to get back out on the lanes with his running shoes. His love/hate affair with fitness was definitely in the hate phase again, and Harry couldn't remember the last time he'd been out for a run.

Maybe running just wasn't for him. Perhaps he needed to find something else. A bike, perhaps, though the thought of squeezing himself into Lycra, then inflicting that sight on the people of the Dales horrified him.

Ahead, Harry saw the world start to turn from low rolling fields and woodlands to high summits further off, as though the land was much like the sea, with shallow waves to shore, and far off a storm approaching.

The road through to Leyburn was quiet, more so because Harry had switched off the radio and was instead, with windows down, just enjoying the cold air gusting in to nip and bite at his skin. The heater was on full, just to make sure that he didn't freeze solid.

Out of Leyburn, he drove on towards West Witton. In Wensley, he was tempted to hang a right and take the back road through Redmire and Carperby, but the urge to stop and see Grace would be too strong; he had work to do and Drake was waiting.

The odd feeling grew stronger as Harry , having driven through Aysgarth and on towards Bainbridge, took a left out of the village to take the home run on towards Hawes. And that was when he realised exactly what it was. For the first time, possibly in forever, Harry felt like he was heading home.

He wondered for a moment if he should've been more bothered about what had happened at the house he now owned but had yet to move into. A murder would put most people off, but the more he thought about it, the less he cared. A big part of it was that to let it bother him was to let whoever had carried out the awful task have control, to win. And that, surely, was the point of it all, in the end. To make sure that his life was forever haunted by what had happened, so much so that he would ease off in the day job, lose his edge.

No bloody chance, Harry thought. Wensleydale was home now, and he wasn't going to allow anyone to ruin it for him.

With Hawes just a few miles away, Harry almost didn't answer his phone when it rang. He didn't like the hands-free at the best of times, but he saw Ben's number on the screen and answered.

'Harry ?'

'Liz?'

He hadn't expected to hear the voice of PCSO Liz Coates.

'I thought you were Ben,' Harry said.

'It's Ben's phone; I can't find mine. Where are you?'

Harry told her.

'I think you need to speak with Ben.'

Harry didn't like the sound of that at all.

'Why? What's happened? What's he done?'

'I think it's best if you just come over now,' Liz said. 'Hopefully he'll be back by then.'

'Back? What do you mean? Where is he?'

Liz didn't immediately answer.

'Liz, I need to know ...'

'He's ... He's gone for a walk,' Liz said.

'Why?'

'That reporter. He was around here, at our place. Ben wasn't very happy about it, if you know what I mean.'

Yeah, Harry thought, I do.

'Right, I'm on my way,' he said. 'I'll be there in twenty.'

Hanging up, Harry spotted a lane to a farm just ahead on the right, slowed down and turned in, swinging the Rav4 around to point the way he'd just come. Then he was heading back down the dale, and a hell of a lot faster than how he'd driven up it.

Driving over Middleham Bridge, Harry entered the small market town and took an immediate right, soon arriving at a small bungalow Ben now shared with Liz. It was a property she had been left by a very generous aunt.

As Harry made his way over to the front door, he realised how few times he'd actually been over to visit. When Ben had moved out of the flat, Harry had decided to give him the space to settle into his new life with Liz, rather than have his big brother constantly checking up on him. Ringing the doorbell, he decided that was something which needed to change. Not that he wanted to check up on him, but he did miss having him around, not that he was about to admit it in public.

The door opened.

Liz hurried him inside.

'He's in the lounge,' she said.

'He's back? I thought you said he'd gone for a walk?'

'Came in just before you arrived,' Liz said. 'I'll put the kettle on.'

Harry headed through to the lounge.

Ben was sitting in a comfy chair, elbows on his knees, hands together, fingers entwined. He was staring at nothing.

'Ben?' Harry said.

Ben lifted his eyes and Harry saw a rare emotion etched into his brother's face, that of pure rage.

'He was here,' Ben said. 'That bastard was here, at our door, Harry ! We were heading out for a bite to eat before popping over to the fireworks in Hawes, when he knocked at the door.'

With everything going on, Harry had forgotten that it was November fifth, Bonfire Night.

'Anderson, the journalist, you mean?'

'I don't know his name. I don't care either. All I know is that he was here, and he was asking questions.'

Harry sat down.

Liz entered carrying a tray with a pot of tea, mugs, and biscuits.

'Tell me what happened,' Harry said, reaching over to pour the tea.

'What's to tell?' said Ben. 'He knew everything about me, my name, that I was in prison, my record, the lot. He knew about Dad, about what happened at your place. Even said to me that I wouldn't miss him. What the hell's that supposed to mean?'

Harry held out a mug for Ben. He didn't take it.

'When was this?'

'When I got home from work,' Ben said. 'He was waiting for me, I swear it.'

'Probably thinks he can use you to get to me,' Harry said. 'Did he say anything else?'

Ben was silent.

'Ben ...'

When Ben spoke next, his words tumbled into each other, like he was trying to say everything at once, but couldn't get the words out quick enough.

'He asked if I thought you did it, if you killed Dad. I said no, of course I didn't. Then he started twisting what I'd said, like I was just protecting you or something. He just kept on and on with his questions, asking about my time in prison, what I was in for, even though he clearly knew. He even said that I asked you to do it because, wasn't it likely that I blamed him for everything, for ending up in prison?'

'Did anything else happen, Ben?'

At this, Ben looked at Harry .

'Like what?'

Harry gave a shrug.

'You tell me.'

Harry knew Ben well enough to know that words weren't enough to have him like this.

'He followed me into the house,' Ben said. 'Just waltzed right in. Then, when I told him to get the hell out, he claimed I'd just invited him. Why would I do that? I wouldn't! And he wouldn't leave. Then Liz arrived, and he was still here and I just wanted him gone, Harry , you know? And he wouldn't, he just wouldn't leave.'

'So, what did you do?'

'I made him leave, Harry , that's what I did.'

'How?'

'I grabbed him and shoved him out the door. I wanted to stamp him into the ground, I'll tell you that for nothing. I was so angry. But I didn't; I just shoved him out the door, then followed him all the way back to his car, just to make sure he was gone.'

Harry looked over at Liz.

'Is that what happened?'

'It is,' Liz said. 'I promise you. Anderson wasn't happy about it. Lots of yelling. But he drove off eventually.'

'And that's as physical as it got?'

'I didn't punch him,' said Ben. 'I wanted to. I still do. But I didn't, I promise you. That's why I went for a walk, to calm down.'

'Did it work?'

'Not really,' said Ben, shaking his head. 'I can feel it, the anger, right in my fingertips. If he came back, I'd rip his face off.'

Harry stood up, resting his unfinished mug of tea back on the tray.

'No, you wouldn't,' he said.

'You don't know that.'

'I do,' Harry said, making his way to the lounge door. 'You're better than that.'

Liz stood up.

'Where are you going?' she asked.

'I need to speak with Drake,' Harry said.

'About this?'

'About this, about a lot of things.' He glanced over to Ben. 'Keep an eye on him.'

'I will.'

'Call me if Anderson comes back. I don't think he will, but if he does, you let me know. Don't let him in, and don't let Ben speak to him.'

'Understood.'

At the front door, Harry paused, then looked at Liz.

'He's lucky to have you,' he said.

Liz smiled.

'You're not getting all mushy on me, are you?'

'No,' Harry said. 'I'm just stating the bleeding obvious.'

Then he was out of the house and walking back to the Rav4 to head once again up the dale, sending a text to Drake to let him know that he was on his way.

Driving away from Liz's house, Harry 's mind wouldn't stop whirling. Trying to get his head around the murder of his father in his own house was difficult enough. But over the last couple of days, he'd seen an old soldier giving up on life while his wife falls apart, another try and strangle him, and now his brother had had a run-in with a journalist who'd somehow found out more than enough about things he shouldn't.

At some point, the week would get better, Harry thought. It had to; there was just no way it could get any worse.

CHAPTER THIRTY-NINE

HARRY BARGED THROUGH THE MAIN DOORS OF THE community centre, leaving the early evening behind him, the sky heavy and black, as though weighed down. He felt much the same, as he continued through the door and into the office to find three people waiting for him. He also saw that the board had been taken down so wasn't on display.

'Anderson knows,' he said, before he had time to register who was there. 'Somehow he's found out about what happened up at the house, about my father. Not only that, the slimy little sod has been over to my brother's place, asking questions. Just who the hell does he think he is?'

DI Haig approached Harry , and quickly, hands up defensively in front of her.

'Harry , before you say or do anything you will instantly regret, I need you to listen to me,' she said. 'Now.'

Harry was confused. Gordy wasn't usually so confrontational, so what was the problem? Also, she'd used his first name, and unless they were close friends or relatives, that was something people only seemed to do if they were admonishing him for something, trying to get his attention, or sharing bad news.

'What? Why?'

Then Harry saw exactly what and why. Except the *what* was a *who*.

'Anderson!' he snarled. 'You—'

Harry made to push past Gordy, his eyes on his prey, who was sitting beside DCI Drake at the far side of the room.

'Out of my way, Detective Inspector. I need to have a little talk with a certain journalist.'

'No, you don't,' Gordy said, holding her ground, voice firm. 'You need to stay right where you are.'

'Who told you, Anderson? Who's your source? And what the hell do you think you were doing out at Ben's?'

Harry tried to dodge around her, but Gordy was too quick. Anderson was sitting in a chair against the wall and attempting to look confident, a smarmy smile slapped across his face. Harry wanted to head on over and slap it right off again.

'You know I can't let you go over there,' Gordy said, a hand up to Harry 's chest, her eyes on his. 'You need to calm down.'

Harry tried to push past once again but didn't get anywhere. And he wasn't about to manhandle his DI out of the way, no matter how much he wanted to. He stepped back, took a slow breath in and out, then eyeballed Gordy.

'You know what he's been up to, don't you?' he said, jabbing a finger over the DI's shoulder towards Anderson. 'He's been out at Ben and Liz's place, pestering, questioning, accusing; he even pushed his way into their house!'

Anderson was on his feet and Harry saw now that the man looked rather dishevelled, his jacket ripped, hair out of place, face bruised.

'I did nothing of the sort! They invited me in,' Anderson said, his voice high-pitched and shrill.

He's over-acting this, Harry thought, roaring with laughter at Anderson's words. The sound, though, was devoid of all humour.

'Invited you in? You talk so much bollocks you should go into politics.'

'Are you accusing me of being a liar, Detective?'

Harry shook his head.

'I'm not accusing you, I'm telling you, that's what you are. And I want you to tell me who told you about the case. Right now. Before I do something everyone in here except me regrets.'

Anderson held out his coat for Harry to see.

'Have you not seen what your brother did to me, to my clothes?'

Harry couldn't believe what he was hearing.

'Ben did that, did he? When, exactly; when you were barraging him with questions, or when you pushed your way into his house?'

Anderson took a step forward and raised a finger at Harry .

'Your brother, he's a liability, a violent man, an ex-con who is a danger to the public. And it's my duty to tell them, to warn them.'

Harry could feel his temperature rising.

'You know what? Forget politics, that's not for you,' he said. 'Writing fiction, though? Maybe you should give that a go, seeing as you're so good at making shit up.'

'Harry , I need you to calm down,' Gordy said. 'Please; this isn't helping.'

'I am calm!' Harry snapped back. 'As calm as a bloody mill pond.'

Harry noticed Drake was now standing and had moved away from Anderson and over to the small kitchen area to busy himself with filling the kettle.

'You don't believe a word of this, surely?' Harry asked, the question directed at the other DCI. 'You can't. It's complete nonsense.'

Drake said, 'Right now, I'm with DI Haig on this. As difficult as this may be, I think you need to calm down for a moment, if you can.'

Anderson, Harry noticed, was smiling again, smarm now mutating to smug.

'I'm pressing charges, you know,' the journalist said, staring at Harry . 'Against your brother. For what he did to me, for throwing me out of his house like he did, pushing me to the ground, dragging me across the pavement. It's assault, that's what it is. And that girl-friend of his, your PCSO, she had a go, too, you know? What's the phrase; put the boot in, I think? Yes, that's what she did.'

'Liz?' Harry was incredulous. 'Where the hell are you dragging this up from? What kind of dark pit of idiocy do you keep in your mind that you can just spout so much shite?'

'It's the truth,' said Anderson. 'Both of them attacked me.'

Harry barked a sharp laugh.

'Oh, they attacked you now, did they? This story is growing by the second. If we wait around long enough, what else can we look forward to hearing? That you were lucky to escape with your life? That you bravely fought them off even though they were armed with knives and you had nothing but your trusty notebook and pen? That way, you can write some bollocks about the pen being mightier than the sword, right?'

Anderson pursed his lips and then said, 'It's not funny. None of this is funny. Assault is not a laughing matter.'

'No, but you are,' Harry said, 'and by going ahead with this, you're making an absolute mockery of anyone who knows what it's actually like. You sicken me, Anderson. Ben kicked you out of his house because you pushed your way in, and you know it. That's what happened and you can't bear the embarrassment of it.'

Anderson clearly wasn't about to give up, though. Harry could see it in the man's eyes.

'Kicked? Funny you should mention that, Detective. Yes, I do remember him kicking me.' Anderson then started to walk around the office and as he did so, Harry watched him develop a limp. 'I was amazed I could walk after it,' he said, rubbing his leg, his face screwed up with pain. 'I'm surprised I can walk now. The physio costs alone are going to be crippling. Not just for my leg, either, but for my back as well; I dread to think what damage your brother's done. He's violent, Grimm. I can see why he was in prison, that's for sure.'

Harry had had enough and was past Gordy before she could do anything to stop him.

Anderson, seeing Harry charge across the room towards him, immediately lost his limp, and dashed behind Drake, pushing the detective in front of him as protection.

'Hey,' said Drake. 'Don't drag me into this.'

'Threatening me won't help,' Anderson said, staring at Harry from behind Drake. 'I'm pressing charges for what he did to me. And I'll win, too, you know that, don't you? I'll win because who are they going to believe? An honest journalist on the side of truth, or an ex-addict who's just out of prison?'

'He's been out over a year now,' Harry said, clenching and unclenching his fists. 'And he's done more in that time, worked harder, than you could ever know. And as for you being on the side of truth? Sounds to me like you're back to talking bollocks again.'

'Harry ...'

Gordy's voice caught Harry 's attention.

'What?'

'You're not going to like what I'm about to say. But I need you to hear me out, okay?'

Harry moved away from Drake and Anderson and walked over to Gordy.

'What are you going to say that I'm not going to like?'

Gordy said, 'Anderson has accused Ben of assaulting him.'

'So?'

'You know what has to happen now, don't you?'

Harry shook his head, unable to comprehend that this was still going on, that they were entertaining Anderson's fictional account of what had happened.

'I've told you, and you know it yourself, that's horseshit,' he said. 'Ben would never do anything like that. Also, that lanky streak of piss over there is lying through his face.'

'Regardless, we have to investigate it,' Gordy said. 'That's the only way we can get to the bottom of what actually happened, isn't it?'

Harry shook his head in disbelief.

'Investigate? You mean—'

'Yes,' nodded Gordy. 'We need to bring Ben in.'

Harry couldn't believe what he was hearing.

'You can't arrest him, not on this.'

'We're not arresting him, we're bringing him in for questioning.'

Anderson let out a gasp of shock.

'Not arresting him? Why not? He attacked me! You have to arrest him.'

'I've already sent Jadyn and Jen over,' Gordy said, ignoring Anderson. 'They'll bring him in, we'll question him, and we will clear this up properly.'

'You can't do this.'

'I have to. You know I do, that *we* do, Harry .'

'Liz was there. She saw what happened.'

Harry heard Anderson laugh.

'Like she's going to say anything else.'

Harry was about to say something, but Gordy turned away from him and walked over to Anderson. She leaned in close enough to force him to lean back.

'If I were you, I'd keep church-mouse quiet,' she said.

'But—'

Gordy cut him off.

'We're going to investigate this properly, find out what really happened. And let me tell you right now that if we discover your accusations are tissue-thin, that you made this up and accused not only Harry 's brother, but one of my colleagues, of assault, there isn't a hole deep or dark enough you'll be able to hide in, I promise you that.'

Harry saw Anderson's confidence seep from him, his shoulders sagging, worry breaking through as nervous twitches on his face.

Gordy left Anderson and walked back over to Harry . She stood in front of him, a hand resting on his arm.

'You have to leave this with me,' she said. 'Trust me, okay?'

'You know I do,' Harry said.

He knew Gordy was right. But that didn't stop him from worrying. Since moving to the Dales, completing his probation after his time in prison, Ben had been doing so well. He had a job, a life with Liz, and was happy like Harry had never seen him before. Now, though, Harry was worried that something like this could send him spiralling.

'I'll be off, then,' Anderson said, now at the office door. 'I'll be expecting a call about all of this, and soon. And you'll be hearing from my solicitor.'

He slipped out of the room, quiet as a snake.

Harry was suddenly weary.

'So, now that you're back from the reunion, any plans for the evening?' Gordy asked.

'I'd head home, but I don't actually have one yet,' Harry said, with a faint laugh.

'Then give Grace a call and have her come over,' Gordy suggested. 'Bonfire Night, remember? Liz'll be bringing Ben over, I'm sure. And everyone will be there.'

Before Harry could answer, Drake said, 'Think I'll give it a miss, if that's okay. I'll get myself back to the bed and breakfast, maybe have a look through my files, think on things a bit.'

With the DCI gone, Harry was tempted to follow suit. But then he remembered Matt and the effort the team and even Ben had put in to replace the missing fireworks. He pulled out his phone and called Grace.

CHAPTER FORTY

Dave Calvert was standing behind a small stall and selling hotdogs.

'Is this your new plan, then?' Harry asked. 'Give up the offshore life to run a café?'

Dave laughed, handing over two hotdogs for Harry and Grace.

'Not a chance of it,' he said. 'I've already eaten a dozen of the buggers myself this evening; can you imagine the size I'd be if I did this full time?'

'And you're not exactly small now, are you?' Grace smiled.

Dave laughed even louder.

'Right, move along, you two; I've customers to serve.' Harry and Grace turned away from the stall, but Dave called after them. 'Keep me posted on the housewarming, Harry .'

The bonfire was held in a field on the edge of Hawes and as far as Harry could tell, most of the population of the small market town, and of Gayle, must have turned up. Families huddled together in the fire-lit darkness, staring into the flames reaching up to toast the sky. The air was rich with the smell of burning wood, barbequed sausages, and jacket potatoes, all of it resting gently in air cold enough to warrant bobble hats and thick coats wherever he looked.

'When do the fireworks start, then?' Harry asked.

Grace pointed away from the bonfire to an area cordoned off with tape.

'Shouldn't be too long now,' she said. 'May as well head over and see how they're getting on setting up.'

Wandering across the field, Harry found himself being stopped along the way for brief chats with people he recognised but wasn't always able to put a name to. It seemed that the entire town not only now knew where he was moving to, but that something was going on. Kind of hard to miss the blue police tape around the house, though, Harry thought.

What touched him, though, was the genuine warmth of everyone he spoke to, whether or not he knew them well. Handshakes were given, they asked after Smudge, wished Harry well, said how good it was to see him and Grace. He'd been there maybe two years at a push, but as he walked across the field it felt as though he'd been there his whole life. With every step he took, that sense of being home grew stronger, until they came to the site of the fireworks and saw the silhouette of Matt above whom a bright light flashed, making him look like a rubbish lighthouse.

'Now then, Harry ,' said a woman close by, and Harry turned to see Matt's wife, Joan looking up at him from her wheelchair. She was wrapped in numerous blankets and looked to be the warmest person in the field. Strapped to her chest by some kind of cunning system of straps and blanket, was their daughter, Mary Anne. The only flesh Harry could make out was the tiniest of noses above a little mouth. On her head was clasped a pair of ear defenders.

'She's fast asleep,' Joan said. 'Frankly, she'll sleep through anything now, which is quite the change from those first few weeks, I can tell you.'

Grace reached out and gently held one of Mary's bootie-clad feet.

'She's beautiful.'

Joan smiled.

'She is.'

Harry looked at the mud-covered wheels of the chair.

'You okay, there?' he asked. 'Doesn't look like you're going to be moving without a shove.'

'I'm grand,' Joan said. 'I've a good view from here. Matt'll sort me out if I need to move or anything, but I'm good. Anyway, how are you?'

Harry saw the concern in Joan's eyes.

'Well, I've had better weeks,' he said. 'But things'll get sorted, I'm sure.'

'If you need anything, you know where we are,' Joan said. Then she looked up at Grace and added, 'If you're ever tired of him getting under your feet, just throw him our way. We've a spare room and a dry shed.'

A shadow cast itself over Harry , Grace, and Joan as Matt strode over.

'Didn't think you'd make it,' Matt said.

'You're all set, then?' Harry asked.

Matt gave a nod.

'Raised more than enough to put on a bit of a show. Though I hope you're not expecting too much.'

'Is it just you?'

'Jim's helping as well,' Matt said, pointing at a figure still standing over by the fireworks. 'The whole team's here, I think. Gordy's on duty, so has to be, really. Can't be working and not show your face at this kind of community event; that's not how it works round here. How's Ben?'

'You heard?'

'The Dales, remember?' Matt said.

Harry explained what had happened, then heard a laugh and turned to see Ben walking towards them with Liz. He gave them a wave.

'Jen's over by the hotdogs,' Matt said, looking past Harry . 'And here comes Jadyn. And he's not alone ...'

At this, Harry turned to see the Okri family striding over. Mrs Okri raised a hand and waved enthusiastically.

'She wants us to go to dinner with them,' he said, leaning over to Grace.

Grace wasn't given a chance to respond as they were then surrounded.

'Mr Grimm,' said Jadyn's dad, holding out his hand to shake Harry 's. 'We've been hearing all about you and the team, and the work you do. We are impressed.'

'Yes, Jadyn is in a good place here,' agreed Jadyn's mum. 'We are sorry, though, that we haven't been able to have that meal with you to hear more about it and how he's doing.'

'Sorry about that,' said Harry . 'It's been a busy week. But I can assure you that your son is doing tremendously. He's a very important member of the team.'

Harry noticed then that Jadyn was staring at him.

'I hear the visit to the hospital went well,' Harry said. Then he added for the benefit of his parents, 'You did some really good work. I'm very impressed.'

He felt Grace's hand squeeze his own at that.

'Actually,' said Jadyn, 'and I know neither of us are at work, but can I have a quick word?'

'Now?'

Jadyn gave a nod.

Making their excuses, Harry led Jadyn away from the others.

'So, what's this about, then?' he asked.

Jadyn pulled an evidence bag from his pocket.

'The missing fireworks,' he said.

'What about them?'

Jadyn quickly went through what had happened the night before.

'And I found this,' he said, and lifted up the evidence bag.

Inside, Harry saw a pale blue tube.

'And what's that, then?'

'It's a disposable vape pen,' Jadyn said. 'It was on the ground where the fireworks had been set off. I thought I smelled it as we chased after them before they hid in the graveyard.'

Harry took hold of the bag.

'We can send this to Sowerby. It may take a while for her to get to it, though; firework theft is going to be pushed down the list of things to do.'

'I don't think we need to,' Jadyn said. 'I know whose it is.'

'What? How?'

'I double-checked as well, just to make sure, but I don't know what to do about it. So, that's why I'm asking you.'

'Asking me what, exactly?' said Harry .

'What I should do about whose it is,' Jadyn said. 'Because, well, it's a little awkward, isn't it?'

Harry remembered something then, from Saturday, and he had a feeling that he knew what Jadyn was talking about. And if he did, then *a little awkward* was a huge understatement.

'How sure are you?' Harry asked.

'Very,' said Jadyn. 'I checked her coat pockets, asked her, too, and she said she'd lost it.'

Harry handed the evidence bag back to the constable.

'This is your call,' he said. 'Have you spoken with the DS?'

'Not yet, no,' Jadyn said.

Harry thought for a moment. On the one hand, crime was crime, no matter how you looked at it, and you couldn't let people get away with it. On the other hand, the theft of a few fireworks wasn't headline news. Harry had dealt with thefts between disgruntled neighbours, disputes which had been settled outside of the courts with the help of mediation as often as they had in the courts themselves. He had a suspicion that there was more going on here than they knew, a story behind what had been done, and he was already leaning towards the thought that someone was looking for attention.

'Here's what we'll do,' Harry said. 'Right now, you have suspicions and possible evidence, but it's not going to hold up under much scrutiny, is it? So, I'll have a quick word with Matt tomorrow morning first thing. You keep quiet for the moment. And then we'll see if we can't work out the best way to deal with it.'

'You sure, Boss?' Jadyn asked.

Harry rested a hand on the young constable's shoulder.

'It's either that or you go over there now and bring your sister in for questioning, which to my mind is a little heavy-handed, all things considered.'

Jadyn shook his head.

'I don't understand it,' he said. 'Why would she do it in the first place?'

Harry looked over at Jadyn's family. His parents were both staring at them and, standing a good few steps away from them now, and all on her own, was Jadyn's sister, gazing down at the screen of her phone.

'I'll leave you to think on that,' he said, and saw Matt heading back over to Jim and the fireworks. 'Now, how about we head over and join them?'

Jadyn gave a nod and Harry led him back over to the small gathering. Jen was there, too, now, and Harry noticed that she smiled when she saw Jadyn and went over to stand with him.

Jadyn's mum came over.

'That looked very serious,' she said. 'Is everything okay with Jadyn?'

'Mrs Okri,' Harry said, 'I can honestly say that I have never been less worried about someone in my entire life. Your son is a superb police constable. If I'd had any doubts previously, I can assure you that I believe he has a bright future ahead of him.'

A smile lit up her face almost as much as the first explosion of fireworks, as Matt and Jim began the display.

Harry moved over to Grace, who reached out and put her arm in his. Then a rocket shot up into the sky to explode overhead, and Harry was fairly sure that in the distance he saw Matt's silhouette do a little dance and a fist pump in the air.

CHAPTER FORTY-ONE

When Harry walked into the office in Hawes, yawning as he went and with Smudge at his feet, all eyes turned to him, and conversations stalled on the partially raised rims of mugs of tea. Smudge slinked off to say hello to Fly.

'Morning,' he said, noticing with a little concern that the whole team was there except for Jadyn. 'How's everyone today after the fireworks?'

Gordy came over.

'You look like you've not slept a wink.'

Harry felt his phone buzz in his pocket and saw Ed's number on the screen. He'd give him a ring later and ignored the call.

'I didn't,' he said.

His mind had been busy all night, and he'd tossed and turned to the point where he'd even got up and made himself a cup of tea.

His phone buzzed again. It was still Ed. Harry thought back to their minor altercation in the cemetery the day before and wondered if that was why Ed was calling him. If it was, now was not the time, and he'd deal with it later. If it wasn't, then he doubted it mattered.

'I think you're a wee bit confused,' Gordy said, as Harry turned off his phone so as to not be interrupted by it again. 'You see, this here is the office, and you and that daft dog of yours are supposed to be at home.'

'Bit difficult when it's still a crime scene,' Harry said.

'You know exactly what I mean, and don't go pretending that you don't.'

Harry noticed a firm edge to Gordy's voice.

'Drake called me,' he said. 'He's heading home later and asked if I could come in, in an advisory capacity, that kind of thing. You won't even know I'm here.'

Gordy laughed at that.

'Well yes, because you're well known for just fading into the background, aren't you?'

Harry heard the office door open behind him and in walked Drake, his walking stick making a dull thud on the floor with each step.

'I hear you're to blame for this,' Gordy said, staring at the man.

'I am, indeed,' Drake said.

'Then if you don't mind, I suggest we get on with things right away so that he doesn't have to be here any longer than necessary.'

Harry went to stand at the front of the room by the board, only to realise he wasn't there to lead the meeting. So, instead, he sat down next to Matt, remembering his chat with Constable Okri the previous evening.

'Any idea where Jadyn is?' he asked quietly.

'Said he was going to be a little late,' answered Matt. 'Had something to sort out first. I don't think he'll be long. Why? Is everything okay?'

'I need to have a chat with you about that, once we're done here,' Harry said, then turned his attention to Gordy who took the floor.

Jen stood up.

'I'll stand in for Jadyn,' she said, and headed over to the board to take notes if necessary.

'Right then,' Gordy said, 'and even though we've all been over it and know what's happened, I'll give a quick recap on what happened over the weekend.'

As Gordy continued to speak, running through the events of the murder of his own father, Harry 's mind refused to sit still. From his own discovery of the body and his subsequent meeting with Sowerby, right through to being taken off the case and heading off to the not-entirely normal or enjoyable reunion, there was almost too much to think about. So, he did his best to dial back into the meeting to hear Drake talking.

'PC Okri and DC Blades had a useful visit to the hospital.'

'How's that, then?' Harry asked. 'We know how he escaped, then, do we?'

'It was definitely organised,' said Jen. 'Someone let off a couple of smoke canisters, which set off a fire alarm, causing panic. In the ensuing chaos, your father slipped the net.'

'What about CCTV?'

'Nothing,' Jen said, shaking her head. 'It's not the failsafe everyone thinks it is, is it? We got hold of the canisters, though, and they're with forensics, just to see if we can get anything from them.'

'Sounds like we're clutching at straws.'

'We've some photos as well,' Jen added, and after a quick shuffle through a file, handed them over.

The photos showed a green canister. Written on it in scuffed white lettering were the words *Grenade Hand Smoke Screening L132A1*. Harry recognised it immediately.

'Military issue,' he said. 'Used a fair few myself in my time.'

'Thought that might be the case,' Jen said.

'You can only get your hands on these if you're actually in the military,' said Harry . 'What else did you learn? What about the officers who were supposed to be looking after him?'

Jen went to answer, but there was a knock at the door and in walked Jadyn. He looked over and saw Harry .

'Sorry I'm late,' he said. 'Had to sort something out. Boss, you got a minute?'

Harry shook his head.

'Can it wait?'

'Not really, no,' Jadyn said. 'Please?'

Harry stood up and followed Jadyn out into the entrance hall of the community centre.

'Through here,' Jadyn said, and before Harry could argue, headed off to the interview room. Harry followed him inside to find Jadyn's sister, Isioma, sitting at the table.

'Ah,' said Harry .

Isioma, he noticed, was for once not staring at her mobile phone. Instead, she looked up at him and said, 'Hi.' Her voice was quiet, as though she hadn't really meant to speak at all.

Harry gestured to the seat opposite Isioma on the other side of the table and Jadyn sat down. He then grabbed himself another chair from over by the wall.

'So, then,' he said, and left it at that. If there was explaining to be done, it certainly wasn't going to be by him.

Jadyn said, 'Isioma has admitted to taking the fireworks.'

'Sorry,' Isioma said, barely audible.

Harry sat forward.

'Saying sorry doesn't make this all go away,' he said.

'I know,' said Jadyn.

'I was talking to your sister.'

Harry looked at Isioma.

'I'm fairly sure I don't need to explain to you the serious nature of what you did. Not just the theft, either, but letting those fireworks off in a public place. You were very lucky no one was hurt.'

'It was just a couple of rockets,' Isioma said, speaking for the first time.

'It was the whole box, Izzy,' said Jadyn. 'What were you thinking?'

'I wasn't thinking,' she said.

'Then why do it?'

'I told you why, didn't I?'

Jadyn sighed.

Important though this was, Harry felt that where he really should be was back in the office.

He stood up.

'You know, I think there's someone you should speak to,' he said. 'Wait here a moment ...'

Harry opened the door to the office and called Matt over.

'Everything alright?'

Harry nodded back down the hallway towards the interview room.

'Jadyn's in there,' he said. 'That thing I said I needed to talk to you about? Well, he's made progress with that fireworks theft.'

Matt's eyes went wide.

'Has he, now? Best I get in there, then, right, and see what's what.'

'You had,' said Harry , 'and I'll leave it to you. I'll support whatever your decision is with how things should progress from this point forward.'

Matt frowned.

'That sounds ominous.'

Harry smiled.

'I'm sure you'll be fine,' he said, then left the DS to head off to meet Jadyn and his sister, as he took himself back into the meeting room.

Inside, Harry found Drake had taken centre stage.

'So, where are we?' he asked, taking a seat again.

Smudge came over and rested her head softly in his lap.

'We're at that point on a map where all the roads disappear and there's just the words *Unexplored Territory* written across it instead,' said Drake.

Harry sat down.

'We were talking about smoke grenades.'

Gordy said, 'We've been looking at everything we've got on what happened in Gayle, comparing it with the other cases Drake has information on. There are similarities, but there are also stark differences.'

'One of those being that this happened in my house,' said Harry .

'Drake leaned back to rest himself on a table.

'All those other cases of mine, there was no torture, nothing like that at all,' he said. 'The point was that the confession was given freely, the victim essentially responsible for their own demise. I just can't fathom why the killer took things to such a violent level.'

Harry had no idea where this was going, but he knew that he didn't like it. A part of him had actually hoped, with Drake's arrival, that perhaps the investigation would move quickly and in a very clear direction, particularly with him being forced by circumstances to not be a part of it. However, it seemed that the opposite was true.

'What's to fathom?' he asked. 'If there's someone out there who's decided it's their job to go around killing criminals, then that's what it is, isn't it? No point trying to dress it up as anything else. I'm sure they have, in their own mind, but it's still murder, regardless of who ends up dead. Maybe they just got carried away.'

'There's more than that here, Grimm, and you know it. We all do.'

'I need you to get to the point, Drake,' he said.

'I am. And the point I'm getting to, Grimm, is that I'm worried. In fact, I think we should all be worried.'

'Give me specifics.'

Drake paused, rubbed his chin.

'He thinks we have a copycat,' said Jim.

Harry snapped around to look at the PCSO.

'A what now? So, we've got two killers, is that it?'

Drake said, 'I think someone was inspired by what I've been looking into, to have a go themselves, crazy though that sounds.'

'And it does,' said Harry . 'But why? What's the motive?'

Drake gave a shrug.

'It's always a fear that someone else will begin their own personal crusade as it were, and that's why I've done my damnedest to keep this out of the eyes of the press as best as I can, but the story is out there, Grimm, if you want to find it.'

'Where, exactly?' Harry asked, though he wasn't exactly listening at that moment. Something Drake had just said was bothering him, but he couldn't work out what or why.

'Not the broadsheets or anything like that,' Drake said, and Harry tuned in again. 'Mainly because I've tried to play this as being a weird conspiracy. Anyone comes in asking questions, it's dismissed, and the deaths are all easily explained as individual events rather than related to each other. But there's only so much you can do, and a few keen eyes have seen similarities, the confessions mainly.'

'The one found in the stomach, you mean?' said Liz.

Drake gave a nod.

'When I read through the forensics report, it just didn't match. No surprise really, as the way the confession ends up in the body has never been mentioned anywhere that would get out into the public domain. So, they wouldn't know, would they, the killer I mean, how it was done?'

'His stomach was cut open,' Harry said. 'That's how it was done.'

'To your father, yes, but not to the others,' Drake replied.

'I'm not following.'

'With all of the others, it was inserted down the throat post-mortem,' Drake said. 'We're assuming with the aid of a long, thin pole of some kind. But they weren't cut open, and that's the key point.'

'Maybe the killer got carried away,' said Jim. 'That happens, doesn't it?'

'They weren't tortured either,' said Drake said. 'They wrote the confession, then killed themselves, each and every one of them. Until we get to your father, that is, where he's burned, cut, deboned, and castrated. And I think it's safe to say he didn't do any of that to himself, did he?'

Right then, Harry had an urge to just leave, to walk out into the rest of the day and get lost somewhere high on the hills. His destination didn't matter, just anywhere that wasn't right here, right now, talking about this.

'Plus, there's the inescapable fact that your father was killed in your house. That's the strangest thing of all, really, because it's so personal. The killer knew when and where you were moving, they stole the keys from the estate agent, drove your father to your house, walked him inside, and the rest you know. And soil samples taken from footprints found at both crime scenes match.'

'I can't get excited about soil.'

'Well, it wasn't just any soil, it was compost and vermiculite, which is a little more specific.'

'I'm not exactly a gardener,' said Harry .

Gordy piped up with, 'It's good for house plants, apparently; mushrooms, that kind of thing.'

'Mushrooms?'

'All you need is a few clean jam jars, a dark space, and you're good to go.'

'You learn something every day,' said Harry , staring at the board, looking for details of what he'd learned from Sowerby.

'Psilocybin,' he said, finding it. 'That was found in his system, along with MDMA and tranexamic acid.'

Drake, Harry noticed, was staring at him with a blank look.

'Psilocybin? Magic mushrooms?' he said. 'Quite the cocktail if it's mixed with Speed.'

'The acid, you mean.'

'The MDMA,' said Harry . 'The tranexamic acid slowed the bleeding.'

'Yes, of course.'

Harry wondered if Drake was growing tired of the whole investigation, which would explain his confusion over the drugs. He wasn't the only one.

Harry then looked at the photos of what had been done to his father.

'Something catch your eye?' Gordy asked.

Harry shook his head.

'Right now, I think I see everything and nothing,' he said. 'That feather still makes no sense to me. The torture, the confession; it doesn't even look like he wrote the damned thing.' He leaned closer and stared harder. No, there was something, wasn't there? About the body, what had been done to it. But what? Why could he still not see it?

'Why would someone kill your father?' Jen asked, knocking Harry from his thoughts.

'Plenty of reasons,' Harry answered. 'Trust me.'

'No, what I mean is, why do all this to him in your house? That's what this all keeps coming back to, doesn't it?'

'Hard to ignore it, really, isn't it?'

Jen gave a nod.

'Well, whoever did it, they certainly weren't doing it for my benefit,' Harry said. 'I just wanted him to go to prison for a very, very long time. I'd never wish any of this on anyone, not even him.'

Harry stood up.

'I think we need a break,' he said.

Everyone agreed, and soon the kettle was on. He wondered how things were going with Matt, Jadyn, and Isioma, but when he went through to check, he found the room empty. Taking that as a good sign, he walked back into the office for a mug of tea. Remembering the call from Ed he'd ignored earlier, he pulled out his phone. Turning it on, he saw that Ed had sent him a message and he opened it.

The words hit Harry with such force he stumbled a little, falling into a chair.

'Still tired from that reunion?' Gordy asked, coming over.

Harry didn't answer; the message from Ed, what it was telling him, he just couldn't take in, not on top of everything else.

'Harry ? Is everything okay?'

Harry shook his head.

'No, it isn't,' he said, and again read what Ed had sent him: *Harry , Andy's dead. Call me.*

CHAPTER FORTY-TWO

HARRY STOOD UP.

'I need a minute,' he said, and left the office, heading outside. The day was grey and cold, but he didn't notice, couldn't feel anything, the shock of Ed's message leaving him numb.

He tried to call back, but couldn't get through. Tried again; no answer. So he sent a message, then another, asking for more information, to know what happened. But no reply came.

'What's happened, Harry ?'

Gordy had followed him out and was now standing at his side.

Harry stared into the middle distance, searching for some sense in all of this, as though out there somewhere a wraith would come to him baring whispers for him alone.

'The reunion,' he said.

'With your old Parachute Regiment mates?'

'Three mates I've not seen in two decades: Ed, Andy, and Ant. And now Andy's dead. Ed found him.'

Harry heard Gordy take a sharp breath.

'What happened?'

Harry shook his head.

'Ed and me, we went to the cemetery, but Andy never turned up. Ed went round to check, see if he was okay. Clearly, he wasn't.

It was Ed who called. I've tried calling back, but there's no answer. I've left a message.'

'Harry , I'm so sorry,' said Gordy.

Harry wasn't really listening. He lifted his eyes to the bleak, drab emptiness of the sky, and wanted to throw himself into it and drown.

'There were six of us,' he said. 'Me, Ed, Andy, Ant, and Tak, with Ricky coming along for the ride as well. We were out on patrol in two WMIK Land Rovers. We'd been sent to clear through some buildings in a compound out in the middle of nowhere. We'd had reports in of some insurgents using it to operate from.'

'WMIK?'

'Weapons Mount Instillation Kit,' Harry explained. 'Between us, we had two Fifty-cal heavy machine guns, a 40mm grenade machine gun, and two general purpose machine guns, plus the usual personal weapons we all carried.'

'Sounds terrifying.'

'I guess.'

Harry fell silent again as he tried to bar the door in his mind to that day, but he was weaker now, and the news from Ed had only weakened him further.

'We'd headed out from the FOB, the forward operating base, to get the job done. The compound didn't look like anything out of the ordinary, not that we would've been worried even if it was; with the firepower we had to hand, we were pretty formidable.'

Gordy stayed quiet for a moment.

'The compound seemed quiet,' Harry said. 'Empty. So, we drove in, parked up, then went through the buildings, clearing them as we went. They were small, and there was only three, maybe four to check out. Ant was on point, with that shotgun of his taking off any door hinges. Ricky stayed with the vehicles and gave us cover with the Fifty-cal. And everything was doing fine until we came to the last building.'

'What happened?' Gordy asked.

Harry could see it all, images racing through his mind like he was there once more. He could smell the desert, the dust, the blood.

'Ant dealt with the door and we were in,' Harry said. 'Like all the others, the building was empty. Just a table and chairs, some kind of stove in the wall, a bed. A couple of National Geographics in the corner as well, would you believe? Then, as I went to say that the place was clear, next thing I know, I'm flying through the air.'

'Bomb?'

'IED.'

'The one that injured you?'

Harry gave a nod.

'There was no sound, though, not right then. Everything was quiet. It was like all noise had been sucked out of the moment, and the world just sort of swirled and twisted around me until I hit the ground.'

'Sounds terrifying, Harry ,' said Gordy. 'I can't even begin to imagine it.'

'When I came to, the building was gone. The roof was, anyway, and a couple of walls. I was outside the building, my head ringing. My face was a mess, not that I knew it right then, though; I had my team to think about. Adrenaline kicks in, your training takes over, you're on autopilot.'

The door in Harry 's mind cracked and splintered, and the memories of that day crashed in.

'I heard Ricky open up with the Fifty-cal; it's a sound you never really forget. Amazingly, everyone was okay; somehow the explosion had knocked us all clear of the building. Well, everyone except for Tak, who was buried in dust and rubble and came out of it swearing and bloody and very, very angry.'

Harry laughed then, the memory of Tak's dust-covered face pushing out of the ruined building.

'So, who was Ricky shooting at, then?' Gordy asked. 'You said this was an IED.'

'It was,' said Harry . 'But it was also an ambush. The

compound was clear, but the local area clearly wasn't. The compound became a kill zone. We weren't meant to escape.'

'They'd been hiding, then?'

'Doesn't take much in a place like that, and it wasn't like we could check every square metre of desert just in case someone had dug a hole to hide in.'

'What did you do?'

Harry really didn't want to remember any of it, but he had no choice now.

'Ed—he's the one who just sent me the message—he sprinted over to the second Land Rover, Tak charging after him to get on the GPMG. Ant jumped into the back and was on with the GMG. A few seconds later, an RPG slammed into it.'

'Bloody hell, Harry ...'

'That's exactly what it was,' Harry said. 'They opened up on us with everything they had. There was sod all for cover, just some crappy mud walls, most of which had been damaged by the blast, a few rocks, and they were everywhere, dug in well. I was bleeding heavily, could hardly see for the blood.'

'What did you do?'

'I was on the GPMG in the other Land Rover with Ricky, when the RPG happened,' Harry explained. 'I don't think they'd expected us to survive the explosion, but that's the trouble with homemade stuff; IEDs aren't exactly that reliable. So, we returned fire, lit the place up. Unless you've been in a firefight, really experienced close-quarter combat, you've no frame of reference. I can't explain it. It's like nothing else; the terror, the exhilaration, everything's so vivid and immediate and you're just firing and all you can think about is taking it to the enemy. We had to get out, though.'

'You said one of your men was hit by an RPG,' said Gordy.

'Ant was a mess. Both legs smashed to pieces, an arm taken off. But he was screaming, so he was alive. That's always a good sign, you see? It's the quiet ones you have to worry about; they're fading or already so far gone there's nowt you can do about it.'

'What about the others?'

Harry closed his eyes. He was sharing an edited version of what had happened, because the true horror of it he couldn't let slip past his lips.

'Andy ended up shot in the bollocks,' Harry said, with a laugh absolutely devoid of all humour. 'Ed I had to half drag, half kick out of the burning Land Rover. He lost a couple of fingers, though God knows how he didn't actually lose his whole arm. While I was doing that, Ricky was still on with the GMG. He emptied it, which is no small task, I can assure you. But that's how hot the battle was; we had to give them everything we had if we were to get out of there. And that surviving Land Rover was our only hope. So, when the GMG ran dry, Ricky was out with his rifle, laying down fire with the rest of us, yelling at us to get over to him so we could just get the hell out of there sharpish.'

Harry paused, breathed slow and deep, squeezed his eyes shut.

'When you're in that situation, it's impossible to keep an eye on every possible corner, every line of attack. Somehow, despite us taking the fight to the enemy as best we could, a couple of them sneaked up behind and grabbed Ricky, dragged him off in all the confusion, the smoke, the flames, rounds flying everywhere. When it happened, I was still trying to sort Ant's injuries. I could hardly see what I was doing because of the blood in my eyes from my own injuries. I had Ed, Andy, and Tak keeping back what we thought was the rest of the attacking force with suppressing fire and trying to call for backup, to get us the hell out of there.'

'Ricky was kidnapped, then?' Gordy asked.

'That was their plan, anyway,' said Harry . 'Had to be. And that was everyone's biggest fear, really, to be taken by the enemy and then end up as the star of your very own horror movie for the evening news. I had Ant stabilised though, realised what had happened, and went off after them.'

Harry fell quiet again, gathering himself for the end of the story. The grey clouds seemed to have grown closer somehow, like they were leaning in to listen for themselves.

'Backup came quicker than anyone expected, including the enemy. They had a choice: stay and die or get the hell out of there. But when I got to Ricky, it was already too late; rather than take him with them, they'd ...'

Harry couldn't, wouldn't, say anymore, not to anyone. What they'd done to Ricky, it hadn't taken long, and their blades must've been sharp as razors.

'By the time it was all over, we had one dead, the rest of us badly injured, one very seriously. One of the vehicles was completely blown to shit, the other had its tyres shredded and the engine peppered with enough rounds to put it out of action for days. We were medevaced out. I didn't think Ant would survive, to be honest, but he did. He's a fighter, wouldn't give them the satisfaction of it. Ed and Andy were patched up, and, well, everyone can see what happened to me, can't they? I just had new scars to add to the old.'

'Sounds like you were lucky to get out of there at all.'

At this, Harry swung round to face Gordy.

'Lucky? Ricky never made it. Tak became yet another PTSD statistic, taking his own life a few months after we returned home. Ant's now starving himself to death, and his wife is in the middle of a nervous breakdown, taking drugs to see her way through, and apparently making lots of jam. Ed's wife left him because his nightmares were violent flashbacks that he was acting out in the middle of the night. And Andy ... Well, Andy's now dead. All I did was manage to survive, that's all; luck had nothing to do with it.'

Harry stopped speaking.

'You should take a moment,' Gordy said. 'You're on leave, remember?'

Harry shook his head, pointed back over at the community centre.

'We should get back in there.'

Gordy rested a hand on Harry 's shoulder.

'You shouldn't even be here, you hear?'

With that, Gordy left Harry on his own. He considered

following her, but instead walked down the lane and into Hawes marketplace. It was busy, and he found himself envying people for their normal lives, busying themselves with little more than grabbing a few groceries, working a nine-to-five.

But who really has a normal life? he thought. Everyone has their own traumas, their own histories, and learning to live with it was just a part of the everyday.

Movement caught his eye, and he saw Matt and Jadyn walking towards him.

'Grabbing some fresh air, then?' Matt asked.

'It's free,' Harry replied, then looked at Jadyn. 'Well?'

'Izzy's with Mum and Dad,' he said. 'They've a lot to talk about.'

'I can well imagine that they have.'

Matt said, 'We had a little chat.'

'Why did she do it?' Harry asked.

'Tried to blame me to start with,' said Jadyn. 'Tired of hearing Mum and Dad always talking about me, about what I was doing. Which is quite the surprise, I don't mind admitting.'

'What about your other brother and sister?'

'That was next,' said Matt. 'I think she was feeling a little left out.'

Harry shook his head in disbelief.

'So, she thought the best way to get attention was to pinch some fireworks?'

'It worked.'

Matt had a point, Harry thought.

'Well, she's going to be out of pocket for a while, paying for them,' Matt said. 'That's what they're talking about now. And I've suggested that Jadyn's parents maybe stop focussing on our police constable here, and instead turn their attention to the child they've still got at home.'

'And how did they take that?' Harry asked.

Thinking about Jadyn's parents, he wasn't entirely sure that a suggestion from the not-exactly-subtle Matt Dinsdale would have gone down all that well.

'We'll see,' Matt said, more than a little cryptically. 'Now, are you coming back in?'

'In a while,' Harry said. 'Need to make a call.'

Matt and Jadyn headed into the office and Harry had another go at calling Ed. Ed answered almost immediately, his voice rough and torn.

'Harry ? I called you, but you didn't answer, and I didn't know what to do, so I called emergency services, and then I called you again and I sent you that message—'

'Slow down,' Harry said. 'Tell me what happened.'

'But I called and there was no answer and I didn't know what to do. So, I went for a walk, and when I came back I realised I'd lost my phone, so I went out to look for it, but I found it when I came home, and—'

'Ed,' Harry said, keeping his voice calm. 'What happened to Andy?'

Harry heard Ed choke back what sounded like a cry, forcing it back down inside, controlling his breathing to calm himself down.

'After we were done at the cemetery, I called him,' Ed said. 'No answer. I kept calling, all the way home.'

'Bit of a long walk, that,' Harry said.

'Did me good. Sorry about ... Well, you know.'

'I do. Don't worry about it.'

'You kicked me in the bollocks,' Ed said.

'Had to stop you from strangling me somehow.' Harry heard a faint laugh down the phone. 'I'm guessing you went round to check up on him.'

'I'd still heard nothing when I got home. I left it, tried again this morning, still nothing. So, I jumped in my car and headed over. He was drinking a fair bit the night before, wasn't he? You must've noticed that hipflask of his. Thought he was probably just hungover to hell and had taken the day off to recover; probably not a great look for a vicar.'

'Then what?'

'Knocked at the door, not a thing. House seemed dead, except there was this radio blaring, so I knew he was in. Ended up round the back, found that the door was open, and let myself in.'

Harry let Ed keep talking.

'I found him,' Ed said, 'in his study. I'm guessing that's what it was, all those books everywhere, and a desk. And there he was, Harry , just sitting there, you know? Staring up at the ceiling.'

'You mean he just died in his chair?' Harry asked.

'He was in his chair and that's where he died,' said Ed. 'He was half naked, just sitting there in his shirt, and ...'

Ed's voice broke.

'In your own time, Ed,' said Harry . 'Just take your time.'

'I ... I don't know if he'd drunk too much or what, but it still doesn't make sense, what he did to himself. I don't know how he could. The pain of it just doesn't bear thinking about. Maybe the booze helped, I don't know. Probably, right? Two empty vodka bottles were lying on the floor.'

'Ed,' Harry said, 'what did Andy do?'

'He ... No, I can't say it, it's ...'

'Ed ...'

'I panicked, Harry . Don't know why. I just saw Andy and all I could think was that they'd think it was me, wouldn't they? So ... So, I took photos, just in case. Don't know if I should've or not, and I know it's a crime scene and I've probably messed it up, but I took photos because I wanted to make sure I had evidence of it, of what had happened, so that I could prove that it wasn't me who did it, because it wasn't, Harry , it wasn't! And they'll think that, won't they? They'll think it was me.'

Ed was making no sense. Harry went to ask Ed to try and explain a little better what happened, when his phone buzzed.

'I've just sent them to you,' Ed said. 'The photos. All of them. Then I can delete them, can't I? I don't want them on my phone.'

Harry opened the images. Andy was, as Ed had described, half naked in his chair, staring at the ceiling. He saw bottles of vodka, an empty mug, trousers soaked with blood at the crotch. He also saw something stuck in Andy's mouth and zoomed in for a closer look.

'Ed?'

'Yes?'

'You said Andy was like this when you arrived, is that right?'

'I didn't touch anything, Harry ,' Ed said. 'I promise you, I didn't. He was just there, dead like that. Why? Why would he do that? What does it mean?'

'Where are you now?' Harry asked.

'Home,' Ed replied. 'And I'm not going anywhere, either, I can promise you that. I'm going to get so drunk that everything I've seen today will be erased from my memory for good.'

'No, you're not,' said Harry , his mind racing now, trying to catch up with something he still didn't fully understand. 'Do you have anywhere you can go that isn't your flat?'

'What? How do you mean?'

'I need you to get out of there, right now. Do you still have a grab bag?'

'Somewhere, yes,' Ed said. 'Used to always have it by the door, but I moved it. It'll be under the stairs.'

'Good. Get it. I need you to pack enough stuff to last you a few days and go.'

'What?'

'I think you're in danger. Ant and Amy, too. I don't know why, or who's responsible yet.'

'I can phone Amy and Ant,' Ed said.

'I'll do that as soon as we're done talking. Where can you go?'

'I don't have anywhere to go. Driving for a living doesn't really help with making friends.'

'What about a hotel, a bed and breakfast? Just somewhere that isn't home, somewhere anonymous.'

'You've still not told me why, Harry . What's this about? Because it's not just about Andy, is it? It can't be. What's going on?'

'Enough talk,' Harry said. 'Grab your stuff, everything you

think you'll need—sleeping bag, stove, anything—and just go, okay?'

'If you say so.'

'I do.'

Ed laughed.

'Seems we really do still take orders from you, doesn't it?' he said.

'Move it, Ed,' Harry said, killing the call and then headed back into the office.

CHAPTER FORTY-THREE

Gordy met Harry at the door, Drake with her.

'You really don't have to be here,' she said. 'Not after what happened. It's fine.'

'Yes, I do and no, it isn't,' Harry said. 'Nothing is. Look ...'

Harry lifted his phone to show them what was on the screen, zooming in close on Andy's mouth, doing his best to ignore everything else, the damage caused, the blood.

'Good God, man ...'

'That's Andy,' Harry said. 'I wasn't sure until I zoomed in, but that's what I think it is, isn't it?'

'It's a feather,' said Drake.

'A white feather, like the one found in my father's mouth.' Harry turned to stare at Jadyn and now Jen's handiwork on the board: the notes, the photos, everything. He needed to check on Ant and Amy. He pulled up Amy's number on his phone. There was no answer, just voicemail. He hung up and tried again.

'Come on, Amy, pick up the phone, damn it.'

Once again, it went through to voicemail.

'No answer?' asked Drake.

Harry shook his head, tried once again, this time he left a message.

He looked at Drake and Gordy. 'I know I'm not part of this investigation, but I'm calling this in. We need someone to go round there and check they're okay.'

'You sure you're not jumping the gun here?' Drake asked.

'I never jump the gun,' said Harry , and rang emergency services. When that was done, he had another try with Amy's number, then turned to Drake and Gordy.

'They've got my number now,' he said. 'They'll keep me posted.'

Drake leaned on his walking stick to push himself up onto his feet, and joined Harry and Gordy in front of the board. The rest of the team quietly came over to stand around and listen in.

'You think there's a link, don't you?'

'Someone is trying to tell me something. They've killed my dad and an old army mate, and I reckon the rest of us from the patrol that day are in danger too. Those two feathers aren't a coincidence, either, no matter what Ian Fleming said.'

'What?'

'Sorry, Goldfinger,' Harry said, remembering a quote from the book he was reading on the Kindle Grace had given him. He'd not read much of it these last few days, but for some reason, a section had popped into his mind. 'Can't remember it exactly, but it's along the lines of: once is an accident, twice is a coincidence, and three times is a pattern, or enemy action. Something like that, anyway.'

'Let's hope we don't find a third feather then,' said Drake.

Harry said, 'Jim mentioned earlier how you thought this was a copycat. I'm inclined to agree, but I don't think any of this is linked to a case we had here a while back. Those feathers mean something else and it's all directed at me.'

'That's quite the leap,' said Matt.

'And we're back to the whole issue of your involvement being a massive conflict of interest, aren't we?' added Drake.

'Conflict of interest or not, we're all here now to work out what's going on, so that's what we're going to do,' Harry said. 'There's a team down south right now heading over to see an old friend of mine who, judging by those photos Ed just sent through, someone filled with booze, stabbed in the crotch so he'd bleed to death, then stuffed a feather in his mouth. But why? What the hell for? And what the hell are those feathers all about?'

The room fell silent, reverberating from Harry 's raised voice.

Gordy gestured to the board with a pointed finger. 'Everyone's been looking through what we have while you were away, and we've got nothing.'

'What about those files of yours?' Harry asked Drake. 'The reason you're here at all is because you thought what happened to my father was connected to your investigation.'

Drake reached for his files from a table close by.

Harry shuffled through the files. They were detailed, unlike anything he'd ever seen before. Particularly when it came to the backgrounds of the victims, who they were, their lives, their families. It was impressive stuff. He then shared the files amongst the team for them to look through once more.

'I've been away since Monday, plenty has happened, I know. So, let's go through that.'

'We already have,' Matt said. 'There's nothing to add.'

Jadyn handed the files back to Harry , who dropped them onto the table behind him.

'The feathers are a message, aren't they?' said Jadyn. 'All of it is.'

'Go on,' encouraged Harry , happy to hear anyone's ideas about what they were looking at.

'It may be a copycat, but what if it isn't? What if all that stuff in the files was just inspiration? It's like fan fiction, isn't it?'

'Is it?' Harry said, with not the faintest idea what Jadyn was talking about.

'No, you're right,' Jen said. 'Someone's emulated what Drake's been investigating and used it to get to you.'

'But I didn't want my father murdered,' said Harry .

'That's my point,' said Jen. 'This isn't about your father, this is about you. Why else would they do all that to his face if it wasn't? I don't know about the rest of it, but that's clearly targeted at you, isn't it?'

Jen's words shone brightly at the front of Harry 's mind. Then he turned and paced over to the door.

'Where the hell are you going?' Matt called over.

'The flat,' Harry said. 'I'll be back as soon as I can.'

Then he was gone.

Racing through Hawes marketplace, Harry 's mind filled with images and memories and thoughts all piling in together, jostling for space. Pushing through it all was what Jen had just said. He'd thought it himself, but now something else was starting to occur to him, mostly thanks to the photos Ed had sent through, but he needed to be sure.

Arriving at the flat, Harry went straight through to the lounge. Boxes were piled everywhere like some mini-metropolis of cardboard. He pushed through it, Godzilla-like, and found what he was looking for: two boxes labelled *Personal Records*.

Harry lifted the boxes over to a clear space on the floor and knelt, cutting them both open with a small penknife he always carried in his pocket. Each box was packed to the bursting point with files and papers dating back decades. What he was actually searching for, he still wasn't sure, but he felt certain he would find it here.

Lifting the files and papers out of the boxes, Harry shuffled through them, taking care to make sure everything was kept in order. He found records of his time in the police, his training, reports on his work, his behaviour. There were bank records, medical records, even reports from school. Really must throw those out, Harry thought with a smile. He kept searching, finding old passports, rental agreements, a warranty for a kitchen-top dishwasher he'd bought for his first flat when he'd started in the police as a constable.

Harry stopped.

What he was searching for, he'd seen it, hadn't he? But what was it?

Harry started to shuffle back through the files, zipping back and forth through the years of his life, until he came again to his medical files.

He opened them, started to read through the various notes and letters and everything else about the various injuries he'd suffered over the years. But when he came to the specifics of the injuries to his face, he stopped.

Harry couldn't remember the last time he'd looked at any of this, and the photos told him why; the cuts and burns from the IEDs looked horrendous; the medical staff who had treated him, healed him, they had done wonders. None of it had been life-threatening, but they'd certainly done a good job of patching him up and making him look almost human again. It couldn't have been easy.

He lifted the photos for a closer look. After that last operation in the desert, those bandages had been an integral part of his life for months, the endless changing of dressings, the subtle plastic surgery to try and smooth things out as best they could, the counselling to help him deal with it all, the worry being that facial scars are so hard to live with because you can never hide them from others or even yourself.

It hit Harry then, what he'd been looking for because he was staring right at it. Not just the medical files, but the photos of what he had suffered, the slow process of healing recorded in colour and in black and white.

Keeping hold of the photos, and heading out of the flat and back along the marketplace to the community centre, Harry pulled out his phone and called Ed.

'You don't need to check up on me,' Ed said. 'I'm a grown man, remember? I'm heading to a bed and breakfast. I'll be fine.'

'Ed, listen,' Harry said, 'I'm not calling to check up on you, okay?'

'Then what the hell are you calling me about, then? What's happened? Are you okay?'

'Your injuries,' Harry said.

'What are you on about?'

'You know exactly what I'm on about. Your injuries, remember?'

'What about them?'

'Can you get your hands on your medical files?'

'Now, let me think,' said Ed. 'Of course I can't, Harry ! Not right now, anyway. It's not like I carry them around with me wherever I go. They're back at my flat which, incidentally, you told me to leave, remember?'

'I need to see them.'

'I don't have them.'

'Fine,' Harry said, not giving up. 'I know this is going to sound weird, but can you just send me some photos, then?'

'What of?'

'Your injuries, Ed. You've not got your files, so I need to see the scars. Right now.'

Ed laughed.

'You're kidding, right? No way can you be asking me to take photos of my hand and my arm.'

'That's exactly what I'm asking, Ed,' Harry said, arriving at the community centre and standing outside to finish the call.

Ed was silent for a moment.

'You're serious, aren't you?'

'Always.'

'That's true.'

Harry heard rustling down the phone. Then, a minute or so later, his phone pinged.

'People usually charge for this kind of service, you know that, don't you?' said Ed. 'Anything else? Did you hear from Amy and Ant?'

'I had a patrol car sent round. Haven't heard anything back yet. I'll check on that.'

'Do,' said Ed. 'Are we done?'

'We are,' Harry said, and Ed hung up.

Harry walked into the community centre. Without a word to

the team, he stood in front of the board, then pulled up Ed's photos on his phone, looked at them, shuffled through the photos of his own injuries, then stared at those of his father's ruined body pinned to the board.

'Bloody hell ...'

'What is it?' Matt asked.

'They're the same,' Harry said. 'The injuries ... they're all the same.'

And he was back on the phone to Ed.

CHAPTER FORTY-FOUR

Ed didn't pick up.

Harry tried again, kept trying.

'Pick up, Ed! Pick up the bloody phone!'

Nothing.

Harry only just managed to stop himself from throwing his phone at the wall. His mind was overloading now with what he was realising.

Thinking back to when he'd first seen his father's body, even before he'd known that it was his father, those injuries had reminded him of his own, hadn't they? Just looking at them had made his face itch. He'd recognised them that evening as well, over at Grace's, seeing his reflection in the mirror. He'd not made the connection, though, not even when Sowerby had told him the identity of the body. But that information had sat in his mind and festered, refusing to die, and now here he was, back in the office with the team and drawing conclusions that still didn't make any sense.

'You need to speak to us,' Gordy said. 'Standing there all moody and quiet might work on a TV crime show, but in real life, it doesn't do a damned thing.'

'Whoever helped my father escape killed him to send me a

message,' Harry said, his mind racing. 'Everything done to him matches the injuries suffered by my patrol.'

'Go on,' Gordy said, encouraging Harry to keep going with what he was trying to explain.

Harry pointed at his own face.

'The injuries to his face match all of this near enough,' he said. 'The missing fingers and damage to the arm, that's Ed.'

'And the other two?' Matt asked.

'Ant lost his legs, which explains the missing bones. And Andy got shot in the bollocks. The photos Ed sent through show that Andy's crotch is soaked with blood, so I'm guessing they took the one that survived.'

'Why would anyone go to all that trouble?' asked Liz. 'Why torture your dad, then go after your friends?'

'And don't forget those white feathers, either,' said Jadyn. 'Didn't you say they meant cowardice or something? Maybe that's what it's about.'

Harry took a deep, calming breath.

'There were no cowards on my team,' he said.

Jadyn, Harry noticed, had gone suddenly very pale.

'I wasn't suggesting ... I mean ...'

'No, I know you weren't,' said Harry , just as his phone rang.

'Grimm,' he said.

'This is PC Mellor,' said the voice at the other end of the line.

'What's this about?'

'Your call earlier. Emergency services have now been called in, fire and ambulance crews are at the scene. I need to check the number of residents at the address.'

Harry shook his head. He didn't understand what he was hearing.

'Emergency services? What are you on about?'

'There's a fire. One body has been found so far, I'm afraid. Are you a friend of the family, a relative?'

This PC's bedside manner needs a lot of work, Harry thought.

'This doesn't make sense,' he said, then told PC Mellor Amy and Ant's address.

'Yes, that's the address,' Mellor replied. 'I'm also on-scene right now.'

'The body,' Harry said. 'Has it been identified?'

'No,' Mellor replied. 'All we know so far is that we have a male, early forties.'

Harry 's world swam.

'Can you confirm how many were at the address?'

'Two,' Harry said.

PC Mellor said thank you and that he would call back if he had any information, then hung up.

Harry noticed then that everyone was staring at him.

'I need to sit down,' he said, and dropped into the nearest chair. Smudge came over and snuggled in, and he stroked her soft head as she licked his hand.

'What's happened?' Gordy asked.

Harry didn't want to say because he couldn't be sure, but it was the only conclusion to draw, wasn't it?

'There's been a fire,' he said. 'Amy and Ant's place. It was Amy who sorted out the reunion, the whole thing was her idea, to try and help Ant, stop him from just giving up.'

Drake said, 'A fire? Is anyone hurt?'

'They've found one body,' Harry said. 'It's Ant. Has to be.'

'What about Amy?'

'Nothing yet,' Harry said, then he pushed himself to his feet and was back at the board. 'Who's doing this? What the hell is it all about?'

The photos of his dead father stared back at him. He saw the white feather, and he remembered Ed's call. Realisation then dawned in Harry that everything was now pointing to Ed.

What the hell have you done, mate?

'Ed's a van driver,' he said, as the team gathered around. 'Travels all over the country. He could go anywhere doing that, couldn't he? Not just to where my father was in hospital either, but here, too, to my house.'

'How did he get the address, though?' asked Jim.

Harry didn't know, but what he did know was that it was Ed who had suggested they go to the cemetery, and it was Ed who had tried to strangle him.

'And those photos he sent through,' he said, now looking at Gordy, having spoken to her about what happened. 'What if the reason Andy never turned up at the cemetery in the first place was because Ed had already paid him a visit?'

'Those smoke canisters used in the escape from the hospital, they're military issue,' said Jadyn. 'Would Ed have access to anything like that?'

'Possibly,' said Harry . 'They're the kind of thing you end up finding stuffed in a random bag somewhere. Stuff always goes missing, no matter how keen the staff running the stores are.'

Harry remembered then the cord used to bind his father. Green nylon, like paracord. And there wasn't a soldier on the planet, serving or retired, who didn't have bits of that still lying around all over the place. He wasn't sure if it was all tied up with the reunion or not. Perhaps Amy's organising it had been the catalyst? Ed had attacked him, blamed him for what he'd become, the failure of his marriage, that he'd attacked his wife in her sleep, every bit of it. And just now, he'd said he was at a bed and breakfast, but he'd not said where, exactly, had he? What if that had been a lie and instead he'd paid Amy and Ant a visit and torched the place? And still, there was the feather. That was one thing Harry still couldn't get his head around. Why it was a part of this? Regardless, he needed to call this in and have someone find Ed and pick him up.

Harry 's phone buzzed. It was Amy. He answered it, stepping away from the team.

All he could hear was sobbing.

'Amy?'

"It's Ant,' Amy said. 'He ... The house ...'

'Amy, I know about the house. Where are you?'

'I went out to grab some stuff from the shops,' Amy continued, ignoring Harry 's question. 'When I came back, the house, it was on fire. There was smoke everywhere, flames coming out of the windows. I couldn't even park near it because the Fire Service were already there, hosing the place down. The heat, it was terrible; I felt it as soon as I got out of the car.'

'Amy, whatever you're doing now, wherever you are, I need you to call the police. Immediately.'

When Amy replied, the tone of her voice had changed; it was flat, cold, emotionless.

'Ant was in the house, Harry . He's dead.'

'I know,' Harry said. 'You need to call the police.'

He nearly told her that he suspected Ed was responsible, but he managed to keep that to himself, unwilling to panic her even more.

'You are the police, Harry ,' she said.

'No, I mean police near your home. They'll be looking for you. I'll call them myself for you as well.'

'I've got your address, Harry ,' Amy said. 'I'm already on my way.'

'What? Why?'

He also found himself wondering how, because he was fairly sure he'd never told her.

'I'll let you know when I arrive, okay, Harry ? I need to see you.'

'No, Amy, you don't,' Harry said. 'You need to—'

The line went dead.

CHAPTER FORTY-FIVE

'That was Amy, Anthony's wife,' Harry said, turning to face the rest of the team. 'She's on her way here right now. I need to put in another call; Ed needs to be picked up immediately. I've no idea where he actually is, but I can send through a photo from the reunion.'

Harry did exactly that, and when he was done, he saw that DI Haig was staring at him, her face serious.

'I think we all need a break,' she said.

Harry had to agree.

'I could do with a coffee,' he said. 'And Amy won't be here for hours.'

'Well, as I'm still the one leading this investigation,' Gordy said, 'even though you're having a good go at taking over, Harry , can I suggest we all take an hour to go for a walk, grab a coffee and a bite to eat, and see you all come back here after?'

'Sounds like a plan,' said Harry .

'You, though,' Gordy said, 'I want heading home.'

Harry went to protest, but Gordy was having none of it.

'You didn't sleep last night, did you? No, don't answer that. I know you didn't. You're still on leave, so I'm going to put my foot down. Either that, or I'll ram it up your backside, if you don't leave here in the next sixty seconds.'

'I'm needed here,' Harry said.

'You're not,' replied Gordy, as Matt and Jim strolled past, heading out the office door, Fly to heel.

'Another call's just come in about that person seen sleeping in their car,' Matt said. 'Going to pop out now and check that they're okay.'

'Where?' asked Gordy.

'Back road out of Appersett, just beyond the old viaduct,' said Jim. 'They're parked up in a field and got themselves stuck.'

'You mean they called it in themselves?'

Matt shook his head.

'Old Alan Dent found him. Whoever it is, Alan says they're not in the best of moods, and a bit worse for wear, too, so I'll go see if I can sort it out.'

'Should be fun,' said Gordy, and Matt and Jim headed off. She looked back at Harry . 'I'm serious,' she said. 'I need you out of here, right now.'

Harry was about to leave when Drake walked past, files under his arm, walking pole clasped in his hand.

'I'll see you all later, then,' he said. 'A bit of fresh air is exactly what I need.'

Harry looked at Gordy and held up his hands.

'I hear you,' he said. 'I'll go. But you'll keep me up to date with it all, won't you?'

Gordy said nothing, just pointed at the door.

With a nod, Harry headed off, Smudge at his side. But as he went to leave the community centre, Jim almost ran into him.

'What the hell's going on?' Harry said.

'Sorry,' Jim said. 'Meant to give you this earlier. Found it on the floor while you were away. I think it must've fallen out of your pocket.'

Jim handed Harry a card. It was the one Ben had given him, the business card of the counsellor.

'Thought it might be important,' Jim said, then dashed back out of the office.

Harry looked at the card with a frown, only to have the frown pulled apart by a yawn. Perhaps Gordy had the right idea after all, he thought, and mooched on back over to his Rav4. Sending a message to Grace to let her know he was heading back to her place, he headed off out of Hawes. When he arrived, weariness hit him like an out-of-control truck on a hill. He headed straight upstairs and a minute later, was enjoying the sleep of the dead.

Harry woke to see Grace sitting on the edge of the bed, looking down at him. Smudge was with her, head cocked to the side.

'Everything okay?'

Harry sat up.

'Not really, no,' he yawned. 'What time is it?'

Grace checked her watch.

'Gone six,' she said, then picked something up off the floor. 'This might be useful,' she said. 'Have you given them a call?'

Harry was confused, so Grace handed over what she'd found; it was the card Jim had found earlier.

Smudge leaned forward to lick Harry 's bare arm.

Harry remembered then that Amy was on her way. He also wanted to know if there had been any news on the whereabouts of Ed, so he checked his phone, but there were no messages.

'I don't need counselling,' Harry said, as Grace moved to allow him to swing himself out of bed.

'Don't knock it.'

'I'm not.'

Harry stood up and stretched.

'It's not a bad design that either, is it?' Grace said. 'The white quill really stands out against the black background. Very classy.'

Harry went to slip the card into his pocket but found himself staring at it.

'You're frowning,' Grace said. 'What's up?'

Harry lifted the card closer to his face and his frown only deepened.

Grace leaned in.

'See what I mean?' she said. 'It's really nice.'

Maybe the sleep had helped, Harry thought, because on seeing that card, he suddenly felt not just awake but fully alert.

'It's not a quill,' he said.

'Of course it is,' said Grace.

'Well, it is, yes, but it's something else, isn't it?'

'What?'

The last few days all piled into Harry , every moment of them filling his mind, but he wasn't overwhelmed by any of it, not now. He was laser-focused and at last starting to see things clearly. It still didn't make absolute sense, not all of it, and there was only one way to find out why. Right now, though, he had a deeper concern.

'It's a white feather,' he said, and pulled out his phone.

'So?'

'Ben,' he said.

'What about him?'

'That's where she's going,' Harry said, 'and I need him out of there before she gets there. Because she's not coming to see me at all, is she?'

'Who isn't?'

Harry was pacing around Grace's bedroom, phone at his ear, waiting for Ben to answer. He checked his watch. How long would it have taken her to get here? There was still time, there had to be!

'I don't think this was what she wanted to happen in the end, not really,' he said. 'I don't see how it can be. But it's her, I know it, I just don't know why.'

The ringing stopped. The call was answered.

'Ben? It's Harry . Are you still at home? Is Liz still with you?' Harry 's voice was clear and fast; he needed Ben to listen and to act. 'I need you to lock the doors, the windows, everything, and don't let anyone in till I arrive, you hear? I'll be there in fifteen. And keep this call open just inc—'

'Harry ?'

'Yes, it's me, Ben,' Harry said. 'You heard what I said, right? I need you to stay where you are, lock the house.'

'She's here,' Ben said.

Harry 's world stopped dead as another voice came on the line.

'Told you I was coming to see you, didn't I?'

CHAPTER FORTY-SIX

'Hello, Amy,' Harry said.

He lifted his eyes to see Grace staring at him. She went to speak, but he hushed her with a stare and a raised hand, then mimed writing something in the air.

Grace dashed out of the room, returning a moment later with pen and paper.

'What's going on, Amy?' Harry asked, taking the pen from Grace.

'You really don't know, do you?'

'No, I don't,' Harry said, and he wasn't lying either. He knew some of it—that Amy was responsible for everything that had happened—he just didn't know why or how.

Harry wrote *Call Gordy* on the piece of paper, then *Amy at Ben and Liz's. Amy prime suspect, not Ed.*

Grace read the note and left the bedroom, already on her phone.

Harry was focused now on the phone call.

'Whatever this is about, you need to stop right now,' he said. 'Let's just talk, okay? You and me, we can sort this out, can't we? Whatever it is, just help me to understand it, and we'll go from there. How does that sound?'

'I thought we could sort it out, you know?' Amy said. 'I really did. That's why I did it all. But it was impossible. I've tried everything, but nothing worked. And it's over now, Harry . Finished.'

'I need a little help here,' Harry said. 'You're clearly way ahead of me. Can we start at the beginning?'

Grace returned, and gave Harry the thumbs up. Harry knew his job now was to keep Amy talking until someone turned up.

'Amy?' he said. 'You're still there, yes?'

'We're all still here,' Amy said. 'Ben and me and lovely Liz. And she is lovely, isn't she? I can see why Ben's with her. He's a lucky man. They could be very happy together, Harry . Shame really, isn't it?'

'What is?' Harry asked.

Amy didn't reply.

'Listen to me, Amy, whatever it is you're thinking of—'

'You know, I was so pleased when Ant came home,' Amy said. 'I'd missed him so much. And it was terrifying having him, having all of you, over there. I hardly slept, hardly ate.'

'Ant couldn't wait to get back,' Harry said, though in many ways, it was a lie. Ant had been flown back home as soon as he'd been stabilised, his injuries too much for the staff and facilities in Afghanistan. Harry had followed soon after once he'd been patched up. He remembered watching as Ant had been lifted into the Chinook sent out to bring them all back. He'd been unconscious, which had been no small mercy, considering the damage wrought on his body.

'I knew he'd been injured, that it was bad, but I just wasn't prepared for the reality of it.'

'No one can be prepared for something like that,' said Harry , remembering it all. 'There's no blame in that, no shame, Amy.'

'It was so long before he came home, to our house,' Amy continued. 'I visited him every day in the hospital, I was there with him when he woke for the first time. When he realised what had happened, how different he was. It was terrible, Harry . You've no idea.'

'You were his rock,' Harry said. 'Without you, he'd have never made it through. You know that, don't you, Amy?'

Harry heard the faintest of sobs.

'But there's only so much you can take, you know?' Amy said, her voice breaking. 'Only so much.'

Harry checked his watch. How long would it take the team to arrive? It all depended on where they all were. He had to keep Amy talking.

'I still don't see how we've ended up where we now are,' he said. 'With you up here in the Dales. It was only two nights ago that we were in the pub, all of us together.'

'None of us are together, Harry ,' said Amy, and Harry heard the deepest sadness in her voice. 'Not completely. You all came back changed, physically and mentally. And what you brought back, what Ant refused to leave behind, it changed me, too. It was bound to, wasn't it?'

Harry sat down on the edge of the bed, rubbed his eyes hard, trying to focus, to get to the bottom of it all, and to keep Amy on the line just long enough. Smudge was still with him, but Grace had headed back downstairs, no doubt to give him the space to focus on what he was doing.

'Whatever you've done, Amy, we can work it out, you and me.'

The words sounded empty, even as he said them, but Harry didn't care. If they kept Amy on the line, if they kept her talking, then it was worth it.

'It was me, you know?' Amy said. 'Your father, I mean.'

Harry 's mind burst with images of what he'd found in his lounge, but he forced them away.

'I did it. I killed him.'

'You didn't need to do that,' Harry said. 'He was in prison, where he belonged.'

'You sound ungrateful.'

There was nothing to be grateful for, Harry thought.

'Why did you do it?' he asked, because he really couldn't work that bit out at all.

'For you, Harry .'

That admission threatened to steal Harry 's breath, but he kept himself calm.

'I'll need more than that,' he said.

Amy laughed, the sound ragged with tears.

'Ant needed you,' she said. 'He was going downhill fast. You saw him! And then I remembered you, Harry , how Ant would do anything you asked of him. But the one thing that took you away all those years ago was your dad, wasn't it?'

'It wasn't just that,' said Harry . 'I needed a change. He gave me an excuse to get out, to do something different.'

Amy said, 'I had this crazy notion that if that bastard was out of your life for good, you might have time for Ant again.'

She was right, that was crazy, Harry thought.

'I'd always have time for him,' he said. 'You didn't need to do any of this.'

Amy laughed once again. This time the sound was cruel and filled with disbelief.

'You've been gone from his life for twenty years, Harry !'

'All you had to do was ask.'

'It wasn't enough, Harry . It wasn't enough at all. I thought your father's death might be, but I guess I was wrong.'

Harry 's breath caught in his throat. What Amy had just said was madness. Had she really killed his father for such a reason as that? How twisted had her reality become to make her think that would ever make sense?

'He was in prison, where he belonged,' Harry said. 'That's what mattered, Amy.'

'Can't you see it, Harry ?' Amy replied, a knife's edge to her voice now. 'He took you away from us, from Ant.'

Harry could think of nothing to say. Deep down, he knew Amy had a point. He just wished she'd thought of a different way to make it.

'Maybe you don't remember, but you were around all the time at the beginning. You used to visit him, read to him when he was still out of it. When he came home, he looked forward to seeing you because there was no bullshit, Harry . He could talk to you about what had happened, tell you things he wouldn't even tell me. I used to hear him crying with you. He never cried with me, Harry . Not once.'

'We all visited,' Harry said. 'Ed and Andy, we all did our bit. Even Tak, before ...'

Harry couldn't finish his sentence.

Another laugh, a short, sharp bark.

'Did your bit? Is that all it was to you?'

No, it wasn't, thought Harry . How could it be? They'd all come back ruined in their own way, but they still looked out for each other. It couldn't go on indefinitely, though. They had their own lives, their own problems. That's just the way things were. Maybe he'd left a little sooner than the others—perhaps there was truth in that and more than he would ever like to admit to—but life had led him in another direction, and he'd followed it.

'You're right,' Harry admitted. 'What my dad did, it took me away. But I'm here now, Amy. I came to the reunion. We all did. This can be a new start, can't it? That's what this is all about, isn't it? Starting again?'

There was no response from down the line, just the sound of Amy breathing. Then, behind it, two voices, quietly talking. Liz and Ben, Harry thought. He wondered what was going through their minds. What had Amy already done to them?

'It was easy. Actually, easier than I expected,' Amy said.

'What was?'

'Getting in touch with your father.'

'You didn't need to do that,' Harry said.

'I did,' said Amy. 'He was my only hope. Can't you see that? If I removed him permanently, then you'd come back, wouldn't you? That's what was supposed to happen, at the reunion, that you'd all be so pleased to be together again, that you'd be back properly, for Ant, Harry . But it didn't happen, did it? It all went wrong.'

'It didn't go wrong,' said Harry . 'It just takes time, that's all.'

'It took too long. It's always taken too long, and I can't take it anymore.'

Harry checked his watch again. Not long now, he thought. The team would be there soon, this would be over, and Ben and Liz would be safe.

'I made your father pay, though, didn't I? It was important, that bit of it, that he knew the pain you had all suffered.'

'You tortured him, Amy,' Harry said. He couldn't help himself because that was the truth of it. No matter what twisted reason she had in her mind for what she had done, she had to know that wasn't right.

'It's because of him that none of you were able to heal properly. Can't you see that?'

'I healed just fine, Amy,' Harry said.

Another laugh, cold and thin.

'What, Ed, with his failed marriage because he nearly killed his wife? Is that what you mean by healing?' Amy said. 'And what about Andy, the sudden epiphany that God was the answer to what he was missing in his life? Except it wasn't, was it? Because the loneliness was killing him and the booze became his only real friend. Tak killed himself because he just couldn't take it anymore. And then there's you, Harry . You turned your pain, your scars into a shield, a barrier to the world, and you've been hiding behind it ever since.'

'Maybe that's how you see it, Amy, but it isn't like that.'

'And what about us? What about me and Ant, you ever think about that? His life was torn apart. It was changed so dramatically that nothing was the same anymore. The bed sores, the nightmares, the pain twenty-four-seven only kept at bay by a cocktail of drugs that would either send him into a coma for days on end, or have him wide awake and screaming and so sure that something was coming through the walls to get him. Have you ever even once spared a moment to consider what that's been like?'

Harry knew life had been hell for Amy, but there was nothing he could do about that now. They'd all been pushed away by a singular event that had blown them apart as effectively as the IED that had ripped apart that building all those years ago and scorched its signature into his skin.

'How did you get to my father?' Harry asked, not only to keep her talking, but because he had to know.

'I read a lot when Ant was asleep,' Amy said, 'which was a lot of the time because of the medication. Books, magazines, websites, anything to pass the time. Television is too busy, too frantic. I kept up with what you were all up to, though you were more difficult, Harry —no social media, almost a ghost—but I'd heard you'd gone north, and I found out where. I read somewhere about these criminals being murdered, and although the police were denying any connection—keen to avoid any suggestion of a serial killer, no doubt —others had linked them together. I thought how great it would be if your dad could end up as the next victim. Except, how could that happen unless I did it myself? So, that's what I did.'

The team had to be nearly at Liz's place by now, Harry thought. Just a few minutes more, maybe, and then this would all be over.

'You contacted him in prison.'

'I'm an English tutor, remember?' Amy said. 'I'm good with words, and I've had a few things published here and there. Nothing major, but enough to sound convincing. I managed to have one of those true crime magazines take me up on an idea because I knew you, so there was that personal element, wasn't there? They were hooked and gave me the necessary kudos to get through the gates.'

Harry shook his head at how easily she'd managed to get to his father. It was simple, and it was clever.

'He was actually very interested in you, still,' Amy said. 'A warden helped put us in touch outside of the official channels. The hospital thing was his plan. I just needed the distraction, and that was provided by all that army kit Ant had refused to throw away. A couple of smoke grenades and we walked out of there so easily. And then I drugged him in my car. A lovely cup of warming mushroom soup.'

Harry remembered the drugs they'd found in his father's body, the jam jars in Amy's kitchen.

'I was going to kill him right away. Just do it in a wood somewhere, leave an anonymous tip with the police, but when I heard you were moving? I couldn't resist it. I just kept him drugged up back at our house. Ant didn't suspect a thing. It was my house-warming present to you, Harry . But you didn't like it, did you?'

'No, Amy,' Harry said. 'I really didn't.'

'Anyway, we've talked long enough,' Amy said. 'Andy, Ed, and Ant are all dead. Now there's just you and me left, isn't there, Harry ? Don't worry, though, you'll live through this. That's the point, after all.'

'What's the point, Amy? Because I'm not seeing one. There's just a lot of pain, a lot of loneliness, and you blaming the world for all of it.'

Amy laughed.

'I don't blame the world, Harry . I blame you! All of you! For coming back like you did, for not just leaving Ant out there to die in the desert, because that would've been the kindest thing you could've done, for him, for me. But you didn't, did you? You had to bring him back, too much of a coward to do the right thing.'

And there it was, Harry thought.

'The white feather,' he said.

'You were all cowards for not leaving him there to die. What he had after that, what I had? It was no life, Harry . You wouldn't let an animal live like Ant did. You know that, don't you? If you found a dog wounded as he was that day, you'd put it out of its misery, because that's the kind thing to do. But the coward's way out is to keep them alive no matter what. You're a coward, Harry . And you deserve to be utterly and completely alone with the pain you brought back, and a little more besides. Which I suppose brings me to Ben, doesn't it?'

Harry was on his feet.

'Don't you touch him, Amy.'

'I'm not just a tutor, you know, I'm a qualified counsellor.

Living with Ant, it's given me certain skills, so I've used them to help others, working freelance with various organisations. Maybe that's when this all started, when I saw that family name of yours come up on a list of clients I could work with, and realised it was your brother Ben.'

How long had she been planning this? Harry thought. Ben had been having counselling for months now. That so much thought had gone into causing so much pain horrified him almost as much as it angered him.

'Ben has nothing to do with this.'

'He told me you were moving,' said Amy. 'All I had to do was grab the right keys, and I was in. I wasn't sure it would all come together as it did, but I was pleasantly surprised. Unlike you, right?'

Harry heard Ben and Liz call out his name.

'Don't you dare touch them,' Harry snarled.

'Or what, Harry ? What will you do? There's nothing you can say or do to me that would be any worse than anything I've lived through for the past twenty years. Nothing! And I've grown rather good at using this little burner of mine, you know? Worked on your dad rather well. Don't think I'll burn myself this time, either.'

Harry remembered Amy flinching when he'd touched her arm, the gloves she'd been wearing.

'Amy, whatever you're going to do, don't. Please, I'm begging you.'

'Begging me? Really? You, Harry ? You never beg. Ed did, though. Cried a little, too, actually.'

Harry 's heart stopped for a moment.

'What? How did you find him?'

'I saw him leave his house, and I followed him,' Amy replied. 'He told me he'd just spoken to you. Can't say he'll be speaking to you again, though. Or anyone. But it's a kindness, really, isn't it? After what he put his wife through.'

Harry was searching for things to say, something that would cut through the crazy and stop Amy from whatever she was planning to do.

'Amy, please, just listen to me ...'

The only answer Harry received was a scream, then a crash.

'Amy? Amy! What the hell have you done? Amy! A—'

'Harry ?'

'Matt?' Relief flooded through Harry as he heard the DS's voice on the end of the line. 'Ben, is he okay? How's Liz? What did Amy do? What's happened?'

'Ben and Liz are fine, Harry ,' Matt said. 'We got here in time. Well, Drake did, actually. He was first through the door; went through it like a steam train. Never seen the like. Didn't think he had it in him, what with that bad leg of his.'

Harry laughed, tears fell, and then Grace was next to him and holding him tight, as Smudge squeezed in between them. He quietly thanked whatever God was up there watching, that he wasn't with the team. He may have been to hell and back too many times to mention, but all of that would have nothing on what they would say if they could see him now.

CHAPTER FORTY-SEVEN

Grace drove Harry over to Liz and Ben's house in Middleham. Harry had assured her that he was fine to drive himself, but she was having none of it, so with the dogs in the back of her own Land Rover, she'd chauffeured them all over.

Arriving at the house, Harry found Amy already handcuffed and in the back of Matt's vehicle.

He made to walk over to see her, but Gordy and Matt barred his way.

'You're not on the investigation, remember?' Gordy said, holding a hand up to stop him from going any further.

'I'm not going to do anything.'

'Of course you're not,' said Matt. 'Because you're not going over there, like our wonderful DI has just said. Ben and Liz are inside, so that's where you should be, isn't it?'

Harry hesitated.

'She murdered three of my friends, my father ...'

'And we stopped her before she could do anything to Ben and Liz because of you,' Gordy said. 'And if she had, and if you hadn't worked this all out, she'd have been after you next, for sure.'

Deep down, Harry knew that the DI and DS were right.

'How are they?' he asked.

'Ben and Liz?' said Matt. 'You'll see for yourself, won't you? But they're fine. Bit traumatised, like, but that's all. They'll be fine, I'm sure. They make a good pair, you know?'

'They do,' Harry nodded. 'You taking her in, then?'

'I am,' said Matt. 'Jadyn's coming along as well.'

Harry smiled.

'His parents will love to hear that, won't they?'

'That's for sure,' said Matt. 'Though right now I think they're probably still trying to patch things up with his sister. Anyway, I'll be off.'

Matt called for Jadyn, who strode out of Liz's house and over to where they were standing.

'You okay, Boss?' he asked. 'There's a mug of tea inside waiting for you, by the way; I thought you'd maybe want one.'

Harry said thank you and watched as Matt and Jadyn walked over to climb into Matt's vehicle.

'What happened about that person sleeping rough in their car?' Harry called over. 'Had they managed to get out of the field when you arrived?'

Matt stopped, halfway into his seat, then came back over.

'I was going to save this till later.'

'Save what until later?'

'You're not going to believe it, I promise you.'

Harry 's look was enough to convince Matt to keep talking.

'It was Anderson,' he said.

Matt was right, Harry couldn't believe what he was hearing.

'You can't be serious.'

'Never been more so in my life,' said Matt. 'Apparently, he got behind on rent and ended up between digs and living in his car. You know, I actually felt sorry for him. Not for long, mind, but you know what I mean. Goes to explain the weird way he behaved when Jim followed him a couple of days ago.'

'How so?'

'Didn't want Jim seeing what was in the back of his car. Jim thought it might be the fireworks, be we know that wasn't him, don't we? Anyway, what it actually was, was his worldly belongings: a suitcase of clothes, a makeshift bed. He'd been kipping around and about, drinking a fair bit as well, I think.'

'We can have him for that,' Harry said.

'We can indeed,' Matt nodded.

Harry asked, 'So, where is he now? And what was all that with him being over here, then?'

'Says he had a tip-off,' Matt said. 'Though he's refusing to divulge his sources. I've told him we will be expecting him at the office in the morning to discuss it all, if you know what I mean.'

'What if he doesn't turn up?'

'Oh, I think he will.'

'Why's that, then?'

Matt stuffed a hand in his pocket and pulled out a set of keys.

'These are his,' he said. 'Out of the goodness of my heart, I booked him in at the youth hostel with some money I found in his wallet. So, come tomorrow, I can't see him going anywhere else, can you?'

Laughing to himself, Matt slumped back down into the driving seat and heaved the door shut, then he headed off into the evening, Jadyn at his side, Amy in the back. Harry watched them go, his eyes on Amy, but she didn't turn to face him, just stared straight forward.

'Come on,' Gordy said, 'let's go and see Ben and Liz.'

Inside, Grace was already chatting with them the pair of them, and Harry was relieved to see that they were unharmed.

Ben saw Harry and came over, and Harry pulled his younger brother in for a hug.

'You're growing soft in your old age,' Ben said.

'Less of the old,' said Harry . 'You're okay, though, right? Both of you?'

He glanced over at Liz, who gave a faint nod, though he could see a wildness in her eyes that spoke enough about what they'd just experienced.

'She turned up carrying this kitchen knife and made Liz tie me to a dining chair,' said Ben. 'I know it was only a knife, but—'

'There's no such thing as only a knife,' said Harry .

'I guess.'

'Then she did the same to Liz?'

Ben gave a nod.

'She looked surprised when you called,' he said. 'I don't think she expected that at all. I don't want to think what would've happened if you hadn't.'

'Then don't,' said Harry . 'I hear Drake came in here at a fair pace?'

'You could say that,' Ben agreed. 'She went for him with the knife, but he had that folding walking stick with him. A flick of the wrist and it was extended and in his hand. He used it to bat the knife away, then rugby-tackled her to the ground before she had a chance to do anything about it. Then she was in cuffs. It was pretty impressive.'

'Where is he now?'

Ben shook his head.

Jen said, 'He headed outside, but that was before you showed up.'

'He left that stick of his behind as well,' said Ben. 'Think he forgot all about it after using it as a sword.'

'I'll go find him, then,' said Harry , and with a nod to Grace to keep an eye on things, made his way back outside.

The street was empty, so he called out for Drake, but there was no reply.

'Something the matter?' Gordy asked, coming to stand beside Harry .

'Drake's buggered off,' Harry said.

'Probably needed a breather after what he did. He'll be back in a few minutes, I should think.' Then she added, 'Swift's going to be a little unhappy to have missed out on this, isn't he?'

Harry laughed at that. Despite their differences, he wondered how their old detective superintendent was doing.

'You heard from him at all?'

Gordy shook her head.

'Walker will know, I should think. And she'll probably want an update, no doubt. Seems a bit late though, doesn't it?'

Harry rubbed his chin then said, 'Well, if she's Swift's replacement, even if it is temporary, there's no reason why we should treat her any different, is there?'

He pulled out his phone and held it out to the DI.

'I'll be calling her tomorrow as the lead on the investigation,' Gordy said. 'If you're calling her now, then that's nothing to do with me, you hear?'

Harry winked as he pulled up Walker's number.

Gordy was back in Liz's house by the time Harry 's call was answered.

'Evening, ma'am,' he said.

'DCI Grimm? This is a late one. I trust everything is okay and that this won't take long. I've a trip to the theatre this evening and I've been looking forward to it for a very long time. I say theatre, it's a musical. I'm not exactly highbrow, I'm afraid.'

'Just thought you'd appreciate an update, that's all,' Harry said.

'On the case that you're not officially a part of, by any chance?'

Harry said, 'Detective Inspector Haig will be doing that tomorrow, but the team has caught the person responsible.'

'Excellent news,' Walker said. 'Then why the call?'

'Have you heard from Swift?' he asked.

'He's doing as well as can be expected,' Walker replied. 'Speaks very highly of you and the team. I think he misses the work, but he needs time to recover. I'll pass on that you were asking after him; I'm sure he'll appreciate it.'

'And he's still thinking of retiring?'

'He is.'

'Fair enough.'

An awkward silence sat between Harry and Walker for a moment.

'Will there be anything else?'

'Yes, actually,' Harry said, thinking back over the last few days. 'If you ever need to replace me, I reckon DCI Drake would be a good fit with the team. It was good to have him around while I was away.'

'DCI Who?'

'Drake,' Harry said again. 'Turned up on Monday after talking to someone on your team.'

'I'm sorry, but I've not the faintest idea what you're talking about. No one called Drake has talked to my team. Where's he from?'

'Somerset,' Harry said. 'And he must've done. He had files on a load of other cases, thought what happened to my father was linked. That's why he was here.'

'I've still got one of those files here,' said Jim, walking over to Harry . 'Drake left it at the office by accident, I think. I grabbed it on the way over. I bet that's where he's gone, hasn't he? Back to the office to pick it up.'

'What cases?' Walker asked.

Harry flicked through the pages of the file, quickly going through the names of the victims it contained. They weren't all there, for sure, but it was only one of the files; Drake's work was certainly detailed.

Harry stopped speaking and heard Walker take a breath or two.

'Grimm, give me a minute or two, would you? I'll call you back.'

Harry , a little confused, hung up, then headed back into Liz's house.

'Your tea's gone cold,' Ben said. 'Fancy another?'

'No, I'm good, thanks,' said Harry , spotting Drake's walking stick. He walked over and picked it up, noticing how light it was, slim, too, as he swished it through the air in front of him. He pulled the sections apart, then let the length of elastic inside snick them all back together again.

Standing with the others, Gordy was looking at him rather seriously.

'Something the matter?' she asked. 'What did Walker say?'

'She's calling me back,' Harry said.

'If you've upset our nice new DSup ...'

Harry 's phone buzzed in his hand and he answered it.

'Grimm, it's Walker.'

'Yes, ma'am,' Harry said. 'Everything okay?'

'No, it isn't,' Walker replied. 'This DCI Drake; you're sure he said he was from Somerset?'

'Saw his ID myself,' Harry said.

'Well, there is no DCI Drake.'

Harry was sure he hadn't heard right.

'I'm telling you, Grimm,' she said, 'there is no DCI Drake. I've checked. No one's heard of him. And no one by that name has spoken to any member of my team. Those cases you mentioned, however, they're legit, but they're all part of a highly classified investigation, so I don't understand how this Drake fellow knew about it at all.'

'Classified why?' Harry asked.

'I'm not at liberty to say.'

'Then I'll say it for you,' Harry said. 'They're all linked, and there's a good chance that one person is behind them all. Am I close?'

Walker said nothing.

Which is answer enough, Harry thought, as he caught sight of something in the file, a small card with a name and a number on it. He'd seen it before, the day he'd been heading off to the reunion and stopped by at the office to speak with the newly arrived DCI. Anderson had handed it to him out in the marketplace, and Drake had taken it instead.

'Grimm?'

'I'm still here,' Harry said, though he was no longer looking at the small card. Instead, he was staring at Drake's folding walking stick in his hand, then scanning the cases in the file, the victim's confessions, where they'd been found, and how they had got there in the first place.

If Drake wasn't a DCI, then who was he? A knot in Harry 's gut told him that he knew, he just didn't want to believe it.

He remembered then a couple of things that had struck him as odd at the time, but not enough for him to worry about, until now; how Drake hadn't known anything about the well in Glastonbury, which anyone who lived there would know about for sure. And then there had been his confusion over the drugs found in his father's body.

'He was right,' Harry said. 'Drake said this was a copycat. That's why he was here in the first place, wasn't it? Because he knew, and he wanted to find out who it was.'

'Grimm,' Walker said, 'whatever information you have on these cases, on this Drake character, I need you to get them to me as soon as possible. Do you understand?'

Harry was understanding more and more. Right at the start, Drake had reminded him of DCI Jameson, hadn't he? And that was no coincidence, he could see that now, but he hadn't been able to at the time. It was all an act, to have Harry trust him, to work with the team, find out who was doing his work for him. Harry almost laughed, remembering how he'd even said Drake should take up counselling, he was so easy to talk to.

He flicked through the file one last time, before closing it.

'I'll have this all sent through to you first thing tomorrow.'

'Good,' Walker said. 'And well done to the team on apprehending the person responsible for what happened to your father.'

'I'll pass that on, ma'am,' Harry said.

Call over, Harry folded Drake's walking stick and placed it on top of the file. The team had done their job. The file and all it contained, well, that was someone else's business, so best to do as Walker said and just hand it over. Though after touching that walking stick, and remembering those confessions, Harry rather felt like he needed to give his hands a good wash.

Grace came over.

'All good?' she asked.

Harry cast his eyes across the others in the room, and then beyond it, through a window, saw the moon casting its glow across the distant silhouette of Penhill.

'I think so,' Harry said.

'What about the house?'

'I won't be able to move in until we're sure no further evidence can be found there. And even then, it'll need a good clean.'

Grace looked thoughtful.

'Look, I think everyone would understand if you decided to not go ahead with it. After everything that's happened, no one could argue living there wouldn't be a little strange.'

Grace had a point, Harry thought, but then moving into an old house would always come with its own ghosts, wouldn't it? At least this way, he'd know who was haunting him, the unquiet bones of his father rattling in the dark.

'It'll be fine,' Harry said. 'But there is one thing ...'

'What?'

'I don't suppose you know a good locksmith, do you?'

CHAPTER FORTY-EIGHT

Harry stared at his reflection in the bedroom mirror, and for once wasn't noticing the scars.

'You look very smart,' Grace said, coming to stand behind him.

Harry had to agree, but he still wasn't a fan of a shirt and tie.

'If this is my housewarming,' he said, 'then why do I have to dress like this?'

Grace laughed.

'If everyone's making an effort, do you really want to be the odd one out?'

'I'm used to it.'

Grace came round to stand between Harry and his unhappy reflection.

'Smile.'

'No.'

There was a knock at the door.

'I'll get that,' Grace said, and left Harry alone.

Harry gave his reflection one final glance, then turned away from it to grab a pair of cufflinks off the bedside cabinet. A few moments of swearing later, his thick fingers having more than a little trouble with the cufflinks, he headed downstairs, voices floating up to greet him.

'Well, look at you,' said Margaret Shaw, who was handing Grace her jacket.

Rebecca was with her and she wore an amused look on her face as she closed the front door to keep the crisp, dark evening where it belonged.

'Thought I'd make an effort,' Harry said. 'Good of you to come.'

Rebecca handed Harry a bottle of wine.

'That's a good one,' Margaret said. 'Save it for a special occasion.'

'This is a special occasion,' Harry said.

'Good point,' Margaret replied. 'Best we get it open then, hadn't we?'

Grace took the wine and Harry led Margaret and Rebecca through to the lounge.

'You're the first here,' Harry said, then gestured to various plates and platters groaning under the weight of an awful lot of food. 'If you can make a dent in that lot, I'll be impressed.'

Sowerby looked around the room and Harry followed her line of sight, taking in the new furniture, the pictures on the wall, the carpet.

'Looks a little different to the last time we were in here,' she said.

The murder of his father in his own house was a few weeks ago now. The crime scene cleaning team had been in and done a thorough job, but then that was to be expected; it was the kind of job you didn't really get a second chance at. The forensic cleanup of a murder scene involved handling not only blood and bodily fluids, but a raft of other dangers, too, all to ensure no biohazards and infectious materials were left behind. As the lead on the team had said through his facemask, 'Just because you can't see it, doesn't mean it isn't there.'

'We had to replace the carpet, do a repaint,' Harry said. 'I'm happy with the place.'

Harry sometimes wondered if there was something wrong with him, because he was sure he should be more bothered by it all than he was. But his father was dead, and worrying about it, or deciding he couldn't live here because of what had happened, wasn't going to change anything. 'Most people would've decided to live somewhere else,' said Margaret.

'I'm not most people,' Harry replied, hearing another knock at the front door.

'Wouldn't have you any other way, either,' Margaret smiled.

Harry headed out into the hall to find Grace coming the other way, a tray of drinks in her hands.

'Margaret was right about that wine,' she said with a wink, then headed into the lounge, leaving Harry to answer the door.

'Now then, Boss,' said Jim.

Harry looked down to see Fly at the PCSO's feet.

'Do you go anywhere without that dog?' he asked.

Jim said, 'He begged to come; bit of company for Smudge, right?'

Behind Jim, other figures emerged from the night, the sky above starless, and Harry found himself staring into the faces of the rest of his team and their various partners.

'Let's get inside, then,' Matt called out over their heads. 'It's brass monkey weather out here.'

Harry stepped back to allow everyone inside, Fly slinking off to meet Smudge, who then led him away to the kitchen. He collected everyone's jackets and pointed them all through to the lounge. Anna had come along with Gordy, and Joan with Matt. Liz was in uniform and on duty but had stopped by to wish Harry well, and was also dropping Ben off. Everyone had brought gifts, the common theme seeming to be something alcoholic in a bottle.

'Spare room is all made up,' Harry said to Ben.

'If there's no He-Man duvet set, then I'm leaving,' Ben replied.

Harry laughed at that and shooed his brother and Liz on through.

Matt was next. 'Managed to get a babysitter in,' he said. 'Haven't been out for ages, just the two of us; even booked a taxi.'

'Very organised,' Harry said.

'That was me,' Joan laughed, as Matt pushed her into the lounge.

Jadyn and Jen were the last to enter the house.

Harry wasn't sure whether to ask after Jadyn's sister or not, but Grace did it for him.

'I spoke to her and my mum and dad a couple of days ago, actually,' Jadyn said, as Jen took his jacket and hung it up with hers in the hall. 'I'm heading home to see them at the weekend.'

'That's good,' said Harry . 'Family is important.'

'It is,' Jadyn nodded, then went through to the lounge with Jen.

'They seem to be getting on well,' said Grace.

Harry saw a look in Grace's eye and was about to say something when there was yet another knock at the door.

'Have you invited the whole dale?' he asked.

Opening the door, Harry found Dave Calvert waiting outside, along with Mary Sunter, his new next-door neighbour, and a few other faces from the houses close by. Dave was wearing more tweed than Harry had ever seen in his life, his shoes polished to a military standard.

'In you come, then,' Harry said.

Dave, rather than carrying a bottle, had clasped in his arms three small metal barrels.

'Beer!' he said, as though the word itself was an epiphany. 'Eight pints of the good stuff in each one.'

'Not sure you've bought enough,' Harry said.

Dave looked immediately crestfallen.

'I'm kidding,' Harry said.

Mary was next. She'd made herself known to Harry almost immediately, gently advising him on how to keep his garden well, and also presenting him with a meat pie and a cake on the day he'd moved in. Harry had also popped around for a visit and had somehow managed to drink all three of the large glasses of the ginger wine she'd offered, despite hating the stuff.

'It's lovely to have a new neighbour,' she said, presenting Harry with a bottle. 'House has been empty for too long. And that's not good for a place like this, not somewhere this old.'

Harry looked at the bottle.

'You really shouldn't have,' he said, and meant every word, but managed to smile regardless.

'Well, you seemed to like it so much when you popped round that I thought I'd buy you your own.'

Harry passed the bottle of ginger wine to Grace, as Mary and the other neighbours followed her through to where the party was now very much underway. Thinking he should probably join them, Harry turned from the door only to hear another knock, this one quieter than the others.

Harry opened the door.

'Good evening, Grimm.'

Detective Superintendent Swift was standing in the door looking up at Harry . He seemed smaller, Harry noted, as though what little extra weight the man had carried before had been eaten away.

'Sir?' Harry said, unable to disguise the surprise in his voice.

'You need at least one Detective Superintendent here,' Swift smiled weakly, 'just to keep an eye on things. And I know Walker couldn't make it, so here I am. I won't stay too long; you don't want me falling asleep on you, I'm sure. So, I've booked myself a room at the Herriot.'

'That's still a bit of a walk,' said Harry .

'Not so far that I won't make it, though,' Swift replied. 'And the walk will do me good.'

Harry stepped back and Swift entered the house. The door swished shut by itself, the wind catching it no doubt, Harry thought.

'How long is it now, then?' Swift asked. 'Since you arrived, I mean?'

Harry wasn't so sure.

'However long it is, it's gone quickly,' he said.

'And now look at you,' said Swift. 'Moving into your own place up here in Gayle. If someone had told you back then that something like this would happen, I don't think either of us would've believed it, would we?'

'I reckon you might've had them arrested for even suggesting it.'

Swift laughed, but the sound cracked with a cough.

Grace came over, and Gordy was with her.

'Come on,' Gordy said, gently taking Swift's arm. 'Let's have you through with the rest of the team, shall we? They've all been asking after you.'

'I doubt that,' said Swift, but when he entered the room, Harry heard the welcome their old DSup received and couldn't help but smile.

Following on behind, Harry was actually looking forward to joining in and having a drink and a natter, when once again there was a knock at the front door.

'But I don't know anyone else,' Harry muttered to himself, as he reached out for the doorknob.

Standing in the dark on the other side of the door was a man Harry didn't recognise. At least not at first. Harry reckoned him to be at least in his mid-sixties, but that was only because of the crow's feet at the corner of his eyes. Everything else about him spoke of someone to whom age was more an irritation than anything, and there was steel in his eyes.

'Can I help?' Harry asked.

'Still catching bastards then, are you?' the man asked.

'What?'

The man laughed.

'It's been a long time, I know,' he said, 'but I've surely not changed that much, have I, Harry ?'

'Bloody hell ...'

'There we go,' the man said. 'You know, I actually think I heard that penny drop. Anyway, are you going to let me in or just leave me to freeze on your doorstep?'

'Jameson,' Harry said, shaking his head in disbelief.

'Well, give the man a coconut,' Jameson smiled, and held out a hand.

Harry shook it, pulling the man into the house and closing the door behind him.

'But how?' he said. 'It's been years. Last I heard, you'd retired.'

'I did,' Jameson said. 'Not sure it suits me.'

Harry was still a little confused.

'How is it you're here, though?' he asked.

'That would be Grace,' Jameson said. 'How I understand it, is that she spoke with DI Haig, I think it is, who spoke with Detective Superintendent Walker, who then spoke with a few other people neither of us have heard of, and now here I am.'

Harry scratched his head.

'Surprised?' Jameson asked.

'A little.'

'Me too, actually,' said Jameson. 'If I'm honest, I wasn't sure about whether I should make the trip or not; couldn't see why you'd want to see me after so long.'

Harry smiled.

'And yet here you are.'

Jameson gave a shrug.

'Always wondered how you were doing,' he said.

'It's good to see you,' Harry said.

'And it's nice to see you're doing alright,' Jameson replied. Then Harry saw a dark look fall across the man's eyes. 'I heard about your father. Bad show all of that.'

'It was,' said Harry .

For a moment, both men were silent.

'So, where is she, then?' Jameson asked.

'Who?'

'This clearly amazing, but also clinically insane, woman who has decided to let you into her life?'

As if on cue, Grace stepped out of the now rather crowded lounge.

'You made it!' she said. 'Lovely to meet you at last.'

'At last?' Harry said. 'How long have you both been in touch, then?'

'Only a couple of weeks,' Grace said, and took Jameson's coat. She then looked at Harry . 'That's everyone, so there's no more reason for you to be out here avoiding your actual party.'

'I'm not avoiding it.'

Harry felt a hand on his shoulder.

'Come on,' Jameson said. 'Why don't you introduce me to your new life? Which, I hasten to add, already sounds like a bloody good one.'

A while later, with the party still going strong, Harry needed a breather. As parties went, he was actually enjoying this one tremendously, but the booze and the chatter were making him feel a little dizzy, so he slipped outside and headed over to stand in his small garden.

'You're a lucky man,' said a voice from behind him.

Harry turned to see Jameson come over to stand at his side.

'I am,' he replied. 'Very lucky.'

'Funny how life turns out, isn't it?' Jameson laughed. 'When we first met, I threatened to arrest you.'

'For throwing a sock at you, if I recall,' Harry replied.

'A sock with a hefty padlock tied in the end of it that you were going to use to brain your father,' Jameson said.

'I was young and angry.'

'And now?'

'Not so young,' Harry said.

Jameson turned to face Harry , his hands shoved deep in his pockets against the cold.

'You've a good thing here,' he said. 'And I don't mind admitting I'm a little jealous. So, if you'll do me the honour of listening to the wise words of this old man again, remember that your father's gone now, isn't he? So that anger in you? It needs to leave as well, I think.'

Harry gave a nod.

'I know,' he said.

'Don't take any of what you have now for granted, you hear?' Jameson said. 'Ruin this, and the only one laughing will be that mean old bastard in his grave. Don't even give his ghost the satisfaction.'

And with that, Jameson headed back into the house.

A moment later, Grace joined Harry , slipping a hand into his.

Harry stared out across Gayle Beck. The water danced past in the dark, white splashes catching pale moonlight, then dashing it apart on rocks in the dark. In the distance, Wether Fell rose into the night, and he saw the flickering light of a vehicle making its way across its slopes, a farmer working hours few others could ever understand or cope with. Voices drifted out of the house, warm conversations tied together with laughter. The air was laced with ice and Harry lifted the hand holding Grace's and breathed on them gently to warm them.

'Wondered where you were,' Grace said, a shiver in her voice.

'Home, that's where,' Harry said, then turned and, with Grace by his side, headed back indoors.

Don't miss out on the next edge-of-your-seat Harry Grimm Crime thriller *The Dark Hours*.

JOIN THE VIP CLUB!

WANT to find out where it all began, and how Harry decided to join the police? Sign up to my newsletter today to get your exclusive copy of the short origin story, 'Homecoming', and to join the DCI Harry Grimm VIP Club. You'll receive regular updates on the series, plus VIP access to a photo gallery of locations from the books, and the chance to win amazing free stuff in some fantastic competitions.

You can also connect with other fans of DCI Grimm and his team by joining The Official DCI Harry Grimm Reader Group.

Enjoyed this book? Then please tell others!

The best thing about reviews is they help people like you: other readers. So, if you can spare a few seconds and leave a review, that would be fantastic. I love hearing what readers think about my books, so you can also email me the link to your review at dave@davidjgatward.com.

ABOUT DAVID J. GATWARD

David had his first book published when he was 18 and has written extensively for children and young adults. *Unquiet Bones* is his twelfth DCI Harry Grimm crime thriller.

Visit David's website to find out more about him and the DCI Harry Grimm books.

facebook.com/davidjgatwardauthor

ALSO BY DAVID J. GATWARD

THE DCI Harry GRIMM SERIES

Welcome to Yorkshire. Where the beer is warm, the scenery beautiful, and the locals have murder on their minds.

Grimm Up North

Best Served Cold

Corpse Road

Shooting Season

Restless Dead

Death's Requiem

Blood Sport

Cold Sanctuary

One Bad Turn

Blood Trail

Fair Game

The Dark Hours

Silent Ruin

Dead Man's Hands

Dark Harvest

Milton Keynes UK
Ingram Content Group UK Ltd.
UKHW041431300824
1448UKWH00022B/50

9 781917 001113